CAPTIVATED

BY
TESSA BAILEY
AND
EVE DANGERFIELD

Copyright © 2018 Tessa Bailey and Eve Dangerfield
Print Edition

All rights reserved. No part of this publication may be reproduced, distributed, or transmitted in any form or by any means, including photocopying, recording, or other electronic or mechanical methods, without the prior written permission of the publisher, except in the case of brief quotations embodied in critical reviews and certain other noncommercial uses permitted by copyright law.

DEDICATION

Tessa

For Dean, who brought us together.

Eve

For the Filomena's. And the Raffella's.

TABLE OF CONTENTS

Chapter 1	1
Chapter 2	19
Chapter 3	38
Chapter 4	59
Chapter 5	69
Chapter 6	92
Chapter 7	103
Chapter 8	116
Chapter 9	134
Chapter 10	155
Chapter 11	170
Chapter 12	191
Chapter 13	206
Chapter 14	230
Chapter 15	251
Chapter 16	272
Chapter 17	293
Chapter 18	308
Epilogue	326
Acknowledgements	339
About Tessa Bailey	341
About Eve Dangerfield	343

CHAPTER 1

Autumn was drunk. Well not *that* drunk, just not that sober either. She hadn't been sober all weekend, as far as she could tell. Such things were hard to figure out when you were drunk. A real chicken or the egg, potato or the vodka situation.

Despite her working class background Autumn had never been one to hit the bottle in times of stress. Alcohol was for celebrating; champagne at weddings, wine with fancy anniversary dinners, the occasional tequila shot with friends. Seven years studying veterinary science had trained her to stay clear-headed as much as possible so she could keep up with her schoolwork. Even once she was a qualified vet she never really felt like cutting loose. Ian came to rely on her to drive them both home from parties.

"You're the prettiest Uber driver in the world," he would slur from the passenger seat. "You're the prettiest taxi."

Which, when Autumn actually thought about it, wasn't much of a compliment. Then again neither was the fact that her boyfriend of six years had dragged her ass to New York, allowed her to support him for months, then cheated on her with a bunch of improv groupies. Improv groupies not only existed, apparently, but were *so* horny for Ian's Kylo Ren impression that they just *had* to suck his dick after the Sunday matinee. Or at least that's how he'd told the story. Ian told a lot of stories, maybe he even believed some of them.

As awful as their break up had been and despite the fact she still hadn't told her family or friends about it, Autumn didn't think the cheating alone would have driven her to spend all weekend locked in her apartment drinking straight gin through a straw and playing Arkham Asylum. What had gotten her was New York.

People had a lot of opinions about New York. Ian's had been that it would make him a star, catapult his comedy career from YouTube and tiny theaters to SNL and movies. Other people praised its architecture, its give no fucks attitude, its 'energy', whatever the hell that meant, but for Autumn Reynolds, the Big Apple was enemy territory and she'd been air-dropped into it without any reconnaissance.

Ian had been the one with the job offer. A reasonably well-known improv troupe—Sparky Spark and the Electric Bunch—had seen a clip of him impersonating Channing Tatum and suggested he fill a vacant position on their crew. Then her boyfriend, the man who swore he wanted to marry her someday, had asked if she'd like to go on an adventure with him. Of course she'd said yes. Moving to New York, what could be more glamorous?

Being thrown into a swimming pool of curdled milk, apparently.

There weren't a lot of adventure novels about working ten-hour shifts putting wealthy people's dogs on anti-anxiety medication while your boyfriend was out drinking and learning the Stanislavski method of pretending to act like a human on camera. With good reason. It wasn't an adventure. It was shit-boring and lonely. All Autumn did was work and go to Ian's shows and think about what a stupid name 'Sparky Spark and the Electric Bunch' was. She told herself to give it time, but as the months passed she only felt more isolated.

New York wasn't the city dreams were made of, it smelled like hot garbage and if she didn't know better she'd think it was personally trying to kill her—loose grates, derailed trains, homeless people wielding broken bottles. The food was crazy expensive and tipping was a nightmare and air conditioner juice kept dripping on her head whenever she went outside. Her work colleagues were nice but they weren't really her friends, and everyone in Ian's improv troupe was awkward around her. In hindsight, that was because they knew he was cheating and felt weird about it, but still, they could have asked her if she missed home or wanted a beer or whatever. She had never been so lonely in her life.

When Ian's cheating had finally come out—one of the improv groupies texted nudes to his phone, which he stupidly asked her to read while he was in the shower—the longest romantic relationship of her life had blown up like a bottle rocket. Ian had packed his bags and moved into a friend's house and she was alone, alone, alone.

It had been two weeks now and Autumn wasn't sure why she was still here, going through the motions of work, groceries and home. She had no reason to stay in America. She could quit her job at the clinic for sad dogs and even sadder people. She could go back to Melbourne where her old friends and family and life were waiting for her. Yet here she was, camped out in her tiny, insanely expensive apartment eating fistfuls of Doritos for breakfast. But that couldn't be mistaken for affirmative action. She hadn't decided to stay, either. Her work visa renewal form had been stuck on her fridge for a month, its final approval date edging closer and closer, yet she couldn't summon up the motivation to fill out her name. She was stuck. Suspended between her past and an unknown future and apparently content to simply dangle there.

Autumn barely understood the mindset she'd gotten herself into. She wasn't the kind of person who sat back and let things go to seed. She was Miss Organized, Miss One Hundred and Ten Percent. If her parents knew what she was doing, they would be shocked. Tears and tantrums and threats of flying out to get her would follow, but for the first time in her life, fear of what her parents would think wasn't enough to spur her into action.

Maybe I don't want to admit failure, she'd written in her comedy notepad on Friday night. *Maybe I don't want everyone to know that the boyfriend everyone thought was way too charming and hot for me cheated and the widely acknowledged best city on earth smashed me into the ground like a tent peg.*

But there was another reason, one she was too scared to write down even within her booze, sodium and video game haze. Ian wasn't the only person who'd dreamed about making people laugh for a living, the difference was his parents hadn't told him he was too smart for that, that he should be a doctor or a lawyer or something suitably prestigious, instead.

Autumn loved her parents. She didn't want to disappoint them, she didn't want to disappoint *anyone*, she just wanted to feel not so goddamn terrible. So, she'd gone to the grocery store on Friday after work and stocked up on junk food, then she'd come home, put a straw in the gin bottle and let everything unravel.

It was Sunday afternoon now. She was avoiding the mirror but whenever she caught sight of herself, it wasn't great. Her long hair was one big honey-colored tangle and her skin was pale and greasy. She'd removed her contacts in favor of the big purple-framed glasses Ian hated, the ones that made her hazel eyes bug out even more than they already did. All weekend, she'd worn nothing but cotton panties and a huge University of Melbourne t-shirt. Bras were for people who gave a shit and for the first time in her life, Autumn soundly did not. She and New York might finally have something in common.

The apartment wasn't the way she usually kept it, either. Once neat and homey, it now looked like a cross between a squatter's den and a trash compactor. The curtains were drawn, empty Dr. Pepper cans, pizza boxes and chip packets dotted the floor, and her vibrator was lying on the couch like a discarded karaoke mic. She had sad feels, sure, but that wasn't keeping her sex drive down. Nothing did. Even when their relationship was going to hell in a handbasket, she'd still tried to initiate sex with Ian most nights.

"You're a teenage boy, Autie," he'd say, and something in his tone had made her wonder if he meant her constant desire or her small boobs and narrow hips. 'Petite', her mother called her, but at twenty-six, Autie knew better. She was tiny, barely five feet tall, and skinny. Everyone envied the way she could smash through a packet of doughnuts and not gain a kilo but she'd happily give up that superpower for an extra cup size or a bigger ass. She'd drawn herself that way in her improvised pornography; curvier and softer, her bare breasts straining against the ropes she'd been tied in.

"Please let me go," her cartoon self begged her captor. *"I'll give you anything you want, just let me go."*

Ah, yes. The improvised, comic-book-style pornography. That had started happening around Saturday afternoon. She hadn't been sleeping much (but wasn't this the city that never slept? hur, hur hur) and Tumblr just wasn't doing it for her anymore. The porn GIFS were all so artificial. All the women looked like busty mermaids with legs, their long hair spilling down to their round asses while celebrity-handsome dudes rode them from behind.

It reminded her of Ian and the groupies he'd cheated with and really, she didn't need more reminders. She'd already seen the nudes. So, since she was already knee-deep in debauchery and incapable of finding anyone who understood her perverted longings, Autumn decided to go all in on her fantasies and make herself some porn. Not with actual pictures—she wasn't that drunk—but drawings. She'd always been a decent artist and she had nothing but time. The problem had been choosing a male figure for her to draw. She tried movie stars but that felt a bit pervy. She tried generic handsome guys but they lacked the realism of her own, if slightly exaggerated, figure.

Then she remembered The Landlord.

Neither she, nor Ian could ever remember his name, so they got in the habit of calling him 'The Landlord.' He'd been the one to give them their keys and show them around the apartment, pointing out electrical sockets and architectural quirks. He was big, like crazy big. Six-foot-four or five and broad as the proverbial sword. Autumn still wasn't sure if The Landlord was hot or not. The entire time he'd led her and Ian around their new home, his face had been scrunched into a perma-scowl, as though the only thing he hated more than his job was newly migrated Australians with comedic aspirations.

Whenever she'd seen him since, he'd looked equally pissed, hulking down hallways carrying ladders and buckets, his boots making a noise like cannons firing. The Landlord's height and bulk would have always been intimidating but he also had a limp, relying heavily on his right leg when he walked. Combined with his shaggy black hair and beard, he cut a rather sinister figure as he made his way around their building.

"All he's missing is a gold tooth and an eyepatch," Ian once said when they ran into him at the mailboxes. "What's the bet he's got about six hookers dissolving in the basement?"

A mean assessment, but Ian was always bitchy about guys who were taller than him. Just call it 'guy who plays Jon Snow' syndrome.

Scary and growly as The Landlord was, he was the perfect man to slot into her dark fantasies. Grizzled like a bear, big and mean. She drew him following her down a darkened New York street, stalking her as though she were a deer. Drawing-Landlord then captured her, threw a bag over her head and when it was removed, she found herself bound to his kitchen chair.

"That's enough out of you," he growled, as she begged to be set free. "If you had any idea how long I'd been planning this, you'd know your blonde ass wasn't going anywhere."

She made The Landlord more beast than man, a hulking collection of shadows. He tucked a clean dishcloth into her mouth and used a set of kitchen scissors to cut through her clothes, first her t-shirt, then her bra, then her—

A sharp knock at the front door.

"*Shit!*" Autie realized it was the first time she'd spoken aloud in hours. She swallowed thickly, wondering who the hell that could be. Ian knew he wasn't welcome and it wasn't like any friends or relatives could have come to visit. Had some electric company salesdouche somehow gotten into the building? Had she drunkenly ordered another pizza and forgotten?

She looked around the room for clues and saw nothing but her own grossness. It was obvious she was home, Courtney Barnett was playing from her Bluetooth speakers, but she didn't have to open the door, she'd just stay very quiet and—

Another sharp knock.

"Ms. Reynolds? Mr. Fletcher? This is your landlord, open up."

Autumn's brain went numb. It was The Landlord. Sweet. Fucking. Hell. Was this some kind of joke? Had life not punched her in the tits enough these past couple weeks? It had seriously come to this? The Landlord knocked again and, remembering he had his own set of keys into her apartment, Autumn knew she was out of alternate options. She was going to need to respond.

"Just a second," she called, flipping her sex-comic notepad shut and shoving her vibrator under the couch. "I'll be there in one second."

"Sure." She'd forgotten what a deep voice The Landlord had. Instantly, her mind flashed to her sex-comic and she shivered. She crammed a couple of the more disgusting food items into the overflowing bin and then ran to her bedroom to yank on a pair of tracksuit pants. Knowing she had only seconds to avoid serious suspicion, she stuck her head into the bathroom. As expected, Harvey, Birdman and Pigioto were still in there, pacing around in the tub, fluttering their grey and white wings. Autumn pointed a finger at them. "You guys need to be fucking chilled in here, you get me? *Chilled*. We could get in big trouble if you cunts don't stay quiet."

The pigeons all cooed politely up at her, which she took to mean yes, and she shut the door.

"Be cool," she told herself as she polished her glasses on her filthy hoodie. "It's probably nothing, don't get paranoid and talk too much, just answer his questions and send him on his way."

"Ms. Reynolds?" The Landlord called again. "I need a word with you."

"Sure! Yes! No problem!" Autumn unlocked the door, plastering a big smile on her face as she swung it open.

Oof. Somehow despite all her sex musings, she'd managed to underestimate both the height and bulk of her landlord. As soon as he stepped into the apartment, he made the place look like it was for elves. His heavy jaw was rigid, as though he was clenching his teeth, and his expression was stern. Mean even.

A little shiver ran down her spine. When she was playing captive in her mind, it had been fun to imagine The Landlord abducting and mistreating her. Now that he was here in the flesh, it was unnerving. It was obvious that he could snap her like a toothpick, she wouldn't have a hope in hell of fighting him off. His enormous hands, thickly muscled body and height gave him power, a power she'd never possess, and that was both impressive and intimidating.

What was a dude like this doing running a building, anyway? He should have been wrestling bears or pounding the shit out of people inside an MMA octagon. He was younger than she remembered, too. She'd thought he was in his forties, but aside from a few wrinkles that were probably the result of his perma-scowl, his skin was smooth. The parts of it that weren't covered in beard anyway. He said nothing as he surveyed what had once been a very clean, relatively nice New York City apartment.

"Sorry about all the mess," she said in her most chipper, everything-is-totally-fucking-fine voice. "I don't usually keep it like this, but I'm having a staycation."

"Okay."

The Landlord continued to look around the room, his gaze falling on the three cans of spray cream on the coffee table. He raised a brow and Autumn was sure she knew what he was thinking. "Yeah, no, I was putting the cream in my coffee, I wasn't doing nangs. I mean…what do you call it in America when you suck the nitrous out of whipped cream cans and get stoned?"

The Landlord stared blankly at her.

"Is it 'whippets?'" she said, a little desperately. "I think it's whip-it's. Two words. Either way we call them nangs in Australia, after the sound your brain makes when you do one, like, that loud whining *nannnnngggggggggg*."

The Landlord's thick black brow rose even higher and Autumn realized what she was implying. "I don't do nangs! I don't do drugs at all! I just live here, and no one who lives here would ever do drugs. Ever. For fun or because they were sad…or for any other reason."

The Landlord stared at her as though she were a gibbering monkey at real risk of throwing fecal matter at him, and Autumn felt her cheeks burn. How fucking drunk was she, anyway? "So uh, what can I help you with?"

He was silent long enough to make her skin start to itch, then he cleared his throat. "Your rent hasn't come through this month."

Autumn clapped a hand to her mouth. "Oh my God, I'm so sorry."

"You and your boyfriend don't answer emails."

The look on his face as he said the word 'boyfriend' told her she wasn't the only person who thought Ian Fletcher was a tool. That helped with her nerves. At least until she realized he probably thought she was a tool, too. As for the rent not coming through, that was obvious. She'd closed her and Ian's joint bank account after noticing Ian was still making withdrawals despite not having put any money in there for six months. She thought she'd transferred all her direct debits, but trust her to forget about the most important one.

"I, um, changed banks," she told The Landlord. "I forgot to

let you know. I'm really sorry."

He nodded unsmilingly. "Give me your new details and I'll get going."

Autumn nearly sighed with relief. This was manageable. "No problem, just let me get a pen and—"

Just then, Courtney Barnett stopped singing about how she was a shitty gardener and the apartment went quiet, quiet enough for a low but very audible coo to emanate from the bathroom.

Autumn's heart stopped. There was no need to wonder if The Landlord had heard the noise. He turned his head in the direction of the bathroom, his nostrils flaring slightly, as though he could *smell* the rental violation. One of the birds, probably Harvey, let out another low coo.

Fuck, fuck, *fuck*.

The Landlord was suddenly bigger and even more menacing than before, and not in a sexy porn comic way. A 'start looking for a new place to live, bitch' way. His broad forehead crumpled into a frown and he turned to look at her with sinister slowness. "Ms. Reynolds, are you keeping pigeons in this apartment?"

She was going to be homeless. She was going to have to live in a Super 8 motel and get stabbed in the laundry room. "Um, what?"

"Pigeons." The Landlord's expression was stony. "Are you keeping pigeons inside this apartment?"

A new Courtney Barnett song started playing, but it was an instrumental and not nearly loud enough to cover the sound of the pigeons which were now cooing in harmony like they were Alvin and the fucking pigeon Chipmunks. Autumn's heart raced and she wished she hadn't drunk so much Mountain Dew spiked with gin. She was getting lost in The Landlord's oddly hypnotic eyes. She'd thought they would be dark like his hair, but instead they were a very pale brown. What was that color even called? The lighter chocolate bit inside Mars Bars? Bright tan bark?

The Landlord decided not to wait for her answer. He strode over to the bathroom door and flung it open to reveal, of course, the pigeons. The pigeons were a new thing. A couple of days after Ian received his fateful nudes, Autumn had been walking down the street to her apartment trying not to explode-cry when she spotted Harvey. He was fluttering across the ground, his right wing stuck out at a funny angle. Something or someone had broken it, which meant he was only hours away from death. She knew that no one would notice or care, and even if they did, they couldn't do anything about it. But she could. She wrapped Harvey up in her jumper and carried him home. There she set his wing and left him to stomp around the bathroom like a tiny, feathery general. Watching him had made her smile for the first time in ages. She knew she couldn't keep him, he was a wild bird who needed to return to the outside world, but thanks to her, he *would* return. That knowledge, and Mountain Gin Dew, had been all that got her through the week. She rescued Birdman and then Pigioto next, the maximum amount of birds she could safely keep in her tiny bathroom. And sure, they were gross New York pigeons but they'd made her feel so much less alone. She hoped that would continue to be the case, seeing as all four of them were going to be chucked out onto the street.

So, do something, you drunk moll! Save them again!

Autumn rushed to The Landlord's side and tapped his bicep. Even in her panic, she couldn't help admiring the definition, the firm swells of muscle. "Excuse me, sir, I know this seems really fucked and you can chuck me out if you want to, but please, *please* don't hurt the pigeons."

The Landlord blinked at her in a kind of angry surprise. "I'm not going to hurt the pigeons. I'd never…" He cleared his throat. "Ms. Reynolds, *why* are you keeping pigeons in your bathroom?"

"Call me Autumn. Or Autie. That's what all my friends call me. Or at least they do in Melbourne. I don't have any friends here. Except the pigeons. But they don't really talk. I mean they don't talk but—"

"*Autumn*. Why are there rabid pigeons shitting in your bathroom?"

The guy did commanding very well. It was no surprise she'd slotted him into her sex-comic. She also liked that he hadn't said 'my bathroom' even though it was so much more his than hers. "Pigeons don't actually carry rabies, that's a myth. I'm a vet."

"I'm aware. I wasn't, however, aware vets took their work home."

Fucking touché. Autumn felt slightly ashamed. Ian had always acted like The Landlord was a Lurch-style dummy, and that impression had clearly rubbed off on her. Now that she was interacting with him, it was clear that wasn't true. The way he studied her with those strangely beautiful eyes said a very sharp mind worked beneath them.

Whelp. Smart *and* fucking humongous. Where had she gotten off turning this guy into a porno comic character?

All over his face, Autumn, old chap. You know that.

"Ms. Reynolds…?"

Right, the fucking pigeons. "It's, um, a side project. Of sorts. Pro bono, that kind of thing."

The Landlord looked her up and down, no doubt taking in her ratty hair and general aura of spackiness. Autumn waited for him to shout, to snarl, to tell her she was a gross failure who needed to GTFO yesterday and wouldn't be getting her deposit back. Then the lines around his eyes and mouth softened. "You okay?"

Autumn was all set to say 'yes, if you don't throw me out of the building' but something about his voice, the sincerity of the question, made the backs of her eyes burn. She turned away from him, unwilling to add 'crying in front of a guy I drew sex pictures of' to her list of failures.

"Forget it," The Landlord said in his rumbling voice. "None of my business."

Autumn, who was wiping her tears away, snorted. "I am literally keeping wild pigeons in your building, I'd say it is your business. And I'm sorry for being such a mess, I'm just having an emotional ripcord moment."

"I…uh…"

"I broke up with my boyfriend," she said, for reasons she didn't understand. "Well, he broke up with me, sort of. He cheated on me."

"Your boyfriend cheated on you." The Landlord's voice was flat. Emotionless. As though he could understand exactly why Ian would do such a thing. After all, she was a crazy pigeon lady, holed up in a batshit apartment. Completely understandable.

Autumn wanted to stop talking but instead she did what she always did when she felt cornered—she tried to be funny. "Yeah, he had sex with some groupies from his improv comedy troupe. That's a thing, allegedly; girls who are attracted to men who pretend to be chickens for lols."

The Landlord was giving her nothing, but that had never stopped her before. "The groupies are called chucklefuckers, which I think is kinda sexist. I mean, they did bang my boyfriend on a pile of old rugs in an improv comedy theatre, but that's on him. He was the one with a girlfriend and, trust me, I've seen Ian's comedy—it's way more likely they fucked him because he has abs."

The Landlord's eyes darted to the door. "Right."

Autumn knew she needed to stop, but she couldn't, she just fucking couldn't. "Ian tried to use the fact that the girls were 'groupies' as an excuse for cheating, but I think that's bullshit. If a hot guy came into the clinic and offered to go down on me because I untangled his Pomeranian's intestines or whatever, I wouldn't be like *'ooh he's a furry-fucker*—or whatever you want to call people who are sexually attracted to vets—*I'd better take him up on the offer! Couldn't possibly say no.'* Ian was just being selfish, the way he was when he said we should move to New York together then refused to get a job because improv comedy is just so much more important than splitting rent."

As soon as she said this, all the funny wooshed out of her. She remembered afresh how much it hurt to come home to an empty apartment, to head out to the improv theatre and see Ian flirting with the comedy groupies. To remember the way she'd pushed her jealousy down because he couldn't help being a handsome guy and of course he would never *do anything.*

"We were in a new place and he didn't have the guts to admit he wanted new women," she said, more tears welling up in her eyes like dew drops. "Or maybe he was just sick of me and wanted me to keep paying the bills. I don't know. I-I feel like I don't know anything anymore, about myself or anyone else."

She looked up at The Landlord, hot water spilling from her eyes. "That's why I brought the birds home, I wanted to help something. I wanted to feel like…I wanted to feel useful."

The Landlord stared at her, unblinkingly for what felt like a very long time. Then he cleared his throat once more. "Look…I'm sorry that happened to you."

Autumn sniffed back more tears. The enormous man in front

of her didn't sound insincere, but it was obvious he was very uncomfortable—and why wouldn't he be? "I—um, I know getting cheated on doesn't mean it's okay to keep the pigeons inside or not pay my rent, but can I please keep the birds in here until they're healed? It should only be another day or so."

The Landlord sucked his lips into his mouth. Very full, pleasant lips, she couldn't help but notice. Then he gently closed the bathroom door and turned to face her. "Give me your new bank details and I'll leave. Whatever happens next is up to you. I won't be back unless there's another issue with your billing."

Autumn grinned. "Thanks so much…"

Shit. She didn't know his name. *Shiiiit.*

"Munroe," The Landlord said, the perma-scowl sinking his face back into a familiar grumpiness. "Blake Munroe."

Autumn felt like this would be a bad time to tell him her brother once had a pet snake called Blake. Blake the Snake. "I just kind of think of you as *'The Landlord.'*"

The scowl grew deeper. "Bank details?"

"Fuck, yes, of course." Autumn dashed over to the coffee table and picked up her notepad, her brain brimming with embarrassment. The guy listens to her whine about Ian, throws her a bone about the pigeons and she lets him know she's forgot his fucking name and internally calls him 'The Landlord.' How was he to know she meant it in an impressive way? He probably thought she was a prissy bitch on top of someone who got cheated on at improv theatres.

She scrawled down her new bank number and BSB as quickly as possible, tore the page out and gave it to him. The hand that took the folded up piece of paper was as huge as the man himself, thick-knuckled and scarred. Autumn imagined it closing around her throat and felt a sizzle of arousal zap through her. She quickly glanced away.

Let's not make this weirder, bitch.

"Thanks," Blake Munroe said and gave the bathroom door a sidelong glance. "I'll let you get back to your patients."

"Cool," Autumn said weakly. "You know, you might not have to deal with me and my pigeon bullshit for much longer. I'm not sure what I'm doing vis-à-vis this apartment, but my work visa is running out and I'm very unmotivated to renew it and continue living in the huge barbershop of horrors that is New York."

"Right." From the look on The Landlord's face, he did not give even one shit, and Autumn watched in numb horror as he stomped out of her apartment, taking the last dregs of her dignity with him.

Slightly dazed, she walked over to the bathroom and checked on the pigeons. They were still cooing cheerfully, testing their healing wings and dipping their beaks into the Tupperware container she was using as a water dish.

"That was great, wasn't it, guys?" she asked. "Being single is awesome. I am definitely not going to die alone."

Birdman crapped on the side of the bath. Autumn felt like that was all the answer she needed and closed the bathroom door.

The realization of what she'd done didn't come at once. It returned slowly, slithering into her brain, not unlike the former snake named Blake. She was lying on the couch, replaying the clusterfuck that was her encounter with The Landlord, when a simple question arose. *Had she written her new bank details down on the back of one of her sex drawings?*

No, she thought at once. That would be insane. It had been a blank page, she was sure of it. Completely and utterly blank.

Although…

Her notepad lay on the coffee table, innocent as a newborn lamb. Autumn snatched it up and flurried through the pages. She'd drawn about a third of her sex comic, five pages in total. She counted them; one, two, three, four—

"Oh my God! No. *No!*"

Page five was missing. It was missing. All that remained were tattered little pieces of paper in the spiral, showing where she'd ripped it out. Panic flooded her body like rain, filling her to the brim with chaos.

"Oh God," she said aloud. "Oh Christ, what the hell am I gonna do?"

She bent down and did the only thing she could think of. She picked up one of the whipped cream cans, pushed the tab down and sucked back some of the nitrous. "Fuck!"

CHAPTER 2

SHE DIDN'T EVEN know his *name*.

Blake gave a sour grunt and limped into his apartment, rattling the door on its hinges with the force of his slam. Once inside, though, his shoulders slumped. What the hell had he expected? The afternoon he showed the tiny Australian and her Prince Charming boyfriend with the sociopathic stare the apartment, Blake was sure he hadn't spoken much, except to amaze them with his knowledge of where the bathroom was located. Or how to turn the radiator knob. When did he *ever* talk? His vocal cords were still reeling from the exchange in Autumn's apartment and that had lasted all of five minutes.

Still…it could have lasted a little longer and he wouldn't have minded.

Blake looked down to find his left hand covering the spot where she'd touched his arm.

Disgusted with himself, he whipped the shirt over his head and stomped through the hallway leading to the back of his apartment. He came to a stop beneath the silver pull-up bar mounted in his bedroom doorway and kicked off his shoes, throwing himself into a set of twenty pull-ups. Finding methods of exercise that didn't include leaving his apartment was nothing new, but this—this intense need to blow off steam was only six months in the making. And it had everything to do with the girl, damn her.

Their verbal exchanges had been minimal, but the day they'd met, Autumn had managed to communicate everything about herself without saying a single word. Their apartment had been receiving a fresh coat of paint and repairs that day, leaving tools and buckets strewn every few yards. Blake's limp, combined with his abnormal size, made navigating the cluttered apartment difficult. He'd watched in stunned silence, though, as Autumn moved gracefully in front of him, toeing items out of his path, silently making things easier for him. Caring for a stranger without thinking, or asking to be acknowledged.

It had annoyed the living shit out of him. Where did this girl get off giving him the assistance he didn't ask for? Why couldn't she ignore the limp like everyone else? And yet from that day forward, every time he saw her, he ached a little. A lot, eventually. Blake didn't want to be fascinated by the girl who'd cleared a path for him. Especially now that he knew she tried to save everyone—including the flying rats of New York. It wasn't a surprising discovery. She always held open the door for her neighbors. Never failed to assist the older tenants with packages or laundry bundles. Always with a smile and an encouraging word. He hated himself for coveting another man's girlfriend. The very idea of unfaithfulness struck too deep a cord from his past. But he continued to watch. To need.

Pointless.

Even if he *wanted* to stop her from going back to Australia—which he *didn't*—such a thing was impossible. She was afraid of him. When he'd walked into her apartment, she'd stopped breathing, froze the way a forest animal did when they sensed a hunter watching them through a scope. They probably heard that rapid tick at the base of her delicate neck in New Jersey. This kind of reception was nothing new to Blake. He was a big motherfucker with a distaste for people he didn't mind showing on his face. Par for the course in someone who didn't leave the confines of his building during the day. No, he'd been built for night and that suited him just fine.

Now, Autumn…she'd been built for the daytime. Looked like she'd been spat out by the sunshine with her long golden hair and an accent that called endless beaches to mind. Lazy barbeques, flip-flop tan lines, kangaroos. She would have to put in contact lenses if she wanted to wear sunglasses. Those big purple specs were cute—even if they barely had room to perch on her button nose—but they couldn't be practical on an Australian beach. It wouldn't matter what she wore, though, nothing could detract from her beauty, the welcoming glow that didn't dissipate one iota as it travelled through the peep hole to his starved eyes. He'd never been drawn to a woman to the point of suffering, but somehow this tiny girl managed to pack a wallop. One that left him dazed whenever they crossed paths.

Blake realized he'd gone well past twenty and let go of the bar. Sides heaving, he dropped forward and rested both hands on his knees. God, what he wouldn't give to stop mentally waxing poetic about the girl upstairs. She'd obviously only felt safe that first day because her boyfriend was there. Being one-on-one with him had distressed her, and therefore conjuring up fantasies where she smiled and touched him was pathetic.

It was a lot like telling someone not to think of a polar bear. Immediately, all they could think about was white fur and big teeth. Blake, though?

He went back to imagining Autumn on the beach. Only this time, his gargantuan hands were sliding the bikini strings free of their knot, loosening the triangles of her top. She turned to him on her knees in the sand and climbed onto his lap, no wariness in her big green eyes whatsoever. Just anticipation. Trust.

There's no one here but us, she whispered, cupping her tits. *No one to see me ride you.*

"Christ," Blake muttered, gritting his teeth and grabbing the pull-up bar again. Out of deference to his height, he bent his legs and lifted them back, forcing himself not to wince at the strain in his right quad. He ripped his way through another set of twenty, continuing on to whatever number would stop his farfetched fantasies of the girl upstairs. The girl who was almost definitely *leaving.*

There was nothing he could do to stop her. Even if he set aside the fact that his job was to collect rent money—at Manhattan prices—which essentially made him the fucking enemy, they existed in different dimensions. Autumn left her third floor apartment at a normal hour, catching the elevator and zipping past his first floor place while juggling toast, headphones and a purse far too large for a girl her size. And although she'd apparently been smuggling pigeons upstairs, she returned home at a customary hour, too. Usually without her cockhead boyfriend…who'd been cheating on her.

His grip on the pull-up bar tightened, his teeth baring themselves to the dark bedroom that lay before him. Who cheated on a girl who nursed pigeons back to health? Sure, he found the whole business of winged rodents in a bathtub pretty goddamn unsavory, but it was likely Autumn put that same compassion into everything she did. That level of caring wasn't something a person could turn off and on like a light switch, was it?

You wouldn't know, would you?

No. He didn't know the first thing about how and why people chose to operate as they did. Even when he'd spent his time in a big circle of friends in his early twenties—and been engaged to be married—he'd always been the odd one out. Quiet where they were outspoken. Content to be alone where his friends couldn't seem to take a shit by themselves.

'You're so intense, bro,' friends would laugh, slapping him on the back. 'Lighten up.'

Trying to 'lighten up' had only been awkward, though, because here was the thing about being on the quiet side. He listened better than everyone else. So when it came time to contribute, his observations were too honest. Too serious.

Being alone was easier. He woke up in the morning, tended to his restoration projects and returned client emails. Inevitably a tenant needed something repaired, so he did it himself or hired the required expert. His meals were consumed beneath the single light bulb in his eat-in kitchen, no sounds to assault his ears, unless you count the omnipresent rush of traffic outside his window. If he left the building, there was a damn good reason. Dropping off a finished project safely with a client, the occasional run if his leg was up for the challenge, or grocery shopping while the rest of the city slept. He didn't *want* to speak to anyone. Speaking meant relating and he couldn't do that without digging into the past.

Blake let go of the bar and swiped an arm across his now-sweating forehead. Pacing didn't help him cool off, though. Being a recluse didn't mean he lacked a temper. Oh no. God help Autumn's boyfriend if he walked down the hallway right now. Blake would lay him out cold. Because for all his and Autumn's differences—sunny versus dark, chatty versus voluntarily mute—they had something in common now. He'd been in the tiny Australian's shoes before. A larger size, of course. He knew all too well the instinct to lock oneself away before any more damage could occur. That instinct was why he'd moved into this building seven years ago and finally allowed himself to quit *lightening up*. There was no *light* involved. There was eating, sleeping, working and exercise. And another activity that had increased of late.

Blake sent a scowl up toward the third floor and unbuttoned his jeans. He headed for the shower where he knew he'd lose the battle against fucking his hand. Autumn walking past, humming along to whatever played in her headphones, made it hard enough to resist the disrespectful practice, but he'd been in her apartment this time. Smelled her girly coconut shampoo and saw her lipstick prints on a coffee mug. There was no way around it.

He was in the process of peeling the jeans down his hips when a piece of paper fluttered out of his back pocket. One hand massaged the twinge in his thigh as he stooped down, retrieving the notepaper with Autumn's account number on it and setting it on the sink.

"What the hell?"

Blake snatched the paper back up.

On the opposite side, there was a drawing. A pretty decent one. Decent enough that he could decipher a naked Autumn. A low groan left him and his cock shifted, pushing through the opening he'd made in his jeans. Jesus, this was what she looked like, wasn't it? Bratty tits and a rounded little ass made for slapping. Some kind of sex-starved librarian with wide, innocent eyes. A girl who'd just realized what she'd gotten herself into, and now her pulse was racing beneath her sun-kissed skin. Picture-Autumn's blonde hair was covering one eye and a bit of her swollen mouth, her knees were pressed to the floor and her obedient, but slightly worried gaze was looking up at…

Him. Blake would assume there'd been a mistake, only there weren't too many people to whom he shared a resemblance. He was towering above a kneeling Autumn in the picture, his hand wrapped around the back of her neck. *Tight.* There were indentation marks on her soft nape, as Picture-Blake guided her closer to the roughly sketched outline of his cock which seemed hell bent on escaping his pants. A lot like his current situation.

Autumn drew this?

Had to be. Her shithead boyfriend wouldn't very well draw Blake about to do debauched things to his girlfriend. No. *Ex-girlfriend.* Funny how one sketch of Autumn preparing to give him a blow job seemed to have communicated to his brain that she was completely free of her ex...and his for the taking. Because that wasn't the case. Definitely not. Their differences notwithstanding, she almost jumped out of her skin when he walked into her apartment tonight. But then, if she was scared of him, why draw them together this way?

Blake's body didn't care about the particulars. Not right now. He set the paper down on the edge of the sink and wrapped his fist around his ready cock. Halfway through that first stroke, he noticed Autumn's hands were tied behind her back.

"*Fuck.*" A breath shuddered out of him and he braced his free hand on the wall, alongside the mirror. Images flooded his mind. Moving ones that started with this picture. When he'd fantasized about Autumn, she'd ridden him on a beach. Or snuck into his apartment for a nasty fuck against the door. The need to be dominant had always tried to bleed into the fantasies, turn him mean, make him hold her down. It had made him feel like a monster, though, so he fought to keep the mental scenes tame. But she'd drawn herself in bonds. Bonds he'd presumably tied.

"You don't want a lazy lay on the beach, do you, Fun-Size?" Blake spit on his palm and brought it back to his cock, choking it top to bottom. "You want a no-mercy fuck with no way to fight me off? I'll make that happen."

Yes, she whispered in his ear. *Please, Blake?*

Sweat slid down his spine. "Your idiot boyfriend let you escape, did he?" In Blake's imagination, he let go of Autumn's neck in favor of wrapping that long blonde hair around his knuckles, pressing her open mouth to his fly. "Don't you dare expect the same from me. You'll go *nowhere.* Unzip my pants and greet your new keeper."

There was a knock at the door.

"No," Blake gritted. He turned to shout over his shoulder, "Come back later."

"Um. Mr. Munroe?" Autumn's voice made him pause mid-stroke. "I'd really like to speak with you. It's urgent."

Blake's head fell forward on a pained laugh. No way could he answer the door to a tenant right now, let alone the very one he couldn't stop jacking off to. Forget the fact that he was mid-jerk job, he couldn't pretend he'd never seen the drawing. It just wasn't in his DNA to play games or soften the truth. Another one of those traits that made people uncomfortable. If he answered the door, there would be a conversation about the drawing. And it would be sexual in nature, no getting around that, considering what she'd drawn.

He opened his mouth to tell her one final time to leave, but something stopped him. *I-I feel like I don't know anything anymore, about myself or anyone else.* She'd said those words to him against a backdrop of garbage, stray pigeons and molested whipped cream cans. Literally the most depressing sight known to man. Now he was going to turn her away? Didn't that make him as big a bastard as her slimy ex-boyfriend? Blake didn't want to be in the same category as an asshole who'd brought Autumn to a strange country and ditched her for something meaningless.

The other far more pressing issue that had Blake zipping himself back up and stomping for the door with a worse limp than usual, was this. He might not have many more chances to be around Autumn. Sure, she'd drawn herself in a compromising position with Blake as some kind of pissed off enforcer, but that only meant...well, he wasn't sure *what* the hell it meant. He only knew whatever *it* was wouldn't keep her in New York. Nothing involving him could have that kind of impact on a woman, especially an adorable, rambling Aussie girl who looked like the sun followed her everywhere she went. Even when she was wallowing in a break up.

"Hold on," he called through gritted teeth, willing his hard-on to subside.

"Sure. Yeah, sure," came her high-pitched response. She sounded kind of nervous. It made Blake wonder if the boyfriend had come back and things had gotten ugly. Well *there* was one way to eliminate an erection.

Decent as could be managed, Blake finally made it to the door, threw the locks and yanked it open. And the sight of her—worse for the wear, but still so achingly pretty—made him angry at her scumbag boyfriend all over again. "Yeah?"

"I—oh. Shirtless. You're that way." Autumn gave a rapid shake of her head, blonde hair catching in the crease of her lips. "Did you...Have you gone anywhere near your pants yet?"

"How..." Cursing himself for forgetting to put on a shirt, Blake held up a hand. "Just tell me what you need."

Was it his imagination or did her attention keep dropping to his crotch? Discreetly, Blake glanced down to make sure his admiration of Autumn hadn't re-manifested and found everything as it should be.

"What do I need?" she murmured, starting to play with the

hem of her shirt. "That's a pretty long list. More whipped cream? Friends? I don't know. Right now, I'd do unspeakable things for a time machine."

When her gaze fell this time, Blake realized it was landing on his pocket. "Is this about your inappropriate drawing of me?"

"Oh *fuck*!" She covered her face with both hands. "I was hoping I could convince you to reach for something on a high shelf and then I would sort of…sneak it out of your pocket."

Blake experienced an odd sensation in his throat. Almost like he wanted to laugh. "Did you expect that to work?"

"Maybe as a back-up plan, in case the time machine wasn't available. I'd settle for a TARDIS. I'm not picky."

He stepped back with a sigh. Casual, when he felt anything but. "Do you want to come in, Ms. Reynolds?"

No one had been in his apartment in a long time. He'd had some furniture delivered years ago and occasionally Mrs. Zhu from the fourth floor would barge in, ranting in Chinese about her neighbors playing loud music, but she was half-blind and therefore couldn't judge. It wasn't so much that Blake was self-conscious about his living space…all right, maybe he was. But only because he didn't want to go through the annoying process of *explaining* things.

Just like when he'd walked into Autumn's apartment, she was clearly hesitant about being alone with him behind closed doors, tucking her hair behind her ear and shifting around in her child-sized sneakers. Her trepidation was likely triple now, knowing he'd found the sketch, but he wasn't making it any easier for her. He stood waiting, trying to look bored. "I don't have all afternoon, Ms. Reynolds."

"I'm sorry. Sorry." She scooted over the threshold, hitting him with the smell of coconut and toast. "Could you…could we leave the door cracked? Not because I think you're a serial killer with a bunch of severed limbs in your freezer or anything, but if I go into a stranger's apartment alone, I'll hear my mum wondering aloud where she went wrong with me. It's not you, it's her."

Ignoring the ridiculous disappointment that settled into his gut, Blake inclined his head and went to kick the door stopper in place.

"On second thought, maybe you should close it? Given the delicate nature of what we're discussing and all. Are we discussing it? Or am I just taking my homemade porn and doing the least satisfying walk of shame ever back to my apartment?"

"What would you like to do?"

"I…are you asking me what *I'd* like to do?" She snapped her open mouth shut and waved a hand. "Never mind, that's literally exactly what you asked me. I'm just not used to being given options." Saying that aloud seemed to jar Autumn and she looked away again.

"You okay?" Blake asked against his better judgement.

She nodded vigorously. "It's fine, you're embarrassing me with riches, but all I can think about is where you've put my drawing and what face you made when you saw it. Was it shock? Disgust? A classic whodunit jaw scratch?"

"Please stop talking."

Her cheeks flooded with color. "Oh."

Jesus, this was part of the reason he avoided people. His lack of a filter offended, even when it wasn't purposeful. Better not to try at all, right? He would already be showing anyone else the door, wordlessly delivering them to the hallway. The idea of Autumn leaving had him feeling flat, though. Her never-ending babble didn't bother him, it amused him. He wanted her to keep going—and he sure as hell didn't like the humiliation he'd painted on her face with his bluntness. "I only meant you need to give me a chance to answer a question before you answer it yourself, Ms. Reynolds. Just come up for air once in a while."

"I can't remember what I asked you."

"I'm still stuck on whether or not to close the door."

"Wow." She pressed her lips together. "I really left you in the dust, huh?"

"Open or closed?"

"Closed," she whispered. "What was the next part?"

"You asked…" He snicked the door shut and turned back to face her, noting her fascinated expression. As if she couldn't believe he'd been listening. "You asked if we were going to discuss the drawing."

"I didn't mean right away," she said, scurrying toward his living room. "We could start with some small talk. Like—"

Blake knew the reason she'd gone quiet even before he joined her in the living room. Stopping beside Autumn, he watched her take in the floor-to-ceiling mountains of books. Most of them were in boxes and plastic sleeves, but a good deal of his personal ones were wedged into shelves.

She turned to him, her eyes the size of hubcaps. "I'm having a Beauty and The Beast moment."

"I suppose that makes me the beast."

"*No*." Autumn laid a hand on Blake's arm and he held his breath.

"No, of course not," she said. "You're actually…that is to say…I don't just go drawing myself tied up for any old landlord, you know?" The last part was barely out of her mouth before her lips puckered. "I don't know what that was. Sorry. I'm being weird. Look, can you just say something? Anything?"

Of all the things she could ask for, it had to be small talk.

"My work station is this way. Don't touch anything." He willed his limp to be less noticeable as he led her around a stack of books, indicating his desk. Before visiting her apartment, he'd been in the process of repairing the binding on an original Dickens, so his microspatula, shears and glue brushes were still out, alongside his magnifying headset. "There."

She tilted an astounded look up at him. "You repair books?"

He hoisted an eyebrow. "You repair pigeons."

"Is it a hobby?" Autumn said, neatly ignoring his rudeness. "Do you keep the books you restore?"

"Some. Others are for clients."

While inspecting titles stacked on one side of the living room, she started to run a fingertip across a spine, but stopped and took it back. "Clients."

Blake wished he hadn't told her not to touch anything. What he wouldn't give to watch that delicate finger trace along the dark red leather. "Yes, clients."

Her tight body seemed to twist a little at his tone. "Is this your life's passion?"

"I don't know what that means. I just fell into it." Watching her move among his things, possessions no one touched but him, Blake had the urge to pick things up and rub them on her skin. His work cloth, the soft bristles of a dry glue brush. Or maybe it would be more to her taste to slap a hardcover against her ass while she whimpered across the top of his desk. As it was with all his darker fantasies about Autumn, he started to feel like a monster. What kind of man would impress his will on someone so fragile?

Blake turned on a heel and left the living room, waiting for her by the door with hands on his hips. He considered retrieving a shirt from his bedroom, but before he could move, she joined him in the foyer, looking anxious.

"Okay. We can discuss the sex-drawing now. We'll do it quick. It'll be like ripping off a Band-Aid." Her shoulders lifted with a big breath. "I'm sorry I stole your likeness and used it without your permission. I shouldn't have done that and it won't happen again. Could I please have it back now?"

"Used it how?"

Her throat moved with a swallow. "Excuse me?"

Blake took one step in her direction, stopping when something flared in her eyes. Not quite alarm, but not quite encouragement, either. "How did you use my likeness?"

"Am I required to answer?"

"No, but I'd like you to."

She wet her plush-looking lips. "Okay, fine. But I wouldn't be telling you this if I wasn't on an emotional roller coaster and under the influence of—"

"Nangs?" Blake suggested.

"Hey! You remembered what they're called!" Her little face fell. "I mean...not that I would ever...what are nangs again? Some kind of rope?"

"Ms. Reynolds, you were telling me why you chose to draw me into your sex-picture?"

Several beats passed as her gaze dipped to his bare chest and traveled the length of him, top to bottom, side to side. "I really hope you won't be offended, but you're rather large and *spectacularly* intimidating and I've always had a-a...wish." Her chest rose and plummeted, her words puffing out like little gusts. "A fantasy, really. To be jailed. Kept prisoner. Your likeness is sort of reminiscent of someone who could—not *would*, just could—do that to me."

The blood running through his body rose a thousand degrees

in temperature. "It turns you on. The idea of me holding you captive."

She crossed her arms over her chest, but not before he caught sight of her stiff nipples poking through her t-shirt. "I guess you could say that. But—"

"Do we *fuck*, Ms. Reynolds? In that little head of yours?"

A squeak left Autumn and he watched as her thighs pressed together. "Um, maybe? I mean yes. Regularly, I'm afraid."

Unbelievable. They'd barely exchanged a word since she moved in, yet they'd been mentally screwing each other's brains out from two floors away. "Do you still want to know the face I made when I saw the drawing?"

"No. I mean yes. I mean…it was a good face, right?"

Blake advanced on her, cataloguing everything. The way she backed up, then steeled her spine and attempted to hold her ground. The way she shivered and glanced at the door. Her very real apprehension forced him to make a decision. "Go home."

Her expression was the physical embodiment of a record scratch. "Wait. What?"

"Go home, Fun-Size." He took the drawing out of his pocket and offered it to her. "I don't hold scared little girls prisoner, even if I look like I do."

Autumn's eyebrows knitted together. "Show me the face you made." She plucked the drawing from its place between two of his fingers. "When you saw this."

What was the point? He rattled this girl. His painful attraction to Autumn was one that should be kept to his goddamn self. She'd just gone through a break up and there was a chance her vulnerability—combined with a very specific kink—could give him a shot at something physical. But he shouldn't take advantage. *Couldn't* take advantage. "No."

The green in her eyes seemed to deepen, like some kind of beautiful female hypnosis. "Please, Mr. Munroe?"

The desperation behind those three seemingly innocent words did him in. Having her throat exposed, head tilted back while she begged him for something, put a huge dent in his reservations. Blake slowly stole back the drawing and opened it with one hand, shaking it out without taking his eyes off Autumn. Seeing the depiction of them with the new titles of *prisoner* and *jailer* made his eyelids heavy. So heavy he couldn't see her from the mouth up. And whatever she saw on his face caused her pink, bow-shaped lips to drop open and a low moan to escape.

"Will you do it?" Autumn whispered. He could feel her nerves vibrating the scant air between them, but still she pushed on. "I know it's crazy to ask, but…h-he would never do those things for me and I've *needed* them—"

"*Quiet.*"

Blake didn't mean to bark at her. It was reflex when she brought up the ex-boyfriend. Jealousy, pure and simple. But it was more than that. It was the right to provide. Autumn needed an itch scratched and couldn't get it from her ex. So she was here, asking him to fulfill her urges. Christ, how many times had he imagined this happening against his usually iron will, never actually believing it would? Having his ultimate craving handed to him on a platter. Could he actually say no? Especially when Autumn had clearly been denied something she needed?

There was one detail holding him back, but it was a big one.

"I…shouldn't have snapped at you." Apologizing was more difficult in practice than in theory. Autumn didn't seem to mind his stilted backpedaling, though. She smiled like he'd just handed her the keys to a Mercedes. "It's fine, Blake."

Her words, the way she said his name, tightened a bolt in his chest. "That's what I do, though. I snap at people. I snap at sunny girls going through break ups. I'm not a nice man and that's why you have these thoughts about me."

"Do you meet loads of sunny girls going through break ups?"

No. No, he would never meet anyone like her again. There wasn't a doubt in his mind. And any day now, she could return to Australia. "I have a condition," Blake heard himself say out loud. "If I'm going to play jailer."

"You're actually considering this," she breathed. "Has the TARDIS idea ship sailed? Because I definitely should have washed my hair."

"Nothing is going to happen today, Fun-Size. Listen carefully." He waited for her nod, before flexing his stiff fingers and settling them on her waist. They almost encompassed the entire fucking thing. It was immediately not enough. He wanted full body contact and her nails ripping his ass cheeks to shreds. Or her wrists rattling in chains against his headboard. But the catch in Autumn's breath reminded him of his resolve.

"Here's the thing." Blake lifted Autumn off the floor, took two strides and pinned her to the wall, his mouth a centimeter away from hers. "If I wanted to kidnap you and keep you as my personal fuck toy, I could do it. I'm bigger and stronger and you live alone now. Nothing to stop me, is there?"

"No," she panted, squirming in his grip. Her pupils were dilated, her gaze fixed on his mouth. "Is that w-what you're doing?"

"If I was, how would you fight me off? Show me."

Autumn twisted to no avail, Blake pressing her tight to the hard surface and looking her in the eye as she struggled, her cunt shifting around on his hard cock like an invitation. "Come on, you can do better than that."

"I *can't*."

Blake eased off on the pressure, his stomach knotting as he heard a whimper of relief. "My point is you're afraid of me. Of course you are, you don't know what I'm capable of, but I don't like your uncertainty." Blake tucked his hips higher in between Autumn's thighs and savored her shaky gasp, the way her knees rose and cradled him, as if she couldn't help it. "I'll tie you up and punish you. I'll fuck you like he never could. But I want you to know I'll let you go home when it's over. I want you wet and naked. Not scared."

"Being scared is part of it, though. I need to believe it's happening in the moment."

"You will."

Her eyelids fluttered closed at those two words, like she knew he damn well meant them. "How are you going to make me less nervous around you in real life?"

Blake had backed himself into a corner without realizing it. Now that he was there, though, he didn't want to be free. The idea of taking a leap with this girl scared the hell out of him, but there was a loneliness in Autumn he recognized. Once upon a time, he'd shut out the world and gone into hiding. Autumn was in the process of doing the same. This new life she'd built for herself in New York would get tossed out with the trash because someone had chewed her up and spit her out. Blake knew that exact shitty feeling. It was none of his business whether she stayed or left…but a sense of purpose he hadn't experienced in a long time prodded him. She shouldn't give up, but he couldn't help change her mind without exiting his cave.

Could he do that? Going out with Autumn would mean talking. In the usual custom of basic human interaction, she *would* ask him questions, about his job, his friends, his past…

Not responding would be rude, even for him. But answering truthfully would mean telling her where he'd come from. He hadn't thought of his former life in so long, the simple act of it now burned his gut with acid. Ironically, that physical reaction is what spurred him into making a decision. He'd deal with the consequences later, but for now…he had to do something to help her. Doing nothing was unacceptable. After all, she'd cleared that path in the garbage for him the day she moved in…

"We go out. We…spend some time together. So you feel at ease with me." When she gaped at him, Blake scowled back. "Three dates. That's my condition. Take it or leave it."

"Take it," she said, arching her back. "But I *am* feeling kind of prisoner-y right now—"

With a monumental effort, Blake sighed and stepped back, steadying her as she slid down the wall. "Go home, Fun-Size." He said a silent apology to his stiff dick. "We start tomorrow night."

"But—"

"Next time you walk into a room alone with me, I don't want you shivering like a scared rabbit." He reached out and gripped her jaw, tilting it for his inspection. "Not at first, anyway."

Closing the door on a sputtering Autumn, Blake stood there for a moment, battling the need to open it, drag her back inside and fuck the damn thing off its hinges. Finally, when he heard her leave, he returned to the bathroom with the drawing. He'd intended to pick up where he left off, but instead he stood staring at himself in the mirror. Had he not only arranged a date, but *three* of them?

CHAPTER 3

Autumn peeled off her disposable rubber gloves and placed them in the hazmat bin.

"She looks good," her nurse, Pauline said, nodding toward the thick brown and gold tabby lying on the operating table.

"Fingers crossed." Autumn held up said fingers. "Are you okay to take things from here?"

"Sure thing, sweetie. You go wash up and have something to eat."

Autumn could barely contain her relief. The operation to remove a paperclip the cat had swallowed had been complicated by multiple haemorrhages and lasted an hour longer than it should have. Her hands and back were cramped and her stomach was growling *'Hostess mini doughnuts are not food,'* at her. She collected her bag lunch from the fridge and sat down at the staff dining table to eat in peace. She was only one bite into her ham sandwich when she realized her head had been far more peaceful when she was operating on cat guts. With nothing to do but chew, she was free to think about the fiasco that had taken place in her landlord's apartment the night before.

After fifteen minutes of straight freaking out—and recovering from the nitrous—she'd decided the best way to proceed was to go to Blake's apartment, fake that the hot water system was broken and steal her sex-drawing back. If he caught her, her plan had been to claim the images were a metaphor for their landlord/tenant relationship and shout something like 'You're making me suck your dick for capitalism, you Big Real Estate shill!'

It was a pretty bananas plan, but it paled in the reality of the craziness that had actually gone down. As she gnawed at her uninteresting lunch, Autumn filed the insanity in order of least to most surprising.

1. The Landlord had come to the door shirtless and revealed he was not only fucking enormous but *ripped*. Cover of a fitness magazine ripped. Just all bulges and biceps and abs and those thick flaring hip muscles.
2. He didn't live in a dank woman-dissolving cave, he lived in a beautiful, leather-bound book paradise. It smelled like sandalwood and non-douchebag intelligence.
3. The Landlord repaired said leather-bound books for money. Not only was that a job, apparently, that was The Landlord's job, in addition to being a landlord. Like, how many size-inappropriate jobs did this cunt have?
4. The Landlord had seen her sex-drawing. He'd just straight up seen it. He'd seen the picture she'd drawn of him making her suck his dick. That was a thing he'd seen. With his eyes.
5. Instead of announcing that she was a sicko and to kindly leave his identity out of her masturbation routine, he'd seemed…well, not *intrigued*. That was too strong a word for a man who had basically one facial expression, but definitely interested.
6. In a moment of severe, nanged-out weakness, she'd sexually propositioned him. She was pretty sure she'd also mentioned that she needed to feel as though she was

being held captive by him and that Ian had been unwilling to go there for her.

Here, Autumn paused to contemplate moving all her stuff out of the apartment without ever seeing Blake 'The Landlord' Munroe again. She ruled it impossible and returned to her list.

7. The Landlord turned her indecent proposal down, claiming they couldn't role play until she trusted he wasn't actually going to hurt her, and they would have to go on not one but *three* fucking dates to get to know each other, first. Autumn had assumed that was just an excuse to get her insane ass out of his apartment, and then…
8. …she found a note taped to her door as she was leaving for work. It read *"Dinner at 8pm."*

Which brought her to the craziest thing of all…

9. She was sincerely thinking of going. On a date. With her landlord. Whom Ian had unfavorably but accurately compared to Blackbeard, famed pirate rapist of the seven seas.

By the time she was done nibbling her green apple, Autumn decided there was no way in hell she could go on the date. For one thing, she and Ian had only just broken up. Surely a period of celibacy was warranted? Also, it seemed unethical of her to use The Landlord—Blake, his name was Blake—as a means to fulfill her prisoner fantasies and maybe read a couple of rare books before her visa expired and she fucked off back to Australia.

Yet, as she drank her strawberry milk, Autumn found herself questioning the validity of those reasons. For one thing, she wasn't sure if she was going home or not, so why shouldn't she go on a date? Sitting around her apartment with a flock of increasingly resentful pigeons wasn't helping her feel better, and Ian certainly hadn't waited a respectful period of time before seeing other people. The fuckstack had a head start of at least three months.

Maybe a rebound shag *was* what she needed to get motivated and stop doing nangs alone in her apartment. And location-wise, it would be very convenient to have a sexy, no-holds-barred fling with a guy who lived in her building.

Plus, she liked Blake. He was scowly but he seemed genuine, something she could deeply appreciate after all of Ian's head-fuckery. Blake seemed like he might be funny, too, in that sardonic, Dylan Moran, way few Americans seemed to have mastered. He was also good-looking, not at all like Blackbeard and seemed more than capable of giving her what she wanted in bed. When he'd pinned her to his door and told her he could fuck her better than Ian ever had, Autumn was surprised her underwear hadn't melted clean off her body.

But a *date*?

What the hell would they talk about? Or would Blake just stare intently at her until she promised she wasn't freaked out by him anymore? He was one concise motherfucker and after six years in a relationship, God knew her dating skills were rusty as hell.

She could barely remember the time before Ian. She'd been so into her studies that her sex life consisted of solo expeditions and the occasional party hook-up. She and Ian had met on a student booze cruise at the start of her second year of university. Autumn was the soberest person on the boat and had noticed the striking blue-eyed jokester right away. Her ex-boyfriend had been in the thick of things, chatting up girls and making everyone laugh.

She'd stared at him a while, wondering if a guy that gorgeous would be any good in bed, then headed onto the deck to talk to her friends and eat cheese puffs. Later, when the boat docked she'd headed below to collect her handbag and found Ian leaning against the side of the ship. He was bleary-eyed and alone, his fancy shirt untucked, his thick chestnut brown hair on end. She wanted to leave him there, but knew she'd feel so guilty if he fell over the side and died and everyone on campus had to attend a really tragic memorial service. She'd edged closer to him. "Are you okay, man?"

Ian had drawn his head up and stared at her as though in a trance, his eyes glittering like cold sapphires. "Do you ever feel like friendship is an illusion and all we do is use each other and get used until there's nothing left?"

Jesus H Christ. She took a step backward. "Uh, no...?"

He smirked. "An optimist, huh? Wish I was one. My outlook's pretty fucking bleak, I'm afraid."

Autumn held up her hands. "Look, dude, I think you're just drunk. Do you want me to call someone? Maybe get you some water or an Adderall or something?"

Ian had come closer, gazing intently into her face. "You're nice, aren't you?"

"I, uh, try to be."

"You can tell." He let out a low whistle. "A hot blonde who's nice. What a miracle. You go to Melbourne uni, right? That's why you were on this shitty boat trip to nowhere?"

"Yeah, I'm in vet-science."

Ian laughed. "Smart, as well! A triple threat! How did that happen?"

A little unnerved by the fact that Ian had called her hot, and the beauty of his gorgeously symmetrical face, Autumn tried a joke. "I have a twin sister who's a hunchback. She does all my homework."

He laughed even louder. "Funny! A quadruple threat!"

His hand found hers then, and when their skin touched, a tingle had shot up Autumn's arm.

"Want to hang out with me?" Ian asked. "I was supposed to go to this after party, but now I just want to sit on my roof with you and look at the stars and discuss life and the universe and everything."

And Autumn had smiled then, because this man was so handsome and his words were so musical and she'd just been going to head home alone. This was so much more exciting. "As long as that's not a metaphor for groping me, sure, we can hang out."

Ian had laughed and wrapped an arm around her waist and steered her off the ship. He did take her up to his roof so they could see the stars, and then he'd kissed her and asked for her number, and then they'd become a couple. *The* couple, really. Everyone was in awe of them, or maybe just that GQ-hot Ian had chosen a short nerd for his girlfriend.

They'd had fun together, her and Ian, but the flaws had been there right from the start, sparkling like the unearthly blue of his eyes. Ian had loved her, but he had also never believed he loved her. In his heart, he really did think people were all out to get one another, that love was chemical and friendship was co-dependency. She wasn't built that way. She thought real love existed, both romantic, platonic and maybe even cosmic love. She thought that people were fundamentally good and that selflessness paid off. Her mistake had been thinking she could change Ian's mind. You could never change anyone's mind, at least not about stuff like that.

As she packed up the remains of her lunch, Autumn wondered what Blake thought about love. Surely someone with as many books as he had was in tune with human nature, or at least had some interesting insights into it? Then she remembered that it didn't matter what Blake thought about love because she'd drawn a sex-comic about him and then *given him the fucking thing* like a complete idiot and she wanted to die.

Autumn had just laid her head on the table so she could really get into her self-pity when Owen and Isabella burst into the staff kitchen. She lifted her head at once. She'd briefly met the dynamic duo when she first came to New York but then they'd transferred to a specialist clinic. The move hadn't stuck and now the two of them were back at Happy Paws, effective today. This was something Autumn had completely forgotten until she'd walked into the lobby to find it full of streamers, balloons and flowers. Not that she'd been up to making cupcakes last night anyway, what with her drunkenness and landlord issues.

"Hey guys," she said as brightly as she could manage. "Welcome back!"

Owen, who'd been peering into the fridge, whirled around. "Autumn! Girl! Did you cut yourself a fringe?"

Duh, it's only the first rule in the 'dumped bitches' rulebook. She ran a self-conscious hand through her hair. "I did. Well, a hairdresser did."

"It looks marvelous. How are you?"

"Good, thanks," she lied. "It's great to have you back."

And it was, if only for the view. Owen was only a little taller than herself and exquisitely handsome in the way only gay men ever seemed to be. He had a chiseled jaw, supermodel cheekbones and a lush mouth he accentuated with dabs of YSL lipstick. All the clients simply adored him. As they were all mildly hysterical rich women, this was unsurprising, but Owen was also insanely charismatic. Autumn was sure he could charm the birds from the sky, if he wanted to.

Isabella was his mirror opposite. She was tall and curvy with thick, dark hair and Lana Del Rey eyes and never said more than five words in a row. She technically worked for Happy Paws, but everyone knew she was Owen's right-hand woman. Wherever he went, she followed. Autumn knew she was some kind of performer, a singer or a dancer, but she'd never spoken to her long enough to ask. She and Owen were so effortlessly New York, the song *'New York, New York'* should have started playing whenever they entered a room. They always made her feel a hundred times more like a floppy Australian fish out of water. She stood up. "Great seeing you guys, I'll let you have lunch in peace."

"Hang on!" Owen seized her shoulders and pushed her gently back into her seat. "We haven't even begun catching up!"

To Autumn's horror, he and Isabella proceeded to sit on either side of her.

"So, we're back," Owen said with a flip of his magnificent hair. "What incredible things have you been up to since we've been gone?"

Autumn couldn't even begin to explain. "Where's your food?" she said, hoping to change the subject.

Owen rolled his bright brown eyes. "Ugh, we're fasting. We have a reservation at Ugly Baby and we're readying ourselves to gorge on brisket soup and rice noodles."

"Oh cool," Autumn said, as though she'd heard of that restaurant. "You know when you fast, your stomach actually shrinks and you can't eat as much as you usually can?"

"Really?" Owen looked intrigued. "Then I will be ordering Pho for lunch after all. The usual, Iz?"

Isabella nodded before returning her caramel-coloured eyes to Autumn.

Autumn swallowed, intimidated as she always was by her size and beauty. "Are you, um, happy to be back?"

"Beside ourselves," Owen said, tapping away at his phone. "The other clinic was *okay*, if you like performing horse tracheotomies all day long, but the commute was a slut, and the money? God, so not worth it."

"That sucks."

"Ah, it's all part of life's rich tapestry," Owen sighed, tossing his phone aside. "Now we're right back where we belong, aren't we, Iz? Two blocks from Hermes, three blocks from Manhattan Beauty."

"Exactly," Isabella said. Her voice was lovely, low and melodious. Autumn wished she talked more, but she seemed perfectly content to let silence—and Owen—speak for her. Maybe she and Blake were a match made in heaven; both of them tall and striking and stoic as fuck. She imagined the two of them kissing and her stomach twisted up like a bag of snakes.

What the hell?

"How's the dreamboat boyfriend?" Owen said, interrupting Autumn's internal horror show. "Has anyone offered him a TV deal yet? They should, I know about three thousand gays who'd watch it for his smile alone."

Autumn—who'd forgotten Ian had once visited her at the clinic to the approval of all and sundry—couldn't work up the enthusiasm to lie. "I don't know about Ian's career, but he cheated on me with a bunch of improv groupies and I kind of hope his dick falls off."

Owen's mouth fell open. "That rat bastard! You threw him out on his ass, I hope?"

"Yeah, a couple of weeks ago. It was kind of a long time coming, though. We didn't have much in common besides…"

She paused. What *did* she and Ian have in common? They both liked mint-choc chip ice cream, but that hardly seemed relevant. Everything else had been complicated. He liked clubs, she liked live music. He took baths, she preferred showers. He liked improv, she loved stand-up. He always wanted her on top and she always wanted to be tied down and—

"Autumn?" Owen enquired. "You okay?"

"Sorry. Spaced out for a bit there."

"Sure." Owen pursed his mouth as though considering a sour thought. "In the interests of post-break up disclosure, I will say your ex was cute, but something about him was straight-up *reptilian*. I told Isabella, I was like 'that guy looks like he strangles the hell out of the homeless in his spare time.' Didn't I, Izzy?"

Isabella nodded gravely and Autumn couldn't help but laugh. It just came out of her like honey, a long joyous spurt. "Yeah, that's Ian. Not about the strangling the homeless thing, he's just a bit shifty-looking."

She noticed Owen eyeing her closely. "What's up?"

He narrowed his gaze. "For someone who broke up with her long-term boyfriend in very torrid circumstances, you seem very, well…not upset."

Well having the object of your sex-comics see the sex comic in question, then ask you on a date, will do that to you. "I have…other things going on."

"Rebound drama?"

"How do you know?" she said, beyond impressed.

Owen tossed his head like a prize racehorse. "Honey, if anyone knows anything about the advantages of getting on some revenge dick, it's the gays. Who is he and what's his damage?"

Autumn hesitated. She wasn't sure it was a good idea to be unloading about this stuff at work. On the other hand, she wasn't in a position to turn down advice from someone that wasn't a pigeon. With her friends and family still blissfully unaware of her break up, Owen and Isabella might be her only shot.

So she told them all about her encounter on her massive landlord, circumventing the sex drawing and making it sound as though she'd gone to his apartment for a logical, landlord related reason and he'd simply asked her out.

"Is he hot?" Isabella asked.

Autumn took a moment to revel in her three-word sentence. "I didn't think so at first because he always looks like someone just punched his mum, but he's really quite sexy. Kind of broad and hairy and angry-looking."

"Mmm," Owen said dreamily. "A bear to call your very own. So what's the problem here? Why can't you have dinner with him?"

"I don't know, maybe because he's my landlord?"

"The enemy," Owen agreed. "Hey, maybe if you fuck him, you'll get a deductible."

She laughed. "It's not about that. Maybe it's just because my future in America is kind of hanging in the balance, now Ian and I have split. Dating just seems a bit pointless. I mean, why bother?"

Owen held up both hands. Autumn had noticed most vets had nice fingers, but his were a work of art. Long and slender, with smooth oval tipped nails. "Up top, don't go back to Australia. We only just got back and your accent is so adorable, I just want to listen to you talk all night and all day."

"Thanks?"

"You're welcome. Also, just because something starts in sex, doesn't mean it's pointless or doomed to fail. You see this?" He flashed his diamond engagement ring at her and Autumn pretended to shield her eyes from a glare.

"How could I not? It's the size of an eggplant."

"Exactly, and you might look at it and think Ryan and I are just the most cookie-cutter couple on earth, but he started off as my dirty rebound."

"Fuck off!"

"It's true," Owen said smugly. "Jeffery, my ex, just dumped me for this twenty-year-old Russian ballet dancer and so I got on Grindr and I was, you know, out for blood basically. And then Ryan came over and we really hit it off and he just…never left."

"Wow."

"It's such a sweet story," Isabella said in her musical voice. "Once you meet Ryan, it's even cuter."

Autumn was even more amazed, but refrained from yelling out 'you can talk!' "That *is* a nice story, but I don't think I'm in the right headspace for a new boyfriend. In fact, I know I'm not."

"So fuck the bruiser," Owen said with an airy wave. "Go out to dinner and then fuck him. Take pictures and text them to Psycho McGroupiefucker. No, wait, he'd probably use them against you. Send them to me instead."

Autumn laughed. She'd missed this, missed fun conversations with people that weren't Ian, pigeons or guys who'd accidentally let their retrievers eat all their weed.

"What's his name?" Isabella asked, pulling out her phone. "I want to look him up."

Autumn, who'd already tried this, shook her head. "He doesn't have any accounts. No Facebook, no Insta, nothing."

Owen narrowed his eyes. "You know what they say about guys who don't have social media accounts?"

"They…like their privacy?"

"Serial killers."

"Blake's not a serial killer!"

"Are you sure?" Owen stared closely at her, as though the truth might be written across her cheeks. "You might have a type, honey. First Cheaty McDeath-Eyes and now Mr. No Face."

"My landlord has a face! And if he *was* a serial killer, he would have made his move when I went to his apartment last night. He's the one who wants *me* to feel safe. I wanted to get right into the rough—"

She realized what she was saying and cleared her throat.

Isabella and Owen shared a significant glance.

"Forget I said that."

"We won't, so why don't you go on…?" Owen leaned closer. "Something about needing to feel secure before you go to the rough…what, exactly?"

Autumn's face felt like it was on fire. "I don't think I can tell you about the…other bits of the story."

"Why not?"

"It's just about sex. Weird sex and I'm just not ready to look you both in the face and say it right now."

Owen let out a plaintive moan. "But I *love* hearing about people's weird sex lives."

"I *want* to tell you, but I don't think I can. At least not sober."

Owen seized her hand in his own lovely one. "At fifteen, I had to look my superbutch father in the eye and tell him I wanted to have gay sex with men. Please believe me when I say, nothing shocks me."

Autumn burst out laughing, then groaned. "I should go. My lunch break is going into overtime."

"Fine," Owen said with a faux-huffy sigh. "I suppose much like your landlord, we also have to earn your trust before we can be rough with you. Shall we get a drink on Thursday? The three of us?"

Autumn was taken aback. A friend date? With the cool people from work? Even if they just wanted to pump her for information about her depraved sex life, she was counting this one as a win. "Um, sure."

"Then it's settled," Owen said. "We'll go to Wilson's, they have decent tap beer. What's your number, by the way? For tonight, so you can text and say you got home safely after you fuck your landlord."

Autumn gave Isabella and Owen her number and promised that she'd text if she went out with Blake. That's if she did go out to dinner with Blake. Although, if she was being honest, she was on such a humongous high from having a successful interaction with her co-workers, she'd probably have gone on a date with Oscar the Grouch. Her sexy, grumpy, pin-you-to-the-wall-and-promise-to-fuck-you-senseless landlord was a whole other story.

※

AFTER A TON of outfit changes, Autumn decided on jeans and converse paired with a sparkly silver tank top. She wanted to look cute, but not *too* cute. If they were headed somewhere Blake looked like he belonged—a dive bar for example—she wanted to be able to run away fast if shit went down.

"Although," she told the pigeons as she fastened the hoops on her purple plastic earrings. "You'd have to have a death wish to try and fight Blake. He's basically a sentient brick wall."

She shivered a little as she remembered the way he'd lifted her into the air and pressed her hard against his door. She liked the contrast of their bodies, him huge and hairy, her small and smooth. It would have been so perfect if he'd just taken her, no questions, no complications. He'd said he could give her what she wanted and she believed him, but so much of his appeal was that he was a stranger. Surely going on a date and having to talk about the weather and where they went to school would ruin that? She didn't have long to contemplate the idea, she had barely put down her hairbrush when there was a sharp rap at the front door. Her pulse spiked wildly.

Enjoy the nerves, she told herself. *Soon you'll be discussing The Landlord's childhood and where he went to college and all the hot chicks he slept with, and then he'll probably try to explain why David Foster Wallace was the one true author and then all the mystery will be gone.*

Wiping her hands on her jeans, Autumn pasted on a smile and swung open her door. "Hi...*what*?"

Blake was wearing a suit. Not a shiny 'it's parole time' suit, a thick luxurious one that bound itself to his powerful body like something out of a blockbuster quality wedding porno. He'd trimmed his beard and his hair was brushed back to expose his broad Kingly forehead. He looked gorgeous and she felt like the dumbest girl alive. "So...I misread this situation."

He eyed her jeans and sneakers with a strained sort of amusement. "Should have said where we were going, huh?"

She held up her hands. "Five minutes. All I need is five minutes and I can be as fancy as you are. Maybe even fancier."

That was bullshit. She didn't own anything in the realm of Blake's suit, but she could do a lot better than she was at present. "Is that okay?"

He nodded, and when Autumn studied his face, she saw he wasn't annoyed at all. That caused her no small amount of relief. Ian could never let her make a mistake without supplying a wiseass crack about it. Maybe it was because her ex had been a comic. Maybe Blake just wasn't a fuckstick.

"I'll just be five minutes," she promised as she walked backward toward her bedroom. "Help yourself to the couch or some…water or something."

Blake raised a brow, something that was apparently a signature move, and dropped his enormous body onto her fake leather couch. "Go."

She couldn't help grinning. He looked so fucking wry and goddamn, the suit. Was there ever a man who looked so good in a suit? Right then, Autumn couldn't think of any. Her unhelpful brain pictured him pinning her down on his bed. *"Don't let the clothes fool you, I'm far from a fucking gentleman. By the time we're done, you'll have the proof all over your skin."*

Heat flickered through her body, making her scalp tingle and her hands curl into balls.

"Something wrong, Ms. Reynolds?" Blake asked.

She shook her head, retreating back into her bedroom. But maybe there was something wrong, specifically with her, because as she closed the door, she let her hand slacken enough so that it didn't click shut. It hung open just a crack, enough for it to look like an accident, enough through which he would be able to see her getting changed.

As she strode toward her closet, Autumn's smirk faded. Somehow, she needed to become Oscars-hot in the length of an average YouTube video. She didn't have time to do her make-up properly, so the hotness would have to come down to the dress. Swishing through her choices—cheap summery maxis and second-hand sailor frocks that would look even worse next to Blake's suit—she realized she'd been mistaken. The hotness would have to come down to the amount of skin she was willing to show. She chose a cherry-red bandage dress that flaunted everything God had given her in the least subtle way possible. It pushed up her tits, showed off her admirably flat stomach and moulded itself to her ass. It wasn't totally trashy, the color was rich and the material wasn't at risk of bursting into flame near a candle, but it was still pretty obvious.

Oh well. Not like you have anything else.

She wasn't poor anymore, not like she'd been when she was a kid, but the move to New York, supporting Ian and astronomical Manhattan rent prices didn't leave much money to spare. She'd have to be careful about what she ordered at wherever Blake was taking her. She was going to offer to split the check and she needed to be able to back that statement up.

She yanked her top over her head and Blake cleared his throat. For a second, she wondered why she could hear him so well, then remembered she'd left the door partially open. He was trying to let her know about it. What a sweetheart. Autumn bit back another smirk and shimmied out of her jeans. "I'm releasing the pigeons tomorrow," she called out.

"Good."

Was it just her, or did his voice seem even thicker than before? Autumn hoped so. Her heart was racing in the best possible way. This date was about sex, right? Why not make it sexier? She reached behind herself and unfastened her bra.

"They'll be happy to go," she said, as casually as she could manage. "They're getting all hyper being trapped in here."

She let her bra tumble to the ground, casual as you please, and heard a low grunt come from the other room. She knew from this angle he could see her boobs, or at the very least some side boob. She pulled off her panties—lines you know—and there came another growl, this one as audible as the knock on the front door. She waited with her heart in her mouth, wondering if he'd burst in and teach her a lesson, but nothing happened. The Landlord was a gentleman, it seemed.

She dressed with care, touching herself far more than she usually would have and fluffing out her freshly washed hair. She tugged on her strappy black sandals and just to be a bitch, bent over at the hips to do them up, her ass facing toward the door. She was disappointed not to hear a response. Maybe Blake was on his phone or something. She picked up her purse and stepped outside. "Okay, I'm ready to—"

The hand closed around her throat before she knew what was happening. Blake, a furious mountainous Blake scooped her up by her ass and pressed her into her bedroom wall, so their eyes were level. His brow was furrowed and his upper lip curled, every inch of him transmitting his anger.

"Let me make something very clear. You don't tease my cock. You're not ready for the consequences that come with teasing my cock."

The hand on her throat wasn't tight, but it was firm. Uncompromising. Autumn felt herself dampen and knew she should have put on underwear. "I'm sorry."

"No, you're not." Blake's voice was like thunder reverberating through her. "If you were sorry, you'd have closed that door when I told you to."

"Told me to? You mean by coughing? Seems a bit vague, if so."

Blake didn't take kindly to her attempted witticism. He leaned in so that their noses were almost touching. "I've used that picture a dozen times since you gave it to me. Thinking about when I'll finally get to see your naked body in the flesh, now I'll have to get through dinner having seen it without touching it."

"Sorry. You still can, though," Autumn supplied helpfully. "Touch my naked body, I mean. Now, or later. Drop by whenever you're in the building."

Blake rammed his hips between hers, pressing their bodies closer. "Yeah, you're funny, aren't you, Fun-Size? That's going to be a problem, because nothing about this is a joke. I wanted to see you naked when *I* tore your fucking clothes off, not because you decided to play pricktease through the crack in your bedroom door."

"Sorry," Autumn repeated. She might have said some other stuff too, it was really hard to concentrate when The Landlord's erection was pressed up against her, and she was ninety-nine percent sure it was as big as the rest of him. "Can we maybe, and this is just a suggestion, have sex now?"

"No." Blake's hand rose from her neck to fist her hair. The kiss of pain that accompanied the shove from his hips felt so good that Autumn's mouth fell open.

"I was already pissed off because I know you used to share that bedroom with your scumbag ex-boyfriend. Now, I'm goddamn furious. What do I do about that, little girl?"

Dear God, do me. Do me right against this wall. "I don't know."

He chuckled, a low malevolent sound, and then something seemed to change. He straightened up a little and released the hold he had on her hair. "You didn't learn your lesson yesterday, did you?"

"Wh-what lesson?" Autumn said, then sighed. She was doing something she never did; playing dumb. She knew what he meant. His lesson had been making her fight him, proving that he could dominate her physically and that he needed to make her feel safe before they got down to any sexy business. A little overcautious by her accounts, but still completely understandable. More than understandable, responsible. Kind. She met Blake's gaze. "Okay, so *maybe* I was messing with your boundaries by showing you my naked ass, but you have to understand, dude, you're fucking scary."

Blake's eyes dulled and he moved to set her on her feet. "I'll go."

"No!" Autumn gripped his shirt collar. "Not like, Freddie Kruger scary! I mean intimidating! You fix old books and you're my landlord and you're wearing this gorgeous suit and you're probably really smart… Sex, I can work with, I can understand why you'd be here for that. But you show up looking like you're going to the Oscars and you want to take me on a proper date…" She exhaled. "It's scary. I've never really dated and I've never, ever dated anyone like you."

"Like me?"

"Classy. Nice."

He stared at her. "You think I'm nice?"

"Hell yeah, man. You're here in a suit, aren't you?"

Blake looked away, brow furrowed. "Huh."

Autumn, operating on an instinct she didn't understand, reached out and touched his cheek. He started a little but didn't pull away, so she cupped his cheek. His beard was very soft. "Can we please just stay here, have a couple of drinks and then fuck, Blake? I'll be so much less awkward, I promise."

He shook his head, looking rueful. "Not the right time. Believe me, though, when you're chained to my bed and I'm riding your pussy on the hour, every hour, I'll make sure you remember what you did to deserve it."

Autumn, whose body was as tight and frustrated as it had ever been, was trying to think of a snappy comeback when he kissed her. The kiss was as much a contradiction as the man himself; firm, yet gentle, furious and yet strangely tender. He was at once exploring and establishing his dominance over her with his lips and tongue and when he pulled away, he nipped hard at her bottom lip, sending a shockwave of pleasure through her.

"Please," she said, not sure what she was asking for, but asking all the same. "*Please?*"

He placed her on her feet. "Not now. Let's go have dinner."

CHAPTER 4

Blake had been reading the classics and watching no television for too long.

Who arrived at a date's door in formalwear? Furthermore, who assumed his date would know to dress in the same way? When Autumn opened the door, her expression had been one of wonder and horror. Blake could still see it as he escorted her to their table at Eleven Madison Park because she had her head tipped back to take in the high, Art Deco ceilings. As he watched, she bumped into another guest's chair.

"Shit! Sorry!" Pink raced up the back of Autumn's neck and Blake swallowed hard, the need to draw her to a stop and taste that color nearly overwhelming. What would she do if he lifted her up onto her tip toes to conform her ass to his lap? What if he pushed her head forward and licked straight down her spine, right here in front of all these diners?

God, he wanted to find out. She would probably go very still, her little sides moving with hard fought breaths. In the end, though, she'd let the moment happen, because for all her timidity around him, Autumn's need for dominating never left her eyes.

Blake had spent a good deal of time lamenting the fact that he scared her. He didn't *want* to scare her. But he'd confirmed again in her apartment tonight that a big dose of that fear was tied up in lust, and Blake supposed he needed to accept that. Her attraction to him was rooted in the fact that she found him intimidating. Perhaps he should be grateful, considering he didn't know another way to behave. Apart from his curt business dealings and the building tenants—who were strange in their own right—no one *had* observed his behavior in a long time. Setting one foot in front of the other and walking through a restaurant shouldn't be difficult. Unless one was focused on not stomping the way he did in his own apartment. Or unless one found oneself maintaining eye contact with other men, monitoring their unwanted interest in his date.

His jacket felt weird, the fly of his pants uncomfortable where it chafed his dick, which was accustomed to loose pants or broken in jeans. Cutlery scraped on plates, chairs scooted along the floor, people talked. Nothing unusual, but all thrown together, they were a soundtrack he hadn't heard in ages.

Growing up in Rockaway Beach, a close-knit neighborhood at the southern tip of Queens, fancy restaurants hadn't exactly been on the agenda. Why travel when beer was cheaper the further you got from Manhattan? He could almost hear his friend Kevin saying that exact thing while performing a tightrope dance on the boardwalk rail, a million nights ago, Budweiser in hand. A night among many he didn't care to remember, but caught him off guard nevertheless.

When Autumn turned to look at him over her shoulder and tugged on the dress's hem, Blake realized he was frowning at the backs of her legs. Her abbreviated attire was on *his* head. Blake knew that. If he'd known these odd strings of possessiveness would tug in his midsection at bringing her into a crowded dining room wearing nothing more than painted on red, he would have been the one to go change. But he wasn't a spontaneous man and the plan had already been made. Now they were here and he'd have to deal with other guys testing their x-ray vision against Autumn's dress.

But he didn't have to like it.

Blake saw the hostess begin to pull back Autumn's chair and cleared his throat, waving her away so he could do it himself. Before tugging back the chair, though, Blake cast a scowl over his shoulder at the two businessmen dining together. Only when they'd gone back to their meal did he ease the expensive piece of furniture away from the table and grunt for her to sit. And then in slow motion, he watched the sweet curves of her ass stick out, the red dress sliding up her thighs, probably revealing the undercurve of her cheeks before planting on the seat. If he wasn't so tall, he'd know for sure. He'd never cursed his height so much.

Autumn spread her white napkin in her lap before tilting her head back to meet his eyes. "Are you going to sit? Or is standing behind your date all night an American custom?"

Even though she was joking, Blake wondered if remaining in place wasn't a terrible idea. As long as he stood behind her, no one else would be able to see the delicate line of her shoulders and the handfuls of blonde hair that said *angel at table nine*. Or whatever the hell number they'd been seated at. God, did she have any idea how sexy she was? Tonight in particular, it was almost too much to bear.

He leaned down beside her. "I can't decide. If I move, your naked back will be showing. If I stay here, I have no way to see your face, unless you keep looking up at me in a way that'll snap your neck."

"And you...want to see my face?"

"What kind of a ridiculous question is that?"

More pink joined the party on her neck. "One that's meant to disguise the fact that I'm basically fishing for compliments."

Her shoulders lifted in a shrug. "You haven't said a word since we left the building and I'm trying to figure out if I did something wrong. Like, besides my whole Sharon Stone pussy flashing act, which seemed way cooler in my head."

"I see." An odd twist in Blake's chest made him straighten. After a moment of debate—and another glare at the men sitting behind Autumn—he took his seat. Autumn was so beautiful in the warm pendant lighting, he had to take a moment to untie his tongue. "Only an idiot wouldn't want to look at your face."

Autumn went from tense to bemused. "Do you have a third career as a greeting card designer? It's never too late."

Christ, he was too goddamn old for this, wasn't he? No, that wasn't right. Even as a young man, dating had been as unnatural to him as flavored coffee. "Was that a shitty compliment?"

"It was…the *best* compliment, actually." A smile curved the edges of her mouth and she picked up her menu and practically buried her face in it, apparently already having forgotten he'd decided *seeing* it was necessary.

"Oh my God. No. They can't be serious with these prices. A hundred dollars for chicken? Appetizers? But it's *chicken*. It's barely even a meat…"

"Why are you worried about the prices?" Blake said, snapping open his own menu. "You're not paying."

"Is that because you're old fashioned or you'd rather not see me cry when the bill arrives?"

His mouth surprised him by twitching. "Both."

He caught her staring at him over the top of her menu and quickly put the kibosh on his almost-smile. "Stop doing math in your head. Order what you want."

She dropped her menu to the table. "How did you know I was doing maths?"

"Your mouth moves when you add." Blake settled on the beef wellington and put down his own menu. "You did the same thing when you wrote out the check for the security deposit, plus one month's rent."

"On the day we rented the apartment?" It took some determination not to snarl over her use of the word *we*, but Blake nodded.

Autumn shifted in her seat. "How close have you been watching me, exactly?"

Jesus, he'd have to be blind not to notice her sudden arousal. She probably had no idea her behaviour had changed, but he did. He watched hungrily as her fingertips traced down the center of her cleavage, her tongue sneaking out to wet her lips. He leaned toward her, his gaze scraping over her firmly budded nipples. "Do you like being watched? Is that why you left the door to your bedroom open, so I could catch you changing?"

"No," Autumn breathed, staring at his mouth. "I left the door open because I thought we could skip the date and go right to you, you know…sexing me up."

"The idea of a date with me is so terrible?"

"No, but I haven't been on a first date in six years. I'm like a prisoner who just got out of jail and I'm gagging for it, but I don't know how dating apps work or how to tell chicks I can't go more than thirty kilometers from my house because I'm wearing an ankle tracker. What I'm trying to say is, I'm flying blind here."

"I haven't been on a date in over a decade." Blake was instantly disgusted with himself for revealing something so pathetic—when Autumn's jaw dropped, it only got worse. "Forget I said anything."

"Wow," she said, her pale eyebrows raised. "*You're* the ankle tracker guy."

"This metaphor is annoying."

"Sorry." Blake watched as Autumn reeled herself back in, fixing her hair and licking her lips in a way he knew had nothing to do with arousal. "So, um, what are you getting?"

Blake opened his mouth to tell her the metaphor was fine, he was just being an unrepentant asshole out of habit—or maybe remind her she'd liked his compliment about her face—but the waiter chose that moment to approach and Blake decided it wouldn't be polite to shout at him to fuck off. The last time Blake was on a date, he'd ordered for himself and his fiancée. It was a week before the accident that led to the injury of his leg. And everything else that followed. His hospital stay. The revelation that everyone he trusted was laughing at him behind his back. It was all so long ago, but the wounds never quite healed. Mental *and* physical. No, the effects hung around and made mockeries of his efforts to try again. Like tonight with Autumn.

Although, this date wasn't about him trying to be a normal, functioning human, was it? It wasn't about him at all, which was how he'd talked himself into doing it. He didn't want Autumn's ex-boyfriend's actions to send her running back to Australia without a fight. He was living proof of where that kind of thing led. *Someone* needed to put on a fucking tie and make Autumn feel important. God knew he wasn't qualified for the job, but he sure as hell didn't want someone else doing it. Hence the suit and small fortune he'd spend on dinner at the fanciest restaurant he knew. He'd wanted her to go to sleep tonight with the understanding that… she was worthy of better. So much better than the cheating dickhead, or even himself.

After Autumn ordered the roasted duck with honey and lavender and Blake, the wellington, they settled on a bottle of

Brunello and were left alone again.

"So..." A sip of red wine left a sheen on her lips and Blake's hands fisted under the table. "I'm guessing you haven't been to this place before," she said. "What made you choose it?"

"The owner is a client of mine. His newest wife is a collector." Blake couldn't hide his irritation. "He thought he was being original, cutting a hole in the center of a first edition Beatrix Potter—a sentimental favorite for her—and planting the engagement ring inside. She accepted the proposal, then socked him in the jaw."

A laugh bubbled out of Autumn. "She sounds like a keeper. Did you fix it?"

"With ease."

Wine glass pressed to her lips, Autumn looked around the room. He followed her gaze, wondering if she was enjoying the view of Madison Square Park or if she'd rather be home sucking nitrous out of whipped cream cans. "You must be very good at what you do to have a client of his caliber. Do you have an office where you meet with them?"

"You've seen my office."

"Yes, but I never see anyone coming and going from your place."

"You've been watching me closely as well, Ms. Reynolds."

Her chest dipped on an exhale, the glass shaking a little in her hand, but he didn't wait for her to respond. "My uncle died a while back and left me the building. The books came with it. Literally. His apartment was filled with half-finished projects. I was only going to complete them to tie up his loose ends, but it went from a necessary pursuit to a profession."

"I'm sorry about your uncle."

Blake took a pull from his own drink and shrugged. "Been

years." Ignoring the jab in his chest, he set down his glass. Due to some differences between Blake's father and uncle, they'd never been close. But he'd liked the man. Respected him. And he'd never gotten a chance to thank him for the unexpected gift of the building. "The reason you don't see people coming and going is I go to them. While you're cozy in your little bed, I'm out doing deliveries or having meetings."

"Really. Never during the day?"

Wordlessly, he shook his head. *I locked myself away from the daylight so I wouldn't run the risk of colliding with the past, until one day darkness was the only thing that felt natural.* What would she say to that? How would she react knowing he'd been outside during the day only a handful of times since moving into the building? This sunny girl was on a date with a borderline hermit who didn't know the first thing about repairing post-break up pride—he had *zero* delusions he could salvage her heart—but was utterly compelled to try.

"I only go out at night," he offered, at a loss for how to explain. "I don't usually bring other people along."

"So you're saying I'm lucky?"

"God, no." He adjusted his cutlery, aligning the fork and knife at an exact distance, top to bottom. "Those weeks I spent wrapping up my uncle's projects, I got used to being in the quiet. Working under the single light. And I didn't see any reason to change my routine once I finally found a way of living that I liked."

"Until tonight, apparently. No pressure or anything." Autumn's gaze skated away and came back. "Wait. I knew you managed the building, but you...*own* the building, too?"

Blake's silence served as his answer.

Autumn blinked. "Looks like I'm ordering dessert."

"I was going to make you order it, anyway." Beneath the table, his palm slid over her knee and squeezed, noting the jump of her muscles, the arch of her back. "We want that mouth extra sweet when I taste the inside of it later, don't we?"

Pulse fluttering at the base of her neck, she nodded. "That's one w-way to change the subject."

"Just needed to get my fucking hands on you, Fun-Size." His hand journeyed higher, stopping at the hem of her dress, rubbing the material between his thumb and forefinger, barely resisting the urge to drag her around the table and onto his lap. "You're too far away from me over there. I need some of your skin on mine."

"If you'll recall," she said in a husky whisper. "I was totally willing to give you some back at my place."

"You should expect *more*." Blake didn't intend his pronouncement to come out sounding so harsh, but it was. Autumn jolted and he cursed, taking his hand back. "Christ. I'm not good at this."

He could feel her watching him curiously, but didn't meet her gaze. Not until she said, "You're...really worried about blowing this date, aren't you?"

What could he say to that? Yes, fine. He was worried. For months, he'd been fantasizing about the beautiful girl upstairs and now she was giving him the green light. Not only to fuck her, but to act out things that—until now—had been relegated to the darkest corners of his imagination. Maybe he should have just taken the offer and ran with it. She could be tied to his headboard right now, screaming into a gag while he rode her sexy little body. Instead of instant gratification, he'd decided to try and give her...more. A reason to believe she was incredible. Incredible enough to tackle this filthy city on her own. It should have been an easy task, because Autumn *was* incredible, but proving that to her might really be outside of his wheelhouse.

"Blake."

"Hmmm?"

She twined their fingers together under the table, all the while watching him as though he might actually be moron enough to pull away. And all the while, he'd forgotten to breathe. "You asked me if I've been watching you."

Her lips pressed and rolled, more of that delicious color filling her cheeks. "I have. And sometimes I feel you watching me through the peep hole and I like it. On those days when you spy on me, I barely make it in the door before my hands are—"

"*Enough,* Autumn." His fingers tightened around hers and she gasped—but it was with excitement, not fear.

"Why did you tell me that here?" he demanded.

"Because you said only idiots wouldn't like my face and you're worried about screwing up this date with me. And no one has ever done either of those things."

Blake's heart rammed into his Adam's apple. Such an alarming physical reaction, he grasped for a way to regain control. "*I'll* be the one who doles out rewards." Slowly, he pressed his thumb into her wrist, deeper, deeper, until it felt like her pulse was beating inside his own body. "Are you asking me to watch you more often?"

"Yes," she whispered, her throat moving with an audible swallow. "Do more than that, Blake." Her eyes closed, the pulse in her wrist kicking into a faster pace. "I-I think I want you to stalk me."

If his cock got any harder, it was going to elevate the table. "Very well, Ms. Reynolds," he rasped, just as their entrees arrived. "Eat your dinner."

CHAPTER 5

IT'S COMPLICATED. FIRST dates didn't require social media updates—at least as far as Autumn was concerned—but if they did, she'd have made her status 'it's complicated.' Maybe accompany it with a picture of her braised chicken oysters or pineapple rum cake. Actually, no, that implied the restaurant was the source of her complication, and that wasn't true. The food had been unfathomably delicious, the décor glamorous, the service wonderful, the ambiance lovely. Ten out of ten to Eleven Madison Park, not that one of the best restaurants in the world needed her fucking endorsement.

No, the complication came from the man who'd sat opposite her, alternatively glowering and looking as though he wanted to put her on the end of his fork and swallow her. She'd been hoping to come away from her date with Blake Munroe understanding him better, or in possession of wicked sex bruises. So far, she'd accomplished neither, she'd just eaten what amounted to half her rent check and told a near-stranger she fantasized about being stalked and taken against her will.

As she and Blake walked down the brightly lit Manhattan streets back to their building, Autumn couldn't help but turn her idiocy around and around in her head. She couldn't blame blurting out her twisted fantasy on the wine, she'd only been a few sips in. Maybe she'd said it because she'd been blindsided by the date as a whole—Blake's gorgeous suit, the eighty-dollar poultry, the fact that old mate was rich as hell—and it had all come as a bit of a shock.

She had only ever told one person about her fantasies; Ian, and she hadn't so much 'told him' as he'd 'caught her reading a fan fiction novel about Hermione being held hostage by a sexy lumberjack and guessed it was why she wanted to be tied up all the time.' It had all been a bit embarrassing, especially when he wrinkled his brow and said, "But you're such a bra-burner, why the fuck would you want me to abduct and/or rape you?"

A fair question, Autie supposed. She *was* a feminist, she wanted same pay for same work and to take back the night and have gender inequality recognized and corrected. Fantasizing about being a man's sex slave was a bit *off brand*, she supposed.

But…

But…

But she wanted it, all the same.

She wasn't deluded, she knew forced seduction fantasies weren't an endorsement for fuckwits to stalk and abuse women, but there was something distasteful about wanting to role play things that had caused such harm. At least in her own mind. Ian felt the same way. For someone so committed to being an actor he once spent a week putting on a Cambridge accent, he did not take kindly to the role of 'consensual pretend lady kidnapper.' They only tried it once, and the whole time he kept swatting her ass and telling her she was a naughty girl. It had just been so, *urgh*. She was not a naughty girl. She was a grown woman who wanted to do some weird shit in bed. Was that so much to ask?

Well you did ask, she reminded herself. *You asked Blake. And he said 'very well.'*

Autumn shivered and looked over at her massive, real estate-owning companion. He'd suggested they take a different route home, presumably because the scenery was nicer, which it was, but he hadn't taken her hand and he wasn't saying a word. He'd been crazy quiet through dinner, too, asking questions and listening intently to the answers while waving aside the same 'getting to know you' small talk she directed at him. By the time they'd ordered dessert, she'd decided he either hated using language or had something to hide.

Complicated. It was all very complicated.

She shot another glance at him as they swerved to avoid a young couple walking hand-in-hand. He was so objectively handsome, it was hard to remember she'd ever questioned her attraction to him, but he felt like more of a stranger now than when he skulked around their building in baggy shirts and a scowl. That such a hot, rich guy was single was strange. That he might be interested in her was downright confusing. She'd have thought he was in it for the easy pussy, but he hadn't needed to take her to a five star restaurant to get that, he could have just done her against her bedroom wall.

As they wove around a card table loaded with knockoff sunglasses, Autumn wondered if New York wasn't done fucking with her—maybe it had sent her Blake to really round out the job.

A young nanny stopped Blake and asked him for directions to some shop Autumn had never heard of. She also eyed him up like he was the last water bottle on the road to hell, flipping her hair and giggling and making sure he knew the crying stroller full of babies weren't hers. Autumn felt a hot flick of jealousy, which would have been a thousand times worse if Blake had flirted back. His expression as he talked to the pretty nanny hadn't change an iota. He still looked like a Persian cat that had just received an injection and could see the needle coming back for more.

He and Ian could not have been more different, she realized. Ian talked a mile a minute and could flirt with on-hold music. He was extroverted and highly aware of how hot he was. Autumn couldn't blame him for that, he'd been daily informed of his hotness since he was thirteen, but there had been a lot of parties when she'd felt invisible, a lot of double takes and *'really? She's your girlfriend?'*s. He'd also never paid for her dinner. They'd either split the bill or she'd picked up the whole thing, what with him being a broke-ass performer and all.

What's more romantic, she thought. *Being treated to dinner by a silent, confusing giant or paying for a charismatic cheater's salmon?*

Complicated.

Autumn didn't want to think about Ian, but it was inevitable, given her lack of dating experience. Lack of sexual experience, too. She'd banged a whopping six men, if you could consider her high school boyfriends and a couple of one-night stands 'men.'

She cast another glance at Blake. He was a man, a fully grown man with money and multiple jobs and contacts to fancy as fuck restaurant owners. He said he hadn't been on a date in a decade, but she bet he was knee-deep in hookups. He probably had crazy high sex standards.

What did men even like in bed? Stripping? That thing where you pulled down their underwear with your teeth?

I know I shouldn't have gone on this stupid date, I should have stayed in with the pigeons and learned how to play Strangers *on the harmonica—really give the neighbors something to bitch about.*

She was considering faking a headache when she caught sight of a neon pink sign that drove all thoughts of sex from her brain. It was The Natch, a stand-up comedy club famous for hosting Amy Schumer and Bo Burnham during their early days on the New York scene. For the hundred millionth time, Autumn imagined herself on the cramped stage saying the jokes she'd only heard inside her head, hearing the laughter of an approving crowd—

"You thinking about him?" Blake said.

She glanced up and was immediately side-swiped by the beauty of his light brown eyes. So bright…

"Autumn?"

"Huh?"

"Your ex. You see the comedy place and start thinking about him?"

Remembering her internal debate of the last ten minutes, Autumn fought back a laugh. The one time she *wasn't* thinking about her dumb ex. "Nah, Ian doesn't do stand-up. He does improv comedy; you know, pretending to be a monkey catching the bus or a waiter who just found out he has ten minutes to live."

One of Blake's eyebrows lifted.

"Yeah, it's exactly as painful as it sounds. I mean, *sometimes* the shows were funny but they were definitely more miss than hit. I used to bring two flasks of bourbon just so I didn't cringe myself out of existence."

"Why'd you go at all?"

'I was being a supportive girlfriend' was the appropriate answer, but just like with her stalking fantasy and her sex-comic, something compelled her to tell Blake the truth. "I never had anything else to do. It felt more productive than sitting at home in New York and watching TV."

"Right."

Worried the conversation was about to wither, Autumn added, "I think I was wrong, though. There were times I'd watch Ian pretend to be a robot lawyer and I swear I could feel my eggs dying."

The corners of Blake's mouth quirked up. "You're funny."

"I...thanks." Autumn frowned. "Wait, you mean in a good way, right? Not like I'm a weird cunt?"

Blake shot her a startled look.

"Fuck, sorry for saying the c-word! It's an Australian thing. I don't mean like 'cunt-cunt', I mean like 'mate-cunt.' Jesus, I need to stop saying cunt. Oh my God, I just said it *again*."

Blake reached over and put a hand on her mouth. "I don't care about you saying any word you want to say. You ever thought about doing stand-up?"

He released her mouth, leaving her free to gape at him. "Why do you ask?"

"I already said you were funny."

"That doesn't mean I should do stand-up comedy. It's a really specific skill. You wouldn't ask an amateur choir singer to perform at the big sporty thing you Americans like so much."

"It's the superbowl."

"Right. Sure. You're into the superbowl, are you? I mean you are enormous. Did you play in a superbowl?"

"Don't change the subject, Fun-Size. You were staring at that sign longer than it took to read the headliner and you had the same look on your face that you got when the waiter brought out the other table's dessert."

"And that look is?"

Blake squinted at her, his eyes bright with obvious amusement. "If I had to go with one word, I'd say 'longing.' Have you thought about trying it out? Stand-up, I mean, since I already made you order dessert."

Autumn, completely unnerved by his observation, kept silent. Forget the weird abduction fantasies, no one had ever known her stand-up secret. Not Ian, not *anyone*. The Landlord had her number and she had no idea how to feel about that.

"You gonna answer my question or not?" Blake's voice was rougher, but Autumn guessed self-consciousness, not irritation, was rubbing it raw.

"What question?"

"Have you ever thought about doing stand-up?"

Autumn licked her dry lips. "I've...written a twenty-minute set. It's about being a vet and it has music in it. I play a Casio keyboard. Pretty sexy, huh?"

Blake's expression didn't change one iota. "What's your show called?"

"I Know Your Dog Ate Your Weed: The Musical."

He smiled, the skin around his eyes crinkling, and Autumn's heart gave an unhealthy lurch. "You think that's a dumb name?"

"No, I think it's funny. Why are you so defensive?"

"I guess..." Autumn swallowed again. "I guess I'm used to men who think women aren't funny. You said I was funny like it was nothing."

Blake said nothing. They walked another block in silence and just as Autumn braced herself to blurt out her headache excuse, he said, "I like Kate McKinnon."

Autumn stared at him. "What?"

"I like Kate McKinnon. From SNL, I think she's funny. You remind me of her."

She stopped dead in her tracks. "You...did you seriously just compare me to Kate McKinnon?"

That got her a smile, a real one. She thought she might have even seen a flash of teeth. Then as quickly as it had come, it faded, and Blake strode on. "Yes, I compared you to Kate McKinnon. Keep moving, Fun-Size, you're blocking the footpath."

Autumn ran to catch up with him once more. "I think that's the nicest thing anyone's ever said about me."

"That's fucking sad." Blake looked at her, his expression unreadable. "Why don't you sign up for an amateur night or something?"

Again, Autumn saw herself on stage, laughter and applause ringing out as she took a bow. This time, Blake watched approvingly from the sidelines, a big bunch of roses in his hands. For a moment she reveled in the fantasy, then her rational brain shut it down. "I don't have time for that. I'm crazy busy with work."

"You might have more time if you stopped bringing sick pigeons home."

"I'm not doing that anymore! Besides, that's the least of your worries, Landlord-wise. I think Ernie on floor seven is making parmesan in his sink again and the smell is fucking horri—"

"You're changing the subject," Blake interrupted.

Autumn threw up her hands like a helpless mime. "I told you. I don't have the time to perform my show. Or enough money for the sign-up fee. It's usually like, a hundred bucks unless you bring ten friends, and as I've already said—no American mates. Unless I train some pigeons to wear hats and trench coats and speak with human voices. You think that'll work?"

Blake didn't smile. "I'll pay your entrance fee."

"That would make me feel weird."

"I just bought you a two-hundred-dollar dessert."

Autumn let out a howl of misery. "There were no prices on the specials board and I didn't know it had gold leaf on it! Why are posh people always trying to eat gold, anyway? It's like, one step away from using it to wipe your—"

"Autumn." Blake's heavy jaw was set, his brow a series of

deep furrows. He resembled a bear that had been forcibly turned human and stuffed into a suit.

"Yes, sir?" She wanted to sound jokey, but her voice came out all nervous. Blake seized her arm and dragged her into the enclave of an abandoned Chinese restaurant.

"Trying to make out with me, huh, big boy?"

Blake's nostrils flared. His gaze dropped to her mouth and for a moment she was sure he was going to snatch her up and kiss her. Instead, he met her gaze once more. "What I want is for you to talk to me honestly, the way you did at dinner. The way you were before I mentioned stand-up."

Autumn licked her lips, the insincerity behind her attempts at humor suddenly obvious. "Your insightfulness is quite unnerving."

"So I've been told. Look, the comedy thing isn't a big deal, I just don't get why a girl as smart and driven as you wouldn't just sign up for an amateur comedy night and do her show."

Another cutting insight, except this time she didn't tell the truth. At least not all of it. "What's the point? Nothing would come of it except I'd lose a hundred bucks and get heckled by everyone's dickhole friends."

"You don't know that. This is New York, weirder shit happens every day."

She groaned. "You're one of those 'New York is the magical place of magical magic dreams' buttheads, too? Christ, you really have been sent by this city to rob me of my remaining self-respect."

"What?" he said, turning his head to the side as though he hadn't heard her, which, considering a huge truck had just driven past blasting The Chainsmokers, he probably hadn't. She decided against repeating the butthead thing. "I don't want to do amateur comedy in New York just because it's a shitfully strange place."

Blake opened his mouth, but before he could protest, a newer, better excuse struck her like lightning. "Besides, I'm probably going home soon. There's no point trying to start a comedy career in NYC if I'll be job-hunting in Melbourne next month."

His gaze cut to the side. "You're leaving next month?"

Autumn forced herself to laugh, though it sounded inauthentic even to her own ears. "Maybe. That's when my work visa expires and the feds'll kick me out. Shit, sorry I probably should have told you I might be breaking my lease in a more professional setting."

"Okay," Blake said, his shadowed face extremely forbidding as he stared a foot above her head. "You're leaving next month. Fine."

Autumn bit her lip, unsure of what to say. She'd come up with the excuse on the fly, but maybe it was for the best. Maybe telling Blake she was moving out was the kick in the ass she needed to finally call her parents and say "Ian cheated on me, Happy Paws Vet Clinic sucks, New York is evil, all the coffee tastes burnt, fuck the Yankees, fuck bagels and fuck that weird thing where people just pack more garbage into already overflowing garbage bins that *no one ever fucking empties!* I'll see you cunts soon."

Without the cursing, of course. She didn't curse in front of her parents, one of the many reasons she could never be a stand-up comic. What if they came to one of her shows?

"You're leaving next month," Blake repeated, though this time he was looking right at her. "You're going back to Melbourne?"

"Yeah. Hey, you said it the right way. 'Mel-bun' and not 'Melbooourne.'"

"I said it the way you said it when you moved in. When I asked where you were from."

Autumn felt a pleasurable squirm in her belly. He remembered a conversation they'd had six months ago and he pronounced the name of her home city the right way. She beamed at him, and he gave a little mouth-quirk back. She realized something—she liked Blake. She liked his scowls and moody silences and his pestering her about stand-up and all. She decided to show him how much she liked him. She moved closer, her head tilted upward, and was gratified to see his face soften. At least she was until he put his hands on her shoulders and said, "Not here."

Autumn tried not to look hurt. "Not a PDA guy?"

He shook his head.

"Maybe you can kiss me back at your place?"

"We're not going back to my place."

"Oh," she said, disappointed. She'd been looking forward to seeing the inside of his apartment again, getting a better look at his books and having hot sex in a new bed, far from the one she'd once shared with Ian. "Why?"

Blake tilted his head toward the street. Autumn followed his lead and began walking again. "You'll feel safer if we're not in my apartment," he said as they resumed weaving through foot-traffic.

"Is that, uh…important? The whole point of my fantasy is that you make me feel unsafe."

"I will."

"Then why—"

"Quit talking and walk in front of me."

She frowned. "Why?"

"Because I want to watch you move."

It was then she finally picked up what he was laying down.

Blake wanted to play at what they'd discussed in the restaurant. Him watching her, her being watched. Conflicting emotions burst inside her like fireworks, but the biggest and brightest was excitement. "I don't know this area. H-how will I know how to get home?"

"It's straight all the way back to the building," Blake said. "Just another ten minutes. That good?"

Autumn sucked her lips into her mouth in an attempt to hide her excitement. "Yes."

"Good." There was a gleam in Blake's eyes that hadn't been there before, and Autumn suddenly understood. She'd told him about the stalking fantasy at dinner, not because she was drunk or lonely or an idiot but because of what she'd felt. She'd looked across the candlelit dining table and seen the bookend to her own desires simmering in those incredible light brown eyes. Blake was excited by this as much as she was, and maybe he was afraid of it, too. Afraid of what it said about him as a man. The realization made her feel braver, less alone. She smiled at him, a goofy, companionate smile, and he smiled back.

"I think you're a good guy," she announced. "Maybe even a *really* good guy."

His smile faded, though his eyes were still gleaming. "Walk, Fun-Size."

So Autumn sped up, moving in front of Blake to strut the streets of New York alone. It was a strange sensation, being followed. At first she just felt self-conscious—what if she tripped and made a complete twat of herself? But as the minutes passed, she relaxed into the knowledge that Blake was watching her. She could almost feel his eyes lingering on her legs as she moved, memorizing the swing of her hips and the swells of her ass.

He's following me, she thought, shivering in spite of the summer heat. *He saw me out all by myself and now he's following me home.*

She remembered the way Blake had looked at her in the restaurant, the hunger in his eyes, and she put a little extra sway into her walk, sliding her legs forward and swishing her ass as though she were a drunk catwalk model. She swore she felt the intensity with which she was being watched increase. Unable to help herself, she turned and looked over her shoulder. Blake's gaze locked on hers. His jaw jutted and somehow he seemed to grow larger. Autumn shivered with excitement. The sizzle of it ran down her midriff and into her pussy. She could feel herself getting wet, wet from being watched and lusted after, stalked as though she were nothing but girl-prey fit to feed this hungry male animal.

I thought you were a bra-burner, a familiar voice muttered in her ear. *This isn't a self-loathing thing is it, Auts?*

Oh fuck off, Ian. Go have sex with someone who likes improv and let me have this.

Miraculously, her brain obeyed. She kept walking toward her building, her skin prickling deliciously and her mind full of thoughts of Blake and what was coming next.

She'd half-hoped Blake was planning to follow her into her apartment and continue their game without another word, but suspected he was far too responsible for that. Sure enough, he caught her at the building door, his heavy hand closing over her wrist. "You liked that."

She nodded, knowing that if she tried to explain why, she'd ruin the mood. "What now?"

Blake bent down and Autumn caught the scent of his cologne, a woodsy aroma that increased her arousal a thousand-fold. Before she could stop herself, she turned and kissed him, a soft closed-mouthed kiss. He kissed her back and she could feel surprise and pleasure in the way his lips worked. His hands found her hips and then she was dangling in mid-air with his mouth pressed to hers. He pulled her flush against him and it was unlike anything she'd ever felt before. Ian was taller than her, pretty much everyone was taller than her, but Blake was *enormous*. Being held by him was like being held in a cage, a gentle, living cage. With another man it might have felt oppressive, but as Blake kissed her deeply, all she felt was warm and safe and turned the fuck on. Within seconds she was rubbing against him, moaning into his mouth. Her landlord couldn't talk worth a damn but god he could *kiss*. He kissed like it was his mother language, like he could tell whole stories with his lips and tongue. She began to writhe against him, desperate for more, and he pulled away, his eyes full of heat. "Not here. Not like this. You're gonna take the stairwell up to your apartment."

"I-I thought it was closed for maintenance," she said, recalling the sign she'd seen on the building noticeboard.

"It was. By me."

"Oh yeah, you're my landlord. Despite the fact that I used to call you The Landlord, I keep forgetting."

Blake flicked her a quick not-quite smile. "Go ahead. Climb the stairs to the third floor and I'll follow."

"What's going to happen?"

"What I want to happen." His gaze dropped from her mouth to her nipples which were poking through her dress like hard candies. It was a leer, pure and simple, and it shot her straight back into her gazelle-being-stalked state of mind. "I...uh, guess I'll go and wait then?"

Blake nodded. "As soon as the stairwell door shuts, you're mine. No one will interrupt us. Nothing will happen that I haven't planned. Start to finish, it's what I want, you got that?"

She nodded, weak at the thought that it was finally going to happen, that she, Autumn Martha Reynolds, would finally experience the thing she'd been daydreaming about since puberty began.

"Say you understand me, Autumn."

"I understand." *Understand that my underwear is ruined now.*

"Pick a word to say if you want me to stop. Nothing you might accidentally say while I'm…" He raised his eyebrows.

Autumn licked her lip. "I choose…gold leaf. *Specifically* gold leaf. If I just say 'gold' or 'leaf' you have to keep doing me, okay?"

Blake's mouth twitched again. "Go."

Autumn walked into the building on wobbly legs. She ignored the 'closed for maintenance' sign on the stairwell door and turned the knob. Just as Blake suggested, it was open, and nothing seemed out of order. She began to climb, the sound of her heels deafening in the empty concrete space.

Ordinarily, she didn't find the stairwell creepy. It was well lit and one of the building whackos was usually rattling around it, doing something inoffensively odd. But tonight Blake had presumably locked the doors on the other floors so that she could hear no one but herself. He'd apparently turned off the fluorescent strips so that the only thing lighting her way were tiny circular floodlights she'd never noticed before, casting everything into monochrome. She moved higher, past the first floor, the second, and then she heard a door slam beneath her.

Blake. Goosebumps prickled on her skin. She began climbing faster, her heart hammering against her breastbone. Her black pumps suddenly seemed much too high, her dress far too tight and short. Blake's footsteps hammered against the metal stairs, his approach as inevitable as that of a coming train. She wasn't sure

, how long it took him to get to her, only that when she whirled around and caught sight of him in the shadows, she gasped like the lead in a 1950's horror film. "Who-who are you?"

Blake didn't answer. He just stood there, his hands shoved in his pockets, looking her slowly up and down. Assessing. "You shouldn't be wearing those shoes."

Autumn's heart was now racing so hard she felt dizzy. Her stomach was tight and all her nerves were thrumming. She simultaneously wanted the moment to last forever and for Blake to make his move so that the tension could split and be over. "Why shouldn't I be wearing these shoes?"

A soft chuckle. "Makes it impossible to run."

And before she had a chance to respond, he was on her, shoving her back into the cold concrete wall. Instinctively, Autumn tried to scream but a broad hand clapped itself over her mouth. "We'll have none of that, Blondie. No noise, no concerned citizens coming to find us out."

His free hand sought her wrists and he pinned them over her head. His scent was stronger now, that woodsy cologne mixed with something subtler, sweat or maybe just Blake himself, warm and powerful and one hundred percent male.

"That's it," he muttered, shoving his hips against hers. "Got you right where I want you. Right where you belong."

His cock was hard against her stomach, thick and eager. It was such a relief to know that he wanted this, wanted *her*, that she pressed back against him. Blake grinned, his teeth flashing in the dark. "Yeah, that's what I thought."

He removed his hand from her mouth and kissed her. This time the kiss was deep and hot and animalistic. He was claiming her, exerting his will over her weaker feminine frame. Autumn strained against his hands and found she couldn't move an inch.

Her arousal ratcheted up another degree and when he pulled away, she had to stop herself from moaning his name.

Blake. He was doing this to her, he was giving this to her. What a fucking legend.

He rubbed his nose along her neck, inhaling deeply. "I was watching you, Blondie. Out on the street. I watched you move in this joke of a dress."

He tugged the front of it down, exposing her breasts, and Autumn bit back a moan. The scraping fabric and cool air on her nipples was making her whole body throb. They'd barely done anything, *anything,* and she was more turned on than she'd ever been in her life.

Blake stared down at her tits and for a moment, the mask slipped. His mouth slackened and he made a soft choking noise, which spoke not of possessive lust but the same desperation she felt thrumming in her veins. The sense that they were both in exactly the right place at the right time.

"Let me go," she whispered, shy but determined to do this right. To do it the way she'd dreamed of it being done.

"No," he said with a snap like a loaded gun. "You're mine now, sweetheart."

"You can have my wallet, my phone—"

"Don't want either." Blake lowered his head and sucked her right nipple. Sensation shot through her like electricity and if he wasn't holding her up, Autumn knew she would have fallen to her knees. Possibly to beg for him to do it again. "Please, let me go?"

He released her nipple with a pop. "Not a chance."

"But, why?"

He sucked her other nipple then blew a cold stream of air over it. "That's not what you want. I knew that as soon as I laid eyes on you. You want a man to pay you a special kind of attention, don't you?"

"No," she said, the huskiness in her voice betraying her excitement.

Blake returned his hand to her mouth. "Shh. I know that's what you have to say, but I saw you walking around in this baby scrap of fabric, your tits jiggling and your ass swaying from side to side for every man to see. That means you're either a dirty pricktease or in desperate need of a fuck."

Autumn shook her head. She was sure her eyes were as round as hubcaps. She would have to take back what she'd thought about Blake being bad at talking. Her insanely monosyllabic date was apparently some kind of filth wizard, taking nothing and spinning it into pure gorgeous filth.

"That a no?" he asked, bending down to suck at her right nipple, harder this time, as though he was angry with her.

Autumn moaned and tried and failed to protest against his palm.

"Can't understand you, honey. Guess I'll have to answer my own question." Her landlord yanked up the hem of her dress and then his hand was against her pussy. He wasn't fucking around either, within moments two rough fingers were rubbing along her insanely wet slit, dipping into her cunt. The stimulation was so unexpected, so dirty and perfect and *rude*, Autumn screamed against his palm.

Blake laughed. "That's just what I thought, Blondie. You're wet. Wet enough to drown in. And no panties either, you dirty little slut."

His fingers moved deeper inside her, curled expertly in a way that had Autumn panting against his hand. He looked feral in the dim light, more animal than human.

A ripple of genuine fear ran through her. She hardly knew this man, not his parents' names nor his family history or even what his favorite book was. Panic slipped its shadowy fingers around her throat but before it could take hold, she remembered the way Blake had kissed her outside of the building, the strength and sweet security she'd felt in his arms. She relaxed into the wall, into the scene. She did know this man, even if what she knew were more feelings than facts.

His thumb found her clit, the rough pad brushing against her with expert precision, and her orgasm just...*popped*. Like the corks on the champagne bottles they kept bringing out at Eleven Madison Park.

She was in a stairwell with her shoes on and her dress shoved the wrong way in both directions, but it didn't matter. This felt so good. Resistance to how good this felt was impossible. She collapsed into the wall, boneless but still humping Blake's fingers, still trying to get more. Blake let out a snarl of satisfaction and began pumping her even harder, wringing more pleasure onto his fingers. "I knew you wanted it, filthy girl."

The elevator came rattling past, loud and unmistakable, and the thought of other residents being so close to where she was ravished by their landlord brought Autumn to the brink all over again.

Blake seemed to know it. He released her mouth to brush a thumb over her painfully sensitive nipples, his other hand working even harder to stroke her clit and dip inside her pussy. He was so coordinated, he felt like more than a man, he felt like a machine designed to extract maximum pleasure from her body.

"No one knows you're here," he snarled. "I could keep you here for hours, fuck you every way I know how, make you scream while you come all over my cock."

Autumn moaned wordless protests, all the while thinking that it sounded like heaven on earth. This entire scene was so wrong, so right, so *everything*.

Blake bent his head, his beard rasping against her cheek. "You give it up easy, and I'll let you go home tonight. I won't drag you back to my place and tie you to my bed, use your sexy little body as my mattress. Fuck your tight cunt whenever I get hard."

Do it, Autumn thought through the delirium of another rising orgasm. *Do it.*

Her legs were shaking, her back and brow studded with sweat. She just needed a little more, a little more filth, a little more stimulation...

"Or would you like that?" Blake's fingers tugged hard at her nipples, biting into them so that she whimpered. "Would you like being my personal pussy, Blondie? Are you hoping I'll take you home and make you my slave?"

Autumn pictured herself tied to his bed, awaiting his convenience, and a hot throb ran through her.

"God yes," she said and no sooner had she uttered the words, than her second climax hit. The first had been fast and intense. This was earth-shattering. White light blistered behind her eyes and as she contracted around Blake's fingers, she ground her teeth so that no sound came out of her mouth. There was nothing but silent sensation.

When she finished, she was limp as a noodle, relying on Blake's weight and the wall just to stay standing. Her shadowy lover pulled his hand from her and sucked his fingers into his mouth. "That's very good, little whore. Now it's my turn. You're going to get on your knees for me, wet me down so I can slide into your pussy nice and smooth. You got that?"

"Oh-okay," Autumn stammered, wondering if she had the

strength to hold her mouth open. He removed his hands from her body and she instantly slid down the wall trembling with pleasurable aftershocks. What had that been? And what the hell was going to happen next? They'd just done third base, *one-sided* third base. How was she going to handle sex without crumbling into a pile of ash? One thing was certain, she was going to try her hardest to give a gold star performance. That orgasm had been—there was no other word for it—mind-blowing.

Blake stood in front of her, his face entirely in shadow, probably wondering how to proceed now she was doing her ragdoll impression.

There was a long protracted pause, and Autumn swore she could hear the cogs in her Landlord's brain whirring, probably wondering how he was going to wring a blow job out of her limp ass. Before she could suggest that maybe she could lie prone on the ground while he fucked her face, he ran a gentle palm over her cheek. "It's your lucky night, honey."

"Nngh?" Autumn said, her power of speech having not yet returned.

"I'm not going to give you what you want tonight," he said. "I'm going to send you home hurting for my cock instead. See if you like waiting and hurting as much as you like doing it to men." He reached down and took her hands, helping her onto her feet.

Autumn stood trembling in her pumps, weak as a teenager after her first bender. "Wait, what's happening?"

"I'm leaving." Blake gently rearranged her dress so that everything he'd revealed before was covered. "You're going home."

"But...but you were going to make me blow you!" Autumn knew she was breaking character but goddammit, she wanted to suck Blake's cock. Sure she could barely lift her arms right now, but they had options, like that lying on the floor thing she'd been about to mention.

"Not going to happen, Blondie. You get fucked on my terms and my terms only." Blake's frowny face told her to give it up, that the scene was over and she could either leave with the fantasy intact or hear him rebuff her request for dick in a more overtly landlord way. She decided to swallow her pride. "Will I see you again?"

"Of course you will." He moved her hand, pressing it against the swell of his cock. "Feel that?"

Autumn whimpered as a sluggish but determined jolt of arousal thrummed through her, a fish trying to flop back to water. "Yes."

"That's all for you, Blondie. I'm not gonna jack it until I see you next. I'll save it all up for you to swallow."

Autumn moaned, closing her hand around his swollen flesh, but Blake pulled away. He gave her another light brush along her cheek and then he was backing away and pounding down the staircase.

What the actual fuck?

"Is this legit?" she called after him. "Is this really the end of the sex thing?"

Blake didn't reply. She listened as he reached the bottom of the stairwell, heard the exit door slam and stood there a moment.

"So fucking complicated," she mumbled, but she couldn't keep from smiling. Whatever weird instincts had driven her eccentric landlord away, she was sure they were well intentioned, and this was still the best not-sex of her life. She slowly climbed the stairs to her apartment and wasn't at all surprised to find the exit door on the third floor unlocked. She *was* surprised to find another note taped to her door, however. She pulled it off and read, *Figured we'd start slow the first time. Sleep well, Fun-Size. The Landlord.*

Next to it was a small drawing of…her. It was only done in pencil but the likeness was undeniable. Her hair was a cloud and her eyes were oversized, she looked delicate and waifish. Was that how he saw her? Did he really think she was that beautiful?

It was then that Autumn felt something truly, sincerely complicated; her stomach fluttered with what could have only been the first stirrings of a crush.

"Fucking hell," she muttered to herself and unlocked her apartment door, determined to hustle all the pigeons out of the bath and take a long hot soak. She'd barely kicked off her shoes when she felt her phone buzz. Wondering—not hoping, definitely not hoping—if Blake had texted, she pulled it out and found a message from Owen. *"Hey lady, how's the date going?"*

She smiled at the message and typed back. *"Good thanks. Over now."*

Her phone buzzed right away. *"Details. All the details."*

She hesitated, then grinned. If he really wanted to know… *"Dinner at Eleven Madison Park followed by multiple orgasms in my apartment stairwell."*

The reply came so fast it was like magic. *"Insufficient details. Coffee. 11am."*

CHAPTER 6

BLAKE STUDIED THE damaged Bible through the hands-free magnifier perched on his head. He'd been contacted late last night by a local financier about restoring a family heirloom and agreed to take it on, mostly out of fascination. In true impatient New Yorker fashion, the man had messengered the book over this morning, bright and early. Blake had never restored a Bible before and the pages were incredibly thin—and there were so many of them. Regardless of the high price such a project would earn, he'd been more interested in the challenge.

Or the distraction, more like.

Normally when he accepted a job, there was between three and six months of lead time. He was damn good at the art of book restoration and scheduled for the foreseeable future. But he'd hoped something new—spontaneous, even—would occupy his mind until he saw Autumn again.

Sweet, delicious Autumn.

Blake took off the magnifying headset, leaned back in his chair and grunted. He was positive last night's date had been a disaster. Table manners and small talk weren't exactly his strong suit, so he'd spent a lot of time staring at Autumn and willing the night to move faster…while having an equally strong urge to slow it down. It was disconcerting, the way he couldn't seem to picture her in the soft restaurant light without his blood racing faster.

The sun followed her at nighttime, too. Their date had confirmed it. This *glow* remained on her wherever she went, catching on stray freckles and white strands of hair among the dirty blond. It was beyond Blake how a man could focus enough to have a conversation while looking directly at her, listening to the little trip in her voice whenever the subject changed directions.

The night had changed direction, too. He'd planned on bringing her to the stairwell, but he hadn't planned on leaving so soon. He'd spent the morning wondering if he was fucking *insane* for doing so. His mouth salivated thinking of her indecently pointed nipples, how they'd plumped on his tongue, so smooth and sweet. He'd been caught between her tits and her mouth in that stairwell, starved for both in a way he'd never come close to experiencing. Starved for her orgasm over his own. He'd wanted nothing more than to unzip his pants and fuck her blind against the concrete wall, her ineffective red dress rucked up around her hips.

So why did he stop? His heavy cock wanted an answer.

For one, as soon as she went all limp and sweet on Blake, he'd felt like that same depraved monster that used to stroke off to increasingly dark fantasies about the petite girl with the happy disposition. The one who chatted merrily with tenants and…cleared that damn path for him the day they'd met. Could he really unzip and use her mouth, when she didn't even have the energy to stand? She wanted him to. He *ached* to take things all the way. His head needed to catch up with his hunger first, though.

And second. He couldn't give Autumn what she wanted right away. Why the hell would she stick around afterward? He was an asshole who reacted to sunlight like a million-year-old vampire just awoken from his tomb, and she was loved by sunshine. If he let the head between his legs make the decisions, she would have been shackled to his wall last night while he wrote a phony ransom note to her family, reading it out loud and making her lick the envelope. He would do those things to satisfy her. Hell, to satisfy himself.

Autumn deserved more than that. Yeah, he'd insisted on three dates so she would be comfortable while they explored these fantasies she'd been harboring about him. Not actually *scared*. Just...on the verge. The razor's edge of nervous. But his ulterior motive for bringing Autumn on three dates was about a lot more. Not that he would ever admit to it out loud, but he might have benefitted from the same kind of guidance all those years ago. It was far too late for him to change now, but Autumn was young. And...incredible. If anyone could shake off a bad break up and strike out on her own, she could.

As soon as he showed her that, Blake could go back to fixing books in the darkness, as he was doing right now. He could go back to *peace* and *quiet*, instead of constantly wondering about the adorable Australian upstairs and whether or not she was cool enough with one measly, second-hand window air conditioner. Or if she still received calls from her shithead ex-boyfriend.

Hence, the age-spotted, torn-up heirloom Bible on his desk.

Blake pushed back from the desk and stood, those first steps toward the living room on the painful side, his leg protesting its use. Perhaps the very act of having a rare, personal conversation with Autumn last night had unearthed other, personal conversations from his past. Because the sharp twinge in Blake's leg sent him back to the weeks he'd spent in the hospital, while undergoing several surgeries to repair bone fractures and torn ligaments.

His hospital room had been a revolving door of activity—fellow sandhogs, union reps, nurses, doctors and family. What he remembered the most, however, was his friends and fiancée. How they'd shifted around him in awkward tableaus, exchanging covert glances and changing the topic before it was completely exhausted—very unlike them. His idiot friends were known for running a subject into the ground and setting it on fire. Leaning back among the pillows, his perceptive abilities had been keener than ever because he was only required to watch. The subtle shift in the air when his fiancée and the head surgeon were in the hospital room together had started a ball of intuition rolling down his spine. He saw the way everyone seemed to go tense as if waiting for them to slip up.

Blake was a man of few words. So on a day when his injury had already made him weakest he'd ever been in his life—and gut-deep instinct told him he'd been thrown over—no exceptions were made. Not at such a sickeningly low point. If anything, he was capable of speaking even less. Blake's fiancée had leaned over to fluff his pillow, locked eyes with him and understood she'd been found out. Hands shaking, she'd removed the ring—but he'd stopped her.

"Keep it," he'd said, already wanting no physical reminder of that time. That life.

Oddly enough, the worst of the pain came on the heels of that sliced-off engagement. He'd turned to his friends. Kevin, Elaine and Tommy in their ice sculpture formations around the room. And he'd roared at them to *get out*, despite the shot of pain it blasted down his side. Elaine burst into tears. Tommy made a belligerent face and stormed off. Always the last one to take a hint, Kevin came forward, palms out, trying to reason with Blake. Reason. To this day, it blew Blake's mind that anyone alive thought they could talk their way out of months of lies. No. Impossible. That was the last time he'd seen any of them and he wouldn't have had it any other way.

Ignoring the acid in his stomach, Blake stalked to the refrigerator, planning to throw together something to eat. Before he could grip the handle, though, his landline rang.

He dragged a hand down his face. "Goddammit."

Already well aware of who was calling, Blake didn't bother picking up. Ross was a young pot-enthusiast who lived upstairs and perpetually roamed the halls in slippers eating bowls of cereal. A while back—and against his better judgment—Blake gave Ross the landline number, but only because the guy's ceiling sprung a leak while Blake was in the process of replacing his broken cell phone. He was the only tenant who had the number. And for some ridiculous reason, Ross thought that made him special. It didn't.

Blake grabbed his tool box on the way out of his apartment, forcing himself to take the stairs to Ross's floor, instead of the elevator. He wasn't weak, like he'd been that day ten years ago, not by any stretch. Giving in, that was weakness.

Ross was waiting at the top of the stairs when Blake reached the third floor, bowl of what looked to be Cinnamon Toast Crunch balanced in one hand. "Hey, man, you didn't answer the bat phone."

"Please stop calling it that," Blake groused, skirting past him. "What the hell is wrong this time? I told you to stop taking the batteries out of the smoke detector. You can never get them back in."

The young man took a large bite of cereal, instead of answering. He raised a finger, the international sign for *hold on* and Blake rolled his eyes. Ross had zero respect for the landlord-tenant relationship. Although, he had to admit, the kid wasn't *that* bad. Sometimes. He had some personal hygiene issues and a parakeet that never shut the hell up. To Blake's surprise, though, Ross had turned out to be one of the few people he could talk to for longer than five minutes without wanting to drill into his own ear. Not that he would admit to it, even under threat of death. They shot the breeze once in a while at the mailboxes or during repairs. They weren't...what did Ross call them? Twin flames?

God, how annoying.

Blake walked into Ross's apartment to the sound of a chirping bird and an applauding television studio audience. He scanned the messy abode for signs of needed repair. "Well?"

The door rebounded off the floor stopper behind him, leaving it ajar. "Okay, don't get mad," Ross said, creeping around the front of Blake. "I have something you're going to want to see, man. It's high quality shit."

Blake set down his toolbox with a clatter. "How many times do I have to tell you? I don't want to buy any weed. And this better not be the reason you called the..."

"Ah!" Ross gave a slow motion fist pump. "You almost said bat phone."

"No I didn't."

"All right, man. But we both know you wanted to."

Knowing from experience that Ross would be content to repeat himself for an hour, Blake decided to change the subject. "Why am I here? And before you ask, no, I'm not asking why we're here on earth. I mean why am I in this apartment right now?"

Ross pointed a sooty finger at him. "I saw you leave the note on that Australian girl's door, you closet Cyrano."

"I think you mean Casanova. Which I am not." Blake scratched at the nerves tingling at the base of his throat. "You didn't read the note, did you?"

"No way. I'm happy to live in the mystery." Ross gestured to a laptop that was open on his kitchen table. "Are you?"

"I'm leaving."

Blake picked up his toolbox and turned for the door, just in time for Mrs. Zhu to walk into the apartment. "What's happening in here?" She breezed past Blake, smelling of dish soap and the hard, green apple candies she always handed out. "Did Wendy start yet?"

"We got ten minutes," Ross answered. "Grab a snack."

"Does anyone in this building work?" Blake asked.

Ross struck a model-esque pose. "Your Australian girl does."

"Her name is Autumn and you should know that, considering she presses the elevator call button for you when your hands are full of laundry." Blake realized he'd said too much. Both tenants were now eyeing him with blatant curiosity. He scowled. "You do too much laundry for someone who primarily wears a bathrobe."

Mrs. Zhu plopped down on the couch. "You're very touchy today, Mister Munroe." She propped her feet on the cluttered coffee table. "I'm usually the touchy one."

"It's true. She is," Ross said in a stage-whisper. "She just shows up now. Like clockwork. Calls me, too."

"I can't imagine what that's like," Blake deadpanned.

Ross waved a hand. "You don't mean that. Come here."

He stepped over a disconnected bike wheel on his way to the kitchen table, Blake reluctantly following behind. He was fully prepared to find something stupid on the screen, like the time Ross faked a clogged sink so he'd come upstairs and watch an SNL sketch about cats that shoot lasers. Thinking of SNL made Blake think of his talk with Autumn last night, so when he saw her picture on the screen of Ross's laptop, he thought he was imagining it. Then Ross looked so smug about his surprise, Blake knew it was real. That was really Autumn in a stadium of some kind, wearing a red and black jersey and carrying a huge flag with what appeared to be a jet plane on it.

"Why the hell is she on your computer, Ross?"

The young man reared back. "Relax, man. She's not, like, trapped in there."

"Touchy," Mrs. Zhu sing-songed from the living room couch.

"Is this a tenant meeting?" Blake turned just in time for Mrs. Fuller to stride in, a pinched expression on her face. "If this is a tenant meeting, notices should be handed out ahead of time."

Blake pinched the bridge of his nose. "This is not a tenant meeting. Explain, Ross."

"Oh, it's your girlfriend," said Mrs. Fuller, peeking over his shoulder. "Is she the topic of this meeting?"

"Not a meeting," Blake said again.

"When I give her a candy, she calls it a lolly," Mrs. Zhu shouted from the living room, laughing to herself. "*Lolly.*"

Blake held up a hand and silence fell. "Okay, no one say another word unless your name is Ross and you've got my...*Autumn* on your computer."

Ross rubbed his hands together and hit a few keys. Just like that, there was a grid of pictures of Autumn. Dozens upon dozens. With her parents. With the ex-boyfriend. Smiling in that sunny way of hers, diploma in hand. Cross legged on the floor, tongue out, navigating a video game. The most beautiful girl he'd ever seen, rendered in a hundred different ways. All of them so...alive. Yet for all the novelty of seeing so many images of Autumn, he was stuck on the ones of her and Ian. Stomach churning, he turned away from the computer. "I don't want to see those. Close it."

"Hold on, man. I had to wade through her profile to get to the interesting part." Ross punched a few more keys and Blake did his damnedest to focus on the television, but his eye continued to be drawn back to the screen. A whole wealth of information about Autumn, sitting right there for the taking. If he learned all her interests up front, maybe he wouldn't bumble his way through dinner next time. "This is an invasion of privacy."

"No, it's not," Mrs. Fuller said, leaning over, her elbow on the table. "Autumn's account is public."

Blake frowned. "Anyone can see that?"

"Yup."

A growl built in his throat, but knowing Autumn didn't mind people seeing these images, he gave up and zeroed in on the screen. A picture of a toddler-sized Autumn holding a book appeared and Ross stopped scrolling.

"Here it is. A post on her timeline from her mom." Ross cleared his throat. "'Hello there, Little Miss New York. Dad and I were cleaning out the shed and we found this picture of you and The Little Princess. I remember how much you loved that book. You cried for days when your cousin drew on it and I chucked it out! Anyway, there's boxes of your crap in the shed and if you don't come and get them, they're going to the tip. Flights are cheap this time of year, lol! Mum XOX'"

"The Little Princess," Blake repeated, something heavy shifting in his ribcage. "That was her favorite book?"

"Moms don't lie about that shit." Ross straightened, looking incredibly self-satisfied. "Do I know you or what, Blake? I wouldn't have called the bat phone if I'd just found her vacation photos or Buzzfeed quiz results, man. I bring you stuff you can *use.*"

Dammit, this is why Blake tolerated the guy. Just when he was ready to disconnect the bat—his *landline*—the idiot did something profound. The valuable information had his wheels turning. Yeah, now he knew her favorite book, that was useful. Suddenly, he remembered what she'd told him directly at dinner last night. She wanted to be followed. Stalked. By him. Heat kicked him in the belly, kindling, spreading. He did his best to keep his features disciplined despite the building hunger. "Can I use that thing to find out where she is?"

"You're dang right you can, man," Ross said, tapping away at his keyboard. Mrs. Zhu and Mrs. Fuller moved in, crowding around him.

"Once you're done finding out," Blake said, giving Ross a pointed glance. "No more looking at her."

For some reason, the women fell all over themselves at that totally reasonable command, giggling and widening their eyes. Blake gave them his best bored sigh, but couldn't help a small smile when they turned back around.

"Okay. Okay, this just in. Autumn likes ice cream. You want to write this down, man?" Ross stroked at the keyboard. "Uh…"

The hair stood up on Blake's neck at his tone. He stomped closer to the trio. "What?"

"She's out with a pretty boy. As of…" Ross squinted at the laptop clock. "Four minutes ago."

Mrs. Zhu looked at the screen and then gave him a sympathetic smile. "He's hot. Probably not too touchy."

"*I'm not touchy.*"

Both women pursed their lips and hummed.

Blake scrubbed at the weight on his esophagus. "Where are they?"

"Everybody calm down. Pretty boy tagged her and I've investigated his profile. He has a husband. *Also* hot." Everyone deflated, especially Blake. Jesus, he needed to sit down, but every available seat was covered in half-finished ceramic sculptures. "She's at the Toasted Bean on West 13th."

"I'll just…" Blake edged toward the door. "Look. Wendy is on."

As soon as they all turned toward the television, he slipped out, plans already formulating in his head. It seemed when Autumn asked, he delivered.

He kind of loved that.

CHAPTER 7

Autumn stared down at her cappuccino, willing herself not to be a douche about this. She was so excited to be on a friend date with Owen. This was his favorite café, she wasn't going to be a dick about the mediocre coffee. She wasn't. She. Wasn't.

"Thank you so much," she said to the barista, who wore the familiar uniform of tattoos, surface piercings and eccentric hair, in this case blue spikes. The barista nodded without smiling, deposited Owen's triple espresso in front of him and departed.

"Cheers," Owen said, raising his phone in front of them in the universal sign for 'let's take a selfie.' Autumn pressed her lips into her photo smile, relieved she'd worn mascara and combed her hair. Owen's phone snapped and he withdrew his arm and began selecting filters. Autumn chose that moment to take a small sip of her coffee. Yeah, that was about what she expected. America did a lot of things well; burger chains, hot wings, gravy, bourbon, but coffee wasn't one of them, at least not by Melbourne standards. Would it be silly of her to go home purely so she could have excellent lattes? Probably.

"My hair looks amazing in this light," Owen muttered. "Are you cool for me to post to sosh?"

Autumn hesitated. "Do I look cute? Ian will probably see them and I've been in a grease coma for two weeks. I need to look cute."

Owen froze. Autumn, terrified she'd offended him, patted his arm. "Forget it. It's all good, put up whatever you want. Ian knows what I look like."

Owen put his electric blue iPhone down. "Autumn Something Reynolds."

"Martha."

"Ooh, unfortunate."

"Tell me about it."

"Well, your first name's nice, that's what matters. Anyway, Autumn Martha Reynolds, what kind of friend do you think I am? I would never post a picture of you not looking cute. I took the thing in the *YouCamPerfect* and I've used three different filters. Look."

He snatched up his phone and showed her the picture. Autumn had to admit she looked awesome; smooth skinned and, yes, cute. A nice bookend to Owen's modelesque beauty. She smiled at the image, thinking not of Ian, but Blake. It was such a shame he wasn't on social media. If he was, he might have seen the picture and thought—

What? What *was* Blake thinking at any given moment?

"Okay, you say the word and I'll go into Facetune and take your face from a nine to a nine-point-nine," Owen said, picking up his phone and opening the app.

"It's all good," Autumn said. "We look excellent, post the picture and we can have coffee and chats."

"Oh, you're so right. Okay I'm posting, the caption will be…'vet's date'."

As Owen played around on his phone, Autumn picked up her spoon and scooped hot milk foam into her mouth. Yeah, nah there it was again, a bitterness that wasn't coffee and a touch of burning as well.

"Something wrong?" Owen asked.

Autumn put down her spoon. "Okay, so I don't want to be *that asshole* but did you know Melbourne is considered one of the best coffee cities in the world?"

"What do you take me for? Some kind of rube?" Owen ran his fingers through his hair, as though to emphasize exactly how un-rubelike he was. "I've never been to Melbourne, but my ex-boyfriend's brother lived there and he was always going on about the coffee. And the drag scene, but that's a whole other story. What makes it better?"

"I don't know. You guys have great beans…The machinery, maybe? Or the milk? Are you allowed to feed cows weird shit here?"

"Honey this is *America*. If you haven't eaten sixteen hundred chemicals before lunch, it must be your fast day."

Autumn laughed. "Well sorry to be a snob, but maybe it's that."

Owen picked up his espresso and took a sip. "Hmm, maybe you have a point. Well, seeing as we're paying eight dollars a cup for subpar garbage, I vote never coming here again."

"Oh we don't have to—"

"Nonsense. We'll try that organic place on 9th street. Isa's always babbling on about it. Sorry she's not here, by the way. She's having sex with some Joseph Heller wannabe on a mattress with no sheets or a bedframe." Owen gave a contemptuous sniff. "What she sees in these men, I have no idea, but that's not the point. The point is how the fuck was your sex date with your beefy bear landlord?"

Autumn felt her cheeks heat. "Is it okay if we circle back to that conversation?"

"Did something go wrong?"

"No, it's just…" Autumn remembered the way Blake had stood over her, his face shadowed, his hands in his pockets. "…it was really intense and I'm not sure how to put it into words just yet."

Owen picked up his coffee and sipped, looking thoughtful. "Okay, as long as you're still feeling good about the date?"

"I am, I promise."

"Then in that case, we're going to have to move on to my other topic of conversation. Why, oh why, are you thinking of leaving this beautiful nation—by which I mean New York—to go back to the land down under?"

Autumn opened her mouth. "I—"

"Wait! If you say coffee, I will slap you! We can find you good coffee." Owen pushed the home button on his phone. "Siri, make a note, I'm going to find Autumn the best coffee in the city or die trying."

"*Making a note*," came the robot reply.

Autumn laughed and grabbed at his wrist. "Relax, you don't need to deliver on that insane promise. It's not the coffee."

"Then what is it? You have everything here, your apartment, a hot bearish landlord who wants to turn you out on the reg, no sociopath eyes boyfriend—"

"And no friends or family."

"Ahh, now we're getting somewhere." Owen put his chin on his hand. "Go on, tell your story."

Autumn felt her mouth retract, her smile pulling itself back into her body. The story started with her family, but talking about her family always felt like giving emotional birth. She didn't want to heap that on Owen, at least not right out of the gate. "Do you have a good relationship with your parents?"

Owen grimaced. Unlike most of his reactions, Autumn could tell it was involuntary, completely without theatrics. She grinned. "Yeah, mine is kind of like that, too."

"You don't like them?"

"It's not that…" she sighed. "I love them, but they're so hard to be around. They're loud and rude and they think that if a waiter doesn't take your order ten seconds after you put your menu down, they're ignoring you and need to get yelled at."

"Yeesh."

"Tell me about it. My parents fucking loved Ian, too. Worshipped the ground he walked on. I mean, sure they thought he was a theatre ponce, but he made them laugh and he was handsome." She looked across at Owen. "My mum is a big fan of handsome men. Grandchildren, you know?"

Owen smiled in a way that said he understood. "Have you told them about the…?"

"About the break up?" Autumn shook her head. "Haven't been able to handle it. Everyone's going to freak out. They thought we were about to get engaged."

"Soo, not to ask the obvious, but why on Christ's green earth would you want to go home to that?"

Autumn sighed, picking up her now-cool coffee and draining half of it. "So a week ago, I get a call from my mother and she's all *'Autie, when are you and Ian coming home? I need to plan Christmas dinner and I'm not buying two hams unless you're both here—'*"

"Does your mother actually sound like the 'dingo ate my baby' lady, post three packets of cigarettes?"

"She does. Anyway, the next item on her nag agenda is to tell me that my uncle's partner is retiring and if I'm not the worst person who ever lived, I'd come home and buy into the family business."

"The family business?"

"My uncle's a vet. He owns a clinic." Autie pictured the faded brick building where she'd spend so much of her young adulthood, the long grass and faded blue and grey sign. "He helped me get a bunch of experience while I was at uni—"

"You mean college?"

"Yeah. I worked for him while I was studying. He paid me like, one dollar an hour and tried to get me to euthanize a dog by hitting it with a shovel, but in my mum's eyes, he's my savior."

Owen's mouth fell open. "Goddamn, girl."

"I know."

"Why couldn't you get away from him when you moved for college?"

Autumn smiled. "Because I didn't move away for college. People don't really do that where I'm from. Rich kids board on campus, the rest of us commute. I lived at home the whole time I was studying."

"Why? How did you party? Experiment sexually? I might still be in the closet if I didn't go to college. I mean, not really but you get me."

Autumn laughed. "I do, but Ian and I got together my second year. That kind of ended my sexual experimentation."

Owen narrowed his eyes. "We'll discuss the hyena later. You don't *want* to move home and become a partner in your uncle's unethical dog murdering business, right?"

"Fuck no, but he's been pushing for it ever since I got qualified and my parents are really gunning for me to do it."

Owen bumped her shoulder with his own. "Who cares what your parents want? Stay in New York."

"You make it sound so easy."

"Because it is! This is the best city on earth and your uncle is someone who, and I cannot emphasize this enough, wanted you to hit a dog with a shovel."

Autumn stared into her coffee. "I know, but if I bought into the business, I could change all of that. I could run things the way I wanted, basically be my own boss. No more overmedicated MILF's telling me how to do my job. No more ten-hour shifts. I could start saving up for a house—"

"And gain mom and dad's eternal approval?"

Autumn looked up, feeling a hot wash of, not *irritation*, but overexposure. First she'd been cut open and laid bare by Blake's knowledge of how she wanted to be dominated sexually, and now Owen was saying all the things she had only heard inside her own head. "You don't know what it's like! My parents put all these crazy expectations on me!"

"Really?" Owen placed a fingertip to his perfectly shaved chin. "Hmm, did my parents put their expectations on me, the gayest little boy ever born in Buttfuck, Iowa? Let me think…"

Autumn winced. "Sorry, I shouldn't have played the 'you don't know what it's like' card. That was dumb."

He flipped a hand through the air. "Don't freak out. I was just being bitchy. I know exactly what it's like to grow up with your parents breathing down your neck, wanting you to be something you're not." He shuddered. "College, honey. It was the best thing that ever happened to me."

"You still talk to your parents, right?"

An uncharacteristically ugly look twisted Owen's handsome features. "I do."

"And they like…accept you?"

"They came to my wedding, but I dunno, it never feels quite right. I still catch them staring at me sometimes with that old look in their eyes. Like they don't know where I came from and they're wondering when the real Owen will show up."

Autumn's heart squeezed tight inside her chest. She'd always felt like she'd been air-dropped into the Reynolds family, the lone nerd in a family of alcoholics and troublemakers—and one weirdo vet—but she didn't feel entitled to go on about it when Owen had clearly gone through worse. She put her hand over his. "I'm really sorry."

He gave her a sad smile. "It's ancient history girl, but thanks. It's always good to meet someone else who gets it. And you do get it."

They held hands for a moment and Owen gave a watery chuckle. "Look at the two of us, sitting here all melancholy, like we're not young, sexy vets. Let's talk about something else."

So they ordered another round of drinks, tea this time, and they gossiped about the Happy Paws regulars and Isabella's dating history. Autumn was having such a good time, she was just about to suggest heading somewhere else for lunch when she spotted him.

She didn't react with dignity. Instead, she let out a yelp and knocked over her tea strainer.

"What's wrong?" Owen demanded. "Did you see Ian?"

She shook her head, admiring how accurate his instincts were. "No, I just bit my tongue, what were you saying about that tech bro Isabella banged?"

Owen returned to the story with gusto, leaving Autumn free to glance at Blake. Her Landlord was sitting three tables away, reading a newspaper he appeared to have brought in himself. He looked different, and she realized she'd never seen him in the daytime, before. She liked it. The natural light reflecting off his plaid shirt and thick black hair made him seem more real somehow. Huge and solid and human.

Minutes passed and he refused to meet her eye, no matter how blatantly she stared at him. He knew she was there, she was sure of it, but he wasn't going to come over. Why? Was he too shy? Did he think she and Owen were on a date? How *had* he found her anyway?

Autumn considered the possibility that his presence was a coincidence, then dismissed it. This was a city of millions of people. Only an idiot would take this as coincidence. She remembered Owen posting the photo of the two of them on Facebook and smirked. That had to be it. Blake might not have social media, but he was definitely stalking her on it.

Stalking...

Her belly drew tight. Of course. He wasn't here to talk to her, he was here on a mission. He wanted to fulfill her fantasy, just as he had the night before. He was here to watch. To stalk.

Her body's reaction to that idea was instantaneous, her pussy clenched and her nipples pricked with arousal. Blake was stalking her, watching, maybe even taking pictures.

"...and that's when we all found out he was on one of those penis websites, like where girls send unsolicited dick-pics to get critiqued by an artist!"

"Seriously?" Autumn said, knowing it would fill the space nicely.

"God yeah, apparently he'd been dick-bombing girls all over Brooklyn and..."

For the next twenty minutes Autumn tried to pay attention. She sipped her tea with shaking hands, and though she liked Owen, she barely heard anything he said. All of her attention was focused on the man sitting adjacent from her, reading the paper and occasionally pulling out his phone and fooling around on it.

Please be taking photos of me, she thought. *Please be taking pictures to look at later when you're lying in bed wishing I was with you...*

She wanted to stay sitting where she was forever, but her tiny bladder, and massive liquid consumption, had other ideas. "Just going to the bathroom," she told Owen. "Be back in a sec."

"Sure." Owen was already on his phone. "God, everyone thinks we look beautiful. And they couldn't be more right."

She smiled, but her attention was fixed on Blake. Was he watching her move? She was sure he was, but knew if she looked over, he would glance away. He was very good at this. As she walked toward the bathroom, she swore she saw Blake's phone flash in the corner of her eye. She smiled to herself.

The café bathroom was in the back of the building and required you to walk down a long, narrow corridor. Autumn used the tiny women's toilet, noting it was immaculately clean. That was another thing Americans did well, the accessibility and cleanliness of public bathrooms. She washed her hands, noting that her eyes were over-bright and her pupils huge. She looked horny, horny and extra alive because of it.

"He's only watching you," she told her reflection. "Don't be desperate, you weirdo."

But that wouldn't erase the brightness from her eyes, nor the knowing curl of her lip. She dried her hands and exited. The hallway was dark—someone had turned off the lights that led back to the café. As her eyes adjusted to the dark, she saw that the person who'd done it was still there. Watching her. She could hear him breathing, slow and deep.

"H-hello," she whispered, fear mixing with her arousal like ripple through ice cream. "The men's is down there."

She pointed as though that wasn't an utterly ridiculous to do in the dark.

The enormous shape in front of her said nothing. He unfolded his arms and took one step, two. Then he was right in front of her. She knew it was Blake but it was still a relief to smell his cologne and the warmth of whatever washing detergent he used.

Murderers use washing detergent too, she told herself. But she knew it was Blake, she could feel it in her bones.

"What are you doing?" she said, sounding exactly as turned on as she was.

He didn't reply. Instead he bent down and inhaled along her neck. All the hairs on Autumn's arms lifted and her knees shook so violently she thought she might fall. Looking down the dark hallway, she could see customers milling around, hear the indie folk playing on the speakers. No one knew she was alone with Blake, no one knew he was not quite touching her. He kissed her neck, raising goosebumps on her skin. His breathing was deep and harsh now, and she knew if she reached out and touched him, he would be rock hard beneath his jeans.

"Is it time?" she whispered.

He said nothing and her heart sank. This wasn't time, she understood, this was foreplay. He was toying with her. She'd gone as far as wondering what his end game was when his hands closed around her wrists, pinning her to the cool, exposed brick.

"Blake?"

She felt him shake his head. Not Blake then, a stranger. A man who watched and followed when the moment was right. Autumn felt more blood flow into her erogenous zones until it felt like all she was, was tingling skin and spiked nipples and a hot, eager pussy. Blake lifted her then, pressed her up so that his hips were pressed into hers. He was every bit as hard as she thought he'd been. A gentle hand covered her mouth and then he began to rock and thrust. To grind. She moaned as the swell of denim between his legs rubbed against her. She was wearing willow-patterned leggings and she could feel every inch of him.

He did it harder and shoved his fingers into her mouth, apparently determined to gag her. It was just as well. If she'd been able to speak, she'd have begged. It just felt too good. The space, his silence, that he was simulating sex on her, as though she were just his little doll. As though he were promising the both of them that he'd soon be back for more. His powerful hips continued to flex against hers as his hand reached down her top and began to tug on her nipples. Pleasure sparked through her, the fluid heat that preceded orgasm. She tilted her head back and the stranger Blake was playing took the message at once, kissing and nipping at her skin so that she whimpered around his fingers. The stars were gathering, her orgasm—as crazy as it sounded—was building. The stranger sank his teeth into her shoulder, his cock stroking firm against her aching cunt.

Come, he seemed to be saying. *Come and then you'll belong to me.*

She was seconds—milliseconds away—when a dark shape appeared in the hallway, blotting the light. Another customer, probably looking to use the bathroom. Blake responded instantly, releasing her onto her feet, turning away from her and striding toward the light as though the entire thing had been staged.

It hadn't though, judging from the hard look the man using the bathroom gave her, but Autumn didn't give even the first fuck about that. She slumped against the wall. "Oh my fucking God…"

That had been…incredible. The entire experience beyond anything she'd ever hoped to explore. She was frustrated, her whole lower half was throbbing with want, but she was kind of happy the stranger had left her wanting. She suspected, wherever he was, Blake felt the same way. She hugged herself in the dark, feeling warm and open and…some other word, she couldn't think of it, but it made her feel as though she'd been washed with gold.

She went back into the women's bathroom and splashed water on her face, needing a few more moments alone with the feeling and then returned to the café.

"You look…flushed," Owen said as she sat down.

Autumn pressed a hand to her cheeks and forehead and felt her damp skin. "No, I don't."

"And you were gone for ages."

"Yeah well…coffee, you know?"

Owen have her a look so penetrating it could have cut steel. "Quick question, did you know that a hulking beast of a man was sitting three tables away from us while we drank our tea?"

"Um…"

"And that he got up when you left for the bathroom, paid for his coffee and then disappeared down that hallway? Turning the lights off after him?"

"R-really?"

"Yes, and right before you came out, he left these premises looking like his whole world had been turned upside down."

Autumn couldn't keep her smile from spreading across her face.

Owen cleared his throat. "Okay, I think it's time for you to tell me about this Landlord of yours missy, but first we pay up and leave, the waitress keeps giving me dirty looks."

"Sure," Autumn said, unable to stop smiling. She and Owen stood, pulling their wallets from their bags and as they made their way to the counter she remembered the name for the washed gold feeling she'd experienced in the hallway.

Cherished. She'd felt cherished.

CHAPTER 8

PEOPLE LOOK STRAIGHT at one another during the day. Blake had forgotten about that.

At night, people scurried past him on the city sidewalks with their heads down, at most they sent him a side eye to assess if he was a threat. Someone who might follow them home or wrestle their purse off their body. What did it say about him that he didn't know which he preferred? Being largely ignored or openly acknowledged in the brittle afternoon light. That's where he was for the second time this week. Bathed in the light. The first time, he'd gone out with the intention of stalking Autumn. And now, he was moved by the ridiculous urge to procure a *present* for her.

If that didn't prove he hadn't a fucking clue how to impress a female, nothing would.

Self-derision curled Blake's lip as he turned off the avenue, moving down the side street toward home, fast as he could manage with his bad leg. Two kids sharing a set of headphones broke their wire connection to get out of his way. He was surprised to find himself glancing back at them, wishing he'd gone around instead. *Damn* Autumn and this effect she was having on him. Making him question his usual behavior, ask himself how she would judge it.

As soon as she went back to Melbourne, he'd go back to normal.

When someone walking toward him on the sidewalk changed directions to cross the street, Blake realized he was scowling. Even worse than usual.

It didn't take a genius to deduce what his bad mood stemmed from. He hadn't spoken to Autumn since the coffee shop. Hadn't spoken to her *in* the coffee shop, either. Granted, it had only been twenty-four hours, but there were things he needed to know for peace of mind. Had he taken it far enough? Too far? Did the coffee shop count as their second date, or did they still have two more to go?

Why the hell was he putting himself out there like this in the first place?

Memories of soft skin and clutching thighs caused a hitch in his step. Lord, he'd almost fucked her in a hallway. And before that, watching her alternately smile at her friend and frown at her coffee…another eight hours of it still wouldn't have contended him. He'd marveled over how she could hate a drink with such passion and still hide her wince every time she took a sip. The amusement she'd inspired, followed by the heat in the hallway had done the impossible of making him forget he was outside during the day time. The whole coffee shop orbited around the sunshine of her and the girl couldn't be more oblivious about it.

Yeah. It wasn't such a mystery why Blake was putting himself out there, was it?

Autumn could make things a lot easier on his sanity by coming home at an appropriate time. Last night, he'd ordered himself to focus on the Bible project. Done pull-ups until his shoulders burned. Beat off twice remembering how he'd palmed her tits in the coffee shop hallway, the little sounds she made in his ear. By the time she'd glided past his peep hole, he'd still been drawn tight as a bow, positive she'd be with the ex, even as common sense loudly disagreed. There was no room for common sense in his jealousy, though. No, it was hot and concentrated. *New*, too. He'd never felt jealousy in his single past relationship. Only shock. Disbelief. Jealousy appeared to be the less controllable of the two. By a long shot.

He wasn't sure how he'd react to seeing Ian, but the acidic burn in his sternum that kicked up every time he thought of the other man told Blake it would be ugly.

Nearing the building, Blake switched the package to the opposite arm, reaching down to massage his sore leg. He did his usual scan of the property, searching for cracks in the sidewalk that someone could potentially trip over and sue him for. Or missing metal guards—required by the city—on any of the windows facing the street. Everything appeared the same as usual. Mrs. Zhu was watering her plants in the fourth floor window. Ross leaned out the window smoking a joint, but he promptly hid it upon seeing Blake, coughing a cloud of smoke into his fist. Blake shook his head and kept going, not in the mood to field questions about where things stood with Autumn. Ross looked disappointed, but eyed the package under Blake's arm with an air of unmistakable smugness.

With an annoyed grunt, Blake took out his keys and started to open the main door when a group of pigeons caught his eye. He hesitated. Were any of them Autumn's? Probably not. There were billions of these gray and black scourges cluttering up the city. Still, he couldn't help but remember the ridiculous way they'd marched back and forth in Autumn's bathtub, as if they were guarding her. She'd needed guarding that weekend, hadn't she? Maybe they'd even brought her some comfort, nasty as they were.

"Jesus Christ." After checking to make sure no one was

watching, Blake took a half-eaten oatmeal bar from his pocket, crumbling it up and dropping it on the ground for the flying rats to feast on. And they did, some silent alarm going out to all the neighborhood fringe pigeons who swarmed in for a nibble. "Disgusting. All of you. This is the first and last time I do this."

"Talking to pigeons now, man?" A hand clapped down on Blake's shoulder. "Do they ever talk back?"

Cold slid down Blake's back, his muscles turning to stone. Without having turned around, everything about the man's voice and the hand on his shoulder was familiar. People who'd met him in the last decade didn't touch him, let alone slap him on the back. No, it was only the people who *used* to know him who didn't think twice about it.

Keeping his features neutral, Blake turned to find Kevin Donahue smiling up at him. His face had aged. A lot. Youth had fled, leaving tracks behind, along with gray hair and heavy cheeks. Not that Blake had any room to judge someone's appearance—not with the pissed off Yeti aesthetic he had going on—but remembering the young guy who'd always looked slightly dopey from a beer buzz, the new mask Kevin wore was a shock. "What do you want?"

"Shit." Kevin staggered back a little, hand to his chest like he'd been wounded. "It's been a long, frigging time. How about a hello? Or a how are the kids?"

"Kids?" Blake repeated, cursing himself for stopping to feed the stupid pigeons, or going out during the day at all. "You?"

Kevin held up four fingers. "All girls. I'm paying for my sins, B-Money. Haven't had a free weekend in years. It's all dance classes and fights over hair accessories." His sigh was long and miserable. "I know way too much about French braids, man."

Silence hung in the air. Blake realized he was supposed to fill it. Ask about Kevin's wife, Elaine, who they'd both grown up with in Rockaway Beach. God, everyone grew up together in Rockaway, it was so close knit. A strip of Queens with ocean on one side, bay on the other. Summers were spent on the boardwalk, riding bikes in the street with a friend perched on the handlebars, scrounging cash to buy slices from Ciro's on 116th Street. A cop or fireman lived in every other house. If you didn't join one of the two lines of duty, you were the member of another union—like Blake's father.

Before he'd retired and whisked Blake's mother away to Florida's world of gated communities, Michael Munroe had been a miner. A sandhog—the nickname given to the men who built tunnels below the city. A dirty, dangerous job, but it paid well. Blake would know, he'd been one himself before the accident.

Obviously Blake had let the conversation lull too long, because Kevin jumped in to break it, gesturing up at the building. "So, uh...this is it, huh? You own this place?"

Blake nodded once.

Ruddy color appeared on Kevin's cheeks. "I've been past it before, but wasn't sure you'd want to see me." His eyebrows drew together. "Looks like I was right."

"Looks like it."

Kevin let out a harsh punch of laughter. "Still a blunt motherfucker. You haven't changed."

Impatience prodded Blake. "You still haven't told me what you're doing here."

"Elaine took the girls to see a show. Lion King. I didn't want to shell out for the extra ticket when I'm just going to snore through the damn thing."

A flash of Kevin in his twenties dozing on the sand after too many wine coolers caught Blake off guard. He didn't like the memory. Didn't like anything that made him feel nostalgic for that time. So much of it had proved to be a lie.

"So I took a walk, got a beer. Ended up here," Kevin finished, looking as though he was at a loss. "We still talk about you, sometimes. Wonder if things could have turned out different, you know? All of us have our shit, man. I'm kind of a drunk. Elaine can't keep a secret. Tommy's a womanizer with, like, a pin prick of morality. You only open your mouth to make everyone feel like idiots. But we were friends—thick and thin—and the rest of us still are."

Blake sighed. "I don't have time for this."

"Fuck you, Munroe. *Make* time."

Fully intending to enter the building and leave Kevin on the sidewalk, Blake found himself stopping with the key halfway in the lock. "I didn't hear you mention Jodie," he said, turning back around with his head cocked. "Why?"

Kevin shifted his weight from one leg to the other. "This reunion isn't going all that well, if you hadn't noticed. Didn't want to throw that into the mix when I know it's a sore spot for you."

"Actually, it's not," Blake enunciated. Already, Kevin was beginning to look defeated and Blake slapped away the guilt it caused. Kevin's expression was one he knew well. *'Here comes Blake to shut us all down. Shut us out.'*

"It happened another lifetime ago. And it gave me an excuse to leave you all behind."

Maybe it was the tiny strand of guilt that caused Blake to add the final part against his will. "I was always the fucking odd one, hanging in the background making everyone uncomfortable. What happened with Jodie just made it easier to get out. What the hell do you want from me *now?*"

Visibly caught off guard by Blake's outburst, Kevin stood there gaping as Blake shouldered his way into the building. But before the door could close, Kevin caught it and stomped through the doorway behind Blake. "You know something, Munroe? Your head is so fucking far up your ass, you can see out of your belly button."

Blake kept walking. "You got that from Elaine."

"You see that? That's why we stay friends." They stopped outside Blake's apartment door, Kevin stabbing the air with his finger. "Because we know each other better than anyone else, even if it's mostly bad shit. Like the time we caught Tommy jerking off in a pair of nylons."

"Jesus, I'd managed to forget about that."

"Yeah. Well?" Kevin said, his mouth spreading into a smile. "Lucky you."

His old friend's smile was *offensive*. The nerve of it slid under his skin like a knife blade. "You knew. You all knew what Jodie was doing and didn't say shit."

Ignoring Kevin's crestfallen expression, Blake shook out his keys and stabbed them into the lock. "If that's friendship, keep it."

One of Blake's feet was inside his apartment when he heard the front door to the building open and close. He glanced over Kevin's shoulder and saw Autumn enter, the sunlight making a halo on top of her blonde head. Goddamn. She was so beautiful. She paused upon seeing him, popping out one of her earphones, her hazel green eyes inquisitive. In her black pants and tight, white button down, she looked different from the girl in the red dress, but she was still her. Painfully, exquisitely her. Yet, Kevin didn't turn to look at their new arrival, as though he didn't know or care that they were no longer alone. "Blake, you've gotta understand..."

Panic trickling in, Blake jerked his head toward the exit. "This has been heartwarming, but it's time for you to go."

But Kevin was clearly still hung up on the last thing he'd said. *You knew. You all knew what Jodie was doing and didn't say shit.* "We were young and stupid, all right? We did things a-and knew things...without understanding the consequences. I'm sorry."

"I didn't ask for an apology," Blake said, his voice low and tight. "Don't want it, either."

"You got one anyway," Kevin's hands went to his hips, then dropped. "Look. We're having the block party—same date it's always been on. 124th on the beach block. You should come."

Blake had no choice but to tear his attention off Autumn where she was attempting to blend in with the mailboxes. "You can't be fucking serious."

"I want you there." Kevin backed toward the door. "Deal with it."

Kevin turned to leave and finally saw Autumn, but she was looking at Blake curiously, despite the high color on her cheeks. And it took Blake a moment to realize Kevin was splitting a gradually knowing glance between Blake and Autumn...because Blake could barely stop staring at her, either. How much had she heard, *goddammit*?

The wounds he thought he'd closed long ago were open. Suppressed memories floating to the surface. How dare anyone see him like this? Especially Autumn. She'd come to him wanting strength, someone to fear, but he felt the furthest thing from her imagined beast right now—and it pissed him off, because that was all he had to offer. Being confronted with the past had taken away his careful control. It was unacceptable.

Kevin left, the door snicking shut behind him, leaving the

foyer silent. Dim, except for the single, muted halogen. Autumn's wary expression told Blake his bitterness was showing on his face. And with the hunger to take back control sizzling in his gut, he decided what he was going to do. He crooked a finger at Autumn. "Let's go, Blondie."

Her steps were hesitant but when she drew closer, Blake could see her pupils were dilated, her pulse tick-tick-ticking at the base of her neck. "Who was that?"

Even through the unfounded resentment he was experiencing toward Autumn for overhearing the conversation, Blake had just enough restraint left to make sure she wanted what he was about to dish out. "If you come inside, I'll be asking the questions."

He slid a hand over her smooth collarbone and closed it loosely around her neck, stifling a growl when her mouth popped open. "Where were you last night? Let's start there."

Autumn's back arched, eyelids fluttering. Oh, she liked that. Maybe she thought his possessiveness was part of the game. It wasn't. "Work emergency. A-a dog got his head stuck in a family-sized pretzel tub and Owen asked me to help him get it off." Blake watched Autumn wet her lips with a nervous tongue as relief speared him. *Just at work.* "If I come in, are you going to let me…do something for you this time?"

"Is that a condition?"

"More of a request," she whispered. "In the spirit of fairness and all."

No, dammit. He didn't want her to be adorable. It gave him a stretching sensation in the region of his chest and it was too much right now, on top of everything else that had happened in the last twenty minutes. He'd closed himself off for so long, feeling nothing, risking nothing. But right now the risk of feeling too much seemed so fucking high, when all he wanted to take was reward. To drop out and forget.

The sound of the moving elevator pierced through the trance only Autumn could put him in and he guided her into the apartment, his hand still around her throat. Her pulse started going wild against his palm the moment they crossed the threshold. Blake could relate. His dick was at a ninety-degree angle, his skin begging for contact with hers.

They stopped in the living room, Autumn shivering as Blake circled around behind her, dropping the package on the coffee table in favor of running a hand over her gorgeous ass, gathering one cheek in a rude squeeze. "You want to get me off this time, is that right?"

"Yes." One shaky breath. Two. "Please."

Damn, there was a part of Blake that wanted to kiss her, gently push her until she was kneeling and praise her while she sucked him off, just for being so brave and walking into the lion's den during feeding time. But that part of him was dwarfed by the need to reassert himself as the one who dominated her. That's what she wanted, anyway. She didn't want the bullshit complications. She wanted her safe cracked and he knew he had the combination.

It might have felt a little *too* good, feeling Autumn tremble as he skimmed his teeth up the side of her neck, listening to her breath catch. Yeah, it felt too good, because the hunk of flesh taken from him today *was* going to be given back tenfold. Too good because Blake was going to use Autumn for that purpose...but when her head lost power and fell to the left, allowing him to feast, how could he stop himself?

"Did you come to tell me you'd be late with the rent next month? Again?" Blake asked, tilting her chin up and to the side, as if inspecting her offering. "Maybe you came here to pay me with this little mouth."

The game veered in out of nowhere and Blake didn't put the brakes on. Couldn't. Not with Autumn vibrating like a motel bed, her eyes glazed with permission to keep going. To let his instinct take over. "I promise I'll have your money next time, but…"

"But?" Blake hit the T hard, snapping his teeth around the syllable as he pressed a thumb past Autumn's lips, sliding it deeper and deeper. "But this time all you have to offer is a wet place to stuff my cock?"

Her nod was vigorous, even as she swayed on her feet.

"Well, go on. Convince me." Blake gathered her hair in his free hand, twisting it around his fist and tugging her head back. "God knows it's a beautiful mouth. It goes with the rest of you…"

He pressed his bared teeth to her ear. "And we both know I've been *watching* the rest of you. Real close. Especially when you give me a show, walking up the stairs with your tight ass on a platter. Little Blondie the building pricktease. Isn't that right?"

Blake sensed the anticipation inside of her pulling tight, tight. She was alternating between holding her breath and taking great big gulps around his thumb. He slid the digit out just long enough for her to say, "I don't mean to be one."

"You know exactly what you're doing." His thumb sunk home once again. "Now show me what your mouth will do around my cock."

The joke was on Blake when Autumn started to pull on his thumb with whimpering sucks, her eyelashes making stark, black patterns on her cheeks. Still holding her hair in his left fist, Blake pulled until her throat was exposed, the delicate muscles moving with her enthusiastic efforts to suck his thumb. And he could no more stop his tongue from bathing and stroking those shifting muscles than he could stop time.

"Good girl," Blake grunted at her temple, removing his thumb from her mouth. "Can you suck that hard from your knees?"

"Yes."

"You've got yourself a deal, then." He eased her to a kneeling position, anticipation licking at his insides, hot and sharp. Autumn—every little detail of her—was definitely the reason Blake was so goddamn turned on, but it probably didn't help his patience that he'd been mostly celibate since moving into the building. It took everything in his power not to push her down to the ground and use her mouth like a depraved animal. "No rent next month, Blondie. Just my personal use of your pretty pink mouth."

Her hands trembled while unzipping his pants. "Thank you, Mr. Munroe."

"Put me between your lips and say that again."

Until Autumn jolted, he'd forgotten it was the first time she'd seen his cock. Her hands seemed unsure what to do, her chin dropping toward the floor. "Oh…I might have to come up with some sort of game plan here. Maybe I can handle it in sections or, like, bring in both hands and my boobs at the same time?"

The sight of cute comedian Autumn peeking through their shared fantasy was like a twig jabbing into his chest, but Blake forced himself to ignore it, lest he pick her up off her knees, hug her and end this scene she needed to find satisfaction. Satisfaction he *needed* to give her to get back in control. "You'll take it all." Blake fisted his cock and pressed it past her lips, stopping after a few good inches had been sunk into the incredible damp heat. "Suck it. Or you'll pay the rent like everyone else."

Her eyelids drooped, but when they lifted again, the incredible hazel green was glazed over and she began to service him. *Oh my God.* Blake must have said it out loud. This gorgeous creature he'd been infatuated with since she moved in was on her knees sucking his dick…and loving it. In many ways, he knew himself to be an arrogant man, but hell if her lips stretching around his girth and the tiny catches in her breathing didn't humble him. This was trust. Kneeling before a man twice her size, delicate and defenseless, and offering her mouth like a sacrifice.

Blake's heart rapped against his ribs like birds hitting a screen door. God, he wanted to lay her on his couch and fuck her. Rip open that prim work shirt so he could wrap his tongue around her jutting nipples and suck them until she screamed. The size of his cock had shocked her. Did that mean she'd whine a little bit and beg him to start slow? Would he even be able to? Or would he lose control and pound into her pussy without restraint, using his mouth to trap her cries?

Need this girl. Need her like nothing else.

He didn't realize his head was tipped back, mouth open, hips rolling forward until he missed the sight of Autumn's eyes. He sought them immediately, finding them lustful, but curious. Somewhat compassionate. His heart stuttered, heat ripping up the back of his neck. Were his open wounds showing?

No. No, fuck that. Blake didn't want her sympathetic. Didn't want *anyone's* sympathy, let alone Autumn's. He wanted her lost in the moment. To see his strengths and not a single weakness. That's what she needed, wasn't it?

He glared down at her. "You've had enough time to get used to it. Take some more, like a good girl."

Panic flared in her eyes, but she wrapped both hands around his base and sunk down another inch, choking a little. *Fuuuuuck* it felt perfect. *She* was perfect. His inner thigh muscles jumped and flexed, the base of his spine beginning to tighten. "Suck it harder, Blondie. Finish me off so I can recover. Then we'll start all over again."

Autumn's hands paused, her body tensing.

He cupped the side of her face. "Oh, you didn't think I'd let you leave, did you?"

Her chest started to rise and fall. Fast. So fast.

"You thought I'd let a sweet, young thing like you walk out of here, now that I know how good you are at sucking cock? That's not how this works." Blake slid his hand around to the back of her head, twisting strands of blonde around his fingers and thrusting crudely into her mouth. Deeper. Harder. The force pushed her knees backward a few inches on the floor. "That's my mouth now. I'm keeping it. It works for *me*. By this time next week, I'll have fucked it so many times, you'll have paid rent for the whole building twice."

Autumn whimpered, her thighs restless. She loved this. Jesus Christ, he loved it, too. Loved watching her get horny while his flesh tunneled into her mouth. And just when he thought she couldn't blow his mind more thoroughly, she scooted closer and began to flat out worship him. There was no sympathy in her eyes now. Hell no. She wanted to make him come. She wanted to taste it. Her hands jacked him off with clumsy twists which grew more confident with each passing second, probably because Blake groaned loud enough to break a fucking window.

"Enjoy using your hands now, little blonde girl. You won't always have them. I've got a rope with your name on it."

Moaning, she cupped his balls with a hesitant hand, as if unsure she should be doing it...and when she looked up at him with obvious nerves, a lump built in his throat. "The only thing you could do to hurt me is stop," he rasped, dropping the game in a split second. Seeing nothing but her. "You're making me feel so good, I can barely fucking stand it."

Blake didn't process his own words until after the fact. And he expected her response to be humor or disappointment over him breaking character. In a million years, he never expected the sort of breathless confidence that stole over her features. Or the rough sucking that followed, her mouth bobbing up and down on his cock in a fantastic blur of pink, her hand massaging his balls.

"Harder," Blake choked out, propelling his hips forward to meet her mouth in a faultless rhythm. A roar built in his throat. "*Harder.* I'm going to blow down your sweet little throat."

Autumn took him deep and hummed, that vibration shaking up his cock and sending shock waves to his balls. His entire body.

"Oh, Christ. *Fuck.*" Blake's lungs seized, scalding, hot come climbing his cock so fast he staggered on his feet, Autumn's mouth still pressed to his lap. He didn't know how he found it in him to rear back and drive deep one more time, only that he didn't want the perfection to end. There had never been pleasure like this. It delved in his bones and spiked his blood cells like footballs in the end zone.

Standing became a challenge, especially when Autumn let go of his cock with a pop and he looked down to see her hand was inside her pants, her face upturned and full of pleasure. Her forearm only moved twice before she went off, her petite body shaking, a harsh whimper echoing in the apartment. Watching her in the throes of a climax sent another spurt of liquid heat up Blake's cock and he couldn't help but jerk off his semi-hard-on, stepping closer to Autumn and letting it land on her lips.

Mine.

Mine.

They stayed like that for a moment, catching their breath. As Blake put his cock away and Autumn wiped at her mouth, he ordered himself to do something. Something had to be done when your lover sat slumped on your living room floor. But all the options he came up with sounded wrong. *Hold her.* Would she want that?

Smile at her. He wasn't sure how.

Talk to her. About what?

"I fed the pigeons outside."

Fucking idiot.

Autumn's lips slowly lifted at one end. "Feeding them is gateway pigeon enabling. Next stop, full on pigeon healing."

Blake scoffed. Wrestling with himself for a moment, he scooped his hands under Autumn's armpits and stood her up, immediately taking a step back. "Don't hold your breath, Fun-Size. I told them it was a one-time thing."

She visibly softened, her eyes glowing and her lips becoming plump, but he had no idea what to make of it. He hadn't told her about the pigeons to please her. Had he? Blake cleared his throat. "Well, then."

"Well, then." She rolled up a shirt sleeve, then shoved it back down to her wrist. "I...I didn't mean to overhear you and that dude out in the hallway, but since I may have heard some stuff in an accidental, completely non-eavesdropping way, was that guy your friend?"

"No," Blake snapped, that hot tide rising a degree under his skin. How had they gotten back here? "Let's drop it."

Autumn's chin lifted—a new show of bravery he loved, because it meant she didn't fear him. But he resented it all the same because he didn't want her asking about this.

"I talked to you about Ian," she said. "I just thought—"

"You thought *what*?"

Blake could hear his mean, brittle tone, but there was no help for it. Even though he hated the way Autumn withdrew, putting distance between them when he hadn't decided yet if holding her was in order. The past had already bit him in the ass once today. The sting of betrayal and shock he'd subdued for a decade was startlingly fresh and he didn't want Autumn to know about *any* of it. Being cheated on by his fiancée while his friends were well aware. Finding out about it while in an uncharacteristically vulnerable state, brought down by an injury, his chosen career—the career passed on by his father—in tatters. These were humiliations he wouldn't be able to stand her knowing about him.

It was a testament to how much better of a human being she was than him. Because even though he'd fucked her mouth like a savage, then snapped at her twice, she reached out and laid a hand on his arm. "I don't know. I *thought*...we could be friends. Since neither of us has any?"

Blake swallowed something the size of a fist, the organ in his chest tightening like a drum. That sweet gesture directed at him when he was at his ugliest? That was once in a lifetime shit. It would never happen again—especially not from an angel like Autumn—and he should be grabbing onto it like a lifeline. *She's leaving, though. She's going to leave.*

That reminder blew out his remaining fuse, powering down any sensitivity he'd mustered. It was a door slamming. A way to keep out any further damage to his soul. Accept this girl's offer, soak up her compassion and tell her the fucked up things from his past...then watch her board a plane back to Melbourne? No. Not in this lifetime. Friends were things that came and went and left him in solitude, when all was said and done. This would be no different.

"I don't need or want a friend, Blondie." Hating himself but moving full speed ahead nonetheless, a train with the brakes cut, Blake reached out and gripped her jaw. "You gave me everything I want from you when you were on your knees."

Autumn ripped her hand away from his arm, her face going pale. "Oh wow. Fuck you," she breathed, turning for the door. Pausing in the door frame, Blake could see she was upset, but still trying to muster a decent parting shot. "You probably...*poisoned* the pigeons, you absolute dick." She turned away. "This is over."

"Autumn," he rasped.

Blake didn't know what the hell he was going to say. *Forgive me. I'm sorry. I don't know how to make people stay or even like me, so I stopped trying long before you showed up and brightened things.* Maybe he would just hand her the package on the coffee table. But she ignored him, the door rattling on the hinges as she slammed it behind her.

And Blake had never felt emptier.

CHAPTER 9

THE WORST PART was that he lied. In the hours of sleepless irritation that followed her encounter-of-the-third-base-kind with Blake, Autumn realized her oversized landlord was lying about only wanting her on her knees. If old mate wanted a strings-free beej, he could walk into any singles bar in the tristate area and take his pick. The unmarried ladies of New York would sniff out his tall, hot, moneyed ass like bomb dogs, but throw in a dick that'd make a pornstar insecure? Forget about it.

No, he wanted something else from her. Didn't change the fact that he'd been a cock. Made it worse actually, because he was the one who passed up casual sex, who was all like *we should go on three dates Autumn! You need to trust me! I'm not a perforated asshole like your ex! I'm super nice!*

"Fuckin' whatever," Autumn muttered under her breath. "Men. Can't live with 'em, can't hurl 'em all into the sun. Useless."

"Did you, uh, say something?" Pauline's usually cheerful expression was drawn and her gaze darted to the clinic door.

"Nope," Autumn said quickly. "I'm just talking to myself. First sign of madness, I know, but I'm sure the patient doesn't mind."

She stroked the tabby she was examining along her fluffy sides. "You don't mind do you, Maleficent?"

Pauline gave a little laugh. "I'm sure she doesn't, but are you sure you're okay, sweetie?"

Autumn didn't blame her for her concern. Unable to sleep after her cunty landlord compared her to one of those inflatable lady dolls you put your dick in, she'd stayed up all night playing Arkham Asylum and awoken on her couch thirty minutes before her shift, looking like deep fried ass. She'd attempted to combat the damage with an icy shower and liberal applications of green concealer, but she still looked like ass.

To make matters worse, the clinic was booked solid and additional walk-ins appeared every fifteen minutes to demand someone heal their beloved family pet, *or else*. She hadn't eaten in hours, had barely had time to take sips of water. Ordinarily, this might have kept her mind off her problems, but memories of Blake seemed immune to distraction. When she wasn't coming up with better lines to have thrown at him on the way out, she was remembering the way he'd looked as he came down her throat.

She'd never been the world's biggest blow job fan. She did it because that was what you did if you wanted to get eaten out; no pussy taxation without cock representation and all that. Yet, when she'd gotten on her knees for Blake, she'd been trembling with excitement. Fucking *trembling*.

He'd looked beautiful standing above her; his thick brows drawn together, his teeth bared in a snarl that was both scary and somehow vulnerable, a powerful man brought low by pleasure. She'd come approximately six seconds after he had and the memory had been making her insanely horny ever since. She'd refused to do anything about it last night though, she couldn't decline to be Blake's summer slam-piece then immediately go back to fucking herself senseless over him. A girl had to have *some* self-respect.

"Got anything on for the evening?" Pauline asked, clearly trying to bring her back to the realm of the aware.

Autumn decided not to tell her colleague she'd likely be rescuing more pigeons or drawing a sex-comic about Blake and then setting it on fire. "I have to Skype my parents. It's my mum's fifty-fifth birthday."

Another task that would challenge her sleep-deprived brain. Knowing her mother, the conversation was going to run smoothly from *'happy b'day mum, what did everyone get you?'* into *'how's Ian? Has he proposed? Are you two coming home?'* and then she would have to lie or say something like, *'no mum, I've not heard from Ian since I kicked him out for cheating on me, but you'll be happy to know I am acting out my niche sexual abduction fantasies with my landlord. At least I was until he revealed himself to be a colossal fuckstick.'*

Yeesh.

She should have ripped the Band-Aid off the Ian break up thing when it first happened but her parents didn't make it easy. She was their only daughter, and when they weren't demanding she make them all proud, they treated her as though she were a stained glass window. Never mind that all three of her brothers had been arrested and one had done time, if she told them she was living alone in New York, they'd be terrified. Who was going to defend her from all the guns, gang violence and all the other Hollywood-inspired problems they imagined taking place in NYC?

Her mother would also state the obvious; without Ian's dream keeping her there, why wouldn't she just tear up the work visa form, come home and buy into her uncle's business?

"We're out of doggie lorazepam," a loud voice said from the door. "I've put in an order but it won't be here until tomorrow.

The anxious doggies of Manhattan will just have to drink chamomile tea or say a little mantra when they get angsty, instead."

Autumn looked up to see Owen lounging in the door frame. He looked insultingly perfect with his freshly shaved face and styled hair, his lower lip all plumped out with whatever serums the FDA hadn't succeeded in getting banned. She instantly felt ten times rattier in comparison. "Are you *sure* the doggie lorazepam is gone? I could definitely use some right now."

Owen grinned. "I'm afraid it's true. Lunch in ten? Isa's still trying to get that Pitbull owner to stop letting Fido lick his lipstick raw and I ordered way too much Chinese. If you're there, I can tell myself I only ate half of it."

Autie glanced at Pauline, desperately longing for free egg rolls but unwilling to abandon her post. "Would you mind if I…?"

"Not at all. I'll get Maleficent in the back before Mrs. Beech comes back. Go."

Autumn didn't need to be told twice. She tore off her gloves, scrubbed out of the examination room and bolted toward the direction of food. Thankfully, Owen didn't appear any more eager to chit chat than she did. They picked up their chopsticks and Autumn dipped her head into a takeaway container of moo-shu pork and didn't resurface until her belly stopped making angry yowling noises. "Thanks, I really needed that."

"No problem." Owen shoved a can of diet coke at her. "Now that your sodium levels are restored, can I ask; did you have a rough night?"

Autumn cracked the can and gulped half the peppery drink down. "Is it that obvious?"

"Yes, quite frankly. You look like you spent the night wrestling a horde of WWE fans. In a bad way."

Autumn winced. "Shit. I knew I should have gone to a department store and pretended I wanted to buy a heap of make-up, so they'd do my face and then lie and say I left my wallet at home."

"It's not that bad, just don't keep me hanging. I want to hear the latest about your bestial landlord, which I'm guessing is what your bad night was about."

Autumn's mood, which had spiked during her rapid sugar and carb intake, instantly crashed. "I wouldn't know where to begin."

"Not this again! Just pick a place and go from there! I just watched you inhale the best fake-Chinese food this city has to offer without tasting it. You owe me."

She grinned, not in the least bit offended by his brusqueness, which she'd learned was part and parcel of Owen, and not to be taken seriously.

"I mince my walk, not my words," he'd told her during their coffee date. "Just tell me to shut up if you think I'm being too bitchy."

But Autumn never did. Paying out your mates was a treasured Australian pastime and even if she and Owen were only work acquaintances, it was nice to experience it again. Still, telling Owen the latest on Blake was problematic. He seemed heavily invested in them having a happy ending. When she'd told him Blake had demanded to take her on three dates so she could trust him, Owen had slithered onto the floor in a mock swoon.

"It's a modern day Beauty and The Beast," he said. "God, I wish it was happening to me but since it's happening to you, you *have* to let me live vicariously through you. I want all the details of this man-beast love connection, live as they unfold."

Autumn had agreed, thinking that it was fun to have a secret to gossip about, but that was before. She didn't relish telling Owen that the strange-but-loveable Beast had told her she was good for nothing but sucking his cock. It made for a very disappointing ending. Disney certainly wouldn't be optioning the rights.

"So last night." Autumn cleared her throat. "He…"

Owen frowned. "The beast fucked up?"

"Yeah," she said with relief.

"Typical. Nothing gold can stay and what have you." Owen twirled his chopsticks in the universal signal for 'go on.' So she told him about the incident in the lobby and how Blake had dragged her upstairs for an afternoon delight gone bad. Recapping the incident had hurt more than she'd thought it would. Describing the scene had brought back details she'd forgotten; the appalled curl of Blake's lip, the way he'd talked to her as though she was the dumbest person on earth. At least Owen was a wonderful audience, the perfect blend of scandalized and intrigued and punctured every third sentence with 'oh my god's' and 'what a dick's!' When she was done, he shoved his Peking duck at her. "Here, you need it more than me."

"Thanks." She picked up her chopsticks and transferred a chunk of duck to her mouth, hoping the sticky-sweetness of it would fill the cavern that had opened up in her chest.

"What a complete disappointment," Owen mused. "Who knew the modern Beast was just some New York douche with man-pain issues."

"Yeah." Autumn had only taken one mouthful of duck but she put down her chopsticks. She felt mildly ill and not because of the takeout. She hadn't realized it until now, but she'd been hoping Blake was the modern Beast, too. Yet, like a newer, burlier version of Ian, all he turned out to be was some entitled asshole.

"Do *you* think he's just an asshole," Owen said, apparently able to read minds. "Or do you think he's nuts? Or both? Or neither?"

Autumn shrugged. "I don't know him well enough to decide. I think he's been hurt pretty bad, though. That's what the guy, his friend who came to see him, wanted to talk about."

Owen nodded thoughtfully as he toyed with a lone beef wonton. "Well, whatever his deal is, you can't keep seeing him. When a man says you're only good for fucking and doesn't immediately follow that statement with 'I'm sorry I just racked a big line of bath salts, which way to the emergency room?' it is game over. The question is, what now?"

"I guess I go back into hiding. Maybe expand my harmonica repertoire. I can do almost all of *'Love Me Do'* now."

"What?" Owen looked utterly disgusted. "No! *No.* You are not becoming a second beast, only much smaller and a female. Not on my watch."

"But I already have the hair for it?" Again Autumn gestured to her scalp. "See?"

Owen slapped her hand away. "I said *no.* What you need is to find some revenge dick to get over your revenge dick. *Double* revenge dick."

"I think I might be all dicked out."

"Bullshit." There was a steely glint flickering in Owen's eyes. "You need to get back out there and move on. And I don't mean sleazy tete-a-tete's with your landlord. I mean real dates with classy men who know how to treat the woman who are so generously swallowing their body fluids."

"But—"

"But nothing." He whipped out his phone. "What's your

type? Your exes swing from model-pretty to papa bear. I have no idea what direction to go in. Enlighten me."

About six-foot-four, dark-haired, handsome, reclusive…Oh and if he manages my building, so much the better…

"I don't think I have a type but I really don't think I should be dati—"

"Dealers choice, love it," Owen muttered, tapping frantically at his screen. "I've been waiting for this, Ryan knows so many hot straights who are trying to find *the one* and Isabella refuses to have sex with anyone who doesn't sell chronic or play the fucking ukulele. How do you feel about men in their late thirties? And are you free tomorrow night?"

Autumn closed her eyes in an attempt to combat the chaos churning in her head. She didn't really want to mope around her apartment pining for Blake but she didn't see how going out with another dude was going to help. In fact, the very idea was making her feel nauseous.

"Am I going too fast?"

"Uh, maybe," Autumn said, opening her eyes. "I appreciate the effort but this is a bit much."

Owen put down his phone, looking apologetic. "I'm sorry, I just like fixing things."

"That's okay, that's why you're an amazing surgeon. I appreciate the effort, I just feel weirdly guilty about dating someone else so fast. What if Blake finds out about it?"

"Why does that matter?" Owen's eyes narrowed. "You think he might pick a fight with you if he saw you waltzing in with a new and improved Beast?"

"Yeah, he'd probably throw him through a wall." Autumn hesitated. Was she giving herself way too much credit? Maybe he wouldn't give a shit. God she wished she wasn't so invested in knowing what Blake was thinking. How had she come to care this much this fast? If she didn't know better, she'd think she was falling—

Nope.

Not going there.

"I don't know," she corrected. "Maybe he wouldn't care. He'd just…look at me all frustrated and disappointed and I'd feel like my organs were being squished into pâté." She shivered. "Just *imagining it* is making my organs feel like they're being squished into pâté."

"Why?"

"I don't know!" But as soon as she said it, Autumn did know. She knew exactly how Blake would look if he saw her with another man. She'd seen it before, when she was with Ian. She hadn't understood what it meant back then, but she did now. He'd been jealous. Or maybe just disappointed that she had such terrible taste, the way he'd been disappointed that she wouldn't do stand-up. Maybe that was why he'd said she was only good for blowing him; because real-world Autumn was no match for the fantasy girl who lived in his head. That idea should have pissed her off. Instead, it just made the hot ache in her chest even worse.

"Girl." Owen's expression was serious. "Do you like the Beast? Really like him?"

Autumn shook her head so hard that grains of rice she hadn't known were lodged in her hair flew out. "How could I? We've only gone on one date!"

He gave her a look. A 'don't-lie-to-me-bitch' look.

"No, I don't like him. I mean I *like* him of course. He's funny and nice and sexy and it's kind of adorable in the way he pretends like he's so mean when really he's a pigeon feeder…"

Owen raised a brow and Autumn realized she was making a

mess of her argument. "But underneath it all, he's a huge withholding dick," she said, with all the conviction she could muster. "But we have this really intense sexual chemistry. It's completely fucked. He's like the living embodiment of all my most psycho fantasies and he does things to me that no one has ever done. Ever. I mean, just thinking about him touching me…" She remembered the feel of Blake's cock in her mouth, the way he'd looked towering over her, telling her she'd suck him off enough to pay rent for the whole building.

"You're blushing." Owen patted her hand with his lovely, turquoise-tipped fingers. "Look, you've danced around what these 'psycho fantasies' are, but if you want a freak, I can find you a nice respectable freak. Your nutty landlord isn't the final word on men who do weird shit in bed."

Autumn smiled, but privately she disagreed. She'd walked the earth for twenty-six years and never come close to meeting a man who compelled her sexually the way Blake did. If she were the kind of hippie who believed in soulmates, she'd have thought their meeting was more than coincidence. That the universe had pulled two perfectly suited people together from opposite ends of the globe. After all, how many places were there to rent in New York City? And how many were owned by the personification of all her secret longings? Yet they'd found each other in a city of millions. Maybe Blake *was* the final word on her fantasies, the only guy who'd make her feel so utterly depraved and yet safe at the same time.

Yeah, except the conductor of your sex orchestra said you were nothing but a cum-dumpster, remember? That's not very 'sage and rainbows and special spirit connections,' is it, Reynolds?

Autumn sighed. She really needed to stop staring into the depths of her own belly button and get with the program.

"Okay, no dates this week, but I'll let you know if I change my mind and want to star in my own low-rent version of the Bachelorette," she told Owen.

"Low rent? How dare you. I only know straight and bisexual men of the highest quality. Handsome, humble individuals who are beloved across the east coast and beyond."

She laughed and was on the verge of telling him to prove it when she felt her phone buzz inside her white coat pocket. Her heart spring boarded into her mouth. Was it Blake? Was he sorry that he'd been such a rampant cock? She pulled out her phone and her mouth went dry.

"Beast?" Owen asked.

"Worse. Ian."

He gasped and clapped a hand to his mouth. "Where have you been all my life? Before you came along, I had to resort to scrolling TMZ for lunchtime entertainment."

Autumn tried to smile, but couldn't quite manage it. Ian texting her had to be a bad deal, it just had to be. "Want to hear what it says?"

"Does the pope shit in the woods?"

She opened the message and began to read aloud. "'*Hey Auts, I don't know if you've told your parents we broke up but I texted your mum for her birthday, I hope you don't mind. I can call you tonight if you want to talk about it, Ian.*' Then he put a smiley face and two kisses."

"Are you serious?"

"As the plague." She shoved her phone back into her pocket. "God, what an anus."

"Hmm." Owen leaned back in his chair, folding his arms across his chest like a wisecracking movie detective. "He's back."

"Huh?" Autumn said, her thoughts having boomeranged back to Blake and his failure to apologize for being such a doucheturkey. "What was that?"

"He's back," Owen repeated. "Your ex. He wants in again."

"No fucking way!"

"Way."

Autumn pulled out her phone again and looked at Ian's message, confused as to how Owen could sound so sure. "Trust me, this is just Ian being a wishy-washy buttplug. He loves my parents. It doesn't mean anything."

"Are you sure? It sounds to me like he's saying he misses you. Sounds to me like he's finally fucked enough groupies to wake up and realize he ditched a natural blonde veterinarian. You'd better not text that little fuckboy back."

"I won't!" She unlocked her phone and deleted the message. "See? Screw that. I've got enough problems."

"Good call, but be on your guard. If I know straight boys—and having been in love with a number of them, I surely do—he'll be back. Try and make sure it's not at a vulnerable moment. Maybe mention that you blew your landlord. Guys hate that. *Anyway.*" Owen clapped his hands. "Time to plan your revenge-revenge dick, are you sure I can't persuade you—"

"Excuse me?" Glenn, the pretty Dutch receptionist poked her head into the lunchroom. "There's someone here to see you, Autumn."

"Who?" she and Owen said at once.

"A very tall man. Blaine, I think he said it was."

Autumn's stomach turned over. Obviously Owen was following the same line of thought because he asked, "Do you mean *Blake,* honey?"

"Oh yes, maybe," Glenn admitted. "It is hard to tell, it is very loud in reception area."

"No, no, no!" Autumn moaned.

He couldn't be here, not *here*-here. Not now when she looked feral and had just pounded half her body weight in Chinese. Not with Owen sitting beside her, practically vibrating with excitement at the chance to confront the fabled beast. She needed to move quickly. So, so quickly. Before Owen could say anything, Autumn clapped a hand over his mouth. "Thanks for letting me know, Glenn, but could you please tell Blake I'm busy?"

"Oh I did, but he said he's happy to wait until you're free."

Sweet lord.

Owen licked her fingers, freeing himself from mouth-jail. "Glenn, please tell Mr. Blake that Autumn can do better than emotionally withholding drama kings and to please never darken these premises with his overly hairy body again."

Glenn shot Autumn a puzzled look, as though wondering if she'd misheard. "I, uh, do not think I can do that."

Owen stood. "Fine, *I'll* tell him. This is *such* an exciting Wednesday."

Autumn tried and failed to grab his arm as he passed. "No! Don't talk to him, Owen! Please, dear God, don't!"

He turned and winked at her. "Sorry lovely, but he slandered you. Also, I have to see what he looks like up close, I just *have to.*"

Owen tore out of the room at top speed, ducking nimbly around Glenn who still looked very confused. "Is this man your boyfriend, Autumn? I'm sorry, I didn't know he was your boyfriend."

Autumn jumped to her feet. "He's not my boyfriend, he's just some cock I rent off of and don't worry, I'll stop this!"

Glenn didn't look very reassured.

She raced after Owen, frantically wondering if crash-tackling a coworker could get her fired. She burst into the reception area and laughed out loud with relief. She needn't have worried about

Owen confronting Blake. He'd been utterly submerged in a group of Armani-clad women. He was the most popular vet at Happy Paws, basically a minor celebrity. He wouldn't be looking at anything except smoothly attractive Manhattanites and their neurotic cats for a long-ass time.

Autumn cackled, then remembered the reason why she'd come out here in the first place. She scanned the room but couldn't see Blake anywhere. Had he cut and run, after all? Had Glenn mistaken the name? Disappointment barely had time to register before she saw him crouched in the corner of the waiting room. He had his back to her and appeared to be talking to a little girl who was crying her eyes out.

Geez, don't tell me he terrifies small children, too...

But that couldn't be the case. The little girl *was* spraying tears all over the place, but she didn't look scared. She was nodding slowly, her expression grave, as though Blake was giving her important medical advice. Autumn slipped out from behind the reception counter and walked toward them.

"You can pat him now," Blake was saying. "Just gently. That's it. He's very happy you're here with him."

"Is he?" the little girl asked in a watery voice.

There was a slight pause and then, "Of course, he'd be stupid not to. And, uh, he's not stupid, he's very smart."

"Really?"

"Yeah. Of course."

Autumn swallowed. "Blake?"

His shoulders contracted beneath his olive-green t-shirt, as though she'd zapped him with a cattle prod. "You...You're here?" he asked.

"I work here."

"Yeah. You do. Uh, hang on a sec."

He rose to his feet and turned, and Autumn felt like someone had swung a sledgehammer into her uterus. Her landlord had not only shaved and put on more of that underwear-incinerating cologne, he was holding a caramel-coloured spaniel puppy. It squirmed in his enormous hands looking both painfully excited and mournful, as only spaniels could. She had a feeling he could have put the dog down and had deliberately chosen not to; a low blow, as far as she was concerned. Determined not to let hormones get the best of her, she leaned around Blake to address the little girl. "Who's this?"

The little girl sniffed. She couldn't have been older than seven. "That's my puppy, Popcorn. He was *freaking out*. Are you a vet?"

"Yes," Autumn said, glancing around for the girl's parents. "Did you come here with your mum or dad?"

"My mummy's over there." The little girl, who had a chirruping British accent, pointed at one of the women crowding Owen, a statuesque brunette wearing a poison-green scarf.

Way to leave your kid and her puppy alone in a nutty environment, lady, Autumn thought, then turned back to the girl. "What's your name?"

"Clover. I'm six and three bits."

"Wow! And can you tell me what was making Popcorn sad?"

Clover shrugged and pointed to Blake who, she was both gratified and amused to see, blushed.

"I think he was just scared by the noise," Blake said, the burgundy on his cheeks and ears intensifying with every word. "He started whimpering and trying to get out of Clover's hands. I was right there and I thought…I just…"

"He helped me," Clover said loudly. "I want Popcorn back now. Can I have him back?"

Without another word, Blake turned around and handed her the puppy. The little girl cuddled him close to her chest. "*Thank yooou.*"

"Anytime," Blake said gruffly. "I think your mom's coming back now."

Sure enough the green-scarf woman was walking toward them looking miffed, which could mean only one thing—Owen was shaking off his fan club and would soon come gunning for them.

Without thinking, Autumn grabbed Blake's hand. "Talk? Outside? Now?"

He'd barely said 'yes' before she was dragging him toward the exit, hoping against hope Owen's vision was still impaired by the dregs of his devotees. They stepped into the sunlight and Autumn became aware she was still holding her landlord's hand. A tingle shot up through her skin and she let go of it at once.

"So," she said, trying to peer up at Blake without being blinded by sunlight. "Come to express your remorse, eh?"

"Yes."

She'd say one thing for Blake; he was abridged as fuck. "Roping a puppy into your apology was pretty cheap."

"I got a lucky break." Blake shifted his weight to the side and suddenly Autumn could see.

"Thanks," she said automatically, then shook her head. "I'm very mad at you, Landlord. Very mad."

One of those infuriating smile-but-not smiles. "Are you sure?"

Damn him. Autumn pointed a finger up at him. "That's because of the puppy. It's very hard to get angry at someone that helped a little girl and her puppy. A puppy called fucking *'Popcorn'* of all things."

Blake glanced away, staring off down the street. "It was crying. I didn't know they could do that."

His obvious discomfort at experiencing such a thing had more of her residual anger ebbing away. "It's the most painful thing in the world, right?"

"No. The look on your face yesterday wins that one. Hands down."

Autumn nudged a crack in the pavement with her rubber-capped toes. "Yeah, well that's what happens when you stick your nose where it doesn't belong. Lesson learned, I guess."

"Look at me." He cleared his throat. "Please."

If he'd ordered her to do it, if he'd even *sounded* like he was ordering her to do it, she would have kicked him in the shins and ran back inside the clinic, but this was no demand. Blake's voice was thin, as though on the brink of tearing. He was in pain, she could feel it, and whatever he'd said to her, she didn't have it in herself to prolong his suffering. She met Blake's eyes, feeling the now-familiar ripple in her stomach that said she was already in too deep. "What?"

"I'm sorry. It wasn't true, what I said. It's more than sex." He swallowed hard, his Adam's apple contracting in his powerful throat. "There are times…"

He stopped again, apparently unable to continue.

For all her idle revenge fantasies throughout the day, Autumn had no appetite for watching this big, silent man slice himself open in the sunlight. She knew words weren't Blake's strong suit but he was clearly going to persevere at all costs, talk until she forgave him, and he'd come here today with that intention. The certainty of it made her chest feel as hot as a baby sun.

"It's okay," she said. "I know you didn't mean for things to go down the way they did."

"It's not okay. If I heard any other man say what I said to you, they'd be eating their meals through a straw." He stepped closer, studying her face as if checking for some secret combination. "I had no right to treat you like that. You deserve better. I'm an asshole. I—"

"*Blake.*" Autumn grabbed his hand again. "It's okay, I was being nosy and you reacted badly. I get it."

"You *don't* get it." Blake's light brown eyes locked on hers. "You're the fucking sunshine and that's how you should be treated. I wanted you to understand that more than anything."

Autumn glanced away, confused by the purity of the happiness coursing through her. He thought she was special and goddammit, the way he said it made her want to believe it was true. This wasn't just gratitude, right? This had to be—

Nope.

Not going there.

Thankfully, before she was required to react to that heart-stopping statement, the door to Happy Paws Vet Clinic burst open and Owen was zeroing on Autumn like the terminator. "There you are, my slippery blonde friend."

His gaze swung from her to Blake and back again. "And just who are you talking to outside on a busy and important day like today?"

Her landlord scowled at him, clearly unhappy to have been interrupted. "I'm Blake, I'm speaking with Autumn about—"

"Rent," she interjected. She really couldn't handle Owen bearing witness to a full blown dialogue about her sex life and she was fairly certain Blake had been about to continue his apology. She moved between the two men and held out her arms. "Owen, this is my landlord, Blake. Blake, this is Owen. He's the very popular vet that everyone around here is always excited to meet."

"Right," Blake said.

"Mmm," replied Owen.

They gripped hands. Both looked like they were doing the old *crushing-this-man's-most-delicate-bones-will-prove-who's-the-manliest-then-eh?* thing. Autumn wasn't the least bit surprised to see Owen holding his own, painted and jeweled as his fingers were. He never had a problem holding down even the largest, most aggressive dogs. She *was* surprised Blake wasn't making some excuse and leaving. Instead, when they finally unleashed each other's hands, he asked Owen how long he'd been working at Happy Paws and an actual adult conversation ensued. As they went through the whys and wherefores of working at a vet clinic, Autumn tried to get a read on how each man felt about the other. It was impossible. Blake was as expressionless as a professional poker player and Owen's face was smooth as a bowl of cream. She, on the other hand, felt like she'd eaten one of those ghost chilies. She wanted to run, scream, drink a lot and go to the bathroom, yet she remained fixed on the spot, her insides writhing like live snakes. Finally, Owen pursed his beautiful lips. "So, what are your behemoth intentions toward my friend?"

Autumn's ears began ringing. Intentions? Friend? "Owen, seriously—"

"We had a three-date deal," Blake said matter-of-factly. "I want the other two."

"In my line of work, if you're scheduled to operate on three schnauzers and you kill the first one, people tend to think you can't handle the rest."

"Owen!"

He turned to look at her. "This man has given you a woeful courtship so far, yes or no?"

Autumn ran a hand through her hair. Now was the time. If she told Blake to fuck off again, she knew he would go, but the thing was she didn't want him to go. "I don't disagree, but I've had a lot of fun with Blake. I just think some conversational, uh, fine-tuning might be required if we go out again."

She expected Blake to smile, but he merely nodded. "Understood. Are you free at eight tonight for date two?"

A whole horde of butterflies took off in Autumn's stomach. To have gone from never seeing him again to a date tonight was just amazing.

Complicated, a small voice whispered in her ear. *So fucking complicated.*

But she ignored it in favour of the bubbling excitement and sheer relief of knowing she had at least two more nights with Blake. "Sure."

"I'll pick you up at eight. No suit this time." He nodded at Owen and then turned away, striding down the street, forging a path for himself through even the most stubborn New York pedestrians.

"Okay," Owen said. "I get it. A little laconic, desperately needs a haircut, but I get it. Very butch, very old world manly. You need to be careful. He's got a six hundred-pound albatross round his neck. I just met him, and I know that."

Autumn, who'd been watching the way Blake's back muscles flexed as he walked, pooled her focus, "I know what I'm doing."

Owen looked skeptical but he smiled at her all the same. "Sure you do. Let's get back to work."

"Oh shit. Yeah. All the people."

Owen held the door open for her on the way back in and Autumn remembered how he'd called her his friend. She hesitated, then gave into her instinct to hug him. "Thanks so much."

"For what? Gay men can be chivalrous. It's a thing."

"I know, but also, you stuck up for me and you and Blake did that uber manly handshake thing…it was nice and just…thanks."

He patted her back lightly. "Anytime. Now let's separate before my fans get jealous. I had to tell them my sister was going into labor just so I could come outside."

"They really do love you."

He heaved a dramatic sigh. "Everyone does. It's a fucking burden."

CHAPTER 10

Autumn opened her apartment door and promptly shut it in Blake's face.

He sighed.

"Seriously, you *need* to give me better advance notice about the dress code for these dates," Autumn called back through the wood.

Blake could hear her footsteps jogging across the floor, dresser drawers being wrenched open. Shoes being kicked off. He breathed out a sigh before reaching into his sweatpants and taking out his keys. When he found the right one, he inserted it into the lock and turned.

"Your exact words were *no suit this time*. But that makes me think jeans and a cute top. Not a T-shirt and runners, for fuck sake. Where the hell are you taking me, anyway?"

Blake gently closed the door behind him without a sound and completed a slow stalk through Autumn's living room. Drawn to her bedroom, he nonetheless paused when something caught his eye in the kitchen. An official-looking form stuck to the fridge, the words 'Application for International Employment Authorization' stamped across the top. Her visa renewal. She'd told him the damn thing was nearly expired—how much time did he have?

He had tonight. All he could do was focus on tonight.

Blake continued on to his intended destination; Autumn's

bedroom. He rested his shoulder on the doorjamb and studied the scene. It was chaotic, Autumn in panties and a purple tank top tugging clothes out of her drawers and tossing them backward onto the bed. She obviously didn't notice him standing there because she continued to mutter under her breath about what an inconsiderate asshole he was.

True enough. Considering his recent fuck up, he probably should have waited outside in the hallway. That would be the polite, gentlemanly thing to do. Truthfully, though…he couldn't stand another minute not having his eyes on her. So here he was. Lucky for him, she had a stalking fetish.

Autumn held up two pairs of leggings, obviously trying to decide which to wear. Had she worn that lace thong for him? It separated the tight cheeks of her ass and wrapped around her slight hips, touching all the places his tongue wanted to be. Every part of her looked so smooth, so sun-kissed, and he wanted to worship her up, down and sideways. Blake's hunger was even sharper than usual and he wondered if this was the almighty need for make-up sex people raved about. Knowing she'd been angry with him made Blake want to give her orgasms. Loud, scratching, sweaty ones.

He should be grateful she'd forgiven him at all. He'd definitely been the asshole she was still proclaiming he was. And when he'd arrived at her job today and seen her covered in pet hair, clearly exhausted but still achingly beautiful…the full magnitude of what he'd done hit him like a ton of bricks. Scraping together an apology on the walk over had seemed like an impossibility until she was standing right in front of him, the sunlight picking up flecks in her hazel eyes and turning her hair to gold. Thankfully, whatever he'd blurted out was good enough to make her agree to tonight's date. Now, hopefully she wouldn't back out when she found out where they were going.

She'd discarded both pairs of leggings and pulled out two more from her seemingly endless supply. "The black ones are frayed," she muttered, "the white ones show my panties. Fucking hell, why do I have so many leggings?"

Blake took two slow steps into the room and watched awareness creep up Autumn's spine. Goosebumps broke out along her neck like lights going on in a city skyline. Her right ankle crossed over the left, then returned to its original place. Jiggling, jiggling.

Oh yeah. He definitely wanted to give her orgasms. And more apologies. The kind he'd issue inside her, grinding his cock against her G-spot. Her accelerated breathing and the flickering pulse at the side of her neck told Blake it wouldn't be a difficult battle, getting her on the bed. Spending the night buried in her pussy, her headboard making dents in the drywall. But something wouldn't let him take her, yet. Not without earning it. Not without her knowing she was worthy of being earned.

Blake slipped his hand around her throat from behind, the tips of his boots pressing into her bare heels. She needed this, too, though. And God knew Blake needed to touch her. He'd deprived himself yesterday and his palms missed the shape of her, the texture and heat.

His fingers cinched tighter around her throat, conforming his body to her back. "I like you in the black ones, Blondie," he said, brushing his mouth over her hair. "The ones you keep in the second drawer from the top."

A shudder went through her at the nickname, a signal the game was beginning. Her swallow slid up and down in his palm. "How do you know where I keep them?"

Of course, he'd been watching her from the doorway. That's how he knew. But that wasn't the answer she wanted. "You think this is the first time I've been in here?"

Blake let his right hand travel down Autumn's throat, his left one joining it at her breasts where he unhooked the front of her bra, tugging the material down her arms and letting it fall to the floor. He clasped Autumn's waist and squeezed hard, lifting her onto her toes. "I've touched every damn thing you own."

He could sense Autumn holding her breath, waiting for him to touch her tits. Cup and mold them. From his vantage point over her shoulder, Blake could see how stiff her nipples had become. He ached to pinch and suck those buds, but knew if he did, they wouldn't leave the bedroom tonight.

Instead, he reached over and slid open the top drawer of her dresser, moving some panties and socks aside until he found a white sports bra with a Nike swoosh across the front. He pulled it down over her head, guiding her arms through each hole and securing the tight material over her breasts, the action jiggling her tight ass around on his lap. "You don't wear this one very often, do you? You're always reaching for the sexy shit that pushes your tits up and makes my cock suffer."

"You shouldn't know what I reach for—"

"If you didn't want me so curious about what's under your clothes, Blondie…" He pressed his open mouth to the side of her neck, taking a hit of her cherry scent. "You'd stop walking around the building looking so…fucking beautiful I can't concentrate on anything. On my work…"

Shit.

Silence bulldozed the room. Realizing he'd screwed up the game, Blake scowled and snatched the leggings from Autumn's hands. He spun her around and—ignoring the adorable O of her mouth, and the twinge in his leg—he hunkered down and held open the waistband. "I was going to say something about you being a dick tease."

"But you said the other thing. The lovely thing."

Blake's frown deepened. He couldn't ignore the relief he felt over her thinking it was lovely. God, that settled it. He was losing his mind. Why not just stick a rose between his teeth and lead her in a tango? This girl wanted to be held prisoner and he was inflicting romance on her. Something he had no experience with.

Stick to the plan. Stick with what you know and what she agreed to.

"Put these damn things on. We're going to be late."

One foot in the air, she swayed. "Are you sure you don't want to stay here, instead?"

He caught her knee and drew it to his mouth, nipping at the soft inner skin with his teeth. "The walls of this apartment have never heard the sounds I want to wring out of you, Blondie. Believe me. But after I was selfish with you…" His tongue soothed the spot he'd bitten and absorbed her shudder. "I wouldn't allow myself to apologize and ask you out again unless I did this right from now on. Did right by you. So put on the damn leggings before the scent of you turns me into a liar."

Autumn complied in a dazed manner, a wet spot spread along the front of her thong. As if leaving the building without mauling her wasn't already hard enough. He tugged the thin, black pants up her calves and thighs and settled them at her hips, swallowing the possessive kick he experienced over dressing her. Goddamn. Why did it feel so nice?

When he managed to drag his attention from her sexy figure, covered in nothing but a bra and skin tight pants, he found her watching him closely. "Where are you taking me?"

"Krav Maga." With a concerted effort, he turned on his heel and left the bedroom. "A beginner's class uptown."

"Are you serious?" She met him in the middle of the living room, her hands clasped together under her chin. "Like, I get to punch and kick things?"

"You'll be a one-woman killing machine within an hour."

Her lips pressed together, but didn't quite hold in her chuckle. "Was that a *joke*, landlord?"

"Obviously it was. You couldn't kill a pigeon." He waved a hand in the direction of her feet. "Go put your shoes on. And cover up."

"Hey, you're the one that dressed me." Her attention snagged on his erection, currently pushing at the seam of his sweatpants. "Um. How long were you standing there watching me, anyway?"

Blake crossed his arms over his chest. "Long enough to know I'm not just an asshole, I'm an arrogant butthole."

"Sorry about that one," she said, dancing off toward a pile of shoes near the door, taking her sweet time sliding them onto her feet. "To be fair, you did sneak in here like giant, pervert ninja."

His mouth threatened a smile. "Tick tock, Fun-Size."

※

BLAKE HAD GOTTEN the idea to bring Autumn to Krav Maga the first time she'd set foot in his apartment. He'd towered over her petite, post-break up twenty-something form as she asked a man twice her size to hold her hostage, and he'd marveled over her courage. It was too much to hope that she'd sensed something in Blake that caused her to trust. Way too much to hope for.

No, she'd obviously reached a point of desperation. A point where her hulking bastard of a landlord became appealing, but he wasn't looking a gift horse in the mouth. No, he was trying not to fail spectacularly at being given this privilege. More than anything, he wanted to take that confidence she'd displayed and…give it room to grow, any way he could.

They'd taken an Uber to the training center on the Upper East Side, because even after Autumn pulled on a tank top, he could still see the Nike swoosh. Honestly, it was as though she'd purchased everything in her wardrobe with the express intention of sexually frustrating him. But he remembered Autumn being self-conscious thanks to his silence en route to their dinner date, so he'd forced himself to form words and ask about her job. She'd proceeded to tell him about a bunny that had accidentally swallowed a tab of acid, and the subsequent tongue-lashing Owen had given the owner, and Blake actually found himself laughing.

Long ago in another lifetime, his friends—Kevin, Elaine, Tommy—would make a huge deal out of how rarely he laughed. 'We knew you had a sense of humor in there somewhere. Take a picture! Doctor Doom is laughing.' It used to annoy him into stopping. Lately, though, laughter made him replay what Kevin had said in the building hallway. *You mostly open your mouth to make everyone feel like idiots. But we were friends—thick and thin—and the rest of us still are.*

When he'd laughed in the cab with Autumn, she'd stuttered a little, obviously caught off guard and he hadn't minded at all. He'd kind of enjoyed surprising her. Had he changed? Or did he just hold his friends to a harsher standard?

Blake and Autumn came to a dead stop upon walking into the gymnasium.

"Oh my God," Autumn said, fanning herself. "It's tropical in here."

"Hi! Sorry." A young man with floppy hair and a mustache jogged toward them, wearing a blue and gold instructor's uniform. "We're not testing out Bikram martial arts or something. The air conditioner's broken. Please don't leave. Free water. I will give you free water."

"Shouldn't water always be free?" Autumn asked. "Like, it does fall from the sky."

Once upon a time, Blake had worked under the ground, locked inside humidity for hours at a time, while wearing a jumpsuit and heavy equipment. This sweltering gym was a cake walk for him. Autumn on the other hand, was unlikely to have endured this kind of damp heat. He turned to her. "Will this be okay for you?"

"I've been promised kicking and punching." She smiled and leaned into Blake, close enough for him to count the scattered freckles on her nose. "No take backs."

Blake nodded once at the instructor. "Lead the way."

While Blake and Autumn stretched on a blue mat that took up the whole gymnasium floor, a dozen more class members walked in, staying only after the promise of free water. At eight o'clock, the instructor took his place at the front of the class, bouncing back and forth on the balls of his feet. "Okay, so. Brief history lesson, folks. Krav Maga is Hebrew for *contact combat*. Its origins stretch back to Imi Lichtenfeld who took his mad street fighting skills and turned it into an art form. Now it's the official military fighting system used by the Israel Defense Forces. And it's badass as *shit...*"

Blake listened with half an ear as the instructor continued the origin story. He'd done his own research before signing up for the class and knew the basic history. He couldn't help but watch Autumn from the corner of his eyes, noting the way she tilted her head when listening, tongue tucked into the edge of her mouth, blonde hair resting on her cheek. It was almost enough to distract him from the swoosh on her tits.

The first fifteen minutes of the class focused on strength

training. Planking, push ups, some mental preparedness guided by the instructor. It had been a while since Blake tested his injured leg anywhere but the privacy of his own apartment, but thankfully no one seemed to notice him favoring it. Mentally, he knew an injury wasn't something to be self-conscious over, but he couldn't help associating it with a time in his life he wanted to forget. A time that had been all too recently thrown in his face.

"Okay, everyone." The instructor clapped his hands. "Partner up. We're going to start with a straight punch combination. On the back wall, you'll find some bags with holding straps. One partner holds the bag, one partner wails on them like Rocky." Everyone laughed. "You're only going to make contact with two knuckles. Forefinger and middle finger. Direct all your energy forward. Maximize the impact."

Autumn retrieved the bag and returned to him, seeming at the last second to remember their considerable height and weight difference. "Um, maybe I should find someone normal sized?"

"You're one to talk. I could put you in my pocket." He took the bag from her. "My fists aren't going anywhere near you. I'll just hold the bag."

"Okay." She hopped around a little, like the gym mat had transformed into lava. "You're not going to rip it away at the last second and make me fall on my ass, are you?"

"Of course I'm not."

"And…" She lost some of her pep. "You're not going to make fun of my spaghetti arms, are you?"

There was a punching bag hanging in the corner of the room. And more than anything in that moment, Blake wanted to go knock the goddamn stuffing out of it. She hid it well most of the time, but it was clear Autumn's self-esteem had been dropped in a garage disposal by her dickhead ex. There was enough of the brilliant woman beneath to know she hadn't always looked down on herself. How else could she not know—and be told on a constant basis—that she was funny and beautiful and perceptive and warm? That prick, Ian, had done this to her. He'd never been surer of it. Or more determined to help reverse the damage.

"You didn't even flinch when I told you about tonight," he said. "This isn't a typical second date. Nothing we've done is typical, but you face it all like a pro. You had no reservations about trying something new. You just got dressed—"

"Again, sir, *you* dressed me."

"I'm trying to be sincere here," he growled. "Kick this bag's ass, Fun-Size. No one is stopping you. *No one* can stop you from doing anything."

Little by little, she started hopping again. "Make the bag my bitch, yeah?"

"Damn right, make it your bitch."

More hopping. "Now?"

"This century. Yes."

She pulled back a fist, screwed up her face and bashed the bag. Hard. It wasn't enough to knock him off balance, but he took a step back anyway—and the lie was worth it when a smile broke out across her face. "Made you my bitch, too!"

"Let's not push it."

Blake could have stood there all day and let Autumn batter him with her fists. After that first punch, she got into a rhythm, getting settled in her stance, focusing on the target and letting fly. With each punch, she stood with a touch more self-assurance. Shoulders squared, chin up. She stopped glancing up at him to gauge his reaction to everything she did. Toward the end of the drill, he sensed she was channeling frustration into the punches. Her hits got harder, came faster, her lips pressed in a flat line. As fierce as she looked while walloping the shit out of the punching bag, there was vulnerability in her expression, too. And it took a lot of willpower for Blake not to drop the bag and...hold her. Or ask what she was thinking, even though it was clearly a private moment. So he contented himself with holding the bag while she had at it.

"Nice job, everyone. Last drill for today!" The instructor circled the room, sweat soaking the back of his shirt. As the class went on, the gymnasium had grown progressively hotter and even Blake had to admit, he could do with some cooling off. So while the instructor pulled a volunteer to the front of the room to demonstrate a takedown maneuver, Blake stripped off his shirt and tossed it toward the bleachers.

"What are you doing?" Autumn whispered, staring at his body like she'd seen a ghost. "You can't just go around looking like that. It's rude."

"How is it rude?"

"This is a beginner's class. People signed up for it secure in the knowledge that *other* out-of-shape people would be joining them. Then you show up looking like Aquaman and shatter their illusion of comfort."

"Yes, if I'm known for anything, it's worrying about the comfort of strangers."

"Actually, you *are* known for that. By me."

He scoffed. Mostly to distract himself from the twinge in his chest. "How so?"

The instructor glanced Autumn's way and she nodded, as if paying close attention to his demonstration. "That's what these three dates are about, aren't they? Making sure I'm comfortable enough in your Blackbeard presence for you to tie me up?"

That was only a fraction of his reasoning, but Blake wasn't

going to clue Autumn in on the rest. "How is that going by the way?"

She gave him a flirtatious shoulder roll, peeking up at him through her lashes. "Pretty good."

Blake felt a heavy pull in his groin. Yeah. His control was nearing the end of the road. If they were the only ones in the gym at that moment, he'd be working himself into her pussy from behind, using the punching bag to prop her hips up. "Anything I can do to help convince you?"

"Depends," she murmured. "Who is throwing who to the mat?"

Blake didn't hesitate. "You're going to throw me down."

"Really? And here I was, ready to accuse you of sexism for making me cover up while you strut around like an aquatic sex god."

"If I threw you down, Autumn, we wouldn't make it home without fucking."

"Explain?" she breathed. "In detail."

Glad they were standing on the outskirts of the group, Blake slid a hand into the back of Autumn's leggings. He found her lace-covered pussy, giving her clit a two-fingered massage. "You were built to be thrown down. And I was built to *throw* you the fuck down. I'm not talking about physically—I'm talking about those dirty damn needs of yours and mine." Speaking directly into her ear, Blake eased the lace to one side and sunk his middle finger inside her, not stopping until he'd given her the whole thing and the sides of her face were fire-red. "If I used my strength on you, you wouldn't be able to hold it together. Your thighs would pop open like goddamn cash registers and everyone would know you want my cock between them. Isn't that the truth?"

Her answer was barely more than a whimper. "Yes."

Blake twisted his finger until the pad brushed her G-spot. He began a slow rub and earned a low sob from Autumn. "Knowing how little I care about strangers, apart from you, apparently, what would I give cute, little begging Autumn if I finally had her on her back?"

"You..." Her hips twisted on his hand, like she couldn't help it. "You'd have sex with me in front of everyone."

"No, I would *fuck* my pretty Blondie while everyone took notes and envied me."

Her flesh tightened up around his finger and she shook through an exhale. She could have come, just like that. Getting fingered in public. But the instructor chose that moment to blow his whistle and Autumn jolted away from him, pressing both hands to her flushed face. "Um. What?"

He steadied her when she swayed toward him. "Shit. I wasn't paying attention. What are we supposed to do?"

Recalling the bare bones of the demonstration, he turned her around and brought her back up against his front. It was a good thing she blocked his lap from view, because his cock was filling out the right leg of his sweatpants—fucking *aching* for her. And he had no choice but to rest it on the sweet curve of her ass, grinding down and tugging her hips back at the same time. He brought his arm up around her neck, holding her in a loose chokehold. Across the room, they locked eyes in the mirror, visible proof of how he dwarfed her, his pecs tensed above her blonde head, his widened stance putting his thighs on either side of hers.

"This is a rear naked chokehold," said the instructor.

"I wish," Autumn muttered.

"If you find yourself in this position, the most important

thing to remember is not to lean back," the instructor called out. "If you do, it's much easier for your attacker to bring you to the ground. Focus your weight forward."

Autumn followed instructions, the move pushing her backside more firmly up against his dick, sending even more blood rushing south.

"Now take hold of your attacker's arm at the elbow, get low and twist. Rotate their shoulder and hopefully they'll lose their balance or at the very least, be thrown off center."

As he and Autumn continued to stare at one another in the mirror, Blake wasn't sure what was happening to him. Undeniable lust pooled in his belly, but there was…affection, too. Maybe it was the reflection showing his arms around her, Autumn leaning back in a show of trust. He didn't know. But the urge to encourage her joined his lust and made it even more poignant. It turned them into the only two people in the room.

"Go ahead, Fun-Size," he muttered in her ear. "Make me your bitch."

He only caught a brief glimpse of her exhilarated smile—and his subsequent hypnotized expression—before she grabbed his elbow, spun in a blur and actually knocked him off balance. Not enough to hit the mat, exactly. But hit the mat he did, even manufacturing a grimace when he landed. "Nice job."

A couple of the other students gave Autumn a round of applause and Blake rested on his elbows, watching her soak it in with pleasure. He waited until the other beginners had gone back to their own exercise before extending a hand. "Help me up?"

"I mean, it's the least I can do after—"

Blake curled a hand around Autumn's wrist and pulled, bringing her down on him. Without pausing, he reversed their positions, rolling Autumn beneath him on the mat, not bothering to support his weight. Just as he'd warned her would happen—just as he'd been fucking craving—her thighs opened automatically for his hips. Her hands flew up above her head, as if seeking an anchor. A rope. A headboard. She went pliant, her breath coming and going through a straw.

"I'm proud of you." He rasped near her mouth. "You were incredible."

"What?" Her mouth opened and closed. "I-I...thank you."

"I think you could do anything, Autumn. You're..."

God, this lust-affection one-two punch was murder. He wasn't even sure he *liked* the damn feeling, but he would have ended anyone who tried to take it away. "You're a fighter, you understand? Even though I'm about to take away your will and laugh at your attempts to get free, I know that will is there. Deep down. All right?"

"Okay," she breathed, her eyebrows drawing together. "Thank you."

Blake angled his hips on top of her clit and punched them forward, listening to the rattle in her throat. "Now nod your head if you're a good, little beggar who does what she's told."

Autumn nodded, her pupils dilating, thighs restless. It was in the back of his mind that they were being watched, but he was growing more and more doomed not to care about a damn thing, except for the trembling girl beneath him.

"I warned you, Blondie. I throw you down, we don't leave the building without fucking. But you had to go dragging your ass all over my cock, didn't you?"

Blake stared at her throat a moment, so she'd know he was thinking about locking a hand around it. "Stay in the woman's locker room until I come and get you. Have your panties off under these bullshit leggings. Understand?"

CHAPTER 11

AUTUMN STOOD IN the sweltering locker room, trying to peel her leggings down her thighs. The tight material wasn't going willingly and it didn't help that her skin was slick and her hands were shaking. She and Blake were finally going to have sex. The truth of that fact had her vibrating beneath her skin, inside her bones. She tried to control her breathing, savor the anticipation, but all she wanted was for the show to start. She pulled her panties down her legs and her skin prickled with goosebumps. She was excited, too goddamn excited.

It's just fucking, she reminded herself. *What are you so worked up about?*

A memory rose; being fifteen years old, her parents away for the weekend. She'd read the Wikipedia entries for abduction movies and gotten so turned on she'd saturated her underwear. Then she'd gone to the shed, taken a length of her dad's orange multipurpose rope and tied her own wrists together. In the face of this overwhelming fantasy, her usual teenage fumblings had honed on one thing—being owned. A farmer, broad and faceless, found her trespassing on his land. He tied her up and kept her in his stable like an animal, coming outside to use her whenever the need arose in him.

Autumn had already known what she liked at that age, but the farmer fantasy had been more vivid than any she'd dreamt up before. It came to life behind her eyes, allowing her to feel the scratch of the rope, the farmer's rough hands on her hips. Alone in her bed, she'd given into the fantasy, slipped inside it like a thread through a needle's eye, but afterward, she'd been so ashamed she'd burned the rope, vowing to never think such gross things ever again. It was wrong to want what other girls had no choice but to endure. It meant she wasn't good, wasn't smart, wasn't the kid her parents needed her to be.

Twenty-six-year-old Autumn met her gaze in the dusty locker room mirror and saw her teenage fears reborn. *I'm wrong. I'm broken. I shouldn't be allowed to do this. Anyone who would want to do this is wrong, too. It'll hurt. Blake will hurt me and then he'll think I'm disgusting.*

In that moment, panic seemed imminent. Then she remembered how she'd felt punching the bag, purging frustrations she hadn't even known were rising in her; Ian's message, her mother's unrelenting demands to come home, the growing feeling that her life wasn't hers, that she'd let everyone else decide for her. She'd hit harder and harder, and while it hadn't given her any solutions, it had felt so fucking good. Blake had given her that. And now, if she let him, he would give her more. He would give her a fantasy turned flesh. Real fear and real satisfaction. The question was, was she ready?

Autumn turned and looked at soft pink marks imbedded in her shoulders. Souvenirs from the mat Blake had pinned her on. She replayed the memory of his weight bearing down on her, the rush of heat that swelled between her legs as he'd done it. She hadn't been scared, not even a little bit—she'd been on fire. She let the truth of that soothe her, encourage her to take deeper breaths.

"No one knows what you want like he does," she told her mirror-self. "He'll take care of us and he definitely won't think we're gross."

She smiled and her reflection smiled back, looking genuinely relieved. For so long, she'd been alone in her fantasies. Now someone had joined her, it was a little overwhelming. When she and Blake had sex in a way that mimicked her secret fantasies, it would be like losing her virginity all over again.

Smiling a little at the idea, Autumn successfully rolled off her leggings and removed her lace panties. They were as wet as they'd been the night she'd first tied herself up, the warm sweet smell making it clear that while her mind was conflicted, her body had no such qualms. It wanted Blake and it wanted the fantasy. Now. She tugged her leggings back up her thighs, adjusting them so they lay flat against her skin. Her mind was now full of memories of Blake without a shirt on, broad and gleaming and almost offensively male. He'd seemed so surprised that she'd been perving on him, as though he couldn't believe she found him attractive. In hindsight, she wished she hadn't teased him about his body, that she'd told him sincerely how beautiful he was. He seemed like a guy who'd be embarrassed, but remember her words forever.

Devoid of anything else to do now that her panties were off, Autumn wandered around the locker room. It wasn't a nice one by any means, just a couple of wooden benches and cracked mirrors surrounded by discarded exercise equipment; bench bars and weight racks and clunky elliptical machines. Maybe the place had been a mainstream gym before it was converted into a Krav Maga one? She had just hauled herself onto a dusty pull-up bar, when she heard footsteps approaching the door.

She released the bar, falling onto her feet. He was here. The fantasy was about to begin. She waited with baited breath, but the door didn't burst open the way she'd been expecting. Instead, the footsteps halted outside the ladies' room. Autumn was sure she could hear Blake breathing behind the wood. Deep breaths like a bull bracing itself to charge. Her heart pulsed hard against her chest, the beat echoing between her legs where her now-bare pussy was pulling in on itself, craving what it knew Blake could give her. She looked sideways and saw her reflection was that of a human deer, all bright eyes and an anxious twitching mouth. "Is...is someone there?"

The door creaked open, the noise as exhilarating as it was in horror movies. The reveal was much better though—a bare-chested Blake, hairy and enormous, cold glinting in his pale eyes. "Evening, Blondie."

There was a beat in which Autumn couldn't remember what was meant to come next. Then she swallowed. "The men's room is on the other side of the hall."

"I know where the men's room is."

"Then why don't you go there? Please?" Autumn loved how she sounded, all frightened and girlish. She'd never been much of an actor but she wasn't entirely acting. Blake looked so big, so mean, so *other*, it was impossible not to feel fear, even if excitement bubbled beneath it.

"I didn't come here to talk." Blake closed the door behind him and dragged the bolt across.

The dull rasp made Autumn's heart rate treble. "No, you can't—"

"Shh." He walked toward her. His weight on the dusty floorboards caused the entire room to quake. He eyed her over, his expression lazy, as though they'd agreed to meet in the women's change room for a date. "Seen you around here a few times."

"I—"

"Shh." Blake picked up an old medicine ball from a shelf and tossed it into the air like it was a balloon, a casual display of strength made all the more sinister by his placid smile. "Once I saw you, I couldn't stop seeing you. But you know all about that, don't you, Blondie?"

"N-no. I promise I don't."

"Yeah, you would say that, wouldn't you? I know your type. You play the good girl, laughing and smiling so no one can call you what you are—a cocktease."

"No—"

"I said *quiet*." Blake dropped the medicine ball. It made a noise like cannon fire, shaking the floor beneath her feet. Autumn wondered if she could lift it if she tried, wondered if she was meant to run. Excitement was a lump in her chest, she couldn't digest it and she couldn't bring it up. She needed to trust Blake to make the next move, even if she didn't trust the man he was pretending to be. He moved closer, his gaze firmly on her tits. "What bra size do you wear, princess?"

"T-that's none of your business." She shifted her body to the right and he shifted with her, pressing her backward with the invisible force field emanating from his height and bulk.

"Please," she whispered. "Can I go?"

He chuckled softly. "Begging already, are we? Funny, I'd say you were begging when you decided to go walking around this gym in your paper-thin leggings, showing off your bare stomach and making every man in here put his sweat towel over his cock."

"I'm sorry," she said, taking another step backward. "I didn't mean to do that."

"I think you did. I think you liked getting us hard, knowing there was no way in hell you'd ever let us slide our dirty pricks in you. That why you picked this gym, Uptown Girl? Why you come here? Cheap thrills with the underclass?"

As he talked, Autumn felt herself sinking into the scene he was painting. She was from nothing and Blake was wealthy but in this scenario she could be rich. Why not? Maybe she was a Park Avenue princess, a brat who slummed it at a blue-collar gym because making rough-looking men like Blake hot gave her pleasure like nothing else. She held up her hands. "I'm sorry about my outfits. I'll find a new place to work out."

Blake's mouth curled in an imitation of a smile. "Too little, too late, Blondie."

Autumn inhaled sharply, her hands and feet tingling with nerves. "What about if I…if I write you a check for two thousand dollars? No questions asked."

Blake didn't laugh, but his light brown eyes glittered with obvious amusement. "A negotiator, huh? That's good to know. You and I are going to make all kinds of deals over the next few days."

"Like, wh-what?"

"Like what you'll do to me in exchange for a crust of bread, a little water, an hour's sleep. Those kinds of deals."

Autumn's whole body was now shaking, the way it had when she was fifteen and reading the Wikipedia entry for *Taken*. She took another step backward and found herself pressed against the chin up bar. She was cornered.

Finally, something inside her whispered. *Finally.*

Blake reached out and touched a gentle hand to her hair. "You're mine now. The sooner you start accepting that, the better."

"Please," she whispered, the bar cold against her bare lower back. "Please, I'll give you anything. Ten thousand dollars, my car, my apartment…"

"Unnecessary. I've got everything I want, except you." He

twisted one of her curls around his finger. "Still, it's nice to hear you beg. You got any more rich-girl offers for me, Blondie?"

Some part of Autumn not utterly consumed with arousal knew what he was saying; 'speak "gold leaf" now or it's fucking on.' She made her lower lip quiver. "Please let me go, sir?"

A lupine smile. "Not a chance. I'm gonna take you home soon, wrap you in my coat so no one sees you go in the trunk of my car. But before that, I think I'm gonna fuck you here, right in the place you put on these skintight clothes. That'll show you, huh?"

"P-please—"

"Shh." He ran a thumb down the line of her sports bra. "Your nipples are always so fucking hard."

Autumn batted his hand away. "I just got out of a self-defense class."

Blake laughed, a short hard bark. "I know, I watched you. Not that it'll do any good. You've got fire, Blondie, but it's the kind of fire that'll make you a hellcat in the sack. When it comes to protecting yourself, you're lacking something very important."

"What's that?" Autumn asked, as she slid her sneakered sole to her left.

He leaned in close, his nose centimeters from hers. "A body to back it up. What you've got is good for nothing but getting a man hard."

It was then that Autumn made her move, darting to the left, intending to make a break for the door. Blake picked her up by her waist and hoisted her into the air as easily as he'd lifted the medicine ball. He laughed as she kicked and struggled. "See? Couldn't get away if you tried. Not that your tight little body's useless, Blondie. In fact, I think there's a whole lot it could do for me."

Autumn wasn't sure how much noise she was allowed to make, but in that moment, she was so pent-up she couldn't help herself. She screamed, needing the release regardless of whether any of the gym members were still kicking around.

Blake's hand descended over her mouth, pressing hard against her lips. He bent in close, his eyes black with fury. "You make one more noise like that and I'll bend you over the bench. I'll blister that ass. Understood?"

Autumn shook her head, kicking out at him. Her foot connected with his side but he was so hard with muscle, it just hurt her toe. "Ow!"

Blake grunted, though she knew it was in anger, not pain. "You want it that way, huh? Fine."

A second later she was on her knees, eye to eye with Blake's groin. Before she could react, one of his hands was cupping the back of her head, the other plunging into his training shorts. And there it was, his cock, thick and purple with blood, even bigger than she remembered it.

"Suck," he snarled, tugging her forward. Autumn parted her lips and took him deep, tasting the sweat and the sheer humiliation of doing this before they did anything else. As though she was a whore he'd picked up on the street and immediately set to work.

His hand fisted her hair. "That's it. You keep your mouth on this while I get ready, understood?"

She nodded, not knowing what 'get ready' meant but unable to care as she attempted to make her jaw go wider, to take him deeper. She had a flash of the last time she'd done this, the hurt that had followed the excitement of sucking him in his living room. His declaration that blow jobs were all she was good for. Perhaps Blake felt her hesitancy because the hand fisting her hair smoothed down the nape of her neck. "Can you handle me, sweetheart? If you can't, I'll spare your mouth. Save it all for your pussy."

It was reassurance, framed as an insult. Autumn shook her head, taking him deeper into her mouth.

"I can't hear you."

"Igh caghn hangle ight," she garbled around the straining cage of her teeth.

A patronizing pat on the head. "Good girl. Now blow me. Show me what you're worth."

Autumn sucked him harder, tasting small salt bursts of pre-come. It was gratifying to know he was as turned on as she was, and she was *turned on*. Her thighs were now slippery beneath her leggings and her nipples were aching points. She knew that if Blake was to lay a finger on any of her sensitive places, she'd come, but he didn't lay a finger on any of her sensitive places, he just let her suck him as he moved above her, doing something she couldn't make out.

She heard the whisper of a rope pulled from somewhere and instinctively wriggled back, needing to see what he was doing. Instantly, Blake pressed a palm to the back of her head, keeping her impaled on his cock. "That's no concern of yours, Uptown Girl. You keep sucking my cock and put a little more effort into it, I want to feel your tongue on my balls."

Autumn returned to her task, all the more frustrated but now incapable of screaming, something Blake had probably factored into the arrangement. Music began playing overhead, mildly familiar rock, she suspected was coming from Blake's phone.

"Just setting the mood," he said, giving her another demeaning pat on the head. "Gave the man on the desk a hundred bucks for some privacy, but I can't have the neighbors wondering about the girl getting her brains fucked out in the gym, can I?"

Autumn moaned around his cock. The image of him taking steps to ensure he wouldn't be discovered screwing her was so perfectly fucked up. Everything about this was.

Blake cupped her cheek. "All done now, sweetheart. One more big suck and you pull your mouth off me, okay?"

Autumn obeyed, diving so deep she gagged a little, before sliding him from her lips. Unencumbered, she looked and saw that he'd strung a thick silvery rope around the pull up bar, woven it into some kind of harness. Her pussy clenched, but she made herself wince a little, because she knew she should.

Blake sneered down at her. "Don't be like that, Blondie. You're going to love it. Sluts like you always do."

The suggestion that she was one of many, that Blake had done this before with another girl, pricked at her ego. "I'm not a slut. You want sex so bad, you'd kidnap someone. *You're* the slut."

Blake's smiled faded. He reached for her cheeks and the next thing she knew, his cock was back between her lips.

"Didn't learn your lesson, did you?" he snarled, driving himself into her mouth. "Unless you're screaming my name, I don't give a damn about what you have to say. Can you get your pretty head around that or am I going to have to smack your ass until you can't sit down?"

Autumn shook her head.

"Are you sure? I'd be happy to show you how a real man deals with a smartass woman."

"Igh meaghn ight," she managed to say.

"Good. Now pull back again."

She let his thickness slip from her mouth and Blake reached down and lifted her into the air. He propped her head against the top of the pull up bar, and wrapped her legs around his waist. "Hold still, or there's going to be big trouble, Blondie."

Autumn held still and he began to strap her in to the harness, the rope winding tight around her rib cage, her shoulders and her hips. Soon, much sooner than she expected, she was dangling from the pull up bar, her arms and legs spread wide. It wasn't uncomfortable. Her weight was evenly distributed and none of the ropes were chafing, but he'd forgotten to take her clothes off. She was still wearing her sports bra and leggings, which would restrict all the things she wanted to come next. She cleared her throat. "Wh-what are you going to do to me?"

A smirk. "Lots of things. Don't you worry about that." He stepped backward, gazing admiringly at his handiwork. "Beautiful girl, aren't you? Bet everyone tells you so."

Au contraire mon frère, said her inner critic, but Autumn ignored it. This was a fantasy, she *was* beautiful and everyone *did* tell her so. "Please…"

"Keep quiet, honey. I don't want to make it hurt, but look at me." He gestured to his torso. "Look how big I am. I could hurt you without even trying and you don't want it to hurt, do you?"

She shook her head. The motion made her sway slightly in her bonds but she couldn't move more than an inch or so. She was bound as securely as a bug in a spider's web. A thrill zapped through her. *Finally. Finally.*

"Are you going to be a good girl, Blondie?"

She hesitated.

"You've had me in your mouth, you know I'm big everywhere. How do you think it would feel if I took you rough from the very start? Just rammed myself into your tight cunt and took you full force, like I'm dying to? Think you'd like that?"

Um, does bro-country music suck? Autumn made herself shake her head.

"Then you need to understand, Little Miss Uptown Blonde, that I'm being a nice guy here. I'm giving you options. You be good and I'll make sure it's good for you. Best you've ever had. If you're not good…" he shrugged. "Who knows what might happen."

Autumn licked her lips, tasting salt and Blake there.

"So what do you say?" he said, reaching out and laying a big palm against her right breast. "You going to be my good girl?"

She nodded. "Yes, I'll be good."

"Glad to hear it. That about brings us to our main attraction." He stepped forward. Tied up as she was, their eyes were almost level. Blake reached down and tugged at the waistband of her leggings. "We've got a problem, don't we? Your fuck-me gym shit, nice as it is, is fucking up my access. Would you agree?"

Autumn nodded.

"I've got a solution for that but it'll mean saying goodbye to your outfit."

Yesssss.

"You can get rid of my clothes," she said in a tiny voice.

"Learning fast, Blondie." He fingered the line of her sports bra again, making the skin beneath it hum. "You won't need any of this where you're going. You're going to be naked from morning 'till night."

She imagined it, being kept stripped on his mattress, turned over and fucked whenever he had the urge. Another zap of electric arousal jolted through her. Her pussy felt independently alive, clenching and fluttering in tiny pulses. Before, she'd been caught up in her expectations and shame. Now a new clarity was rising. She'd given herself over to Blake and now all she wanted was to get fucked. To be a good girl and receive her award.

Blake grasped her sports bra with two hands. "Here we go."

He pulled, and Autumn wouldn't have believed it possible, but the thick mesh material tore open, exposing her nipples. The exposed air felt better than she thought possible. She struggled in her bonds, needing more.

"Easy, Blondie." He bent down and sucked her into his mouth, the heat and wet of his tongue making her hips buck against her harness. "Please stop!"

Instead, Blake sucked harder. His hands moved from her waist to her legging-clad hips. "I think it's almost time, Uptown Girl. What do you think?"

Autumn could only whimper, terrified talking would result in more delayed gratification.

"Sounds like a yes." He cupped the place between her legs. "You're fucking soaked and no panties either, huh?"

She shook her head. "I'm sorry."

"No, you *will* be sorry." He fisted the crotch of her leggings and pulled. The seam split and Blake tugged at the material, stretching it wider, exposing her pussy in a way that felt more revealing than if she was wholly naked. Her landlord dropped to his knees so that he was at eye-level with her cunt. "You're smooth. You let someone wax you, Uptown Girl? Let another person get you ready for me?"

Actually, she'd de-haired herself with a bunch of men's razors Ian left behind, but this hardly felt like the time to reveal such things. "Yes."

"Not anymore, you don't. From now on, the only person who touches you here is me. If I want your tiny cunt smooth, I'll shave you myself, you got that?"

Autumn nodded.

He wrapped her legs around his shoulders like she was nothing but a doll, staring intently between her thighs. "You still going to give it up?"

"Yes," she whispered, but it wasn't until he lowered his head toward her that she realized what he was intending to do. This wasn't a part of the plan. Sucking his cock and getting tied up, yes. But oral? How was that showing her who was boss?

"No!" she said. "Not that."

Blake glared up at her. "Not your fucking call. You're going to get eaten out, Blondie, and I'll make you hate how much you love it."

"No! Please! I don't want that!"

His answering smile was malevolent, but there was also something of her landlord in it, the man who'd taken her to a fancy restaurant and forced her to order what she wanted. The man who was determined to bestow pleasure on her, regardless of whether she thought she'd earned it. *You'll take, Fun-Size,* that smile said, *you'll take because you deserve it.*

"I'm doing this," he said.

"But—"

"No buts. You've had me in your mouth, you know what I've got and if I want to get it inside you, you'll need to be sopping wet. Besides..." He ducked his head and licked a long hot line through her cunt. "...I've been wondering what you taste like for months."

He pressed his hands into her ass and buried his face in her pussy. For a few seconds he seemed to inhale her rather than do anything else, pressing her scent and taste into his mouth, rubbing her across his lips. She cried out, the sensation pleasurable but too sharp to make her come. Then his fever seemed to die down and he slid his tongue inside her while his lips circled and worried at her clit.

"Tiny little pussy," he muttered, making her flesh vibrate. "So wet, so fucking warm. My new favorite place."

He'd said he would make her love it and he kept his promise. His mouth was so large compared to her that he covered everything all at once, licking and sucking and making her thrash in the rope harness. Autumn had never received oral standing up, but the view was spectacular—Blake's dark head between her thighs, devouring her.

The head Ian gave had been perfunctory, almost clinical in its precision—get her off so that she could get him off. Blake moaned into her pussy as though there were nerves chained from her clit to his cock. He was constantly glancing up at her to gauge her reaction and as she edged closer to orgasm, he pressed one big finger inside her, then two, the rough invasion of it in strange contrast with the soft, fluid motions of his tongue. Autumn fought climax for as long as she could, scared of the noises she'd make, the total abandon she knew she'd feel. Then another of his thick fingers began toying with her asshole, making her scream. "No, please, Blake, *no*. Not everything, not all at once."

He didn't slow for a second. "Don't fight it, Blondie. What I'm doing to you has your greedy little cunt on fire. There's nothing for you to do but come."

"No," she moaned, "No."

But it was already ending. Molten pleasure rose up inside her. She was so aware of everything, not only her pussy but her aching nipples, the ropes binding her fast to the pull up bar, the dust in the air, Blake's low moans of satisfaction. Everything. All at once.

She came hard, shuddering and shaking and screaming Blake's name. Her limbs went stiff and she felt wetness gush into his willing mouth. She wasn't sure how long she stayed lit up from the inside before slacking limply into her bonds, nothing but shuddering flesh and willing bone. It felt like eternity.

"That's it," Blake growled, his fingers pumping hard inside her. "That feels nice doesn't it? Having the bad man make your pussy come? Knowing you've got no choice but to take it?"

She moaned helplessly, knowing it would turn him on more than any limp sentences she could summon.

Blake got to his feet, his chest gleaming with sweat and his cock straining through his shorts. He pulled a gold square from his pocket and tore it open.

"No," she pleaded, even as everything inside her said 'oh fuck yes.'

"Shut your fucking mouth," Blake snarled. "Shut your mouth and look at my cock."

She dutifully watched him roll the condom down. His shaft was heavy and dark with blood and though she wanted nothing more than for him to take her, she wondered if this would work. He was so fucking *big* and it had been months since she'd done Pilates…

"You're getting a condom now because I'm not leaving a mess for the cops to find," Blake growled, bringing her back to attention. "Once you're in your new home it'll be nothing but bareback, Uptown Girl."

Autumn's cunt contracted at the thought of this huge man raw and pumping inside her, feeding his fluids into her body. "I'm not on birth control," she lied.

Blake smirked, a perfectly evil smirk that spoke of his pleasure in the face of her powerlessness. "I'll pull out and come on your tits. At least half the time anyway. Now, legs up."

She disobeyed for the pleasure of having him grab her and force her tethered legs around his waist. His cock was pressed at her entrance and it felt like a battering ram poised in front of a spun sugar fence.

"Ready?" he asked and Autumn really didn't know. Then he gave her a look, a look that said he wouldn't hurt her, that he would sooner die than hurt her. She couldn't explain how she knew he meant that, only that it bled away the last of her reservations. She was a woman and women gave birth to watermelon-sized babies. She would take all of Blake inside her, revel in it, claim him even as he claimed her.

"Do it," she whispered, playing the part of the terrified captive. "Please just do it and get it over with, please."

A smile that was not a smirk, but something more. "Whatever you say, Uptown Girl."

He pressed forward and she parted like butter. The spread of her cunt around him was exactly what she'd needed and she rocked her hips against him, needing more. "Blake. *Blake.*"

"Look at me, Autumn."

Her name, he'd called her by her name. She opened her eyes and looked up to see Blake staring at her, his gaze so hot, it burned. He slid deeper, making her mouth fall open as her pussy burned and throbbed around him. Blake could feel it, she'd bet her life on that. His hands as he grasped her hips were shaking and there was a muscle leaping in his jaw. It was clearly taking everything he had not to plunge inside her, but still he went slowly, taking care of her.

Inch by inch he spread her wider, deeper, and soon Autumn was the one who was pushing against him, humping him, trying to get more, faster. The heat stoked by her first orgasm was back, burning like a flame between her legs. She needed to come again, to feel her landlord fuck her with the brutality of a man who'd abduct a girl from his gym.

Yet, Blake wasn't playing that scene. He held her firmly and drove in slowly. When at last he'd seated himself deep inside her, their hips locked, and Autumn felt a fullness that had nothing to do with Blake's cock. She stared into his incredible eyes and for reasons she couldn't explain, said, "Thank you."

His mouth twitched the way it did when she told a joke, but his eyes blazed hot. It looked like he was going to say something, but then he shook his head and it was gone. He didn't shut down exactly, but Autumn could see he was putting whatever he felt aside. Storing it wherever this big silent man stored unwanted things. His eyes darkened and his brows lowered, making his handsome face unkind again. He thrust his hips and Autumn whimpered at the throb between her legs.

"You like that, little whore? You like my big dick inside you?" She shook her head and he laughed. "Girls like you always want this. They want a man to fuck them hard. Take them rough and make them like it. And since you can take all of me, it's time I took all of you."

"N—" she barely began the word before he clapped a hand over her mouth. "It's time to get fucked, Blondie. Nothing left for you to say."

He plunged inside her, setting the fast, brutal pace she'd imagined ever since she'd slotted her landlord into her darkest fantasies. It was an explosion, a cavalcade of pleasure force-fed directly into her cunt. She hung in her harness, unable to move or resist. Every thrust reinforced her helplessness, her subjectivity to Blake's will. Time sped up as her heart began to pulse hard and sweat spread across her still-clad body. She made noises she barely recognized, mewling, whimpering, feline noises as she tipped ever closer to a devastating orgasm.

Please say more, she thought, and like a mind reader, Blake lowered his mouth to her ear. "You're loving this, aren't you,

Uptown Girl? Taking my cock deep?"

Her protests were muffled in his palm but it seemed Blake got the gist. He fucked her harder, his flesh slapping hers, striking her clit in rhythm and making her whole body thrum.

"You're a fucking liar, Blondie. You didn't want it, you wouldn't come, and you're about to gush all over me. You'll love being my sex slave, cooking my meals and draining my balls. It's all brats like you ever want."

It wasn't true, but Autumn trusted that Blake knew that, that this was smoke and it was mirrors and it was lovely sexy lies. She threw her head back, orgasm welling like a ripe fruit between her legs.

Blake's tongue lapped her neck, tasting her sweat. "That's it. Come for your owner, baby. Make him proud."

She did, bucking so wild and hard against her restraints that if Blake was any other man, she'd have worried about hurting him, but seeing as he was huge and hard, she decided not to be worried. Instead, she focused on the bright trickles of pleasure threading through her body like veins. She was *flying*.

Blake let out a harsh bellow, removing his hand from her mouth to grab both her hips. He fucked her rougher, thrusting in and out with abandon, chasing his own climax. She moaned to see him so wild, her stern, distant landlord coming apart at the seams—and all because of her. "Finish inside me, Blake. Please?"

He swore, his handsome face screwing up in a mixture of pleasure and pain.

"Please," she repeated. "Please come inside me?"

"I will," he moaned. "I'll fucking fill you up. Make it so you never need another man again."

Something about this rang strange in her ears but she was too caught up to give her much pause. "More? Please more?"

"You'll get more," Blake said, his gaze locked on where his thickness was vanished inside her. "I'll ride your body every hour, wear you out like a fucking jacket. You're a slut, Blondie, you're my slut."

Autumn knew he was about to come and while she'd fantasized a thousand times about watching this, she closed her eyes, letting herself feel it all instead. He poured himself between her legs with a strangled, almost wounded moan. "Autumn. *Autumn.*"

For a moment they hung, suspended in the frameless window that followed climax. She kept her eyes closed as she nuzzled Blake's shoulder, tasting the salt of him. She wanted to say thank you again, but knew that wasn't right. They'd just shared something, and while she was grateful, thanking him would be silly. They'd built it together. Whatever it was.

She was just starting to worry about the condom when Blake placed a gruff kiss on her forehead and pulled out. She listened, her eyes still shut as he snapped off the rubber and swooshed the material of his shorts back over his cock.

"Autumn? How do you feel?"

She opened her eyes and smiled at his look of mild worry. "I feel…"

"Yeah?"

"I feel so fucking free."

And she rolled her head back and laughed because it was true, she was suspended in midair, half-naked and covered in sweat but she felt so *free*.

Blake shoved his hands in his pockets and gave a sort-of smile. "Glad to hear it."

"I'll bet you are. How do you feel, by the way?"

"Good," Blake said, which she chose to believe meant 'extremely fantastic Autumn, you're the absolute fucking best.'

"That's good."

He reached forward and touched her cheek. "I liked giving you what you need."

"You did." She sat up in her bonds and looked at him, ignoring the hot pressure in her chest, that feeling that continued to encroach whenever Blake said anything sweet. "Okay, so…what now?"

Another of her landlord's trademark smile-but-not-smiles. "Now we go for a drink."

CHAPTER 12

AUTUMN STARED AROUND the bar. Once again, Blake had surprised her. The place wasn't dingy and it wasn't ultra-high end, it was…cool. Floating pink lights, garish oil paintings and black leather lounges filled every space not taken by New York natives coalescing with their usual glamour. Autie was thankful for her magenta lipstick, black camisole and crimson cigarette trousers which, in the semi-darkness, could pass for chic.

"What?" Blake asked as he settled in the velvet tub chair across from hers.

"This isn't what I was expecting when you said 'grab a drink.' But then, I rarely expect anything you do, so maybe I should expect this."

"Don't like the place?"

"No I really like it, it just doesn't seem very…you." Autumn picked up the single sheet cocktail menu and almost choked on her tongue. "Okay, this? The unbelievable sticker shock? *This* seems like you."

Blake laughed, the sound like the lower notes on an oboe. "Then I shouldn't have to say 'order whatever you like Fun-Size, and don't bitch about the price tag.' But I will. Order whatever you like Fun-Size, and don't bitch about the price tag."

Autumn tapped the menu. "Have you seen how much they're charging for a shot of vodka? This is *offensive*. I'm gonna organize an occupy movement inside this bar."

He chuckled again. He seemed so much lighter tonight. He'd smiled multiple times on their way from the Krav gym to the bar and when they crossed the road, he'd taken her hand. As they walked, she'd felt completely safe on the streets of New York for the first time, secure the way she'd felt secure dangling in her rope harness. Blake had her, and he wouldn't let anything bad happen. Except paying thirty-two bucks for a cocktail, apparently.

Her landlord rubbed his hands down his granite thighs. "Right, what do you want?"

Autumn glanced at the menu again and its choices swum up at her like drunk, highly expensive fish. "I...can you pick for me?"

Blake didn't even hesitate. "Sure."

He stood up and headed to the bar. Alone for the first time in hours, she tapped out a quick text to Owen informing him she was fine and the second date was going well. She'd barely put her phone down when Blake returned, two drinks in hand. His was a highball; hers was what looked like a bright green milkshake full of pink flowers and pineapple chunks. She stared at it in wonder. "What *is* that?"

Blake shrugged. "Something with pineapple."

He placed it in front of her and Autumn bent forward and took a small sip through the bamboo straw. It was cool and sweet with a slightly astringent aftertaste. "It's nice, thank you."

Blake nodded.

"How did you pick it? Did you just tell the bartender to make something girly?"

"No."

Autumn waited, knowing if she stayed quiet he would say more. A few seconds passed and her landlord's eyebrows drew together. "Someone else ordered it and I thought you'd like it. The flavors looked tropical. Sunny. They seemed like they'd suit you."

Autumn smiled down at her cocktail, remembering how he'd compared her to the sunshine outside Happy Paws. "You've never seen me when the Bombers, my football team, are losing. You wouldn't compare me to the sunshine, then. I set new records for the number of swears per second."

Blake's lips curled a little as he sipped his drink and she wondered when a compliment had ever felt as good as that little half-smile. Never, she realized. And silence had never been so sweet. She had never understood the appeal of the strong silent type before, but being with Blake meant she didn't have to keep up a constant stream of chatter the way she did with her vet clients. She didn't have to listen to endless self-focused stories the way she had with Ian. She was free to really taste her drink, to look around the bar and study the art and people without worrying she was losing the thread of a conversation. It was very…peaceful.

When Autumn was nine, her cousin Jessica had brought home a Brazilian boyfriend. Josef spoke almost no English and Jessica spoke almost no Portuguese but they soon got engaged and moved in together. Autumn's family had found the situation utterly bizarre.

"How can you love someone if you don't understand a bloody word they're saying?" her mother moaned into the landline. "It'll never work."

Autumn, too young to be tactful, had gone up to Jessica that Christmas and asked her how she could have a boyfriend if she didn't know what he was saying. She'd never forget the look on Jessica's face, the mysterious smile, the warmth in her eyes. "Everyone's gossiping about me, aren't they?"

Autumn had nodded.

"Well you can go tell them all I don't care. Love isn't just saying words. What we feel is real."

At the time, Autumn had assumed her cousin meant kissing or possibly—*yuck*—sex, but now, looking at Blake, what she said rearranged themselves in the context of this lovely, confusing man. True, Blake spoke English, but only reluctantly. His words were blunt and, dirty talk aside, came in clusters of three or five. They meant exactly what the most literal interpretation of those words were, nothing more or less. That should have been a problem, but it just wasn't.

As she drank her drink in that same companionable silence, she realized it didn't matter because what he said paled in contrast to what he did. He'd taken her to a five-star restaurant, asked her about comedy and come to her workplace to apologize for being a cocklord in person. Those things talked. They said he thought she was special, interesting and worthy of his time. Their sex spoke, too. The connection between their bodies was so fluent, it could have served as a UN interpreter. She'd never felt so utterly wild, yet completely safe.

Love isn't just saying words, Autumn thought. *What we feel is real.*

He leaned forward. "What are you thinking?"

"I was thinking that for a quiet guy, you actually say quite a lot."

She expected him to smile or make a two-word crack, but he stared at her, his eyes hot with the same intensity that had burned when he was inside her. She was sure he was going to say something profound. Then he looked away, and despite her earlier acceptance of his impassive nature, all Autumn could think was: Talk to me fuckhead! Say what your brain is doing!

Instead, Blake took another swallow from his highball. "Why did you become a vet?"

Autumn bit back a sigh. Small talk. She and Blake had lived in the same building for six months, sucked each other's intimate areas, shared a two-hundred-dollar cake, taken a self-defense class together and *now* they were doing rudimentary small talk. Christ.

She stared at her date and wished she knew what she was feeling. She liked him; she liked having sex with him, but as much as she appreciated his stoicism, the fact was Josef knew enough English to ask Jessica to be his girlfriend and then agree to come to Australia. Though he had a far better grasp of Autumn's mother tongue, Blake had done neither. She was getting all crushed out on him, while he'd given her no indication he saw this as anything more than a fling. He knew she was thinking of leaving. She'd told him about her work visa that day in her apartment with the pigeons. But he'd given her no indication, in English or otherwise, that he was invested in her as anything other than a valued fuck-buddy.

She licked her lip, inwardly chiding herself for thinking on such silly things. This was a whirlwind fuckfest and Blake was wonderful. Couldn't she just enjoy that for the weeks—days, really—that she had left before she either renewed her visa or allowed the fates, or more homeland security, to take her back to Melbourne?

"I love animals," she said, the practiced lines slipping off her tongue the way they always did. "I mean, I know everyone loves animals, but I got a lot of hands-on experience helping my uncle when I was a kid—he's a vet, too, so I knew what to do. That's about it really…"

Feeling dumb about her answer, she took a massive sip of her drink and almost choked. Blake either didn't notice or chose to ignore this failure to be a human. "What else?"

"Huh?"

"That's not the whole reason you're a vet. There's more."

It wasn't a question, it was a statement, and all the more grating for the fact that it was a true one.

"I don't want to talk about it," she said, then felt stupid. What was she, fourteen? "I don't want to talk about it without knowing something about you. Something personal."

Blake frowned. "Why?"

"Because if I open up, I don't want to feel alone."

There was a short silence and then he exhaled loudly. "I told you I haven't been on a date in ten years. That's because I used to be engaged."

Whoa.

Autumn worked hard to keep a straight face as the truth of that statement washed over her. Blake had been engaged. He could have been someone's *husband* more than ten years ago. How fucking bizarre. "What the hell…what happened?"

Blake cast his gaze around the bar to settle on a painting of a merman with aqua blue hair. "She cheated. I found out at a bad time. Not that there's ever a good time."

Autumn, thinking of Ian's phone nudes, nodded, even as she struggled to process the idea of someone doing that to Blake. Not only was her landlord lovely, he was so goddamn *perceptive*. How had his ex managed to pull the wool over his eyes long enough to cheat? She wanted to say something but found she had no words that didn't sound like pity—something she knew he'd resent. God knew she had. *'Oh you had no idea, huh? Not even a clue? Nawww, better luck next time, sweetie.'*

"Sorry," she managed, because she was so very sorry someone had hurt him. "That must have been shit."

"It was." Blake sat back in his chair. "You said one personal thing, Fun-Size. Time for you to talk."

Autumn attempted a pout. "Why do you want to know why I really became a vet?"

"Because I do."

"Care to elaborate at all?"

Blake just stared at her.

"Fine." Autumn took a fortifying drink of cocktail, realized she was almost at the bottom of her glass and drained the rest of the foamy green liquid into her mouth. When she resurfaced, Blake was grinning at her. "Need a napkin?"

"Shut up." She swiped a forearm across her mouth. "I'm nervous."

He watched her over the rim of his glass and sipped his drink.

Autumn waited, realized he wasn't going to tell her not to bother telling him about her past, and then sighed. "So my family is poor. Like really poor. Growing up, my mum's go-to phrase was, 'that's too expensive!' My dad's was, 'turn off the lights! Electricity isn't free!' Me and my brothers can laugh about it now, but it wasn't very funny when I was a kid."

Autumn took a deep breath, appreciating Blake's silence anew. She rarely paddled in the pools of her childhood memories, and for good reason. They were swampy with affection and confusion and resentment. To talk about it, she needed to go at her own pace, process her thoughts and memories as they came up.

"I can't explain what it was like living in that house," she said after a minute. "I have three brothers and they were always in and out of jobs and relationships and rehab and sometimes jail. My mum ran a hairdressing salon out of the spare room and my dad was always letting some divorced asshole friend of his sleep on our couch. Then my racist grandma moved in and started all these fights with our Korean neighbours..." Autumn drew a deep, shuddering breath. "It was insane. Everything was always insane. Morning 'till night, it was noise and people and fights and drama."

"And where were you in all this insanity?" Blake asked. His voice was low and Autumn loved how calm he sounded, how unaffected.

"I was drawing something in a corner or at the library doing my homework. Staying out of everyone's way."

"You didn't fit in."

"Never. I was nothing special, but I did *not* belong in that house. I hated the noise. The fact that anyone could show up and do anything at any fucking time..." Another shudder ran through her.

Blake inclined his head. "You make good grades?"

"Straight A's."

"Ever get in trouble?"

Autumn tried to laugh, but it came out as a kind of huff. "No."

"I bet your parents were proud of you."

"They were." She looked into his eyes and was relieved to see he understood. How she was the good kid, the one Shane and Patricia could look to and reassure themselves they weren't shit parents. How their love always felt cut with obligation. They were so sold on her being successful, they basically shoved her at Uncle Dan and told him to make her a vet. Well her mum had, her dad wanted her to be a doctor. To this day, she was grateful her dad didn't personally know any doctors or she'd be Autumn Reynolds, brain surgeon at large.

"So, why did you become a vet?" Blake asked. His voice was

light, but his gaze said he wanted to know the truth and, goddammit, autumn wanted to tell it to him.

She swallowed. "I became a vet...because I wanted to make my parents proud."

"And if you could do it all again?"

She stared out at the bar without seeing anything. Wasn't that the very question?

"It's hard to say," she said slowly. "I like being a vet, but I feel like I missed out on those chaotic early years where you change jobs seven times and have no idea what you want. Maybe that's selfish, but I never really had a choice. While I was studying twelve hours a day, my friend Candice was on the quad pretending to be a cat—she did drama."

"You ever think about studying drama?"

"Not really. I was Beatrice in my school's production of *Servant of Two Masters*. I wasn't a good actor, but I liked making people laugh."

"You stopped, though."

"I couldn't handle plays once I was at university. And then..." She hesitated, not wanting to needlessly mention Ian.

"Go on," Blake said. "Whatever it is, you can tell me."

"And then, Ian came along, and being the star of the show was his thing." She laughed at Blake's grimace. "Yeah, I didn't want to mention him, but it's relevant."

Her landlord looked like he was going to say something then shook his head. "Can't imagine you not being center stage, Fun-Size."

"You calling me—"

"I'm not calling you a drama queen," Blake said, correctly predicting her next words. "But you're more interesting than that...*your ex*, could ever be."

She smiled. "Owen said something like that. I think only people who met me now, in New York and after Ian, could say that. Before that, I was always the quiet, responsible one. At least in contrast to him, or my family."

There was a short silence, and Autie felt so suddenly and overwhelmingly exposed, she buried her face in her hands. "Forget I said any of that. I'm so fucking embarrassed I'm not even drunk. Ignore me. Please stop looking at me. Just let me die."

"Fun-Size, look at me."

"No thanks."

An impatient sigh. "You deserve to be the center of attention more than anyone I've ever met."

"Cheers," Autumn said into her palms. "But that would mean a lot more if I hadn't just fucked you."

"I mean it. You're sweet and funny. Thoughtful. You care for sick animals, for godsake. I'm starting to think everyone you've ever met was a moron not to make you aware of this. You're...incredible. Okay?" Another sigh. "I'll be back in a minute. I'm getting you another drink."

She opened her mouth, her eyes suddenly overbright. "Um, thank you, The Landlord. That was really sweet and, um—"

"You don't need to go on about it."

She smiled, adoring him. "So, about my next drink..."

"It'll be different. You liked the first one but you didn't love it."

Autumn frowned. "How do you know so much about what I want, The Landlord?"

He shrugged and the feeling of overexposure rose again. Was she that obvious? That basic? "Seriously, how do you always know what I want? Isn't men not knowing what women want, like, a whole thing?"

Blake pulled a grouchy face. "People always act like women are another species. Like they're cats or planets or whatever the fuck else. It's not hard to see what people want if you actually look and listen."

"That's not really an answer."

Blake bent down so that their faces were close, their bodies contained in a private bubble of this noisy, trendy bar. "You're a busy woman," he said. "You feel obliged to give all of yourself all the time, to those dirty pigeons, to the gym instructor, to the other tenants. Now I found out your parents leaned on you pretty hard and that doesn't surprise me at all. The day you moved in, you were the one making everything happen while your ex was on his phone. You…"

He broke off.

"What?" Autumn urged.

"You cleared that path for me to walk through," Blake muttered. "You saw my leg and you knew…that's just not something a lot of people would have done, but you did. You care, Fun-Size, you notice things. You run the show and you do it well so people assume that's what you want."

"And isn't it?" she whispered.

Blake shook his head. "Nope. You want me to order your drinks, pick where we eat and choose how we fuck. You don't care if I pick a pink drink, or a blue one. If I screw you standing up, or on your back. You care about not having to decide. You want someone else to be dependable for once. To make you feel like if you fall, someone else can catch you. That's why being tied up makes you feel free. It puts the burden of responsibility on me, that way you can relax and enjoy yourself without feeling guilty. That's what you want, Fun-Size. To feel like you matter enough for someone else to try."

There was a rushing in her ears, like an ocean tide crashing onto the shore. Blake met her gaze squarely, his incredible eyes locked on hers. He was still ruddy from their sex, his color high beneath his beard, his smell more earthy and masculine. Staring at him, she felt a deep vibration within her. A recognition of something old and new and terrifying and wonderful, but when she reached for the word to describe it, the feeling slipped away and she was left with what Blake had said about her wanting him to take care of her. "I think that's…that's pretty dead-on," she said.

Blake nodded, stood and started toward the bar.

"Wait!"

He turned and raised his eyebrows.

"If what I want is to put the burden of responsibility on you, why do you take it? What's in that for you?"

She got the same unfathomable look he'd given her when he was sliding himself deep inside her. "Be back soon."

When he returned, Autumn had decided to move the conversation along. His revelations about her needs had struck something deep and uncomfortable inside her on what was supposed to be a casual post-fuck drink.

"So, what did you do before you were a landlord?" she asked as soon as he handed her a tall, peach-colored cocktail. "Or have you been running the building since your late teens?"

"I was a sandhog." Clearly reading her confusion on her face, he added, "Slang for an underground construction worker."

"Oh, what does that invol—" Autumn's phone buzzed within her bag, the loud vibration snapping her train of thought.

"Call?" Blake asked.

"Text I think? Do you mind if I check it? It might be Owen."

"Go ahead. I like that you've got a friend keeping an eye out for you."

Autumn smiled, feeling another flash of that strange new-old sensation. "I'll just be a sec."

She pulled out her phone and lit up the screen.

Fucking...what?

It took everything Autumn had not to yell something out loud, but she managed it. Unfortunately, she must have showed a physical response to the very unwelcome picture message she'd received because Blake bent over the table. "Everything okay?"

"Totally fine," she lied, shoving her phone back in her bag.

Goddammit. So much for thinking Ian was over it, that he'd be content with his shiny new fuckbuddies and leave her alone. Owen was right, he'd had his fill of easy sex and now he wanted his body pillow back. Jesus Christ, what was she going to do? He was already sending nudes, what if he called her parents to petition for her to get back with him? Or her brothers? Or their friends? God, what if he showed up at her door naked and holding a dozen roses? That would be so like him...

"Autumn." Blake's tone was colder than the ice in her drink. "Who was that message from?"

She knew then that he already knew, or at least strongly suspected, but she couldn't help herself. "Owen, he was just...saying hello."

Blake's face was blank, utterly void of emotion. "It was him, wasn't it?"

Autumn couldn't lie in the fact of the direct question, nor could she ask 'who's him' when she knew Blake already knew. "Yeah."

"What did he say?"

Tricky, considering he didn't really say anything. With

words, anyway. The fact that he was shirtless on his bed with a hand shoved into the dark blue briefs she'd bought him implied a great deal. "Um…well…"

"Autumn, I swear to god if he's trying to hurt you—"

"It's not like that, okay? It was just a text."

Blake sat back in his chair, his shoulders swelling, his chest expanding. His face was still blank, but now he looked like a man preparing himself for a bar brawl.

"And what," he said, his tone icy, "was in that text?"

She took a deep breath. "It was a picture."

Blake's silence was more deafening than a thousand church bells clanging at once. His upper lip curled and she knew that he knew. Knew and that he was beyond furious.

She pulled her phone out again. "I'll delete it."

"Autumn." Blake's voice was surprisingly level. "Are you still sending him that kind of thing?"

"No," she said, so quickly the word came out more like 'nurghh.'

"You still talking to each other?"

"No! I haven't spoken to him until today when he messaged about my mum's birthday. I don't know why he thinks I'd want to look at his dick after what he—"

About two seconds too late, she realized she shouldn't have mentioned the dick thing. Really shouldn't have mentioned the dick thing.

"Your ex-boyfriend just sent you a photo of his cock?"

"No. A bit. It's kind of like from here to here," Autumn said, waving a hand from face to groin. "You can only see a bit of the head. I can show it to you if you want, it would totally serve him right."

Blake's face grew dark as a surge of roiling storm clouds.

Fucking hell, Reynolds.

"Actually, I'm going to delete it," she said. "I'll empty the trash, too. And uh, you're a lot bigger, if that's any consolation."

Blake's expression told her it wasn't even close. "Finish your drink."

"You're not gonna kick his ass, are you? I know he's a prick, but I hate violence."

Blake drained his whiskey in a single swallow and banged his glass down. "I have no interest in seeing that little prick. This involves you and me, Blondie. We're going back to my house. I'm going to show you what I consider consolation."

CHAPTER 13

WHY WAS BLAKE always blind to one hill of the landscape when it came to women?

He listened. He watched. He didn't pride himself on too many things, but perceptiveness was one of them. At thirteen, he'd noticed his parents going through a rough patch. They had money issues, which wasn't unusual for anyone in the neighborhood. Blake's father was particularly stung by his low bank balance, because Blake's uncle, his brother, had invested in real estate at a young age. Was making money hand over fist, living the bachelor life across the water in Manhattan, while Blake's father worked himself to the bone in an underground mine for far less pay.

All of this had been apparent to Blake at age ten. It had been impossible to miss the twist of his dad's mouth every time his uncle came up in conversation. Or the dimming enthusiasm his father had toward the job. During that time, Blake let his mother maneuver him around the house to escape his father's black moods. He humored her when she told him to go ride his bike outside, a tight smile pasted on her face, but he'd seen and heard everything. Known what was happening, including the day his father received a promotion and the heavy fog lifted in the house.

Or so he'd thought. One morning on the walk to the bus stop, his mother burst into tears. She'd thanked him for being so patient while they'd dealt with some things.

"It's okay, mom. Dad has the promotion now. Everything's fine."

She'd seemed surprised. "Right. He didn't get it in time, though. I needed some money to go into business with my friends. You know the new spa on 129th Street?"

She tugged her coat higher around her neck. "It's okay. There's always next time, right?"

Somehow he'd missed his mother's end of the struggle. Been completely blind to it. Over a decade later, he'd been blind to the true feelings of his fiancée. Apparently this was to be a running theme in his life. He could see *everything* but the shit that mattered. Like his fiancée fucking someone else a month before their wedding—someone who spoke in full sentences and knew how to be social—while he got up every morning assuming their lives were going to plan, that he'd found someone who didn't exactly accept his quiet moods and odd ways, but had learned to live with them.

Blake glanced at Autumn, trudging beside him. The cab had dropped them off on the avenue and they were walking the remaining distance to the building. She hadn't said a word since the bar and he wondered if she was thinking about her ex. The idea made him want to hoist her over his shoulder and scale the side of the brick structure, like some deranged King Kong. Every sinew of strength in his body was pulled tight as a violin string, ready to be plucked in the wrong way so he could go off.

Jealousy was a puny little word. Right then, there was enough of it in his pinky finger to power the fucking city. So taking his whole body into account, the experts would have to think of a new phrase to describe how Blake felt over Autumn receiving a dick pic from her asshole ex-boyfriend. But he supposed berserk was a decent start.

His hands fisted in his coat pockets to prevent him from ripping the cell phone from Autumn's purse and stomping it into a non-existence. Yes, of course, he didn't want this girl looking at anyone's cock but his own. He'd allowed himself to wedge himself inside her tonight for the first time, slipping deeper and deeper into obsession as she pulsed around him, her thighs straining in the ropes. Calling it the best sex of his life was on par with describing his current state of mind as 'jealous.' With Autumn tied up and moaning, her tight, slippery body welcoming him home, he'd been a king and a lucky bastard at the same time. Everything all at once.

Emotions were things he could manage, like a teacup game, moving them around and hiding the prize until his adversaries gave up. But for the first time in his life, he'd lost track of the prize. Maybe because Autumn held it in her hands and didn't realize it.

Blake reached over and took Autumn's hand, without a formal command from his brain. He didn't understand the move, he was pissed as hell and planned on exacting retribution in the form of nasty sex. Since the beginning, though, he'd needed her to know…to understand he'd die before hurting her. And even in his somewhat unhinged state of mind, her being confident in him was still the most important thing.

Especially when she let out a slow breath and tucked herself into his side. Cannon balls started firing inside his rib cage. Boom, boom, boom.

Goddamn, she could send him to the height of anger and bring him plummeting back down with one cheek nuzzle. Did she realize that? Was she even halfway aware? Yes, the idea of her looking at someone else's dick was like a spike to his right eye, but more than that it didn't make sense. What kind of stupid prick tried to win a woman like Autumn back with something so ridiculous?

His rage swooped back in, spiky and metallic-tasting. The image of a smirking Ian reclining naked on his bed was haunting him. He had intended to tempt Autumn, *had* tempted her, at least at one time. Maybe he still did, because what the hell did Blake know? He could be missing another hill within the landscape, just like he'd done in the past. Did she like getting pictures from her ex? Did she miss him? Did she consider their three-date deal a mere distraction?

As Blake unlocked the building's front door and guided Autumn inside, he greeted the anger and uncertainty with open arms.

The better to fuck you with, my dear. There wouldn't be a millimeter of uncertainty in her mind with him filling her up. She'd know her master, call him by name and her flesh would react accordingly. Sex was the only weapon he had right now, when everything felt stripped down to the bone. So he'd use it.

There was just enough rationality inside him to acknowledge he had no right to be that jealous, or hold Autumn responsible in any way. None whatsoever. They'd struck a deal to *fuck*. Everything they did with clothes on was at Blake's own insistence and God, there was every chance she found that pathetic. She'd just come out of a relationship with a man who resembled a boy band member yet lacked an ounce of character. Still, Ian must have had more redeeming qualities besides looks to land a bright girl like Autumn. What did he have? A cave on the first floor, heaps of books and an aversion to sunlight.

No. He had one more thing. The ability to make her his captive.

Blake squeezed Autumn's hand once and paused at the inside door, letting her walk through the hallway alone. Almost even with his apartment, she sent him a timid look over her shoulder and his blood started to pump hard through his veins. No holding back tonight. She wasn't going to see anything but him. Wasn't going to feel anything but what he chose her to feel. Yes. Control over the situation with Autumn was exactly what he needed. Based on the little shiver in her walk, the slide of her palms along her hips, she needed it, too. The voice of reason told Blake they should talk about what happened, but he ignored it.

When Autumn would have ventured past his apartment to the elevator, Blake started after her at a fast clip, paying no attention to the throb of his bad leg. He twisted a fist in the back of her shirt, throwing her off balance and tucking her into the front of his body. She gasped and struggled, planting her hands on his apartment door and pushing back with her hips. Her tight little ass pressed back on his hard cock and it felt so fucking good, he let out a genuine groan. God, he needed to fuck her.

He wrapped her hair around his knuckles and tugged Autumn's head back, pressing his mouth to her ear. "You'll only make it harder on yourself if you fight me, Blondie. Do you understand?" He rammed his hips forward, pinning her to the door. "I want pussy. And I'm going to get it."

"No." Her fingertips clawed at the door. "Please. I—I don't..."

"You don't what?" Blake's right hand plunged into her pants, gripping the source of his lust. "You don't have a pussy? Then what's this tight, little thing, huh?"

"Please, sir." Her flesh heated right there in his hand, ripe and obedient. "I just want to go home."

"That's too bad. You have a new home now." He massaged

her roughly, grunting at the wetness spilling over his fingers. "I have a new home, too. Can't wait to get settled in."

Autumn renewed her struggles, giving Blake no choice but to remove his hand from her tight pants, unlock the apartment and drag her inside. She fought him—*hard*—twisting in his arms and kicking at his shins. And from the way his cock swelled, he understood once and for all that this wasn't just Autumn's thing. Yeah, he'd fantasized about being rough with her, but her specific needs had sharpened his own. They were both *in* this together. Deep. Autumn needed to be a prisoner and his desire to give her everything made him crave the role.

It's mine.

She's fucking mine.

Blake was ready to devour her. His muscles rippled and shook, fingers flexing on either side of his hips. Something gave him momentary pause, though. Maybe it was the fiercer than usual struggle from Autumn or the fact that they hadn't spoken about Ian's text. God, everything non-sex related between them had a giant question mark stamped over it. Was she going to renew her visa? If she stayed, could this ever realistically last longer than three dates? Whatever the uncertainty, he felt compelled to remind her she was safe. Always safe with him.

"What's wrong, Blondie?" He razed his teeth up the side of her neck. "You were expecting your new home to be nicer, weren't you? Maybe some gold leaf furniture?"

At the mention of her safe word, Autumn's struggles ceased. They both breathed heavily, the sound like gun shots through a silencer in the quiet apartment. When she turned to look at him over her shoulder, he allowed himself a split second of tenderness before clapping a hand over her mouth, lifting her off the floor and lumbering toward his bedroom. He didn't want false hope.

Didn't want to watch her pretend to return his infatuation, if it was all just in his head. No. This is what they had that he could *count* on. That *she* could count on. And Autumn must have understood that, because she began to struggle again.

Blake carried her, thrashing and screaming into his bedroom. Once inside, he waited for her to see what he'd set up before he got her for their date. After his terrible treatment of her last time she was inside this apartment, he'd been reasonable with his expectations for the night. Yeah, there was every chance she could decide he didn't deserve her body—and want to go home after Krav. That said, he couldn't be in her presence for any length of time without needing to fuck. He knew Autumn was no different. Not with this mutual kink spread out in front of them like a playground.

He knew the exact second Autumn saw the pictures taped to his bedroom wall, just over the nightstand. Her body went limp but he could see the pulse point at the base of her neck going wild, she was a baby deer secretly thrilled at being trapped in the headlights.

Normally, Blake only used the camera of his cell phone to send his clients pictures of their works in progress, so he'd been somewhat new to stalking with the damn thing. But he'd managed to get three of Autumn, without her being the wiser. Two from the corner across from her job, after he'd left her standing with Owen. Another from their first date night, walking in front of him in the too-short, too-tight red dress and heels. Finally, he'd drawn several rough sketches of her in various states of undress, taping them haphazardly to the wall around the cell phone shots he'd printed.

"Y-you," she stammered. "You've been…?"

"That's right. I've been planning this for a while."

He pushed her face-down over the bed, keeping her pinned with a hand to the center of her back. With her cheek pressed to the comforter, she watched Blake from the corner of her eye. He stepped more clearly into her line of vision and stroked himself through his pants. "I know every fucking thing about you. Your route to work. How you take your coffee. Your work schedule. The fact that no one will notice you missing for a couple of days." Blake dropped forward, supporting himself with one elbow on the bed as he licked straight up the center of her ass, wetting the material and savoring her shocked whimper. "Might have to risk people noticing you're gone, though, won't I? Can't see me getting my fill anytime soon. I'm going to wear my cock out taking you."

"What do you want?" She tried to turn over on the bed, but Blake held firm, drawing a frustrated sound. "I can give you anything besides...beside me."

Blake chuckled. "Then you *can't* give me anything. I'll have to take it."

"*Please.* This isn't fair."

"*Fair?*" Blake straightened and started to unfasten his belt, whipping it through the straps. Her ass muscles clenched up in anticipation, probably expecting him to bring the leather down. He drew her wrists back, instead, securing them together at the small of her back. And while she sucked in gulps of oxygen, trying to get free, Blake laid a resounding slap on her backside, hard and unexpected enough to make her scream. "Fair is giving up what you've been advertising, Blondie. That's fair."

Blake's cock was stiff and uncomfortable in his pants. He unzipped with a grunt and left it free to escape through the V of material and settle on the waistband. Keeping Autumn in his line of sight—her beauty and absolute trust gave him no choice—he went to his dresser, taking out the only silk tie he owned. The one he'd bought for their first date, while wondering if he was being a fool. She stiffened at his approach, but he wasted no time wrenching the pants down her legs, revealing the taut swells of her ass and the stretched out thong between them. Heat licked at his temples, the insides of his veins.

Fuck her, fuck her. Take. Show her you're the only man who satisfies her.

He wouldn't take her yet though. There were boundaries that needed to be pushed first. Ones that she'd trusted him to test and he *ached* to obliterate.

Autumn was pantsless, fighting her wrist bonds and hiccupping pleas in front of him, looking like a dark porn video beckoning from the far reaches of the internet to make men feel both horny and guilty. But Blake felt nothing but lust and responsibility as he knelt down, gathering Autumn's kicking ankles and tying them together with silk.

"You'd like me to part those whore cheeks and fuck you now, isn't that right?" He traced his index finger down her backside. "Deep down, you want to be the reason for that one *sickening* moment only men have to go through. The one where we're living for nothing but getting the come out. The moment you *drive* me to every hour while I look at your pretty pictures."

Blake slid an arm beneath Autumn's waist, taking note of her dilated pupils, the intense, pink flush of her skin. The shallowness of her breath. He lifted her off the bed, keeping her aloft in one arm.

"There's some relief. But it builds right back up, doesn't it? The pressure *you* cause, Blondie. And then I'm back to looking at the pictures and rubbing my cock raw. A vicious fucking cycle that's your fault. You and this body you flaunt all over town." He kicked open his closet door, laughing against Autumn's ear when she started to sputter. "This isn't going to be over fast, like you were hoping. No, you're going to spend some time thinking about what you've done."

Her middle twisted, her feet seeking the floor. "Don't put me in there. You can't. *Please.*"

"Shut up, Blondie. I can do whatever I want."

Blake couldn't quite bring himself to toss her in like a rag doll, but he was rough as he secured her beside an upright suitcase in the bottom of the closet. The second he let her go, her neck seemed to lose power and her head hit the wall with a thunk. Blake almost jumped to cushion the light blow after the fact, but then he saw the moisture between her thighs. It was slicking her folds beneath her thong and gleaming on the insides of her legs. Jesus Christ, and he thought she'd been hot back in the gym...

"Goddamn, if your hands were free, you'd be fingering that little pearl between your legs, wouldn't you?" Blake reached down and captured her chin. "Listen, carefully. You're here to be my personal fuck princess. I'm going to take you as hard and as often as I want and any enjoyment you get out of it will be an accident." He loosened his hold and gripped the knob on the closet door, preparing to close it. "Now be a good girl and think about all the ways you owe me."

"Uh...um." She found her voice just before the door closed, but it was rusted and hoarse. "*Wait—*"

He shut her in the tiny space before a half-smile caught him off guard. Good Lord. He'd just locked a woman in his closet and he wanted to grin. It made sense, though. Nothing made him happier than knowing Autumn was almost too turned on to be a convincing hostage. Blake stood outside the closet for a full minute, just in case Autumn so much as whispered the words gold leaf. The longer she went without saying them, choosing instead to shuffle around like a trapped mouse, the harder it was for Blake to breathe, to concentrate on anything but the full, burning pressure gathering in his groin. In that moment, he was the jailer and he had his prisoner bound and ready to give him relief. Relief that felt somehow physical and mental at the same time. Yes, the pumping on either side of his forehead and the clutch in his throat were new. Specific to the now. To *Autumn*.

Following his instincts, Blake toed the closet door open a couple of inches. He caught a sliver of Autumn's face, tight with excitement before he walked slowly to the bedside table. He ripped the picture of her in the red dress off the wall, the severing tape slicing through the silence. He slapped the photo down on the table and tossed away his shirt, leaving himself bare-chested. Then he wrapped a hand around his cock, concentrating on the spot in the picture where Autumn's hem licked the backs of her thighs. Hunger slunk low into his stomach, drawing his balls up tight to his body. Blake had no choice but to beat off. Hard. Did it make the need more urgent knowing Autumn was watching him from the closet floor? Only about a thousand times more urgent. More wrong. More right. More *them*.

"Look what you do to me." He choked the base and slid his fisted hand roughly to the tip, squeezing a bead of moisture from the tip. "Look at it, you teasing little brat."

Autumn's breath see-sawed in and out. "L-let me out of here and we can discuss it?"

"Discuss it? Sure." Blake's laugh lacked all humor. His fist found a rough rhythm in its journey up and down his length. "First let's talk about that wetness dripping down your legs."

She shuffled around some. "I'm...n-not sure I'm open to

that."

"No?" Blake braced a hand on the wall and chanced a look at the closet, finding Autumn watching him in a daze. "If you want out of the closet, you need to admit you get off on making my cock hard, all day and night. I want to hear those words come out of your smartass mouth."

It took Autumn a moment to respond. "If I say that, what will you do?"

"I'll give you what you've been asking for." Blake groaned as a spear of pleasure hit its mark, sending unbearable, sticky heat to the lowest section of his belly, making him stroke faster. "I'll teach you a lesson for wearing a dress so tight, I can see the outline of your pussy when I zoom in. Unless you admit you wore it for me. You knew I'd be watching."

"No, I didn't," she protested, sounding winded. "I had no idea."

"You always know."

"No—"

Blake cut her off with a groan. A clamp tightened around the base of his spine and the outer edges of his vision began to spark. Operating on an instinct he'd never thought he'd show another person, he picked up the photo with his free hand and licked it, top to bottom, listening to the muffled whimpers coming from the closet.

"Please," Autumn wailed. "*Don't.*"

"Don't what, Blondie? Finish myself off?" Blake tossed the photo down on the bedside table, fixing a hand on the wall and angling himself over the likeness of Autumn, his fist jerking at high speed, preparing to defile the red dress. "Why? You want it for yourself?"

"No!"

Blake gave a strained laugh. "Tell you what, Blondie. Admit you want me to save it for your tight, taunting pussy, admit that's what you've wanted all along, and you can have it."

"I've wanted it."

"Louder," he growled.

"*I've wanted it.*"

Blake was across the room in one lunge, jerking open the closet door to find Autumn on her knees, teeth marks on her lower lip. She was a human tangle, her thighs shaking, her shirt twisted and hiked up. He took a mental snapshot of her unimaginable beauty, the vulnerability and strength of her, before dropping to his own knees. Pain? What pain? He could be *missing* his fucking leg and he would have found a way to kneel in front of her. To join himself with this girl.

Unable to spend another moment without being inside her, Blake reached just beyond her shoulder and knocked the piece of luggage sideways, dragging it close.

"Turn around and bend over the suitcase. Ass *high*. You'll get your first fuck in the closet for making me impatient."

Autumn's knees skidded as she turned awkwardly on the floor, a shudder passing through her head to toe. With her wrists and ankles tied together, she could only fall forward over the suitcase, her blonde hair covering her face, a curtain of light in the darkness that was their game. "I'm sorry. Please don't hurt me."

Blake positioned his knees outsides hers, taking his cock in hand and using the weight of it to slap her ass cheeks a few times. "Prisoners don't get a say, Blondie. But it's cute listening to you try." He dragged the tip of his cock through the split of her ass, stopping at her drenched pussy and rubbing it there. Grinding it. Growling like a fiend. "*Mine.*" The word came straight from the core of him, imploring and desperate and commanding all at once. "Mine, Autumn. *My...*Autumn."

The admission left him so stripped, he almost took it back until he felt her fingers flex between their bodies. She had limited use of her hands, but she used it to caress the skin of his stomach, slowly. Not the same as having Autumn make a claim on him, but more than he could have hoped for. More than he needed to stay grounded in the moment with her.

Blake sunk his teeth into her shoulder and drove his cock deep, until he could go no further. He began to pump inside her, slowly at first but his thrusts rapidly grew faster. The slick friction, her sharp inhale, the bounce of her ass where it slapped his stomach...all these things happened at once, shooting Blake to the end of his rope. Already. Fucking *already*, even though he'd been inside her only hours earlier. That trickle of frustration was what he needed to bring Autumn along and he embraced it.

"What kind of girl gets this wet for her kidnapper?" Blake reached around her hip and spread her perfectly excessive moisture in circles around her clit. Just as she began to moan, pressing herself against his touch, Blake drew his hand back and slapped her between the thighs—hard. "Yes. What would your mommy and daddy say about their twisted little girl?"

"I don't know," she sobbed. "Don't stop."

"Better yet..." Knives sharpened themselves inside of Blake, heightening his hunger, his slippery ride of Autumn's body, but most of all, his possessiveness. That particular blade rose up and stabbed him between the shoulder blades. "Better yet, what would that asshole ex-boyfriend of yours say? If he could see you now, getting what you've needed all along? Getting something he was too much of a selfish limp dick to give you."

He gathered Autumn's hair in a fist and continued to ride, to thrust, the smell of their attraction turning to musk in the air.

"I don't care what he'd say," she whispered, arching her back. "I only care about this."

Blake cared, though. He cared a fuck ton. If Autumn was his, he'd eventually learn to get over the jealousy. Be the bigger man, because he'd earned the girl. As of now, though, he hadn't earned her, had he? He had the illusion and he would cling to it, for as long as he could. "I won't stop, Blondie," he rasped, giving her pussy a series of quick slaps. "But you're going to say the name of the man who brings it. Brings what the *fuck* you need."

"Blake," she sobbed. "*Blake.*"

They were halfway to dropping the act and he didn't care. No, he relished the fact that they had a breaking point. That *something* real couldn't help but bleed through. "Who's bigger, Autumn? In every goddamn way?"

"*You.*"

"My fucking *name,* Blondie." Blake pumped deep and held, sawing his middle finger against Autumn's clit. "Who will drop a grand on your dinner and still fuck you like a slut? Say the name."

"*Blake!*"

Her pussy began to ripple and constrict around his cock, the muscles in her back and shoulders firming up and thank Christ, because if he had to go another minute without coming, it was going to shave years off his life. She was the most incredible thing he could imagine, her body bound and writhing between him and the suitcase. Mind-blowing and delicate and fierce. Knowing she was poised right on the edge, he took her clit between two knuckles and dragged them up and back on either side, his hips slapping over and over against her bent over ass.

"Get used to this, dirty girl. I'm going to keep you in my

closet. Only take you out when I get horny. What will that make you? My personal what?"

"F-fuck princess." She heaved a scream, her body trembling, milking his cock so hard, Blake couldn't contain his own grunt of pleasure. "Oh my *God*."

With Autumn safely over her peak, Blake followed, every molecule seeming to drain from his body, starting in his head, centering at his groin and flowing down, down, like fast-forwarded sand in an hourglass. There was a stunning, undeniable need to get as close as possible to Autumn, the source of his everything in that moment. So he hunched forward, wrapping both arms around her heaving middle, yanking her back into his lap for one final thrust, his throat muscles straining from the force of his shout. Just when Blake thought there was nothing left to give, she grinded back and tempted another spurt from his body, the warmth of it dripping and clinging to her inner thighs, his stomach.

Blake was still trying to find his footing in the wake of what they'd done when Autumn began to cry. Not loudly, but the small, soft sobs of someone who was utterly lost. Panic sliced his throat and his hands flew to the belt binding her wrists, unlooping it in record time before he moved to the silk around her ankles.

"Goddammit, Fun-Size." He brought her against his chest, shoving her hair out of the way so he could see her face. "Tell me I didn't hurt you."

Autumn gave him a watery smile. "No. I swear you didn't. It's just the release of it all, you know? There was all this…I don't know, like, a buildup, and now there isn't. I'm just floating."

Blake slumped back onto the floor in relief, taking Autumn with him. Without missing a beat, she turned sideways in his lap, throwing her freed legs over his thigh and wrapping both arms around his neck. Blake didn't know what the hell he was meant to do now. There was a crying female in his lap, but she was happy, but it still seemed as though she required comforting.

He settled his right palm on her hair. "You're okay."

A laugh burst out of her, followed by more tears. "Yes, landlord. I know I'm okay. Are you okay?"

"I'm more worried about you." He gave a testing stroke of her hair, his heart thudding when she angled her head. Was she asking for more? "Do you like this?"

"Yes," she mumbled into his chest. "It's nice."

"I'm just sitting here."

"You haven't run off to the kitchen or checked your phone yet," she said, her fingers slipping through his chest hair. "Maybe you're better at this after part than you think."

Blake had only recently escaped from the ninth circle of jealousy hell but her innocuous comment threatened to send him back there, because it was a hint about what she was used to. Proof she hadn't been getting what she deserved. With Autumn rubbing her cheek on his chest and her body limp from sex, though, he was able to remain in one of the outer circles. For now. Autumn seemed content to sit there forever and Blake found he was too. Just sitting in the quiet, his arms around Autumn in a protective shield, watching the flush fade from her skin. This was something else he could give her. Something beyond the fantasies.

What if there was enough inside him to give? Enough that she would stay in New York?

Blake gave an inward scoff, but looking at the sunshine-laced crown of Autumn's head, he couldn't stop himself from picturing it. He wanted to keep her. Might as well admit that. He'd been wanting to keep her for some time—long before she'd broken up with the scumbag, and now that he had her in his lap, her lips parted, her cheek pressed to his heartbeat, the possibility had never seemed more real. Christ, if she went away, he'd spend every minute wondering if she was safe, warm and happy. Razor sharp stones clogged his throat just thinking about it.

Autumn's breathing changed and Blake realized she was staring up at him, her hazel eyes tired, but curious. His instinct was to look away, make a suggestion about getting off the damn floor and putting on clothes. But he didn't. He stared right back and did what felt right. What his gut told him they both needed. He tightened his arms around her and rocked, right to left, leaning down to kiss her forehead every so often. In stages, she loosened even more. Her shoulders, neck, knees, like he'd waved a magic wand over them. Blake didn't know how long they stayed there on the floor rocking her in the dark, it could have been five minutes or forty. When he sensed Autumn was ready, he stood, tucking her against his chest and walking toward his bedroom.

"What are you doing?" she mumbled.

He looked down at her. "I want you to stay."

Her gaze widened and Blake cursed under his breath. "Tonight. I mean I want you to stay here tonight. In my bed."

Autumn's mouth curved into a smile against his bicep. "I think it's for the best. These hallways aren't safe at night."

Knowing she was referring to their game, Blake gave her a gentle squeeze then laid her down on his bed. She immediately burrowed into his covers with a sleepy yawn and the natural step would have been to join her. Yet, seeing her there froze him in place. No one besides him had ever slept in his bed and she looked so *tiny* on the king-sized mattress. The protectiveness over holding her in his arms kicked up another few notches. There seemed to be an endless number of notches where this girl was concerned.

"I'm guessing you haven't had many sleepovers," she murmured into his pillow, blonde hair framing her face. "Seems like a missed opportunity to have pillow fights with Mrs. Zhu. Or maybe you're more of the facials-and-boy-talk type."

God, she was adorable.

Stop staring at her like an idiot. Blake shook himself and climbed into the bed, holding his breath as Autumn slipped an arm across his chest, tucking her head into the crook of his neck. "I've gone to one sleepover and it involved zombie movies and a Sharpie mustache being drawn on the first to fall asleep."

"When you were just a baby boy?"

"Yes."

He felt her smile. "Were you the mustache recipient?"

"There's a reason I've only gone to one sleepover. It was a handlebar with curls at the end. I didn't go to school for two days."

Autumn's giggle tugged at the corners of his own lips and he didn't bother hiding it in the darkness. "The one I draw on you tonight will be much more fashionable. You'll be able to wear it out to brunch and blend right in with the hipsters."

"Just what I've always wanted."

Her fingertips drew patterns on his chest. A hexagon with a smiley face inside, if he wasn't mistaken.

"Blake?" He was trying to be discreet about smelling her hair, so he only hummed. "Maybe this is a stupid thing to bring up when everything is so lovely, but I'm sorry about what happened tonight. With…you know. The text that shall not be named. On the walk back, I was trying to imagine how I'd feel if the same thing happened. You know, if you got a nude right while I was sitting there. I think it would have hurt, way more than it should have."

Surprise had Blake's formally heavy eyelids wide open. "You'd have been jealous?"

"Are you serious? You told me you'd almost been married, like a gazillion years ago and I didn't even like hearing that. Add photo evidence and I'd…" She trailed off, her fingers drumming on his chest. "I'm trying to stop myself from being seriously masochistic and asking for more details about this woman."

"What would that accomplish besides upsetting you?"

She tilted her head to eye him in the dark. "Some guys would enjoy a girl being jealous over them."

Blake examined how he felt about Autumn coveting him. "I'd like knowing you were…interested enough to be jealous. But I'd want to make it stop at the same time. I wouldn't want you to be hurt."

Autumn nuzzled her face into the crook of his neck. "There's no one like you, landlord."

"Considering I just put you in a closet, you're not far off."

She laughed. "The crazy thing is if you were holding me, I could probably hear the whole fiancée story and be fine. Something about the way your hands feel on my skin…It makes me calm."

Satisfaction kicked him in the belly, freeing a grunt. "Then that's where I'll keep them."

Beneath the covers, Autumn's hand traveled down over his hip, the pads of her fingers brushing his thigh. "Will you tell me how you injured your leg?"

His instinctual reaction to having his weakness discussed was to shut the conversation down. Or change the subject to something he was far more interested in discussing—her. But just like earlier, when he'd rocked Autumn on the floor, he found himself trying to give her more. "My injury...it's part of the story. I broke the engagement right after it happened."

"I knew it. She stabbed you."

"What?" Blake looked down to find her smothering a teasing smile. "No stabbing, but we should probably discuss what you've been watching on TV."

"It's not TV's fault. I'm cheating on it with a *lot* of true crime podcasts. Did you know that it's almost impossible to identify someone at a crime scene through genetic evidence? Like, unless you blow a load all over the floor *and* you're already in the criminal database, all the cops can do is collect your cum and hope you strike again."

Blake couldn't believe it. Discussing one of the darkest periods of his life and this angel—yes, fuck it, Autumn was an angel—could still make him want to laugh. "We should discuss your stand-up routine, Fun-Size. You're the first person in a long time—hell maybe ever—that's showed me the humor in every situation."

As he spoke, her smile gradually faded. "Thank you."

He tucked some of her hair behind her ear. "Will you perform it for me?"

"I...I'll definitely think about it." Her expression turned suspicious. "Are you petting me and telling me I'm funny to distract me from your murderous ex-fiancée?"

"No. I mean it." Blake sighed and drew her closer, closing his eyes as memories rushed back, a decade old and still so fresh. "I told you I was a sandhog, right? Up until about ten years ago. We were working on the second avenue subway tunnel. I'd been on the job about a month when there was an explosion. A slow gas leak and a spark was all it took. A metal bar embedded itself in my leg."

"Shit! Ouch! Oh my God, Blake."

Not used to sympathy, Blake gave her another awkward head pat. "It doesn't hurt very often, anymore," he lied. "Anyway, she was a nurse at the hospital where they brought me. A big one across town and it must have been fate or karma or something, but they paired me with the surgeon she'd been seeing behind my back. She wasn't assigned to me, but she came to visit…and when I saw them together, I just knew."

"I'm sorry." Autumn was quiet for a moment. "We've both been fucked over. Is that why you get so upset over Ian? You remember what it was like?"

"No. I get upset over Ian because I hate the thought of him touching you, or holding you, or *anything* with you." The outburst was too telling and he immediately wished he could take it back. "But I guess that's part of it. Being blindsided hurts, whether you're in love with the person or not."

"You weren't in love with her?"

He shook his head, snippets of memories coming back to him in blurs of shadow and light. Walking on the boardwalk in Rockaway, bikes weaving in figure eights, laughter and arguments, all the moments that made up his youth. "Me and Jodie grew up together. Breaking up would have fractured the group. The group is everything when you're twenty." Discomfort spread in his throat. "It's the betrayal itself that hurts most, isn't it?"

"Yeah," came Autumn's voice in the dark. "Everything stops counting. All the time spent, all the conversations and meals and milestones, they all feel like they mean nothing, or at least mean way less." Her head lifted. "That guy in the hallway…I could tell he was an old friend. That time I accidentally eavesdropped on you? He said something about knowing things and not understanding the consequences. Your friends in the group...they all knew?"

Blake let his silence serve as a response.

"And that c-word had the nerve to invite you to a party?" Autumn breathed. "I guess we could go. And stab them. And we could get away with it because of everything I know about true crime."

This time, he just let himself laugh. "I had the right idea binding your hands."

She waggled her light eyebrows. "Sleep with one eye open, landlord."

He could almost hear her pondering a more elaborate plan. "Maybe going to the party would be a good thing. We could walk in like Bonnie and Clyde and glare them into dust. They would rue the day they ever crossed Blake Munroe." She paused. "It's been a long time. And if your mate is still coming around after a decade, you must have been good friends. Is it maybe, conceivably, perhaps, within the realm of possibility that we could do that?"

There wasn't a chance in hell he was setting foot in Rockaway, but he couldn't blame Autumn for trying to help. It was in her nature. "Good night, Fun-Size."

She sighed. "I'll take that as a no. Night, Blake."

It was new, but natural, settling in with Autumn against him. He assumed she must be freezing with the way she wiggled closer and closer, until she covered at least half of him. About twenty minutes was spent covering her with the comforter, then doubling it up, adding his arms around her to keep it in place. Yet, still she burrowed, her feet finding holds between his calves, her hands resting on his chest. Was she even aware of what she was doing? Why couldn't he stop smiling? Sleeping would be difficult if he couldn't make his mouth go back to normal.

Finally, she got settled and stopped moving. Just before she drifted off, though, she drew one final smiling hexagon on his chest with her finger, adding a squiggly goatee this time. "Okay, landlord. I'll show you the routine."

Turned out, a man could sleep while smiling, because when he woke up it was still there.

CHAPTER 14

A UTUMN'S GAZE WAS unfocused as she stared at the packed bar. In her mind, Blake was braced over his bedside table, his powerful hand clasped around his cock. He was jerking off to her picture, preparing to spray himself all over it and degrade her image while she watched. Her only choice was to beg for his cock, to be ridden in the closet and take that salty fluid inside herself. God, she could almost feel him bearing down on her again, his thighs hot against hers, his hard flesh pressing against her sopping—

"New love, Isabella. Does anything in the world make straight people look so stupid?"

Autumn snapped out of her daydream and focused on her now smirking colleagues. "Sorry, I was thinking about—"

"Dick?" Owen enquired.

"No!"

"Your landlord's big bear dick?"

"No!"

Owen nudged Isabella in the ribs. "Look at her, she's so moist."

Autumn was going to object when she noticed she *was* sweating a lot. She wiped a hand across her forehead, collecting the budding droplets. "I hate that word."

"Everyone does. Everyone except the person who says it with

the intent to gross other people out. They can tolerate it."

"Very wise." Autumn drained the last of her IPA out of her pint glass. She, Owen and Isabella were having after-shift drinks at a small pub near Happy Paws. It was grungy but laid back and cheap. She was excited Blake was meeting her here, giving her a chance to show him a cool New York location for once. She'd seriously needed to up her game on the date front. By rights, they should have gone on their third and final date ages ago, but Blake was dragging his feet, claiming he was waiting for a special event. Meanwhile, they were hanging out every night at his place or hers, ordering takeout and having sex until their bodies gave out. Frequently, Blake came up with elaborate excuses to take her to tiny Thai restaurants, indie rock gigs and cupcake boutiques after sex. If she really wanted to match him, she'd need to plan a solid month's worth of dates.

Which might be hard to do once you run out the clock on your visa, Reynolds. Or have you forgotten about that?

She cringed. This morning she'd gone as far as taking the form off the fridge and filling out her name before putting it back up there. What was her fucking problem? Why couldn't she commit to anything? What would she tell Blake if in a week's time his new lover was being deported? But it wasn't like he wasn't playing games, too, fucking around with their dates and refusing to discuss their future...

"You're still thinking about him," Owen said loudly. "I can sympathize, but I must insist you either focus up or say what you're thinking out loud. I have not heard nearly enough details about your landlord's body."

"I told you, he's hairy and jacked," Autumn protested. "And he has a bad leg."

"Three things? Pfft. I could wax poetic about Ryan's ass for *hours.*"

"And I would gladly listen, but I don't have that skill. Anyway..." Autumn looked over her shoulder. "He should be here soon, I don't want to freak him out."

"What is that supposed to mean?" Owen demanded. He was five beers in and a little punchy. "Do you mean that we're freaks? That we're *inhospitable?*"

"No! It's just that Blake's shy and you're very..."

"Not," Isabella said, laying a hand over Owen's. "You guys want another round?"

They all agreed that was an excellent idea. In a flash, Isabella returned with fresh beers. Autumn wasn't the least bit surprised. Her colleague looked cool and gorgeous in spite of the New York heat and the tattooed bartender practically fell into her cleavage.

"That bar guy definitely wants in," Autumn said, accepting her pint. "He's on his phone right now. I bet he's trying to Tinder you."

Isabella didn't bat an eyelid. "I deleted Tinder a month ago. He'll have to work a lot harder."

"God, you're cool," Autumn said, too drunk to stop herself. "You don't say much but when you do it's like..." she held up a circle made of her thumb and forefinger. "Perfect."

Isabella laughed, the sound as buttery as her speaking voice. "Thanks. I'm glad you didn't move home after your break up."

Autumn sipped her beer, feeling awkward. She didn't want to lie, but the truth about her visa situation was far too complex to broach on a Friday night. Thankfully, Owen pulled them all into a conversation about the recent subway strike, leaving the subject of her future firmly in ambiguity where it belonged. Twenty minutes later their beers were growing dangerously low again. Autumn was on the verge of getting another round when Owen pointed over her shoulder. "There he is, the conquering beast! Look at him, Isa!"

Autumn turned and saw Blake had indeed arrived. He looked fucking divine in his checkered shirt and jeans and she had to actively work not to let her mouth stretch into the lovesick smile she knew Owen would call her out on. She also stayed in her seat to avoid looking like one of those girls who ditched their mates the instant their dates showed up.

Isabella whipped around to give Blake a once-over, then smiled at her. "Very handsome. You must look great together."

Autumn was absurdly flattered. "Thanks! Also I love your voice, please talk more."

Isabella and Owen laughed.

"If you like the way she sounds, you should come to her performance on Sunday." Owen slung an arm over his friend's shoulders. "This little Brooklyn baby is gonna be singing her heart out at the Essence Theatre. You got a, what, twenty-minute set this time?"

Isabella nodded her glorious head.

"Congratulations," Autumn said. "What kind of music do you—"

"Come to the show and find out in person," Owen interrupted. "Bring your man bear. Ryan's coming, we can all hang out as a group."

"That sounds awesome!" Autumn was so excited at the idea of being in a group once more, she leapt off her barstool and ran toward Blake, who was still weaving his way through clusters of drunk businessmen. Throwing aside all dignity, she wrapped her arms around his waist and hugged him tight.

"Hey, how are you? Thanks for coming! Are you free on Sunday night?"

Blake frowned at her. "Are you drunk?"

"No. A bit. Yes," she admitted. "But more importantly, are you free on Sunday? It's very important that you tell me now because I want you to come hang out with us at Isabella's performance thing. It's perfect third date material, a group of us all hanging ou—"

Blake picked her up and kissed her, not a big kiss but enough to make her eyes close and her knees quiver. Enough that she completely forgot where she was. He pulled away and smiled at her, his expression very soft. "Hey."

"Uh, hey," Autumn whispered, more than a little dizzy. "What was that for?"

Blake put her back on her feet. "I need a reason to kiss you?"

"No it's just…" She felt herself flush and refused to finish that sentence with 'you said you didn't like PDA and it seemed like you really wanted to kiss me.' "Come meet my friends. Or meet Isabella, seeing as you've already met Owen. My New York City friend stock has risen to three and I am loving it."

She grabbed his hand and began tugging him toward the table. Blake, of course, didn't budge an inch. "Hang on, Fun-Size, does the table need drinks? And who's your third friend?"

"I adopted another pigeon Blake and this time it's for real." Autumn laughed at the horrified look on his face. "It's you, you big silly landlord. You're my third mate."

Maybe it was the pigeon joke but Blake didn't seem very impressed by this.

"I'm going to the bar," he said, his mouth turned down at the corners. "I'll get a pitcher of something."

It turned out to be a pitcher of white wine sangria, which went down amazingly well. Autumn had been nervous about introducing Blake, a self-confessed recluse with no social skills to a wider circle of company but he was completely at ease with Owen and Isabella. He didn't talk very much, true, but he asked a lot of questions and he and Isabella immediately struck up a strong/silent type rapport. There was still a slight tension between him and Owen, but not an unfriendly one. Autumn guessed it was a kind of manly rivalry with some competitive nuances thrown in. Also, Owen probably hadn't forgiven him for fucking up his 'Modern day Beauty and The Beast' story. Still, the conversation flowed and one round of white wine sangria merged into a second. Before long she was feeling pretty damn tipsy. It was only when Isabella asked if she and Blake were still going out alone or if they wanted to join them for karaoke in Alphabet City that Autumn realized it was nine o'clock and they'd been at the bar for hours.

She was keen for karaoke but since Blake looked like he would rather saw through his own foot, she cheerfully declined. After agreeing that he would join them again for Isabella's performance at the Essence theatre, Blake hustled her out of the bar and into the cool evening air.

"That was fun, wasn't it?" she asked. "I had a lot of fun. You and Owen and Isabella are very fun."

"Well, we are your three mates."

"Hey, don't tease me for only having three mates. Or saying the word 'mate.' It's an important part of my culture."

"I'm not teasing you, Autumn."

She scrutinized his face under a passing street lamp and decided he definitely looked grumpy. Or grumpier. "What's wrong, Blake the snake?"

He turned and stared unblinkingly at her.

"Okay, I won't ever call you that again, but seriously, are you mad at me? Is it because I'm drunk? Because that might be your fault for ordering delicious sangria and then getting a refill. It was generous and charming, but did you ever stop and think who would drink it all? And that that person would definitely be me?"

Blake snorted. "I guess I didn't. Let's get you something to eat."

Without waiting for her response Blake stopped and bought two hot dogs from a nearby vendor. Autumn *had* been feeling a bit snacky after all the drinks and happily accepted her fake meat product. A minute later it was gone. She was just going to ask him for a bite of his when Blake stopped to buy her a pretzel with the seemingly infinite bundle of cash he kept in his wallet.

"Where do you keep getting all this money?" she demanded. "And you know you don't have to keep feeding me, right?"

"I get money from ATM's like everyone else and you were eyeing my hot dog like a rabid raccoon." Blake handed her the salt studded pastry. "I'll buy you all the food you can eat, Fun-Size, but I draw the line at sharing."

Autumn bit into the pretzel. "Fargh enoghff."

They walked in silence for a bit, eating their street food when Autumn realized she had no freaking idea where they were going. "Where are you taking me this time, The Landlord? Opera? Hot air balloon racing? Drug deal?"

"We're going to the park."

"Like… to break up an illegal dog fighting ring?"

Blake frowned at her. "Sometimes I worry about what goes on inside your head. No. We're just going to the park."

"That's fine, I guess." She stared at the ice cream food truck parked on the opposite side of the road and instantly Blake was gripping her arm and steering her toward it.

"At least let me pay for this one," she protested. "I want to get four different flavours and I'll feel bad about making you spend too much, otherwise."

"Are you forgetting about the two-hundred-dollar gold leaf cake?"

"Why? Why do you always remind me of that? *Whyyyy?*"

He chuckled. "It's always funny to see your reaction. Get as many flavors as you want."

Fifteen minutes and a banana, chocolate, peppermint, cherry, rainbow ice cream later, they were in the park. It was large and not nearly as nice as the more touristy commons Autumn had been to. The stone benches were covered in graffiti and the flowerbeds were weedy and overgrown.

Everything had a slightly ominous look, yet she could observe all of them without the slightest trace of fear because of the man next to her. Nothing bad was going to happen while Blake was there. Not only was he the size of a pyramid, he was hyper-alert, always scanning the perimeter for possible risks and guiding her into his side whenever anyone remotely dodgy approached. He was like a huge, free bodyguard who was also an incredible fuck.

"What do you think?" Blake asked.

"I think you're like a huge, free bodyguard who's also an incredible fuck."

He grinned, the spread of color on his cheeks obvious even through the beard. "Maybe you're not so bad drunk."

And maybe you're not so bad ever, she wanted to add, but chomped the last of her ice cream cone instead. Her mushy, gold tinted feelings for her landlord were becoming harder to fight down. She didn't believe Owen, she wasn't, *couldn't* be in love with Blake, but the feelings, the ones that stole her sleep and made her chest ache, *were* getting harder to hold in.

He led her to a park bench on the edge of the perimeter, apparently placed so that visitors could stare intently at the thick bull brush hedge.

"Terrible place for a park bench," Autumn commented.

"The view isn't important." Blake sat down, pulling her onto his lap. "What do you think of the place?"

"It's very..." Autumn scanned the park, trying to come up with adjectives that weren't 'unkempt' or 'random.' "Private."

"It is. Which is exactly what I wanted."

Autumn put a hand on his chest. "Hold on, I don't want to give you more examples of my true-crime brain, but are you going to murder me tonight, Landlord? Choke me out so no one can discover you've been illegally fucking me in exchange for free pigeon meat?"

He scowled at her. "No."

"Well, that's a relief." Autumn shifted in his lap and felt a hot heavy weight she'd grown very familiar with over the past month.

"If that's the case, is there perhaps another, more sexful reason for bringing me here..." she leaned in close to his ear, "...owner?"

She had the satisfaction of hearing Blake's strained grunt, feeling him thicken between her legs. He was more responsive to her than any man she'd ever met. It seemed like everything she did turned him on—something she'd been exploiting on an almost nightly basis. His large hands closed around her hips, fisting the flowy knee length skirt she'd worn to the bar. She closed her eyes for a kiss, but it never came.

She opened her eyes and saw Blake shaking his head. "Much as I'd love to play, that isn't why I brought you here. I've decided you're going to perform your routine for me."

At first Autumn thought he meant a striptease routine. She was all set to tell him that she was an incredibly shitty dancer and wouldn't do that kind of thing even if they weren't in a freaking park, when she realized he meant comedy, and that was even worse. "No fucking way."

Blake let go of her skirt. "Not an option, Fun-Size. You want to pay me back for all the food I've bought you, you'll do your routine."

Her mouth fell open in horror. "Paying for my food was a sincere gesture of gentlemanliness!"

"And now I'm using it to get something out of you. I want to see that routine, Blondie, stand up."

When she refused, he gently hoisted her onto her feet. "Come on honey, just do it. I promise not to heckle you."

Autumn gaped at him. "You can't seriously be—"

"I am. Routine. Now."

"But it has singing and music and I don't have my Casio keyboard!"

"Do it without the keyboard."

"But it'll be embarrassing!"

Blake rolled his eyes. "I already told you. There's no one here but me."

"Sure, you do realize you're the most intimidating cunt on earth, right? Ian used to avoid going to the mailbox whenever you were in the lobby."

Blake gave a little snort of derision but didn't say anything. Autumn felt a hot wash of discomfort. They hadn't spoken about the dick pic thing since it had happened but she'd noticed a renewed possessiveness about her lover. He held her hand whenever they walked together and when they were playing in her bed last week, Blake had kept her orgasm at bay until she screamed that he owned her pussy. It had been hot and completely in keeping with their role play, but it also felt like a fuck-you to the man who used to live there. Ian, for his part, hadn't sent any more messages and Autumn lived in hope that he had really, truly, given up on her and gone off in search of greener groupie pastures.

Oh, Ian. The thought of what he would say if he found out she wanted to do stand-up and had actually performed a routine in the park made Autumn's skin crawl. She wasn't the funny one. So few people were the funny one. Stand-up comedy was one of those things everyone imagined themselves excelling at; like writing a novel or winning a quiz show, but only ten percent would ever do it and one percent would do it well. She wasn't the one percent, not in terms of money and not in terms of this. "Blake, I can't do my routine for you. I mean it."

"Yeah you can."

Autumn held up her hands. "Okay, let's compromise. How about...and this is just a suggestion, we kill ourselves, instead?"

He frowned. "Don't say shit like that."

"But I'm scared!"

"Of what?"

"Seriously, man you *barely* smile and I have literally never heard you lol. You're a stand-up comic's worst nightmare. I don't know if I can do a single bit of it without freaking the fuck out!"

Blake scratched the bridge of his nose. "Okay, what about this, you go behind the park bench and perform. That way I won't be looking at you. How does that sound?"

That would be better, she thought and then stomped on the idea. "No. I can't do it."

Blake leaned forward, clasping his hands between his knees as he looked at her. "Fun-Size, I saw the way you looked at the poster for the open mic night. You spent, what, hours? Days, preparing a routine that no one'll ever see? Why would you bother to do that if you didn't think that someday someone would hear it?"

"I don't know."

"I do. I think you want to perform and you're scared. That's understandable, but if you don't push yourself, you'll regret it some day."

That was a good point. Autumn scuffed the toe of her flat in the dirt. She knew however bad she was, Blake wouldn't tease or hold her routine against her, he wasn't that kind of guy. And she had to admit there was a squirming jellybean of excitement inside her, something that did want to perform, if only to see what it was like.

"Tell me something embarrassing about yourself," she demanded. "We'll call it the price of admission."

Blake didn't even hesitate. "I fell asleep in history class in middle school. Woke up with an erection. My friend Kevin saw and almost pissed his pants laughing."

She laughed. She couldn't help it. It was just too endearing to picture the mortification on a young Blake's face.

"Okay," she said, walking around the park bench to face Blake's back. "I'll start now. If you still want to see my routine. You don't have to see it. We could just go home and fuck, you know."

"We're doing that either way. Go."

"Fine." She took a deep breath, and knowing that it would be easier to just start and keep going, she began. It wasn't hard to remember the words. She'd long since committed every letter to memory.

"Hi everyone, I'm Autumn Reynolds and I'll be making you glad you're not following your dreams tonight."

Blake chuckled.

Autumn pointed a furious finger at the back of his head.

"Don't you fucking token laugh at me, man!"

He waved a big hand in the air. "Keep going."

"So I'm not trained in comedy law, a thing that I don't think exists and if it exists, definitely shouldn't exist. I am a practicing vet. Yes, that's right, if your dog can't shit out that Lego brick, I'm the girl who can help you out."

Blake laughed again and the sound was like balm to Autumn's nervous system because she could tell, really tell that he wasn't faking. Her skin tingled all over and her belly became hot and tight. This wasn't pleasurable the way ice cream or an orgasm was pleasurable, it was too sharp, too terrifying, but, it felt so, so good. She cleared her throat. "Yeah you might laugh, but that is seriously what I spend my days doing. I studied for seven years, spent thousands of dollars and my main thing is extracting small toys from the bowels of overweight golden retrievers. Some people get upset when I say that. They ask 'surely there's more to it than that?' and I say 'yeah, you ever see *"Marley and Me?"'* That's every day of my fucking life man, just watching kids and grown men cry as I exterminate their beloved family pets. Sometimes I feel like I signed up to be an apprentice of the grim fucking reaper…"

As she talked, Autumn could feel her voice growing louder, more confident, falling into the familiar clicks and grooves she'd rehearsed so many times in her bedroom and lounge room, or on her way home from work. She wasn't perfect, she forgot a couple of lines, but it didn't matter, the spiky energy flowing through her continued and when she finished and took a bow to Blake's tumultuous applause, she was grinning from ear to ear. "That felt amazing."

"It sounded even better," Blake said and she could hear his smile in his voice.

"I only did it because of you. *You* made me feel all of this. Can I come give you a hug?"

"You *better*."

Unable to contain a girlish squeal of over-excitement, Autumn dashed around the bench and threw herself into Blake's arms. He caught her, pulling her close to his beefy chest. "I'm so proud of you. You were so clever. So brave."

"Did you like the thing I said about lizards?" Autumn asked. "You didn't think it was too dumb?"

"Not at all." He kissed her forehead. "I think you should call Netflix and see if you can get a special."

"I don't care about that, I just can't believe I actually said my whole routine out loud in front of another person!" Autumn buried her burning face in his shirt. "You promise you really liked it?"

"I did. And if you wanted to perform it facing me, I'd be happy to hear it again."

But the glow of having successfully completed a stand-up comedy routine was already starting to fade in the presence of being so close to Blake. It was insane to think she'd hung out with him for a little over a month. He'd not only met her friends tonight but bought her a hot dog and laughed at her jokes. God, she would miss him if she went home. She allowed a little of the mushy feelings to slip through and ask how she'd manage go back to a life filled with men who talked all the time and never pushed her to do new things. The thought was so terrifying, she kissed Blake hard, trying to prove that he was there and she didn't need to worry. Their mouths molded perfectly—no longer strangers to what the other liked. As she sank deeper into his hips she again felt the thick swell of his cock. "Tell me you didn't get that from my jokes?"

"You're funny, but no one's *that* funny."

She laughed, rolling her hips against him. "You know we're still all on our lonesome, Mr. Landlord?"

"I might have noticed." His hand rose and wound itself into her hair. "You shouldn't be out here so late at night, Blondie. There's a lot of bad men around, they might get the wrong idea."

Autumn felt the familiar arousal that came from Blake all hot and raspy in her ear, but to her surprise, she didn't have the same anticipation. She opened her mouth. Closed it again.

"What?" he said at once. "Say it."

She licked her lips, stupidly nervous for some reason. "Can we just do it like, normal? I mean, not normal, but vanilla? Like maybe I could go on top and ride your dick?" She made a face. "Sorry that's not the sexiest thing in the worl—"

He kissed her hard and deep, his hand slipping from her hair to gently clasp her neck. "You can have whatever you want from me. Always."

"I just thought…because when I came to you I wanted it to be all about my fantasies…"

He gave her a soft smile as his hand cupped her spine. "I know there's more to you than just your fantasies, Autumn."

She thought about what he'd just done, pushing her gently toward one of the best experiences she'd ever had in New York. "You do, don't you? You always know everything I want."

"So what do you want now?" he asked, his voice low. "You want to fuck me on this park bench? Take control of me. Make me suffer?"

She nodded shyly. "I don't want to risk our jobs and reputations, though."

He smirked. "Stand up and take your panties off."

Autumn did what she was told, shimmying her underwear

down her legs and putting it in her handbag. She watched as Blake unzipped his fly and produced his cock. It was thick and dark-red, straining inside his fist. Her mouth immediately started watering but when she lowered her mouth toward him, Blake gently nudged her away. "I don't mind breaking the rules, Fun-Size, but we can't risk being here all night. I've never had a blow job from you I didn't want to last an hour. Come sit on it before I change my mind."

Autumn put her hands on her hips. "I thought I was going to be in charge?"

"You know what they say about old habits. What do you want me to do?"

"Sit back with your hands behind your head."

He obliged, still looking like a lazing god. "Now what?"

Rather than respond, Autumn climbed onto his lap, arranging her skirt so that what they were doing would be concealed, even to the hedge. She reached between them and fisted Blake's cock, sliding it between her soaking lips.

"Fucking hell," he grunted. "Not shy with it anymore, are you?"

"Not even a little bit." She sank down, impaling herself on him inch by inch. "We see or hear anyone, we start kissing and pretend we're just making out, okay?"

"Yes, boss."

The idea that they'd get away with this became slimmer and slimmer as she sank down and they both let out deep moans.

"God, don't move," Autumn said, gripping his shoulders and using them to raise herself up again. "I want to use you. You don't move unless I tell you to."

He nodded, his lips pulled into his mouth in concentration. She could tell it went against his instincts to let her do all the work, but still he sat there, allowing her to ride his cock. Within seconds he was slippery from her wetness. She experimented with her speed, taking him fast before slowing down and grinding herself against him. As she played, he watched her, a king allowing a subject to play with his toys without ever losing an ounce of power. Their gaze met and she shivered. "You look so good."

"Goddamn, so do you. Now, take my fucking dick, Fun-Size. Take it all the way down like I make you take it."

The use of her usual nickname while they were having sex made her smile. Blondie was the woman he screwed in a closet. Fun-Size was the girl who did stand-up in the park. She sank down on him as deep as she could go, moaning into the night air. "You're so big."

He chuckled, making both their bodies shake. "Like hearing that. You know I used to picture this. Before we knew each other."

"What? Me humping you in a park?"

"Something like that."

Autumn leaned forward and kissed a line along his neck. "How did you picture it? Tell me exactly and maybe I'll let you live."

Another chuckle. "We were on the beach, you came crawling up to me in this tiny string bikini begging for my cock, so eager, you sat on it the second I got it out."

She closed her eyes, her arousal accelerating. "I can be eager."

She rode him fast, her hips slapping down on his. He was so deep this way it was hard for her to keep it going. She was a vet and amateur comedian, not a spin instructor.

"Blake," she whispered. "Can you help me?"

Instantly, his hands were on her hips and she was being raised up like she weighed nothing, brought down with more speed than she could have ever managed on her own. She moaned into Blake's shoulder, slightly embarrassed.

"I wish I could do that," she mumbled. "Fuck you the way you—oh—fuck me."

"Don't think about it," Blake said, his hand weaving into her hair. "No one can make me laugh the way you do."

God, this man. This man and his body and his words, it was more than a girl could take. Autumn closed her eyes and just let herself feel, the flutter of her skirt, the prickle of her sweat, the roughness of Blake's hands as he ground her against him, rubbing her clit against the thatch of pubic hair that covered his groin. "Feel good?"

"Yes," she said, unable to add anything else. "Yes, yes, yes!"

There was something different about this sex, but she couldn't put her finger on it until her orgasm was closing in around her like the darkness. They might have been on a park bench, fucking where everyone could see them, and Blake might have been doing most of the work—she probably needed to do some squats or something—but they were connected in a way that went deeper than their bodies. Fully clothed, she could feel herself revealing something to Blake. Something that went beyond their shared fantasies. The *like*, maybe. The like she felt for him. The knowledge that from now on, the hardest thing about leaving New York would be leaving him.

The knowledge hurt. It made the sex sweeter and more painful. Her orgasm, as it swelled, made her feel the way she did when she received a beautiful bouquet. It would bloom and then burst and then it would be gone, leaving her a little emptier for knowing such beautiful things faded away.

"Can you grab my hair?" Autumn asked, needing to feel pain,

to escape the crushing void of all this intimacy. Blake complied and with his fist tight in her hair, she imagined him as he had been before, a brooding outsider who watched her with an intensity she now knew was lust. She pretended her landlord had found her wandering the park and decided to use her for his own selfish purposes.

As soon as the fantasy wrapped itself around her brain, she felt better, more in control. She ground against him, imagined him cursing and taunting her for being such an eager little whore, even as the man inside her kissed her cheeks and moaned his encouragement. She came that way, her mind grasping at the filthy and impersonal despite the glow in her chest that said it was so much more. Her orgasm detonated like a bomb. It was a mercy the way it dulled out all her thoughts in a hot glow of sensation. He followed her a few seconds later, pressing her down and coming deep, deep inside.

They sat together, still joined, waiting for their breathing to slow.

Blake tipped his face toward the night sky. "How was that for you, boss lady?"

"Really good," she said, which was the truth, but not all of it.

"Autumn…?"

She looked up at him. "What's up?"

He stared at her for a long moment, then shook his head. "It's late, we should get you back home."

They untangled themselves with some difficulty, mopping up with the tissues Autumn kept in her handbag. It was pitch black now, and though she could still hear distant traffic it felt like she and Blake were the last two people in the world. She amused herself for a second, imagining the two of them trekking through a post-apocalyptic wasteland. Funnily enough, Blake was the first person she'd ever met that she could see surviving in that scenario. Big, tough, resourceful. He knew all the streets and would probably know how to get food, too. If she was lucky, he'd agree to let her tag along with him. He didn't seem to mind her more irritating personality traits and she had some medical knowledge. Surely that counted for something?

Her mind still on the apocalypse, Autumn absently checked her phone. When her brain processed what she was actually seeing, her heart felt like it stopped dead in her chest. "Oh fuck!"

"What?" Blake said sharply, but she was too distracted to answer.

"Fucking *shit*!"

She had over two hundred Facebook alerts. Doubting that meant anything good, she opened the app to see she'd been tagged in a photo Owen had taken at the bar. The background was a blur of people and little fairy lights but she and Blake were crystal clear. They were standing so close together she was sure they'd just kissed hello. Blake's hands were on her waist and he was frowning down at her in that familiar way that said he was amused and concerned at once. She was smiling up at him, her eyes huge as an anime character's. She looked smitten. As though she thought he'd hung the moon and every star in the universe.

A lump rose in her throat and she swallowed, trying to force it down. This wasn't the time. This wasn't the fucking time for that. She kept scrolling and discovered Owen had captioned the picture *'A tale as old as time'* and included a bunch of hashtags including *#summer* and *#NewYorkRomance*. It had over three hundred likes but that wasn't the problem. The problem was that her account was public and a ton of her friends from home had commented.

"*OMG where's Ian? Did you guys break up?*"

"Fucking hell Autie are you and Fletcher opening things up?"

"God we're out of the loop! Upload more pictures you spaz!"

"New York Romance? So you're not coming home? Your mum keeps saying you're coming home!"

She had twenty direct messages, all of them asking similar things, but that wasn't all. She had nine missed calls from her parents, two from her uncle and multiple texts. She sank down on the stone bench and found they all said the same thing; *what the hell is going on?*

Then it got worse. Her mum had apparently called Ian, forced the truth about the break up out of him and was now in the process of *booking her a fucking flight home.*

"Oh god…" Autumn moaned. "Oh god, they all know, everyone knows. I was waiting for the right moment and now everyone knows."

Her stomach heaved upward, threatening to eject her ice cream/vending cart dinner. She'd not only been outed as single, but clearly dating another man. Everyone knew and anyone who didn't already would soon be told. This entire situation was out of control.

"Autumn," Blake said. "What's wrong? What do you mean everyone knows?"

She turned to look at him. In her horror, she'd almost forgotten he was there. "There are some things I need to tell you. About my parents and my uncle and Ian and a deadline date I've let get very, very close."

CHAPTER 15

Blake leaned back in his chair and regarded the finished book sitting on his desk. Not the Bible project that had grown overdue. No, this restoration hadn't been on the schedule, but it was by far the most important one he'd ever worked on. The rich pinks, reds and greens of the cover glowed in the lamplight, the embossed golden letters polished to a shine. There was no sign of the frayed spine or uneven pages that had been there when he purchased it. It was as perfect as he could make it and yet, he was less confident than he'd ever been upon completing a restoration. Usually when he finished a project, there was a sense of relief. He looked forward to dropping off the item and having it out of his life, the association with his client done. Clean cuts. His life had *always* been about clean cuts.

When his job had quite literally blown up in his face, he'd changed lanes.

When his friends proved to be untrustworthy, he'd walked away.

When his fiancée slept with someone else, he'd canceled the wedding.

Walking away without a backward glance was so much easier than forcing a square peg into a round hole. Maybe it was one of the pitfalls of a brain that operated on pure pragmatism. If a man's leg is busted, he finds a job that doesn't require him to use that leg. If people take away more than they add to a man's life, cut them off. Simple. He'd always wondered why others didn't find concise, necessary changes easy.

Blake had read enough of the classics stacked in his apartment to know there was an answer to why others chose to stick out an uncomfortable situation, instead of using their brains and God-given sense of self-preservation. Romance. Love. But *love* would suffice.

Looking down at the book he would give to Autumn, now he understood.

Love made people do uncomfortable things.

He'd never loved anyone before—obviously not even his fiancée—because he'd exited his comfort zone for Autumn. It got easier every time, mainly because of her. The way she held his hand and allowed him to be his grumpy self, even celebrating it. And on the opposite end, when he made jokes or couldn't quite hide his happiness, she celebrated that, too. She had restored something in him, as sure as he'd restored the book on his desk. Then again, she'd made him better than he'd been before. She'd made him believe he had the capacity for love and now...now he couldn't lose her.

Blake loved Autumn.

Admitting his feelings, especially in the midst of this rare cluttering of his usually cut and dried mindset, wasn't easy. In fact, it was difficult acknowledging that he'd opened himself up *this much* to someone else. At first, he didn't know why, until he realized she could be the one making the clean cut this time.

Isn't that what it boiled down to?

For the first time in his life, he was on the other side of the knife. He'd never taken the time to consider what it must be like, having a loved one's presence hanging in the balance. Knowing you were unworthy of them and that the decision to stay paired or separate was in their hands.

An uncomfortable knot tied itself in Blake's stomach and he pushed himself out of his chair, beginning an agitated pace behind his desk. For so long, he'd maintained a brick wall between himself and the past, but the mortar began cracking now, letting daylight through. On the other side were faces he'd left behind, without so much as a second thought.

Although now Blake wasn't so sure if he was devoid of second thoughts, or if he'd just blocked them, never acknowledging the hurt it caused to carve out vital parts of the past and toss them away. For the first time, he tried to imagine things from his friends' point of view. His fiancée. If they'd tried to communicate with him, to make him listen to things he didn't want to hear, would he have cut them off anyway? Before they even did anything wrong?

He didn't have time to think about this now.

Blake snatched up the book and slipped it into the waiting plastic. Christ, why the mental torture when too many things already weighed in the balance tonight? As soon as he gave Autumn this book, she was going to know he loved her. Even without the inscription he'd written on the title page, she knew him well enough that the gift would say it all.

She knew him well enough.

How long had it been since anyone knew him well?

Never. He'd...never let anyone know him like Autumn did. Tonight he would show her the reverse was true, too. When they'd met, she had been in a state that reminded him of his past, yet he could see the girl beneath still burning so fucking bright. If all went according to plan, everyone would see her burn that way tonight.

Blake slipped the book into his inner coat pocket, switched off the lamp and tucked his apartment keys into his pants. He intended to pick Autumn up at her door, but when he opened his, there she was, her hand poised to knock.

"Hello," he said, surprised. "I was just coming to get you."

She dipped her chin. "Thought I would pick you up for a change, landlord. Men deserve to be courted, too."

It was hard to speak for a moment, she looked so beautiful in her sparkly tights and black lace dress. Part of him wanted to drag her into the apartment and forget tonight's plans. It would be so easy to continue as they had been for the last couple weeks; eating dinner together while she scratched jokes into a notebook with her purple pen, occasionally asking his opinion about one. And since the night in the park, she'd grown more and more confident with the delivery each time. Sometimes she sat on his knee while he prepared rent statements for the building or worked on a restoration.

Then there was the fucking. God, the fucking. He couldn't help going at her like an animal at the smallest encouragement. Or lack of encouragement, as was often the game between them. Every time he thought the edge had been taken off, it came back sharper and more demanding. It always would for this girl, he knew it in his gut. His heart. Where his bedside drawer had once been empty, it was now filled with rope, handcuffs, a gag, a notepad for ransom letters, new pictures he'd taken of Autumn on the sly and panties he'd confiscated. But when she left her joke notebook there, such a private part of herself, that had been the most satisfying item of all.

"Blake?"

He realized he'd been staring at her in the hallway without commenting for too long. "You look beautiful," he said, clearing his throat. "What is that? New lipstick?"

"Yes. Electric coral."

Blake waited for her to make a joke or lay a lipstick mark on his cheek. Either of those things would be typical Autumn behavior. Instead, she just stood there. There seemed to be an air of distraction about her. He didn't like that, especially when there was so much on the line tonight. That went double after what happened in the park. She'd explained her reaction to whatever popped up on her phone away by summing it up as family drama she didn't want to discuss, before he'd walked her home in a thick silence. He'd only pressed enough to make sure it wasn't another dick snap from her ex-boyfriend, then let it drop, hoping Autumn would explain when she was ready. Maybe that had been a mistake.

He stepped into the hallway and caught her chin between two fingers. "Something on your mind, Fun-Size?"

"Who, me?"

"No, the miniature candy bar behind you."

A light warmed the hazel green of her eyes. "Hey, I thought I was the aspiring comedian."

He let go of her chin to lock the door. "Maybe you're rubbing off on—"

Autumn's arms wound around his waist from behind. "Can we stay home?" She squeezed tighter and the beating organ in Blake's chest lifted and snared in his throat. "I can pretend to be a school girl disobeying her principal again. That was our best, yet."

Remembering the innocent white panties she'd worn beneath a plaid skirt, Blake stiffened in his trousers.

Whatever you do, don't think about the pigtails. Jesus. Throw lust into the mix with his suffering heart, and not dragging her into the apartment was becoming impossible. He could tell her right here and now how he felt. They didn't have to go to Essence Theater for the variety show. He could forget the plans he'd made once they got there. But words weren't enough for this girl he'd fallen in love with. She would get the world from him.

Blake turned around, catching a glimpse of distress on her face before she hid it in his chest. "Autumn, tell me what's wrong."

"Myphrodion tulk prow—" He took a handful of her hair and tipped her head back. "I can't hear you when you talk into my shirt."

"And that's...a bad thing?"

He kept his hips angled away, because God knew if she used her hands to persuade him to do anything, he wouldn't be able to deny her. Tilting his head, he considered her pout, remembering she'd been called in to work today. "Something bad happen with a patient?"

"No. Apart from a turtle with diarrhea."

"Glad I asked. Are you stuck on a joke?"

"Did you just hear me? I just treated a turtle that couldn't stop shitting itself. If jokes were gold, I would be King actual Midas."

"Right." Blake leaned down and kissed her mouth, long and slow, not giving a fuck if he ended up with a face full of electric coral. And if remembering the name of her lipstick didn't prove he loved her, nothing would. Using a technique he knew would work wonders, even if it was kind of unfair, Blake pulled her hair harder and dropped his voice. "Talk."

Autumn's eyelids fluttered. "My parents...no, *everyone* I know found out." She swallowed hard, the angle of her neck showing off the slide of muscle.

"Everyone found out what?"

"About the break up. That I'm living alone. Every time I get a second to myself I'm messaging my friends and reassuring my parents that I'm surviving the shipwreck that is my adult life."

Blood swam in Blake's ears. "You hadn't told them about the break up?"

"No."

"Why not?"

Autumn broke free of his hold, mostly because he was taken off guard and didn't have the wherewithal to keep it up. "I came here to support Ian getting into comedy. If that's not why I'm here anymore...then why *am* I here?" She looked up at him quickly. "That's what they're all asking me. My friends want me to come home and my parents want me to buy into my uncle's business. That's what they've *always* wanted."

No.

It took all his willpower not to roar that word at the top of his lungs. The book sitting in his jacket felt ridiculous in that moment. Ridiculous. Autumn's adult life had been shaped by a relationship with another man, one that had lasted years. There was no reason to be surprised that she hadn't called home about him—a man she'd simply asked to fuck her the right way, before he'd managed to make it more. After all, who had Blake told about Autumn? A couple of tenants? There was no one in his life *to* tell. He was just a solitary asshole with a book to offer.

What a catch.

"What do you want, Autumn?"

She tripped toward him, throwing her face back into his chest. "I want to go inside and smell the leather of your books and let you undress me. I just want to ignore my phone and get lost for the night."

So easy. 1-2-3. Giving Autumn what she wanted was such a temptation to him, it physically hurt to shake his head no. He hadn't been asking what she wanted for *the night*. He'd meant in general. For the future. Did she want to go back to Australia? Did she want her parents to know she was dating a former hermit with only rudimentary social skills? Could she see him as a legitimate reason to stay in New York?

He would never know unless he asked. Unfortunately, he sucked with words. And whatever ones he'd mustered for tonight seemed trite and ineffective in the face of what she'd just told him. There was every chance he wouldn't be enough to keep her in this town. He had to come to terms with that, but he would be damned before he allowed Autumn to believe she couldn't stay on her own. That she couldn't make New York a better place than it was before she arrived. If she didn't already believe, he would damn well believe enough for the both of them.

Blake forced an easygoing expression onto his face. "In what world am I the one making *you* go outside, huh? It's supposed to be the other way around." He stooped down and threw Autumn over his shoulder, ignoring her yelp and giving her backside a squeeze. "Suck it up. I was promised three dates and I'm damn well collecting, Fun-Size."

"Landlord!" She twisted on his shoulder. "I don't like this kind of hostage taking."

"You will."

He hoped. He hoped like hell.

※

AT SOME POINT during his sabbatical from the human race, they'd stopped assigning seats at concerts, allowing it to become a free for all. There *were* actual seats at the Essence Theater, but only in the balcony sections, everything else appeared to be general admission and nothing about this seemed surprising to Autumn. She ponied up to the bar in front of him, her feathers still a little ruffled from being denied her night at home. To tell the truth, Blake liked the feisty side of her on display. Their first few encounters, she'd been ready to pass out every time he came close. Now she was comfortable enough to eye roll him and know she could get away with it. She knew not only that he wouldn't lay a fucking finger on her, but that he would still be there waiting. When she decided she'd made him suffer enough.

That's how he knew his plan tonight was the right thing to do. Autumn had always been an extraordinary woman with talent and resilience. Not in a million years could he take credit for traits that were so essentially *her*. But his original goal in taking her out and showing her New York had worked. First, she was no longer a timid mouse around him. And second, the sparkle that had been dimmed by her break up was back. If he'd thought her beautiful before, he couldn't look at her now without wanting to get on his knees. She'd grown. He'd had the privilege of watching it happen. After tonight, she'd have no doubts about herself, her ability to thrive on her own and just maybe…her desire to be with him.

Blake passed a twenty over Autumn's head to the bartender before she could pay for the drinks. She turned around with another adorable eye roll and handed him his beer, deliberately not looking at him. It was a thing of beauty.

Blake dropped his mouth to her ear, breathing against it for a few seconds, settling into the flavor of her. "I know you're mad with me. But I need to tell you, Autumn, that I'm…proud to be here with you. To be the one who walks into a room holding your hand. Every time we go anywhere together, I'm proud you'd choose to be here with me over someone younger." He laughed quietly into her hair. "Or *nicer*."

She made a sound. "Goddammit landlord, you've messed up the truly satisfying mope I was having."

"Good. It worked."

Her fingers crept up and down his chest. "Did you mean all that?"

"Do you think I say things I don't mean?"

"No. Except for that time you told me I was only good for a blow job."

"You had to bring that up."

Autumn gasped. "I just won a *current* argument by bringing up a *past* argument. That does it. We're officially a couple!"

Blake knew she meant it as a joke, but that didn't stop his heart from aching, needing that statement to be a reality. It was possible the universe had decided to speed up his timing, too, because right on the heels of her declaration, Autumn's knuckles bumped into the book in his coat pocket. "Whoa, what the hell is that? You packing heat?"

This is it, he thought. *I'll tell her everything right now.* He took a moment to marvel over his newfound spontaneity and knew it could only be attributed to Autumn, then reached into his coat to take out the book—

"What's up, assholes?" Owen said, sliding into a vacant spot beside them at the bar, his arm linked with a man with a neck tattoo and an indulgent smile. "Go ahead, compliment my outfit and we can move on to introductions."

"It's lovely!" Autumn said, clearly forgetting all about the object in his coat. "Toast of the nonexistent red carpet."

"I know." Owen dragged his companion closer. "This here is the old ball and chain. Ryan, meet Autie and her pouty man bear,

Blake. Status: It's complicated."

Ryan gave them a dissecting look. "Only if they let it be."

Owen signaled the bartender. "You right, baby. You so right."

God save Blake from wise-beyond-their-years millennials. He'd shown enough vacant apartments and overheard enough rent disputes between people in their mid-twenties to know they had a startling sense of self-awareness. It might even be impressive if it didn't make him wonder what he could have done with the same attribute at their age. Only, he hadn't started wondering about that until recently. The last few days, to be exact.

A memory of Kevin Donahue outside the building rose without warning. Why was he thinking about his old friend now? His past had nothing to do with tonight. It had nothing to do with anything. He'd made sure of that.

"Should we battle our way up to the front? I want Isa to know she's loved and supported." Without waiting for an answer, Owen gestured to the crowded stage area, which was growing denser now that the lights were out. "Just kidding, she'll castrate me if I'm not front and center. Move it, folks."

Blake settled a hand on the small of Autumn's back and guided her through the crowd, putting the fear of God in anyone who complained about them pushing to the front. When they reached the stage, however, Blake took mercy on the significantly shorter population and led Autumn to an alcove just off to the right. She leaned back against him, natural as breathing, taking their linked hands and crossing them over her body. Blake enjoyed the moment of easy intimacy as Autumn laughed at the emcee on stage who was introducing the first act—a beat boxing harmonica player.

Sure, why not?

They were around five acts into the show when Isabella's turn came. She didn't smile as she glided toward the microphone, plucking it out of the stand and waving away the wire, as if she'd done it a thousand times. Most of the acts talked to the crowd or told a pointless anecdote before cueing the music, but not this girl. She held up three fingers, counted down in silence, then slid right into At Last by Etta James.

"Holy shit," Autumn whispered. "She's amazing. I mean, of course she is. She makes eating noodles look elegant. Seriously, can you imagine going on after her? I'd want to die."

Blake ignored the rock that had just formed in his stomach. Just a figure of speech. Although, when he'd made that phone call to the organizer a couple days ago, he hadn't pictured the Essence Theater being quite this large. Or that such a high volume of people would show up to a variety act on a Sunday night. He'd thought it was going to be on the casual side.

A tick started in his temple as Isabella's song drew to a close, thunderous applause following the final note. Autumn took Blake's hands and clapped for him. All he could do was let her, watching as the emcee approached the microphone again.

"Was that not transcendent, you guys?" The emcee waved his hat in front of his face. "She goes by Isa. I-S-A. CDs are available in the lobby, but honestly, what are CDs anymore? No one knows. Download that shit right now while you're thinking of it. I'll wait." Someone yelled something from the audience, making the emcee frown. "No, *you're* a CD. Okay."

He clapped his hands and another spectacled young man ran out on stage. He was holding a Casio keyboard and he handed it to the guy on the microphone. "Our next performer is here to make you laugh. She comes from the land down undahhhh. Please put your paws together for Autumn Reynolds!"

Autumn tensed up and a nervous laugh hissed out of her. "Isa must have asked him to play a joke on me backstage. I mean...right?"

The crowd started murmuring, clearly confused as to why no one was walking out on stage and Autumn turned to look at Blake. "Where'd they get the keyboard, though? Oh God. What should I do...?"

He watched in horror as the color drained from her face. Had he gone too far too soon? No. They were there in the correct moment together, weren't they? They were there, there was no going back and she was fucking *good*. He knew if she got up there, everyone in the room would fall in love with her humor. Was he biased? Yes and no. He was in love with the girl so he found her every inhale amazing, but he could still listen objectively and recognize her comedy as the real deal.

"Autumn, you can do this."

Her expression remained dazed. "No I can't."

Blake turned her, shaking her a little by the shoulders. "You've practiced a million times. Just go up and perform like you're with me in the park. Or in front of your mirror. I know you can."

"You..." She shook her head, trying to get free of him. "How *dare you*. How could you do this to me? What fucking *right* did you have?"

All around them, the crowd started chanting Autumn's name, at the encouragement of the emcee. Autumn started to tremble and she clenched her small white hands into fists. It tore Blake straight down the middle.

I have fucked up huge.

"Autumn..." he rasped.

"No." Using one of the moves she'd learned in Krav Maga, she twisted and elbowed him hard in the ribs, breaking away.

Blake went running after her, no choice but to tunnel straight through the chanting crowd. There was nothing he could do but go after her, his leg protesting as he wove through the crowd of tightly packed bodies. Regret clogged his throat, panic blurring his vision. He'd thought all she needed was a push to realize her dream, but once again, he'd miscalculated. He'd missed one hill of the landscape, same as he always did. This time, though, it could cost him everything.

Blake saw a flash of blonde hair barreling through a side exit and followed, bursting out onto the street behind a weeping Autumn. She whirled on him, her hands shaking to stave him off. "Don't come near me."

He knew an apology would fall on deaf ears, so he went with an explanation. "I thought—"

"You thought what, Blake? We're sleeping together, so maybe that gave you the right to make a huge decision for me? To push me into something I wasn't even *close* to being ready for?" She turned in a circle, hands on her head. "At least before tonight I could *pretend* it was a possibility. Getting on stage and actually trying to be funny. But you threw me into this a-and now I *know* I'm a fucking coward. It's fact."

"You're not a coward," Blake growled. "There's never going to be a right time. It's always going to be too soon until you just do it."

Perhaps not the right thing to say—as evidenced by the bright red spots of color that bloomed on her cheeks.

"Know what, Blake? You're right. I'm not a coward." She took two steps and shoved him, but unlike in Krav class, he didn't have the presence of mind to feign a loss of balance and his refusal to budge seemed to piss her off even more. "*You* are. Hiding in your stacks of books and holding a grudge for ten fucking years. Turning your nose up at your friend's apologies. Whatever happened, it happened another lifetime ago and you've just shut yourself away and licked your wounds. *That's* cowardice."

Autumn's mouth snapped shut and she turned away. She was clearly still awash in her anger, but aware that what she'd said had crossed a line. Not that Blake could process much besides the jagged gash in his chest. It gaped and bled, right there onto the sidewalk.

She was right. Christ, had a more accurate truth ever been spoken? He'd spent a month trying to essentially fix Autumn, but she'd never been broken in the first place. He was the broken one. Instead of looking inward and sorting through his bullshit, he'd put pressure on her to heal in a way he obviously never had.

"If I want to go home, it will be *my* decision. If I want to make a go of comedy, it'll be *my* decision." She swiped at her damp eyes. "You just maneuvered me around without a thought to what I wanted. Just like he did."

A clamp tightened around the back of his neck. "Don't compare me to him."

"Well then who should I compare Ian to? *Your* ex-fiancée?" She pushed a jerky hand through her hair. "Is that what this rehabilitation project was all about? Sticking it to the people who betrayed us? Are we some kind of sad club? Because I didn't sign a membership form."

"I understand why you're mad at me, but that's a load of shit and you know it." He tried to catch her arm, but she evaded him. "We're together because we want to be."

"I know there's more to it." She peered up at him. "Were you trying to use me as your second chance, Blake?"

"No, Jesus…"

But he couldn't say with full certainty that he hadn't done so without realizing it.

More than anything, he wanted to pull Autumn close and tell her everything he'd done for the last month was because he'd been falling in love with her. She'd walked into his apartment seeking her drawing and she's brought in sunshine. Sunshine he couldn't help coveting and eventually soaking in like a selfish bastard.

The book inside his coat felt like it weighed as much as a lead cannonball. He couldn't give it to her, now. Maybe he never could. The last month had been the best of his life, but when Autumn looked back, what would she see? His pathetic attempts to make her be better while everything in his rearview still laid in shambles? No. No, that wouldn't work. It never would have worked. He lowered his head. "I'm sorry, Autumn."

Blake sensed someone behind him and turned, half-hoping it was Owen. If Autumn wouldn't let Blake comfort her, at least her co-worker could stop her from crying. God, he just wanted her to *stop crying*. But it wasn't Owen, it was, horror of all fucking horrors, Autumn's ex-boyfriend. Ian swaggered down the sidewalk with a shit-eating grin plastered all over his face.

"Evening, kids," he called out. His overly loud voice and loose stride all said he was drunk, but he was, as Blake remembered, hatefully good-looking. Sleek as a brand new BMW, classically handsome in the way he'd never be. Denial froze him in place. Not now. This couldn't be happening now.

But it was.

Autumn's ex met his gaze directly. "That didn't go well, did it, mate? I mean, I've seen some shit attempts at romance but that was just…" He put two fingers to his lips and kissed them. "Staggeringly incompetent."

Blake couldn't talk. The immensity of his feelings was so strong, so overwhelming, he had no idea what to say. If Ian had shown up yesterday, Blake still would have wanted to shatter his perfectly straight, white teeth, but at least he wouldn't have been at such a disadvantage. His gut told him he'd lost Autumn, and then the man she'd moved continents for had arrived to point that out. And as much as it pained him, Autumn's ex was right. He'd fucked up. He'd fucked up so bad.

"Ian?" Autumn said with a sniff. "What the Sam fuck are you doing here?"

He frowned as though having to account for his presence at this shit-show—instead of having it celebrated—had never occurred to him. "A…friend of mine is performing a one-minute, one-woman show. It's usually an hour, but she—they condensed it. It's about…vines. The plants, not the six-second video thing."

"Shouldn't you be inside watching it?" Blake snarled.

Ian turned to look at him, his discomfort melting back into amusement. "Trust me, this is way more interesting."

He turned to Autumn, grinning widely. "He doesn't know you at all, does he? Not like I do."

"You need to leave," Blake said through gritted teeth.

Ian raised an eyebrow at him. "Seriously, man, seven years we were together. Walks in the park, family dinners and no public humiliation or anything."

"I wasn't trying to humiliate her," Blake rasped. "She had a dream. I just wanted to…help her realize it."

Ian laughed again, but his eyes had gone hard. "Get fucked, Landlord, you spend a couple of weeks putting your dick in my girlfriend, and you think you know her better than I do?"

"I'm not your fucking girlfriend, Ian," Autumn said. "Please, can you just piss off?"

The words were harsh but Blake was devastated to see she was still wiping tears from her cheeks. "Fun-Size, please—"

"Fun-Size?" Ian leaned backward, cackling at the moon. "Is this guy for real? That's the stupidest fucking pet name I've ever heard."

Ian straightened up, his bright blue eyes finding Blake's again. "I call her sugar, because of the way she tastes, but you'd know all about that, wouldn't you, Landlord?"

"You shut your fucking mouth."

Blake barely recognized his own voice, it was so pumped with hatred. His fists were clenched at his sides, poison flooding his veins. God, he wanted to hurt this asshole, give his anger and confusion somewhere to go. Ian didn't seem to realize the trouble he was in because he took another step closer. "You been doing my girlfriend in my bed, big guy? Or have you been taking her down to your murder basement or wherever the fuck you live?"

Blake barely registered the insult. It was his calling Autumn his girlfriend that had him breathing through his nose, telling himself he shouldn't hit him, shouldn't, shouldn't, *shouldn't...*

Autumn groaned. "Ian, I mean it, you need to leave. This *really* isn't a good time."

Blake watched as the younger man's face contorted into a look of boyish empathy. "I know you must be embarrassed, Auts, but trust me, no one knows it was you who was meant to be up on stage. Do you want to go get a coffee? We could go to the place that does the red velvet cake stuff you like?"

Autumn's forehead contracted, another tear splashing onto her dress. "I don't want to get a red velvet anything with you, Ian! Can you please just fuck off?"

With a pout, Ian started toward Autumn, but Blake stepped into his path. "You're good where you are."

Ian scoffed then bent around him to keep addressing Autumn. "Autie, I forgive you for fucking Shrek, okay? I just want to be able to talk to you again. I miss you. And you never reply to my messages, even *the* picture and that took fucking ages to do, by the way. I had to take like nine until I got the lighting right and then—"

"Are you clinically insane?" Autumn interrupted. "No, wait, I know that one; yes you are. Now can you please fucking listen to me and just go away? Just go back inside and watch the show about vines."

Ian made an impatient sound. "I didn't really come here for the one-woman show. I came because I knew you'd be here. I'm here for *you*."

Autumn didn't say anything, just stared at her ex-boyfriend for a long, long moment. Blake's blood bubbled and snapped. No. This wasn't happening. Was she considering going somewhere with him? If she did, Christ, how would he be able to stand it?

"Autumn…" Blake started, swallowing the shake in his voice. "Please."

"*Autumn. Please,*" Ian mimicked approximately eleven octaves lower than his own tone. His bravado faded somewhat as Blake bared his teeth but despite the guy taking a hasty few steps backward, the slimy fucking smile never faded. He held up his hands. "Okay Frankenstein, let's not get all fuckin' violent. You've just got to understand that novelty sex time is over. Autie and me are soulmates. Just because you slipped her some strange while we were on a break doesn't mean she actually wants to be with you."

The words were so close to what Blake had been hearing in his head for weeks, his anger spiked even higher. He could taste copper in his mouth and knew the end of his tether was approaching.

"Leave," he growled. "This is your last fucking warning."

Ian bent to the side, addressing Autumn again. "I can't believe this is the guy you fucked while I was gone. Seriously, was Chewbacca not available or something?"

"Just go away," Autumn sobbed and Blake was about to pin the man's hands behind his back and march him off when a light dawned in Ian's eyes. "Oh my god, I get it now! I fucking get it! This idiot is about your whips and chains thing, isn't it?"

"Shut up," Autumn whispered, sounding so hurt it made Blake's heart contract.

Ian sniggered, his eyes bright with malevolent glee. "It is. I fuckin' knew it *was* a novelty fuck! That's my mistake, I should have taken your whole captive thing more seriously. If you really want a Neanderthal in bed, I can—"

Blake's fist flew before he could stop it. He didn't *want* to stop it. Inflicting damage to the man who referred to himself and Autumn and sex—in the same breath—needed to suffer. Nobody touched her but him. Nobody satisfied her but him.

Blood spurted from Ian's nose like a geyser, landing on Blake's sleeve in a haphazard pattern. The rest splashed onto the sidewalk, because that's where Ian landed. On his side in the fetal position, moaning into a crooked elbow. "*Fucking hell, it's broken. He broke my fucking nose.*" He tested the bridge with a finger and howled. "Autie, Jesus, help me. It hurts."

Not really giving a shit about the writhing excuse for a man on the ground, Blake looked to Autumn and saw her staring at her ex-boyfriend in horror. "Fucking hell, Blake, what did you do that for? He doesn't have health insurance! And he could go to the cops! God knows he's a big enough sook."

She pressed her face into her hands for a moment. "You know what? Please just go. I-I don't want to see you right now."

"I can't leave you with him," he said, feeling ragged and wrung out.

Autumn shot her ex a disgusted look. "Someone needs to take him to the emergency room and stop him from suing you. You haven't left me with a choice." Frustration wrinkled her forehead. "That's twice in one night."

That was the knockout blow. In an instant, he was an outsider standing on the edges of a scene he'd written himself out of. Maybe he never should have been a part of it in the first place—maybe he'd been a fool to believe he could. Autumn stood watching him, tears poised to fall, the hurt he'd inflicted clear. She was waiting for him to leave. *Needing* it.

In the end, knowing Autumn needed something forced Blake to take one final look at her, before turning and walking away, passing a concerned and newly arrived Owen and Ryan as he went. Half of himself remained in pieces on the sidewalk, scattered in his wake. He thought he'd known loss, but he hadn't known the fucking half, had he? This was loss.

Twenty minutes later, on his way into the building, Blake was too numb to register greetings from Ross, Mrs. Zhu and Mrs. Fuller where they stood congregated near the entrance. He simply took the book out of his pocket and threw it into a green metal trash can. Then he went back inside where he belonged.

CHAPTER 16

THE EMERGENCY ROOM smelled like work—antiseptic wipes, floor cleaner, the faint tang of blood and body fluids. All that was missing was the jungle fug of animal hair and Autie would feel right at home. Except she wouldn't fucking feel like that because she was at the emergency room with her dickhead ex-boyfriend and this was the worst night of her life. If she closed her eyes she could still see Blake's expression when she called him a coward.

He shouldn't have signed me up for that show! What kind of cockhead does something like that? There were people *there. I could barely do my routine in front of him, how could he think I was ready for that?*

She thought about her Casio keyboard on the stage and shuddered.

"Are you cold?" Ian asked through the thick wad of toilet paper covering his nose. "I can give you my jacket, if you want?"

Autumn didn't reply. As they were walking to the hospital she'd explained to Ian that she was only helping him because if he bled to death on a New York sidewalk, his mother would be sad and she would feel guilty.

"Autumnnnnn…" Ian moaned, giving her pleading puppy dog eyes. "Can't you at least look at me?"

Without turning her head Autumn raised her middle finger at

him. Ian made a sulky noise and lapsed back into muteness.

Good, she thought. *Be silent, you useless prick. Haven't you done enough?*

The entire clusterfuck at the theater couldn't be pinned on Ian's deluded sense of self, but it certainly hadn't helped. His showing up reminded Autie of the movie *Gladiator*—two warriors were doing bloody battle when the emperor was like 'this is boring, I want *surprise lions*!' and released enormous man-eating beasts into the fray to liven things up. Not that Ian was a lion, more like a raccoon with a new, untreatable form of hepatitis.

Autumn wondered where Blake was, then realized she didn't need to wonder, he would have gone back to his apartment to seal himself in his safe space, to work on his books and listen to his music and drink whiskey from a smudgy glass. Once, she'd been granted passage into that beautiful place, but no more. It would be like she never existed. She hugged herself, feeling as though she'd been kicked in the chest by a mule. Blake shouldn't lock himself away from the world. He was too interesting and funny for that. Why did he have to ruin everything by signing her up for that stupid show? *Why?*

"Auts, I know you don't want to talk to me, but just let me say what's on my mind? Please?"

Ian had adopted what he undoubtedly thought was a soothing *'hey baby, everything is love, y'know?'* voice. It was even more irritating than his pout. Autumn replayed the way Blake had decked him in the face and willed the satisfaction of that memory to keep her from turning and seizing her ex-boyfriend by the throat.

He prodded her arm. "Look, *seriously*—"

Autumn snapped. She turned and began slapping him all over his body and shoulders. "Shut. The fuck. Up. You fucking.

Moron. Just shut. Up."

"Hey, whoa, hey!" Ian wriggled away from her. "I'm injured, remember?"

"Yeah, and you fucking deserve it! You shouldn't have come to the show, you shouldn't have approached me and you sure as hell shouldn't have said what you said to Blake."

"Ooh, Blake," Ian said in a mocking tone, all faux-sincerity gone. "I knew that dickhead had a crush on you. He was always staring at your ass whenever we walked past him."

A strange heat twisted through Autumn's body. After all their games, it was impossible to think about Blake watching her without getting turned on, but feeling that in front of Ian was just wrong. He was so much of her past, it felt wrong to have him in her present, where she and Blake had role played stalking and had sex in a public park.

Ian pulled the now crusty scrunch of toilet paper from his handsome face. "What the fuck do you see in that guy? You suddenly developed a beard fetish? Or was the in-house convenience too much to resist?"

Autumn ignored the sting in her chest, the urge to shove Ian and say Blake was so much more than either of those things. "You do realize I could ask you the exact same question about the women you cheated with."

Her ex-boyfriend had enough self-awareness to look embarrassed. "Christ Auts, I know I fucked up, okay? I know I was an asshole. I just got so caught up in finally having my dream—"

"Being in an improv troupe named after a Mark Wahlberg ensemble?"

Ian scowled. "Performing in New York, going to auditions, having people we *didn't* go to uni with tell me I was gonna be someone. All these girls who hang around the theatre…they think

I'm a legend and part of me knows that's bullshit, but having them treat me that way was a fucking chemical high. I got addicted to it. I kept wanting more."

Autumn rolled her eyes. Only Ian could turn a story about drilling a bunch of sexy nineteen-year-olds into a victim narrative. She edged as far away from him as the plastic seats would allow. "Just shut the fuck up, okay? I'm here because you're physically injured and every word that comes out of your mouth makes me want to physically injure you more. If you have even a smidgen of sense, you'll shut your dumb face."

"But—"

"Stop. Talking."

"Why would you come here if you didn't want to talk?" Ian leaned closer, his expression almost earnest in its delusion. "You don't mean it."

She saw red again, solid, crimson red. She whirled around and prodded him hard in the chest. "Yeah, fuck what I say, right? Why would you actually listen when I talk? Why would you take my break up seriously? That would only get in the way of you doing whatever you want, wouldn't it?"

"Autumn—"

She poked him again, right in the pectoral muscle. "You never fucking shut up, you just talk and talk and talk until I'm too tired to argue. You want to know what I saw in Blake? Someone who lets other people say things. Who knows how to listen."

Ian gave an indignant huff, then clutched his nose. "Ow! So that's the appeal then? He *listened* to you?"

"Yeah. Although he was also the best sex I've ever had. Just FYI."

It was a cheap shot but it landed. Ian's face screwed up so it resembled the toilet paper in his fist. "You were never this aggressive when we were together."

She laughed. "And yet you were still a massive toolbox. You hurt me and you didn't even care."

Ian's eyes grew wide. "I did care! I do! Life doesn't make any sense now you're gone. You're the only person I can always stand to be around. Everyone else can die in a plague resurgence for all I care."

Autumn let her head hang to the side. He was so ridiculous she could barely hold up her brain anymore. "God, you're a fucking edgelord."

"Edgelord?"

"Yeah, an edgelord. You make everything all dramatic and nihilistic because you think it makes you look deep when all it does is remind people you've got the emotional depth of a five-year-old."

Ian's upper lip curled. "Which makes you, what? A sex offender?"

Autumn was preparing to poke him again when a doctor walked briskly toward them. "Okay, what seems to be the problem here?"

The obvious answer was every-fucking-thing, but Autumn decided not to go with that. She pointed to Ian. "He's got a broken nose."

The doctor, an attractive brunette, made a sympathetic noise. "Okay, follow me."

She led them to a small, even more antiseptic-smelling room. She pointed Autie onto the faded blue armchair and guided Ian onto the narrow plastic bed.

"So," she said, tugging the toilet paper away from his face. "What happened here? You get yourself into some trouble, mister?"

Ian gave the weary smile of a brave solider who'd just been dragged in from a battlefield, sans leg. "Just a little disagreement with a very unreasonable man."

The doctor gasped. "That's awful, Mr....?"

"Ian."

She smiled. "Ian, then. If you'd like me to call the police, I certainly will. I'm so sorry this happened to you, I apologize on behalf of the entire city."

Autumn fought back a bitter laugh. Somehow she doubted the doctor would be saying that if she were treating someone other than Ian, with his sculpted torso and electric smile. If she were treating someone like Blake, for example, bearded and gruff, looking like he hadn't smiled for a million years.

That hurt to imagine. She pictured him coming in after his accident. How helpless he must have felt to be trapped inside his broken body, knowing he was facing months of rehabilitation. With a jolt, she remembered he'd discovered his fiancée was dicking someone else that same day. She couldn't even imagine how painful that news must have been. Was it really that surprising that he'd spent the next decade lost in his own world?

She remembered the way she'd called him a coward and winced. Who the fuck was she to level that accusation at him? She'd never had to endure that kind of pain, physical or mental. Sure, the stand-up attempt had been terrible, but God she just wanted to *hug* him.

Ian let out a loud catlike yowl of pain and Autumn rolled her eyes. He was always such a baby when it came to pain. The doctor was lapping it up though, swabbing him so gently she might have been dressing a baby. "Is that better?"

Ian gave another hero's grimace. "Yeah, it's fine. Just stings a little, is all."

Autumn resisted the urge to say she'd mopped up braver corgis. She figured it wouldn't be constructive. The doctor continued dabbing at Ian's face. "Say, are you an actor?"

"At times," Ian said, dropping the walking wounded act in a heartbeat. "I do improv at a local theatre."

The doctor beamed. "I knew it. You just have that kind of face. I've been trying to guess who you look like the entire time we've been in here."

Ian laughed. "What have you come up with?"

"Oh, a young Paul Newman, James Dean, Chris Pine…"

"I love Chris Pine."

The doctor blushed. "I love him, too. Where are you from? I'm so terrible with accents."

Her ex-boyfriend grinned like he'd just been named Miss Universe. "Melbourne."

"Is that in New Zealand?"

Ian cast Autie a wicked smirk she refused to return.

"No," Ian said. "It's the second biggest city in Australia. Chris Hemsworth, Hugh Jackman, Thunder from Down Under. That kind of thing."

The doctor laughed and Autumn gave a small cough that she hoped would let Ian know she thought he was a knob-skin. The only way he could be laying the accent on any thicker was if he smeared Vegimite all over his mouth. Her ex had no qualms about using their nationality to charm 'the ladies.' He had once bemoaned that the Australian lexicon didn't have a charming appellation with which to refer to women. American southerners could melt hearts with 'ma'am,' the Scots had 'lass,' the French purred 'mademoiselle,' but all they had was 'mate' or something dumb and bogan like 'sheila.' Not that it affected his pull rate, the doctor looked like she was a touch on the arm away from orgasm. She seemed to realize this herself, clearing her throat and turning to address Autie. "Are you Australian, too?"

"Yeah."

"And is this your boyfriend?"

"Yep," Ian said, before she could respond. "Autie's my soulmate."

The doctor's eyes became cartoon hearts. "Oh how lovely. And her name is Ortie? Is that German?"

Ian laughed like a merry psychopath. "No, it's short for Autumn. You know, like fall?"

"Oh Aaaaautie," the doctor said, clapping her hands. "That's so adorable. You're both adorable."

Autumn gave her a big, orange-juice commercial grin. "Thanks, doc. Hey, if you get a moment, have Captain Edge over there tell you how many times he cheated on me before I dumped him. Warning; it's somewhere between thirty and a hundred times."

The doctor looked like someone had just clubbed a baby seal. "I...um..."

Ian immediately donned his victim cloak.

"Doc," he said, his tone dripping with salty male misery. "I made a mistake, but I promise I'm making up for it. I'm not going to give up until Autie sees I'm truly sorr—"

"Yeah, cool story, bro," Autumn interrupted. "Here's the thing, it's not even the cheating that makes you the shittest person on earth. There are worse things you can do to someone you love than rub your genitals on a teenager and lie about it."

Both Ian and the doc looked genuinely surprised.

"Like what?" he asked.

Autie tapped her chin in mock thoughtfulness. "Um, try

ignoring me, never encouraging me to pursue my dreams, dragging me to New York and leaving me at home every night unless I wanted to come to a club and watch you do dumb shit for no money—"

"Autie's obsessed with money," Ian said in a loud, conspiratorial whisper.

Autumn stood up, pushing back the arm chair. "Fuck off! I'm not *obsessed* with money, I just know that it matters, unlike some entitled assholes who've never worked more than a five-hour bar shift in their lives."

"I've worked longer hours than that!"

"In plays. About pubescent choirboys cutting their own dicks off."

"You never understood that was a metaphor!"

"I understood that it was fucking weird!"

Autumn could see the doctor's eyes going from her to Ian as though watching a ping-pong match. She knew she was embarrassing herself, but she was too angry to care. Blake was gone, her whole life was a smoldering garbage fire and it was all Ian's fault. He'd brought her to New York, the land of anti-dreams. If she'd just stayed at home and been exactly who everyone wanted her to be, this never would have happened. "You know what, Ian? You're a trashbag."

"Very mature." Ian turned to the doctor. "She's fucking our landlord. He's the one who decked me in the face."

The doctor gasped.

"You-you f-fucking asked for it," Autumn said, literally spluttering with rage. "And he's not your landlord, anymore, because you don't live with me."

"You're right, I live in an artist's residence where I *belong*."

"Yeah, you definitely belong in someone's asbestos lined

basement."

"Okay, that's enough, you two!"

Both she and Ian fell silent. The doctor put aside her bloodied swabs. "Ian, we're going to need to do a CAT scan of your face to make sure there's no loose bone fragments. There shouldn't be any problems, though, it was only a minor fracture."

"Cool," Ian said.

"So I can go?" Autie asked.

The doctor walked over to the small sink and pumped hand sanitizer into her palm. "You can, but first I'm going to give you guys a moment to talk. You seem like you need it."

"We don't," she and Ian said at once.

The doctor smiled. "Whatever happened between you two, it's clear you guys have a lot of history and as my mom used to say, 'never leave angry.' I'll just be five minutes and then you can go, Autie."

She swept out of the room, smiling to herself. It was pretty awkward without her there. Ian wouldn't look at her and she had no idea what to say. He felt like a stranger to her, like they hadn't spent years living in each other's pockets. So strange how life could flow that way, turn someone you once loved into your nemesis. Autumn could only remember affectionate facts about him, not feelings. She couldn't recall what it was like to look at this man with his handsome face and his evil smile and not want to leave the room. Especially not now that she'd met Blake and learned what it was to be cherished. Ian had never cherished her, but maybe that wasn't his fault. He wasn't the kind of guy who knew how to cherish, just like he'd probably never be able to make a monogamous commitment. Things had ended badly, but maybe she should be glad. At least it had happened before they had kids, or did something equally impossible to take back.

"So…" she said. "Good thing your face isn't all messed up? Acting-wise."

"Yeah."

There was a short pause.

"We're never getting back together, are we?" Ian said.

Autumn dropped her ass back into the guest chair. "No, Taylor Swift, we're not, and if you'd paid any attention to me when I was turfing your ass out, you'd know that. But you chose to not take me seriously and think you could come running back whenever you wanted."

Ian ran a hand through his carefully cropped hair. "That's fair, I guess. I just…I miss you."

Autumn was very proud of herself for not saying 'tough titties.' "You don't get to miss me after what you did. Or I guess you do, but I am under no obligation to give a shit."

Ian rolled his eyes. "I know."

"Do you? Because you shouldn't have sent me that dick pic and you definitely shouldn't have showed up at Essence. How did you even know I was there?"

"That gay dude tagged you in the photo. When I saw you were with your landlord I just kind of…lost it." He looked up at her, his blue eyes made even bluer by the redness of his nose. "So many people texted me after that stupid picture of you two hugging made the rounds. Everyone thought you were cheating on me. Do you know how humiliating that was?"

Autumn took a deep breath, willing her good temper to hold. "I don't want to lose my shit at you again, but seriously, use your head. How do you think *I* felt when I found out you were actually cheating on me *while we were still fucking living together?*"

"That was different!" Ian said, with predictable hypocrisy. "None of those girls meant anything. This, you and our fuckin' landlord, it means something, I can tell."

His words thumped down on a space inside her that was already aching.

"It's complicated," she said, because that was what she'd been saying from the start. "You wouldn't understand."

Ian snorted. "Yeah okay, only I've never seen you look at anyone the way you looked at him, but sure."

Autie didn't reply, couldn't reply. It was too big, too much to process on a night when so many things had happened. All she'd wanted to do was be with Blake in his bed again, delay the reality of her future for at least a few more hours. How had she wound up here, rehashing her life with her ex?

Ian drummed his fingers on his thigh. "Since we've got at least four more minutes and I'm bored, I'm gonna ask—what's the deal with you and The Landlord? You guys a couple now?"

She looked up at him. "Are you for real?"

He gave her the cocky shrug that once set her heart a-flutter. "Why not? There's nothing else to talk about."

Autumn shook her head. "You're a knob, but we're not a couple, we've just been dating."

"Seriously dating?"

Autumn thought back to all she and Blake had done together, the experiences they'd shared, how she'd peeled back his layers, found he was so different from anyone she'd ever known before. It was all so, so complicated. "I don't know. It's been weird. Good and new and scary and…weird."

"Jesus, you like him. You really fucking like him." He grinned at her. "Shame he signed you up for that show. That was dumb."

Autumn rubbed a hand over her forehead. "Yeah, it was."

"Not very tactful. Disrespectful to your feelings, even."

"Yeah, you can shut up now."

Ian did so, though he started whistling 'Everybody Hurts' by REM. Autumn ignored him. The doc would be back soon and then she could leave, head back to her stupid apartment and take a shower. Maybe there was an injured pigeon she could pick up on the way home. Take care of it and make herself at least the smallest bit useful again. Or would Blake chuck her out for doing that, now they were through? Seemed likely. He would revert back to his old self, maybe become even grumpier. That was it, she would have to put in her notice at Happy Paws and go back to Melbourne with her tail between her legs. A perfectly tragic fairytale. Like if Belle stayed in her hometown and read the same nine books and took care of her nutbag dad forever.

"I knew you wanted to do comedy."

Ian's voice came in loud and clear, but Autumn still couldn't believe she'd heard him right. "Huh?"

He scratched the side of his neck. "I, uh, knew you wanted to be a comedian."

"No you didn't."

"I did. I read your notebook, you know, the one with the stars on the cover."

Autumn's belly clenched. God, just when you thought you had truly suffered enough, life hit you in the head again. "You fucking suck, Ian!"

He shrugged. "Sorry. I just wanted to know what you were always working on. I knew it wasn't a beat poem."

Autumn shook her head. "Fucking unbelievable. Why didn't you say anything?"

Her ex looked out of the darkened window, still scratching his neck. "I don't know."

"Oh, sick. Wonderful. Glad you brought it up then."

"I was jealous or something," he burst out. "It was good, what you'd done. Not great, but good."

Her mouth fell open. "You're serious?"

Ian looked more uncomfortable than she'd ever seen him, his shoulders hunched and his mouth turned down. "Kind of. You know I find it hard to write my own stuff. I take workshops, I spend hours going over the same jokes and then I open up my girlfriend's notebook and she's better at it than I am."

Autumn could barely process what she was hearing. It had been insult enough that another guy she'd fucked had taken liberties with her private comedy work, let alone that both of them thought it was *good*. She'd appreciated Blake's enthusiasm and believed him when he said it. Ian, her ex-boyfriend that she'd just permanently rejected, was under no obligations to tell her that her jokes were good. In fact, he looked bitter as lemons about it. "Are you taking the piss?"

Ian screwed up his eyebrows, turning his lips down at the corners. He was good at that. He could tell entire sonnets with his rubbery face. The crux of this one was *'fuck you, yes I mean it. You're funny.'*

"Okay, so, you think I'm good." Autumn grinned. "You think I'm good at comedy."

"Don't get smug."

"Why, because it'll distract from you?"

He smiled and just like that, they were caught in a very bittersweet moment. In her ex's smile, Autumn could see both the man she once loved and the man she didn't know at all, but that didn't matter. They were all just…Ian. Scheming, clever, handsome asshole Ian. She'd already known they were over, but in that instant, it became canon.

"You don't have to worry about writing your own stuff," she

said. "You're an actor, you've got great timing. Other people'll write the lines."

"That's not the same. I want to be the creative genius. It's unfair you get to have that, too. You're already a vet..." Ian made a face. "Anyway, forget all that shit. I just wanted to say The Landlord was definitely a cock to sign you up for a fucking live show, but maybe he was just...you know...maybe he had your best interests..." Ian began to cough violently, blood spraying from his ruptured nose.

"Jesus, is being nice actually killing you?" Autumn got up and filled a paper cup with sink water. "Here."

Ian accepted the cup, downing the entire thing. "Thanks."

"No problem," Autumn said, and meant it.

He thinks I'm good at comedy, too.

The thought was a hot glow in her chest, a glow that faded when she remembered that Blake was gone and her future in America was over. A moment of pleasure to give the stupid darkness more depth.

The doctor came back into the room and beamed at them, clearly happy they were standing so close together. "Worked things out, I see?"

Autumn looked at her ex. "Yeah...I guess."

"As much as we could," Ian agreed. "But you've gotta go, right, Autie?"

"I do," she said gratefully. "So, uh, good luck? With your nose? And your life?"

"Thanks." Ian contorted his rubber face into a hammy glare. "Here's looking at you, kid."

Autumn smiled. "I told you, you'd be great at other people's lines. See you later."

She walked out of the emergency room feeling far less shitty than when she'd walked in, which was saying something. She paid for Ian's visit at the front counter. It was only a couple hundred bucks and it felt like a parting gift to the man who used to mean so much to her. Plus, she was still pretty happy Blake had broken his face, which made her feel guilty.

She returned to her building in a daze and walked past Blake's door. She couldn't bring herself to knock but she did press and ear to the wood and listen for signs of life. There was nothing, and though she couldn't prove it, she'd have bet money he wasn't in. Feeling decidedly empty, she continued to the elevator and went up to her floor.

Her apartment was exactly the way she'd left it, everything poised in their neat and orderly positions, as though everything was normal. That would have to change. Autumn kicked off her shoes, knowing she should go to bed and knowing it wasn't going to happen. She cracked open a can of off-brand energy drink and was contemplating what things to toss around the room when there was a knock at her front door. Her heart stopped. Surely it wasn't...could it be?

She ran a hand through her unwieldly hair and wet her lips before racing to the door and yanking it open to find...various people from her building. "Uh, hey...dudes...?"

"Hey, Autumn," said Ross, the perpetually stoned guy from downstairs. "What's going on?"

"Uh, nothing, though that might be because it's one in the morning." She took in the rest of the group who were all staring at her in a very horror-movie fashion. "If you guys are forming a committee or something I'd be happy to hear about it, but, like, in the morning or maybe via email?"

"It's not about our committee, though I will be filling you in on our petition to have Mr. Munroe provide us with a new hot water system," said a sharp blonde woman Autie thought might have been called Mrs. Fuller. "Right now we're all here to talk to you about Mr. Munroe, himself."

There was a general jostling of agreement.

Oh fucking hell. In spite of the fact that she'd just drunk half a can of guarana flavoured crack, Autumn was suddenly so, so tired. They knew about her and Blake and were probably here to complain about their inappropriate building relationship and demand to see the receipts from her rent payments to make sure she wasn't getting a better deal in exchange for her pussy. "Guys, I really don't want to talk about—"

"You need to stay with him," Mrs. Fuller said. "You're not *allowed* to break up."

Vigorous nods from all of the nine or so residents outside her door.

Autumn gripped the sides of her head. "What the fuck is happening? Am I dreaming?"

"No," said Mrs. Zhu. "You and Blake should be together because—"

"What she's trying to say," interrupted Mrs. Fuller. "Is that we've noticed ever since you and Blake started...*dating*, he's a whole new man. He's agreeable, he's friendly, well *friendlier*. He even smiled at one of my boys. *Andrew*'s been terrified of him since he was a baby and I can't tell you how good it's been for his self-esteem to know—"

"You need to keep, like, brightening his life, Autumn," Ross urged. "Not only because he doesn't scare kids anymore but because we all know he's a cool guy and he was like, drowning in loneliness before you showed up. It's sad, man."

Another murmur of agreement.

Autumn rubbed her face. "Okay, um, thanks guys. Maybe.

But the problem is Blake and I *are* over."

"How?" Mrs. Fuller demanded. "Why?"

"He, uh, signed me up for a comedy night without me knowing and when I got mad at him, he tried to be all like, 'seize the day Autumn, my shitty surprise is totally helpful!' and then he punched my ex in the face—"

"Ian?" Mrs. Zhu asked. "I thought he was an asshole?"

"He is, but, you know, violence is never the answer. And more importantly..." She swallowed hard. "Blake doesn't actually like me, you guys, I think I was just some weird project for him. Some way to make up for his past."

It hurt, saying it out loud, but that was the thought that had terrified her most since leaving Essence. Hell, since Blake had shown an interest in her in the first place. She'd benefitted so much from his particular brand of tough love, but she'd never wanted to be his mission, she wanted to be his—

"That's not true," said the sharp blond. "We've seen you two together. He's a new man."

"That doesn't mean anything."

"Well then what about this?" Ross knelt before her, holding up a book as though he were a squire offering a knight a sword.

Autumn stared at him. "Umm..."

"What the fuck are you doing, Ross?" Mrs. Fuller grabbed the book and handed it to Autumn. "We found this outside. We think it's for you."

Autumn turned it over and all the air rushed out of her lungs. "This is...how did you...?"

"We think he repaired it for you," Mrs. Fuller said. "Does it have any kind of significance?"

"It's a first edition," Autie breathed. "It's my old...it's my *favorite...*"

The entire group beamed at her. Clearly thrilled. Autumn traced a hand over the book's cover. How had he known? And when he'd known, how had he found this? She knew he had money and connections but this would have required so much work.

"Open it," Ross said. "There's something written on the inside cover."

With her heart in her mouth, Autumn did just that and when she read that one word, tears filled her eyes. It was a simple message, befitting an uncomplicated man, but it also said everything.

Stay, he'd written.

Just, *Stay*.

"Oh, Blake," she whispered. "Love didn't exactly run right for us, did it?"

"So like, do you love it?" Ross enquired. "Do you want to like, be his twin flame now?"

Autumn wiped her eyes. "Yes. I don't know, that sounds kind of fucking silly, but I do have to go and see him."

The group shifted uncomfortably in front of her, all of them avoiding her eyes.

"What?"

Ross gave a mournful sigh. "Blake's not here. I saw him come back tonight. I was the one who got the book out of the trash—"

"It was in the *bin*?" Autumn looked down at the book in horror. "This is so fuckin' valuable. Tell me he didn't throw it in the fuckin' bin?"

"He did," Ross said earnestly. "I saw him and I got it out. Then I rolled him a joint—thought it might help, you know—and then I gave it to him and tried to talk about you and he was all 'does everyone in the building know about me and Autumn?'

and I was like 'yes' and then *he* was like 'I hate all of you, you're all evicted, this is the worst night of my life, Autumn's going back to Australia, blah, blah, blah', then he threw the joint at me and left."

"Like I *told you he would*," Mrs. Fuller said huffily. "Who knows where he is now, probably drinking himself into oblivion somewhere. *Very* unsafe. He's a sensitive man and he's gone through a lot. You really shouldn't have tried to discuss Autumn with him, Ross."

"I know," the stoner said, looking chagrined. "I'm sorry."

"So, how do we find him?" Autumn said, feeling desperate. "Does anyone know where he hangs out when he's not at home? Has anyone called him?"

"He's not answering," Mrs. Zhu said, offering Autumn some green apple candy, which she took and crammed into her mouth. "Thanks."

"Anytime. But we have no idea where he goes. Until he started dating you, none of us ever saw him leave the building."

Autie winced. As much as she wanted to launch a city-wide search for Blake, she knew she was going to be no help. She barely knew the streets and she had work tomorrow. Owen had already requested a day off to spend his anniversary with Ryan. If she skipped her shift, Happy Paws would fall into utter chaos and she could be fired. Once, that might have struck her as a good thing, a way to get out of making a decision about her future, but now...

She looked down at the book, at the word, *Stay*. The man who had given her this cared for her more than anyone ever had or he wouldn't have done it. She had to trust the word he'd written, she had to stay and believe that he would return. And if he returned, it would be good to be gainfully employed. The job market in New York was fucking crazy.

"Thank you, guys," she told the not-quite-strangers at her door. "Thank you so much."

"You won't leave?" Mrs. Fuller pressed. "You won't go running away once our backs are turned?"

Autumn smiled. "No. I promise I'll stay."

CHAPTER 17

B LAKE STEPPED OFF the A train into the pitch black of Rockaway Beach. The only other soul on the subway platform was the weary conductor who'd ambled off, presumably to take a leak or get something to eat before turning the train back around toward Manhattan. The fact that he'd just gotten off on the dead last stop was symbolic as a son of a bitch, but he was in no mood to appreciate irony.

What the hell was he doing here? He hadn't been back to his old neighborhood since collecting his things from the apartment he'd shared with his fiancée. But he'd been poised to go stark raving mad waiting for Autumn to return to the building. It was either search her out and make a fool of himself—again—or get the hell out and collect his fucking head.

So he'd ended up here, the only other place besides Gramercy he'd ever called home; the northernmost tip of Queens. Stepping out of the station, he saw how much had changed since his early twenties. Commercial franchises had made their way into little spots, in between the Korean market, Rogoff toy store and the Tobacconist. Ciro's pizza shop still stood at the end of the block, toward the beach of 116th Street. Same awning, if he wasn't mistaken, but it was right next to a brand new Wendy's. All the same places he'd frequented in his youth with pops of modernisms to prop them up.

Listening to the Atlantic break in the distance, Blake walked up the silent street, not really sure where he was headed. He only knew Autumn had accused him of using her to get over his own past. It wasn't true. Hell, he was sick in love with the girl and frankly, there was a significant part of him that was annoyed she hadn't picked up on it, ridiculous as that sounded. When they'd started seeing each other, he'd been a certified hermit that could barely string two sentences together, though. Now he was a man who attended fucking variety shows and spooned in public places and ordered silly drinks from bars just to see her smile. There wasn't a soul on earth he would do those things for besides Autumn.

Where had he gone wrong? Because he most definitely *had* screwed the pooch—and not just in registering her to perform stand-up in front of a crowd.

Blake thought back to the other times he'd failed to see one hill of the landscape when it came to women; when his mother wanted to open a spa with her friends and when his fiancée cheated. He didn't want to relate either of those situations to Autumn, though, because this heartbreak was so much more severe. So he trudged up to the deserted boardwalk and kept walking, hoping the answer would come to him while he stared out over the breaking whitecaps of the ocean.

Yeah. His past might have played a part in wanting to help Autumn recover from her break up. He'd watched this glorious little ball of sunshine bounce up and down the hallway for months and couldn't stand that glow dimming down for even a second. Not that Blake had ever glowed in *any* sense of the word, but he was the product of a dimming down, to be sure. The same thing happening to Autumn had been unacceptable. He'd pushed so hard, though. Had he thrown himself so completely into her recovery, he'd failed to see his own was needed?

Blake pushed off the metal rail and started walking again. He passed some kids sharing a joint on the bench, waving a hand to let them know he couldn't give less of a shit. They reminded him of his friends. How they would sneak up to the boardwalk to do all manner of nefarious activities while their parents slept. The couples made out on the sand, while everyone pretended not to look. Beers inside paper bags were passed around. Initials were scrawled on the surface of the closest lifeguard tower.

Maybe it was the reminiscing that brought Blake to Kevin Donahue's house. At least, Blake assumed the two-family, red brick house with union stickers in the ground floor window still belonged to Kevin. It was entirely possible he'd moved now that he was raising four daughters. When Kevin visited him in the city all those weeks ago, though, he'd told him the block party would be here, the same place it always was.

"What are you doing?" Blake muttered, turning back in the direction of the boardwalk. Would it just be the icing on this shit cake of a day to get arrested for loitering outside of a house where four underage girls resided? Seriously, what was he doing in Rockaway in the early morning hours before the block party? Was he actually planning on showing his face?

It wouldn't fix what he'd broken with Autumn, it wouldn't bring her back to him or stop her from going back to Australia. For all he knew, she'd decided to give her relationship with Ian another try.

Misery lanced his chest as his strides ate up the sidewalk. He flexed his bruised knuckles thinking of how satisfying it had been to deck the little asshole, but how the satisfaction had faded so fast. Too fast, until all that remained was the loss of her. Fuck, his skull hurt thinking about it. Just hours ago, he'd been the man who had the privilege of escorting her places, tucking her into his arms at night, kissing her, reading her comedy notebook. Now he was left with nothing but questions. If he had a chance in hell of winning her back, where did he even begin sorting through his past to find the source of what had caused him to drive her away?

"Hey." A screen door slapped behind him. "I'm calling the cops."

At the sound of Elaine O'Leary—now Donahue's—voice, Blake turned and found Kevin's wife under the harsh glow of the porch light, elbow propped on hip, cigarette in a limp right hand. Same pose she'd stood in since they were kids. Same stoop, too. They'd probably only changed the light bulb twice since the last time he'd seen her there. Not so much time after all. A warm skitter of nostalgia went through him. "Elaine."

She went still, then jerked into motion, stubbing her smoke out on the brick wall. "Don't even fucking play with me right now. Blake Munroe?" Her steps were quick, yet hesitant down the steps. "If that's you, I'm going to kick your ass."

Blake sighed before stepping into the glare of the streetlight. "It's me."

Elaine ran back up the steps and smacked the wooden edge of the screen door. "*Kevin!*" She jerked a thumb over her shoulder as she descended the steps a second time. "He's inside watching American Pickers. Get over here and give me a hug, you big asshole. I haven't seen you in ten years."

On the rare occasions he'd actually allowed himself to envision a reunion between himself and the people he'd grown up with, there had been awkwardness, stiff greetings and maybe an accusation or two. Apparently he'd been wrong to make those assumptions, because Elaine Donahue launched herself into his arms and rubbed his back in circles…and against all odds, Blake was comforted.

He'd come here to be comforted.

Unbelievable. His intention might have been to heal Autumn, but she'd been the one to heal him. An awful scab with layers of Band-Aids had lived inside him for a long time, but her spirit and optimism had made this hug possible—made it possible for him to accept and need it. If only he'd known while it was happening.

"I'm so glad you're here," Elaine whispered, stepping back. "What took you so long?"

The answer was Autumn, but Blake didn't know how to say that out loud without wanting to die, so he swallowed.

"You're a little early for the block party," Kevin called from the stoop. "You're lucky we've already got the beer on ice."

"Come on in and we'll crack one open." Elaine slung her arm through the crook of his elbow, pulling him forward. "There's shit that needs to be said, but we don't have to say none of it tonight, if you don't want to."

Kevin greeted him at the door with a slap on the back. "B-Money."

Obviously still recovering from the surprise of seeing him there, Kevin stepped back, gesturing awkwardly to the cluttered hallway, which was lined with dozens of mounted jackets. "You always knew how to catch everyone off guard."

"I didn't know I was coming," Blake said, his voice like rusted metal. "I'm not even sure why I'm here."

"You fucking missed us, that's why." Elaine took his jacket and hung it beside a collection of matching pink raincoats. "Come in. Sit. Sit. Tell us what's new. Kevin said you have a girlfriend."

Kevin hissed at his wife, slashing a hand across his neck. "You don't bring those things up until after the first beer."

"Don't tell me how to talk," she breezed, guiding Blake into the living room and pushing him down into a brown, leather recliner. The living room was different than when Kevin's parents owned the house. The wallpaper had been stripped, replaced with sheetrock and painted a tasteful blue. Family photos adorned the walls in white frames. Shoes. There were shoes everywhere, all clearly belonging to girls. The television flickered in the dark room, lighting up the room and darkening it at will. Two cats peeked out at him from beneath the staircase, making him think of Autumn's animal patients and twisting the knife in his ribs.

"Blake." Elaine sat down across from him on the L-shaped couch, leaning forward and clasping both hands between her knees. "I just found you outside our house at midnight. Not that I'm not freaking over the moon to see you, but you gotta give me something." She flicked a look at Kevin, who was in the process of handing each of them an opened bottle of Bud Light. "I'm afraid to apologize. I'm afraid to say anything in case you leave again."

"I think I'm the one who should apologize," Blake said and miracle of miracles, a joint seemed to loosen inside him. He'd spent all this time angry, thinking he was owed an apology and when it came down to it, he didn't even want one. Maybe he'd spent a decade getting angrier and angrier at himself for not being able to cope with his own mistakes. Staying away from his friends so long had definitely been wrong. He could feel it as he sat across from them. If Blake was being honest, his missteps had been obvious when Kevin showed up at the building weeks ago. Autumn was the reason he could acknowledge that now and not throw the world into a tailspin. Losing her was the only thing that could do that. "Yes, I'm…sorry. Staying away this long was selfish of me. It turns out I'm a selfish man."

Both Elaine and Kevin drained half of their beers, avoiding his eyes.

"I want things done on my own timeline," Blake continued. "And I don't stop to consider that I could be wrong. I don't talk…" Thinking of Autumn's face when they called her name onto the stage, prickly energy rippled at his skin. "I don't talk or ask questions. I just do. Just make decisions without a conversation."

"Like cutting us off and disappearing without letting us explain our side?" Elaine reached out and squeezed his knee. "You were in the right, Blake. You should have been mad at us. We weren't good friends. We should have told you what Jodie was doing."

"I think we were hoping it was a phase." Kevin shrugged. "That she would snap out of it before any damage was done. And we could just keep things the way they were. The prospect of change was too scary."

"Nothing stays the same, though, does it? No matter how hard you try." Elaine leaned back against the couch cushions. "Most of the group are still living in the same place, but we barely have time to wave at each other in Stop & Shop. When we get together, it's a rush to fill each other in and details slip away. That old feeling slips away, no matter how hard you try to cling to it. But once in a while there are moments. Someone says an old joke or calls you by a nickname and you remember why you make an effort to stay in touch. We're all made of memories, but we can't remember them all on our own."

Kevin laid a hand on Elaine's thigh in absent gesture. "She turns into a philosopher after one drink, this one." Elaine punched him in the shoulder, but he only gave a fleeting smile.

"You, uh…you're part of our memories, man. Your parents' old house is down the block. It's impossible not to think of you every time I drive past it."

"Me too. Makes me think of how one hard phone call could have made you stay. And that much Catholic guilt isn't healthy." Elaine's laughter was hesitant. "Jodie's going to be at the block party tomorrow. She's my friend, Blake. She's all of our friends. What she did was wrong, but we still love her like we love you."

"I'm glad," Blake said and meant it. "I'm glad you all still have each other. I hope she's happy, too." He paused, letting the past merge with the present. "Maybe if I hadn't been injured, I would have been able to get past the lying, but I was low, already. Knowing I'd been walking around blind made it so much worse. That's on me, though."

Elaine blew out a breath. "It's weird to think of what could have been. If the explosion never happened and you'd stayed. If you'd been here all along…"

"I never would have met Autumn." Blake said the words automatically, and his heart climbed into his throat. "She definitely would have been better off. Not me, though. I'm better for having known her, even if it was for too short a while."

"This is the girlfriend?" Elaine rubbed her hands together. "Now we're getting to the good stuff."

Blake raised an eyebrow. "My decade of angst wasn't the good stuff? Tough crowd."

"Look at you, laughing at yourself." Kevin tapped the necks of their beer bottles together. "Back in Rockaway for an hour and you're already getting your sense of humor back."

"Did I ever have a sense of humor?"

Elaine hummed. "Sometimes…it was kind of weird. But it counted."

Blake smiled, even though it hurt. "Right."

"That day I saw you in Manhattan—"

"What?" Elaine snacked Kevin in the chest. "You didn't tell me about this."

"It was man to man stuff," Kevin shot back.

"Oh fuck off." She waved at her husband, looking disgusted. "Continue."

"Thank you," Kevin said, not without a truckload of sarcasm. "When I saw you in Manhattan, there was a girl in the hallway. Blonde, about yay high." He gestured to his shoulder. "That's Autumn?"

"Yeah." Holy shit, talking about her with these people who used to know him better than anyone...even just broaching the subject was cathartic. If someone had warned him a couple months ago that locking himself away was bad for his well being, he would have scoffed. Now he knew it was true. He'd needed his people. He had...people. "Yeah, that was her. I beat up her ex-boyfriend tonight."

Elaine whooped. "Atta boy."

"She left with him."

Kevin winced. "Ohhh boy."

"Yeah." Blake massaged the bridge of his nose, marveling over the fact that he'd sunk so deep into jealousy over Ian it felt like an extension of him, just sitting on his shoulder like a hundred-pound tumor.

"I was never like this over Jodie. I realize now that the anger was at me for not seeing it coming. What she did. And I'm back in that place right now—just fucking angry at myself. But the consequences are worse. Much worse. She's...it for me." Blake exhaled, then filled them in on what he'd done at the variety show, volunteering Autumn without consulting her first. "No surprise to anyone, I did things on my own timeline. I didn't…"

"Communicate with her." Elaine waited, but Blake wasn't sure for what. "Ask her what she was thinking. What she wanted."

Blake frowned. "No."

"Why not?"

"What if she told me she wanted something—"

"That wasn't convenient for you?"

"Yes," Blake returned sharply. "What if she never realized how strong she was? What if she never got on a stage and lived her dream? That might have sent her back to Australia. I needed her to stay. *I* needed…" Blake stared down at his beer. "Fuck."

Elaine made a big show of crossing her legs. "I bill by the hour."

Kevin snorted. "She only knows the answers because I do the same thing. I forget to look her in the eye and ask what she's thinking."

"It's easy to do when your head is up your ass." Elaine chuckled. "Ah, I'm guilty of it myself. We don't want to hear what we don't want to hear. It's human nature."

"I decided what she needed." Blake set down his beer. If he drank another drop, he was going to be sick. Sicker than he already was, which was saying something. Where was Autumn now? Did she hate him? "Kind of wishing I'd taken the train here yesterday."

Elaine stood and leaned down to give Blake a hug. "Give her some time to cool off, then go apologize. And for the love of God, *listen* to her. That's an order."

When Elaine straightened, Kevin put an arm around her shoulders. "So this is it, huh? You're done making us feel like shit?"

Blake looked around the room, wishing he was in bed with Autumn, smelling her hair as sleep hit him...while at the same time, feeling pretty damn lucky to still have his friends. "I guess I have no choice, since I need to sleep on your couch."

※

IT TOOK BLAKE hours to finally fall asleep and when he did, he woke up to an earthquake. Although he hadn't experienced very many of them, he couldn't recall squealing being a part of the scenario. A sharp object gouged him in the stomach and he jackknifed on the couch, toppling a...*child* onto her back?

"Who are you?" Another little girl screeched, holding a throw pillow at the ready to bash him in the face. "*Dad!*"

The pillow connected and Blake saw stars.

"Hold on now..." He shook his head, trying to clear the cobwebs from his brain. "I'm a friend of your parents."

"Nope." Another girl—bigger than the others—tapped her foot. "We know all their friends. You're, like, a vagrant or something. *Mom!*"

"If I'm a vagrant, you shouldn't be engaging with me."

Another pillow was swung at his head, but he ducked in time to avoid it. "*Kevin!*"

Laughter trailed down the stairs, revealing his old friends, dressed in their bathrobes. "Girls," Elaine said, wiping tears from her eyes. "You were trained better than this. Why aren't you waterboarding him?"

Kevin reached one of the girls and swung her up onto his shoulder. "Ladies Donahue, meet your Uncle Blake. He's a crabby piece of work, but for some reason, we put up with him."

Elaine winked at Blake. "You'll be seeing him around more often. So let's feed him and make him feel at home."

Just like that, he went from enemy of the state to object of curiosity. Blake wasn't allowed to get up from the couch until he'd answered several questions from each girl about his place of residence, his favorite foods and what he wanted to be when he grew up. In order from oldest to youngest, they wanted to be a dolphin trainer, a Kindergarten teacher, a YouTube star and a bow maker. By the time he was allowed to get up and enter the kitchen, both cats were asleep on his lap and he couldn't get up anyway, so Elaine handed him a bowl of cereal over her daughters' heads while they all settled in to watch something on the Disney Chanel called Descendants. Within the hour, he found himself settling disputes about which girl got to recite which characters' lines and weighing in on which of the male leads was cuter.

Blake looked up to find Elaine and Kevin smiling at him from the doorway. He rolled his eyes, but couldn't help but acknowledge he'd done the right thing coming to Rockaway last night. How long had he needed this sense of home without realizing? There were loose ends inside him that were connecting and growing solid…even as his heart remained in tatters.

Had he figured out how to offload his baggage too late to fix things with Autumn? God, even having a speck of hope was miles from the state of ruin he'd been in last night. After the block party, he would go home and knock on her door. If she refused to open the door, he'd let the whole building know he was in love with her. Whatever the consequences of that were, he would accept them, even if she didn't love him back.

It was unbelievable how long it took to get a house of seven people ready just to go outside. Hours of crying and bargaining and rejecting of clothes, Kevin, Elaine, Blake and the four girls walked outside to help their neighbors set up for the block party.

Same as always, the set up amounted to mismatched folding chairs, a bouncy castle and a couple of rolling barbeques. The block began to fill out and by noon, every house had emptied into the street. Music pumped from multiple sources—some traditional Irish, some Journey and Bob Seger—and hoards of children tore through the crowds like packs of wild dogs. Blake found himself concerned when the Ladies Donahue were out of sight, but Elaine told him to relax, that the girls had hundreds of babysitters looking out for them.

Blake ran into several people he'd grown up with, all equally shocked to see him in the neighborhood. He really did want to focus on what they were saying to him, but his mind continued to drift back to Autumn. He didn't want to be rude, but an anxiousness churned inside him, urging him to get back to Manhattan and repair the rift he'd created between them. After talking to Elaine and Kevin, he wanted to look her in the eye and beg for her thoughts.

What did she want?

Would she let him help get it for her?

Would she stay?

A tap on the shoulder distracted Blake from his thoughts. And he turned around to find his ex-fiancée staring back at him in shock. Blake waited for...something to happen inside of him. A kick of the nostalgia he couldn't seem to stop experiencing since getting off the A train. Sadness or anger or regret over how he'd handled the situation. But as he looked back at the redhead who'd softened into maturity and finally embraced her ample height with heeled sandals, the strangest thing happened. Blake found himself laughing.

He laughed, because they'd been kids who'd made mistakes. Because they were adults now and there were bigger, scarier things in the world than their break up. Because he'd wasted time being angry and thinking himself superior when the easy way out of that shitty pit of quicksand was to just leave it behind.

"Jodie," he said with a nod. "You look great. How are you?"

She sputtered, but recovered fast. "I'm well. I just...never expected to see you here. How...?"

The answer to how he'd gotten there was too long—and he couldn't bring himself to talk about Autumn, so he went with simple. "I just got on a train." A little girl ran up and clung to Jodie's leg, the strawberry of her hair giving away their relationship at once.

"Is she yours?" Blake asked.

"Yes," Jodie said, with a slight unevenness to her voice. "This is Brianna."

"Dad is getting me a hot dog!"

"Ooh. Yum." Jodie smoothed a hand over the little girl's hair, while still looking right at him. "It's not...it's not the same guy. I'm not sure why I'm mentioning that, except I don't want you to feel uncomfortable."

A punch of surprise caught Blake in the gut. He'd always assumed Jodie had married the doctor, but she hadn't. She'd had a child with someone else. He wasn't sure how to feel about that—but there was regret in him. Regret that he hadn't been more sensitive to Jodie, despite the fact that she'd been unfaithful. In her early twenties she'd been with no one but him. If he'd been easier to talk to, maybe she would have told him marriage was too much, too soon, especially when she hadn't explored yet. So many pitfalls in his life could have been avoided just by asking questions. Communicating. He didn't intend to make that same mistake again.

Please God, just let his little Australian give him another shot.

"What about you?" Jodie asked, seeming more comfortable now that Blake hadn't hung a scarlet letter around her neck and openly mocked her. "Is there a girl?"

"Yes." His throat grew tight. "I wish she could have made it."

Jodie pressed her lips together, her eyes bright. "I'm sorry, Blake," she whispered. "No hard feelings?"

He shook his head. "None."

Blake watched Jodie carry her daughter toward a man and accept a hot dog from the three he was carrying, the three of them looking happy. Content. For the first time in his life, Blake could see himself in their position. An arm around Autumn's shoulder while one of them fed a child. A tall, moody one, or a funny blonde with hazel green eyes.

Did Autumn want that some day?

He'd have to ask her.

Blake was jostled from his thoughts when the cell phone in his pocket buzzed. His mouth went dry when he saw the caller ID. Autumn.

"Hey, Fun-Size," he answered, dying to hear her voice. But it wasn't Autumn's that spoke, it was an unfamiliar man who sounded stressed as he tried to yell over the sounds of traffic and sirens. *"Hello, sir…?"*

"Autumn," Blake shouted into the phone, his lungs seizing.

"Sir, there has been an accident. I was told to call you…"

Blake was demanding Kevin's car keys before the man even finished his sentence, sprinting to the vehicle parked one street over in deference to the block party. What he'd just heard was a roar in his head.

No, no. Please don't take her away from me. I've just figured out how to do this right.

CHAPTER 18

THE TEXT CAME at four in the morning. Autumn was awake to hear it arrive. She was lying on her back dreading the shift that was due to begin in a few hours, knowing her eyes would throb and her head would be puffy and stupid. The familiar 'bing!' was a welcome distraction.

Please, she begged as she scrabbled beneath her pillow for her phone. *Sweet Lord, please let it be Blake, safe and sound and missing me.*

With a jolt of excitement, she saw it *was* a text from him. She opened it with trembling fingers, confused even within her elation. Blake never texted. He barely called. He was old school 'we agree to meet at this place and time and then we show up, without all this unnecessary electronic technology using.' When she'd shown him some of the memes Owen had sent her, he had seemed genuinely baffled by the concept: picture messaging a person you spent forty hours a week with dumb jokes? For *fun*?

Her heart plummeted as she read the first line of the text, '*Hi honey, this isn't Blake…*'

"Fuck," she muttered.

'*…but don't worry, I'm an old friend of his. I'm Elaine from Rockaway, where Blake grew up. Your man's with us tonight, he's fine. He's on our couch snoring like a friggin' bear, which was how I managed to steal his phone…*'

Though still genuinely baffled, Autumn grinned. "What even

is this message, lady I've never met?"

Elaine seemed to be thinking along the same lines. '...*I'm hoping I don't freak you out here but Blake talked to us about you tonight and while it's very clear he fucked up—I swear to God if my husband did that to me he'd be sitting down to piss for a month—it's obvious you two have something special. I don't know you but something tells me you're as hung up on him as he is on you. If that's true, then I also know I'd want to find him as soon as possible and make things right. That's why I'm reaching out. We're having a block party up here tomorrow and I think you should come and surprise Blake. Maybe slap him a little for being a clueless asshole, but come see him too. I'm sending you a dropped pin as soon as I figure out how to do it...*'

Autumn's phone buzzed, showing Elaine had indeed just figured it out.

...I hope I get to meet you tomorrow! Blake's always been an odd duck, but he's a good man and he deserves to be happy. Ps. I need to hear why he popped your ex, Blake wouldn't tell me anything. If you come tomorrow we can talk it over with some wine.'

"Elaine," Autumn whispered. "You sound great."

She locked her phone and lay back, considering what she'd just been told. A block party? Like, one of those American street fairs? And Blake was going? She smiled at the idea of her big man wading through the crowd eating a hot dog. Of course she would go. She would ask her boss to leave early, catch a Lyft to Rockaway and throw herself into Blake's big, bear arms. She would ask him to forgive her for calling him a coward, then come hell or high water, they would make up. She yawned, her tiredness hitting her like a fog. Secure in the knowledge she would make things right, Autumn fell dead asleep.

Five hours and four coffees later, she wasn't nearly so confident. From the minute Happy Paws opened its doors, she and all the other staff had been smashed with clients. There was some kind of doggie stomach virus going around and the waiting room was full of extremely miserable shih tzus and their even more miserable owners.

Autumn pushed through her lunchbreak, desperate to cut down the waiting list, but even without taking any breaks, her chances of her getting out early for the block party seemed as likely as flying to the moon on the back of a fucking swan.

As soon as she sent away a gloomy spaniel owner with a script for doggy antibiotics, she got another hysterical Persian owner insisting her cat had eaten her 'caffeine pills' which, after some gentle prodding, turned out—as it always did—to be MDMA. As soon as she got a moment's respite, Autumn pulled out her phone and checked the time. Her pulse spiked as she realized the block party had already been going for an hour. Elaine hadn't said anything about Blake's state of mind. What if he left the block party and hit the road? Went where she wouldn't be able to find him? The temptation to just grab her shit and bail was so strong.

She let out a shaky breath trying to remind herself that ditching her job for Blake would mean the sack, which in turn would mean her work visa would be invalidated. Although, if she didn't go to Blake, she might not get to be with him, which meant she didn't need her stupid job. The situation was a complete fucking catch 22. As her next client knocked on the clinic door, Autumn ran to her bag and pulled out her first edition copy of The Little Princess. She left it propped on her desk, looking at it every time she was sure she was going to go insane. It was a reminder that Blake cared about her and probably wouldn't leave the block party with the intention of going off-grid in South America. Probably.

She was skulling from her water bottle, having just assessed a hamster with epilepsy, when Isabella came gliding into her room. She looked lovely as a spring morning, as usual, and was carrying a large takeaway cup. Autumn almost moaned at the scent of fresh espresso. "How are you holding up?"

"Good," Isa said in her ethereal voice. "Have you taken your break?"

Autumn shook her head. "I can't. I have like, ten more clients lined up before I can leave."

Isabella put her coffee cup down on Autumn's desk. "Did you get any sleep last night?"

Autumn smiled weakly. "Not as much as I'd have liked."

"Yeah, Owen told me about you and Blake. And you and Ian. Sounds like you had a bad time."

"That would be correct." Autumn checked her phone and swore. "Sorry, I'd love to talk but I'm super late for a block party, of all fucking things. I need to get back to work."

Isabella didn't move, instead she stared at her in a way that reminded Autumn forcibly of Blake. There was a solemnity to their everyday features that made them seem more in tune with human pain than other people. As though they'd both lived very long lives and seen all manner of ugliness.

"Are you okay?" Autumn asked. "Is something wrong?"

Isabella leaned over her desk, laying a long fingertip on the cover of the book Blake had given her. "Is this The Little Princess?"

Autumn smiled, even though it felt like all of her intestines were falling out. "Yeah."

"I like this book."

"Me too. It was my favorite when I was a kid. It's probably still my favourite now, if I'm being honest. I, uh, don't read much."

Isabella bent forward, examining the cover. "It's very old."

"It's...it's a first edition. From 1905."

She whistled.

"I know." Autumn pressed her hand even harder to her chest. "Blake got it for me. He must have repaired it, or else someone owed him a hell of a favor. I looked up the asking price and it's a fuckton."

"Clearly, he thinks you're worth it. Does that make you happy?"

"Yes," Autumn said, even though she didn't know if that was true. Was happiness feeling utterly breached by a man who'd once been a stranger? Did it feel like you had nowhere to hide but you wanted to be looked at anyway?

"I like Blake," Isabella said, stroking the cover of The Little Princess. "He's very…"

"Big?"

The tall girl smiled. "Genuine. That's rare. Underrated."

"It is." Autumn's chest compressed. "I still really wish he hadn't signed me up for the show last night. I don't know if Owen explained what happened—"

"He did," Isabella said. "That coffee is yours, by the way."

Autumn was so touched, and caffeine deprived, she nearly started crying. "You didn't have to do that."

"I know. I wanted to."

It was an answer so reminiscent of Blake that Autumn did start crying. She leaned against the desk for support and let every ounce of pain and frustration run out of her in hot bursts. Isabella walked toward her and wrapped an arm around her shoulders. She smelled amazing and Autumn instantly relinquished all dignity and began sobbing into her shoulder.

"Everything's okay," Isabella said in her measured voice.

"You're allowed to have your own limits. I'm sure Blake didn't mean to hurt you by signing you up for the variety show, but you *were* hurt and you're allowed to still be hurt even though he gave you an expensive book."

"It's not that," Autumn sobbed. "Okay, it's kind of that, but it's more like…disappointment."

"Why?"

She cried harder, her thoughts veering from Blake to her family, to her secret joke notebook, to the years she'd wasted with Ian despite knowing deep down that it would never work.

"I should have tried harder," she told Isabella. "I shouldn't have let myself become this person who just does whatever's asked of her. Goes along with everyone else. If I was in a better position when I met Blake, he wouldn't have tried to make me his project. I would have been standing on my own two feet, without Ian, maybe doing comedy. Instead, I let him push me out of my comfort zone and then I got angry at him for taking it too far. I let myself down."

Isabella was silent, though her arms stayed tight around her. They swayed on the spot and Autumn was amazed to find it wasn't awkward at all, hugging Isa. It reminded her of being held by her mum, when she was very small, rocked and sung the Postman Pat theme song. They were some of the only sweet family memories she possessed and she welcomed the nostalgia in a way she rarely did.

"You can't change the past," Isabella said eventually.

"No."

"But there's always a path to what you want. I've never seen you do stand-up but you must be good for someone like Blake to put you in that position."

Embarrassed, Autumn toed the floor with her shoe. "I dunno…"

"I do. The way he looks at you, you can tell he thinks you're perfection. I think he wanted everyone else to see you that way, too. I think you're his little princess, Autie."

Autumn's tear ducts began stinging again. "Please don't say stuff like that to me, man, I'm so tired I'm gonna explode-cry all over you again."

"It's okay to cry."

Autumn didn't need much encouraging. The stress of the last twenty-four hours welled up in her and within seconds she was gasping and hacking and leaking salt water everywhere again.

"I'm not sad exactly," she mumbled into Isabella's shoulder. "I'm just really raw and I love Blake and I didn't realize it fast enough. Also, I've been at work for so long and I'm hungry and tired and I can't get to the block party. Also you're so incredible and nice and beautiful and you smell like vanilla icing."

"Thank you," Isabella said, with the calm of someone who got told that a lot. "I think you should leave."

Autumn's heart sank. "Do you hate hugging me?"

"No. I mean you should leave work and go find Blake. Say you've got stomach pains and go see him."

Autumn gaped at her. "I can't do that! Owen's counting on me to cover his patients and—"

"Happy Paws will be fine. Owen will understand. Work isn't a big deal, this thing with Blake is a big deal. Go."

"But—"

"No buts." Isabella nudged her toward the door. "Go chase your happy ending. And take your coffee with you. It cost twelve dollars."

"Jesus!" Autumn felt so guilty, she picked up the disposable cup and immediately took a sip. The instant the coffee hit her tongue, she almost spat it out. "What the fuck?"

"Something wrong?"

"This is…" Autumn stared down at the disposable cup. "Delicious. Like so delicious."

She took a big swallow, wondering if it was her hunger and panic that was making it taste so good but no, it was just *lovely*, bitter and creamy and rich. It tasted like home.

"How?" she begged. "How did you get this?"

Isabella shrugged. "Stay in New York and I'll take you some time. Now go catch your landlord."

Autumn hugged her again, one-handed because she wasn't going to let go. This coffee was a sign. If she needed to stay in New York, she *could* stay in New York. All she needed was Blake and friends and good coffee. She squeezed her new mate tightly. "You're an angel of goodness and I love you."

Isabella was silent, her lovely face thoughtful. Then she smiled. "I love you, too, Autumn. Now, go."

Autumn gathered up her stuff in record time, yanking off her white coat and deciding to skip the bit where she told everyone she was sick. She dashed out of the front door. Glenn the receptionist called out but Autumn ignored her. She was on a mission. The sunshine outside was thick and bright, the feel of it filled her with an emotion she couldn't quite name. It made her heart feel three times its usual size. She turned her face to the sky. "Blake! I'm coming for you!"

It was a testament to New York that not one of the dozen people walking the footpath even looked at her, though a bleary-eyed bro gave her the finger. "Quit yelling, bitch."

Autumn must have been running on pure adrenaline because she whirled on him like a tornado. "Don't tell me what to do, cunt!"

The bro's mouth fell open. He looked so horrified she almost felt bad for him.

"Whatever," she said, adjusting the collar on her jacket. "I'm Australian, fuck you."

She looked up at the sky again. "Blake! I'm coming!"

The gold sunlight beat down on her face and, her mission affirmed, Autumn pulled out her phone and ran toward a better pick-up location.

Her driver, another bro with slicked back hair and a thick gold chain, was pretty pumped to be taking her to Rockaway during a surge. The trip would be expensive as fuck but there was no way around it. She didn't have a car and it would be just her luck to get lost on the subway during an emergency, and time was of the essence. Blake could get uncomfortable and leave the block party at any moment, escaping into the wilds of Queens like a slightly less hairy Bigfoot. She needed to get there and make sure that didn't happen. She also needed to look like someone who slept well and hadn't spent the whole day examining the insides of pets.

She had a bunch of loose cosmetics in her bag and she made up her face as best she could, smoothing petroleum jelly over her eyebrows and lids and using dabs of lipstick as blusher. She wanted to look good when Blake saw her, especially if she had to meet his friends at the same time.

They'd been on the road for less than two minutes when Autumn began to feel decidedly unsafe. Her driver took a call from what sounded like his extremely unhappy girlfriend and as he yelled into his device, his driving grew increasingly erratic. He started speeding up and slowing down at random, changing lanes without indicating. Normally, she would have asked him to pull over but she was sure she wouldn't be able to get another ride walking the highway, at least not one that wouldn't leave her murdered. She'd just have to sit tight and give him an incredibly shitty rating when the ride was over. At least that's what she told herself until he drifted halfway into the parallel lane, earning himself a loud honk from another driver. Then she decided it wasn't worth the risk.

"Excuse me," she said, in her most authoritive vet voice. "Can you please finish your call and pull over?"

"Who's that?" the driver's girlfriend shrieked from inside the guy's iPhone. "Who's that bitch?"

Autumn didn't appreciate being called a bitch by a stranger for the second time in an hour. "My name's Academy Award winner, Helen Mirren. I'm in my seventies and I still look fuck-hot in a bikini."

"*What?*" the girlfriend screamed. "Marcus, who the fuck is she?"

The driver turned and gave Autumn a dirty look. "Can you, like, butt out? She's going through some stuff."

"Can you look at the fuckin' road?" Autumn screamed, but the driver continued to stare at her. "You assholes are so ungrateful, it's like, I'm a person, too. I have the right to call my fuckin' girlfrie—"

Autumn knew it was going to happen before it did. The car was idling into the left hand lane and the driver of the white Nissan beside them wasn't watching, she had earbuds in and was staring straight in front of her. They were going to crash. She kicked the back of the driver's seat, aware she was screaming, unsure of what the words were. It didn't matter. They were going to crash.

There was an explosion of glass and a crunch of metal. The car reared up and slammed down. Her seatbelt locked tight around her chest and neck. Autumn bent over, instinctively curling her hands around her face to protect the meat clockwork that kept her alive.

I never got to tell Blake I love him, she thought dimly. *I should have texted it. I shouldn't have waited to tell him in person.*

Time went a funny for a while, then. It clipped past like horse hooves, bursts of sound and movement, the driver's wet moans, her mouth making the same sounds, the screech of tires as other cars pulled up around them. Then came a man's voice, soft with what she thought might be a Japanese accent. "Ma'am, are you okay?"

A good question. Not one she was sure she could answer. She could feel blood running in thick streams down her face and she didn't have the strength to wipe it away. Didn't even have the strength to open her eyes.

"Driver," she said. "How's the driver?"

The man said nothing, which made her think it was bad, maybe worse. "Did he go through the front window?"

"Yes," the man said. "I...I don't think he was wearing a seatbelt. He's okay, though, that's what this guy who's a doctor is saying. But he's a foot doctor so maybe he's wrong..."

Autumn screwed her eyes shut even tighter. The man kept talking, saying the woman in the white Nissan was fine, that she was walking around with barely a scratch on her, but as he continued to talk, she was struggling to stay focused. She was getting very sleepy, something she knew couldn't be a good sign.

Blake, she thought. *Where are you? Come save me. I know I was meant to come save you, but there's been a slight change in plans.*

"Ma'am." The Japanese man's voice was loud in her ear. "We've called an ambulance but do you have a phone? Anyone I can call for you?"

Autumn swallowed. Her mouth was very dry and tacky, like old gum. She nudged her foot against her satchel, wincing at the pain. Her leg couldn't be broken, that would hurt much more, but she'd definitely done something to it. Or the stupid crash had, anyway.

"What are you doing?" the man asked, sounding nervous.

"Phone. It's in my bag, my code is…one, four, eight, seven."

Autumn closed her eyes as she listened to the guy follow her instructions. Everything was so bright and her head was pounding.

"Who should I call?" the man said. "Who's this guy who texted you? Should I call him?"

She licked her cracked mouth trying to remember who that had been. "What…what did the message say?"

"He's asking if you've seen his old copy of Mad Magazine, the one with George W Bush on the cover. Before that he asked you to forgive him and before that he said you were his reason for happiness and before that, *oh my God* he sent you a picture of…" The Japanese man cleared his throat. "Is this your boyfriend? Do you want me to call him?"

"Noooooooo!" Autumn summoned up the last of her inner strength. "Do not call that cocksheathe. Call Blake. Blake! He's listed in my phone as…" She yawned involuntarily, her head throbbing with dull warmth.

"As what?"

"…The Landlord…keep forgetting to change it." She tried to stay awake while the man called Blake, but she couldn't. She let her mind curl into the surrounding blackness and went to sleep.

❋

WHEN AUTUMN CAME to, the first thing she noticed was she was still by the side of the road. That was irritating. She'd been hoping to have been airlifted to the hospital. Still, considering America's health care system, that was probably for the best. She could stand to not be billed for a helicopter ride. She swallowed and realized that while she was still by the side of the road, she was no longer in the car. She was lying flat on her back in a van. Probably an ambulance. She swallowed again, pleased to find she was noticeably more clear-headed than she'd been right after the crash. Maybe her little sleep had helped her heal—

"Ow!"

She tried to move her foot and pain shot up her right leg. It still didn't feel broken, though, and her face was no longer sticky with blood. She took a deep breath and tried to focus on what was happening around her. There was a lot of honking and traffic sounds, and she could hear someone getting yelled out by an angry guy.

"…how is someone like that allowed to work for Uber?" the man was saying. "Aren't there regulations? Ways of stopping these dangerous assholes from driving other people around?"

"I don't know," a woman replied in a neutral voice. "I'm sorry, sir."

"Well I'm gonna find out. If that prick wasn't already in the hospital, I would have put him there myself. Given him more than bruised ribs, too. He's lucky Autumn wasn't seriously injured or *worse*."

Hey, she thought, *that's me, I'm Autumn.*

She licked her lips and discovered she was crazy fucking thirsty.

"Hello?" she called. "Can someone please get me a water or some mineral water, or a Capri Sun or something?"

The man and the woman instantly stopped talking. Autumn's

surroundings began to shake as someone climbed into the back of the ambulance with her.

"Excuse me, sir! You're not allowed—"

A fingertip ghosted the curve of her jaw. "Baby, please be awake. Please be okay."

No, it couldn't be...he was here? Autumn opened her eyes. White light blinded her for a few seconds, and then it grew softer and revealed she was right. Blake was there with her. He'd gotten the call and he'd found her, just as she'd hoped he would. She beamed at him, but he didn't smile back, his brow was furrowed and his beautiful light brown eyes were narrowed. He looked utterly terrified.

"Sir!" the woman said firmly. "You're not authorized to—"

"Blake, I love you," Autumn said before anyone or anything else could stop her. "I love you and I think you're great and I want to stay with you in New York and be your girlfriend and stuff."

Her landlord's mouth fell open.

"I guess I'll, uh, give you guys a minute," the woman said. "Give her a couple sips of water from that bottle."

The ambulance shook as she got out of it and then they were alone. Autumn was hoping for a love confession from Blake—or at least an acknowledgement of hers, but instead he placed a straw in a bottle of water and held it at her lips. "Drink."

Figuring it was easier not to argue, she sucked the straw and a couple of deliciously cool pulls of water burst in her mouth.

"Thanks," she said, when Blake removed the straw. "But why am I in an ambulance parked by the side of the road?"

"They wanted you to wake up before they moved you again." His fingers prodded different areas of her body, as if searching for breaks or reassuring himself she was alive. "They said you weren't concussed, you were just asleep."

Autumn giggled and closed her eyes again. "I guess I did have a really late night. Still, it's kind of bananas I went to sleep after a car crash."

"I assumed you did it to turn me into a madman." Blake's voice was lower, as though he were kneeling beside her. "How do you feel, Fun-Size?"

"Good. Pretty awake. At least twenty percent awake."

"They gave you a stimulant."

"Ah, that's why I feel awesome. Cool. Oh my God, guess what I did?"

"What?" Blake brushed the hair out of her eyes and the sensation made her shiver. "Some guy called me a bitch on the street and I totally yelled at him."

"Excuse me?" Blake's hand left her hair. "What exactly did he say to you? Where was this?"

She laughed, reaching around blindly until Blake did her a favor and put his hand in hers.

"Don't get angry," she said. "It was just New York bullshit but that's what I wanted to tell you, I can handle New York, now. This guy was an asshole and instead of getting upset, I just called him a cunt right to his face!"

There was a short silence. "Good for you."

"Thanks! You know what this means? It means that New York can't fuck with me, anymore. I still think it's a hole full of bin juice, but I kind of like it. And when I totally freaked that guy out, I felt like it kind of liked me."

Someone, probably the woman from before, climbed into the van and cleared her throat. "Are you…feeling okay, Ms. Reynolds?"

"Totally fine. Can I go home?"

"I should probably, um, come back in and examine you?"

"Okay," Autumn began, then a thought occurred to her and she opened her eyes. "Hang on one second," she yelled to the waiting woman.

The EMT turned and faced her. "Yes, ma'am?"

Autumn pointed at Blake. "Did you hear what I just said to him? About loving him? Or did I imagine saying that? You have to be honest, even if it was really embarrassing."

The EMT avoided her eyes. "I think, um. You did."

Autumn stared at Blake. "What the hell, man? You just ignored my love confession?"

But Blake seemed more concerned about her upcoming examination. He was eyeballing the EMT as if he might ask to see some credentials. "We don't need to talk about this right now, baby, you've got a sprained wrist and ankle, and you need to go to the hospital and—"

Panic pumped through her veins, a thousand times more potent than whatever had gotten her to wake up. "Do you not love me, too, Blake? Do you not love me, as well?"

Her landlord stared down at her, his expression unreadable, and Autumn's feeling of dread soared. Then she saw the sheen in his light brown eyes.

"Oh my God, I'm such an asshole," Autumn said. "We don't have to talk about it now, we can wait, *I* can wait. As long as you need."

"How can you…" Blake broke off, shaking his head.

"What?"

He took her hands in his. "Do you know how I felt when I heard you'd been in an accident?"

"Sad?"

A humourless laugh. "Try frantic. I thought I'd lost the girl of my dreams. I thought I'd—" He broke off, shaking his head. "Of course I love you, I've loved you from the moment I laid eyes on you. You made me want to be in the sun again. You made me want to be the one who…gave *you* the sun."

Autumn felt the backs of her eyes burn. Words might not be Blake's strong suit but he could string them together perfectly when he wanted to. She reached up and touched his stubbly jaw, reveling in the feel of her big lovely man. "You don't need to say any more. I love you, too. Plus, I knew how you felt about me the second I saw The Little Princess."

He stared at her. "How did you get that? I got rid of it."

Autumn smiled through another yawn. "Turns out the rest of the tenants want us together as much as your friend Elaine does. She texted me from your phone, by the way. That's why I was coming to the block party."

"I know," Blake said, looking ominous. "I found the message she sent after I got here. I'll be having words with her."

"Don't be mean. She helped bring me back to you."

Blake's hard expression softened. "You're right. Are you sleepy?"

"A bit," Autumn said, closing her eyes again. "I have a sprained ankle, huh? Maybe we can incorporate it into our role play, pretend like you did it to me to keep me from leaving—nah, that's way too dark, hey?"

"Yes." He leaned down and kissed her mouth softly, dropping his voice low. "We might have to take things slow for a little while, sweetheart, but we'll get back there, I promise."

Autumn smiled. "Blake…?"

"Yeah?"

"When I was a kid, I pretended I was the little princess, like this magical special girl that no one realizes is a princess until the end, but I was wrong, you're the little princess. You're the magical person who looks like a hobo, and I helped discover you and reveal you to the rest of the world."

Blake chuckled. "I'm glad to hear that. I think."

"You should be, all the tenants really care about you and so..." she yawned again, "do I."

"Thanks, Fun-Size," he said in a voice so soft she could barely hear it. "You're..."

He whispered something she couldn't quite make out. Sleep was rising up like a velvety shroud, covering her. "Will you stay with me? Make sure that no one steals my watch or makes me pay for a helicopter or something?"

The lightest of cheek touches. "Of course I will. Sleep well."

Then he leaned in close and said it again, the thing she missed before.

"You're everything to me, Autumn."

EPILOGUE

Blake stood in the doorway to the green room, giving himself a moment to study Autumn without her being aware. Goddamn, he was a lucky man. The luckiest. How had he gone from a solitary, anger-fueled existence to this? A man watching his beautiful girlfriend pore over notes for her first open mic. Her Casio lay propped against the ratty couch where she sat, her mouth moving along with the words she read. Blake knew them by heart, since she'd been rehearsing them in bed for the last month—they accounted for some of the best moments of his life.

"Pretend the crowd is in their underwear. Isn't that the old trick?"

Notebook in hand, she'd knelt in the center of the bed. "Pretending is no fun. Strip for me, landlord."

And that was how Blake had become her nightly, mostly naked audience. At this point, it was going to feel unnatural wearing clothes while she performed, but he'd dressed up for the occasion, nonetheless, in black slacks and a gray button down. When Kevin and Elaine had arrived so they could drive to the club together, he'd taken quite the ribbing over going Hollywood, but he wanted Autumn to know the things that were important to her mattered, especially to him.

They hadn't spent a day apart since the accident. There'd

been no discussion about whether Blake would get to hold Autumn in his arms at night, either, but they'd quickly come up with a solution for *where* that would be happening. Autumn's brighter apartment served as home, meaning he now paid himself half the rent. His apartment was being used as their mutual office. Blake used the space to restore his books and exercise and Autumn generally napped on the couch and brought home the occasional sick pigeon. Against his will, Blake had formed something of a kinship with the winged rats, even taking over nursing duties while Autumn worked at the clinic. They were little reminders of his girlfriend when she had the nerve not to be there.

Christ, if he'd known love like this was waiting for him, maybe he wouldn't have spent a decade being such a surly bastard. Autumn showed him the bright side of everything. Daytime was no longer a period to hide from the sun and unpleasant chores. It was a time to try new things, like drinking from paper bags in the park and walking home tipsy, laughing for no reason. It was time for making their story, one experience at a time.

His friends had fallen in love with Autumn within minutes of their first meeting, Elaine dragging her off to gossip and hide from the four little girls who now referred to Autumn as Auntie Autie. They'd even gone down to Rockaway and taken surfing lessons one weekend, crashing at Kevin and Elaine's afterward. Blake was surprised to find that not only could he stand on the board with his bad leg, the continued movement forced him to stretch the damaged area and ease his limp. He'd caught his girlfriend looking up online deals for surfing getaways that night…a prospect that would have made him scoff once. Now, he couldn't wait to get Autumn out of the city, be in a place when he could focus on nothing but her.

Maybe they would even visit her parents in Melbourne. Their Sunday Skype call was growing less and less awkward, mostly thanks to Autumn's unflagging positivity. It was clear her parents wished she would come home—and Blake couldn't blame them. The thought of parting with Autumn after knowing her for twenty-five years was a grim prospect—he couldn't live without her after a few months. Blake had a difficult time conversing with a screen, but last week, Autumn's mom said she'd never seen Autumn happier. Her dad had agreed. And the tense atmosphere had eased. It would continue to ease, because Blake's mission in life was to make sure Autumn remained happy. Having her parents understand and approve of her decisions was part of that.

Enough mooning over your blissful existence. Tonight was about her. Autumn telling her jokes in front of an actual crowd. Blake opened his mouth to tell her that she had a full room waiting for her to perform. Kevin and Elaine had wrangled a babysitter for the night, against all odds. Mrs. Zhu, Mrs. Fuller and Ross were in the house, too, all of them having surpassed the two drink minimum—they were his crazy-ass tenants, after all. Isabella, Owen and Ryan were in the front row staring at their cell phones, and some of Autumn's patients had shown up, too. Or the *owners* of her patients, rather. Which was a testament to the affect she had on everyone. They all wanted her to succeed.

He thought better of telling her she had a packed room when the tension in her shoulders registered. It dawned on him that Autumn already knew he stood behind her. Across the room there was an ancient stereo system with a glass door, his reflection in the doorway clearly visible. So why hadn't she turned around to greet him?

Awareness crackled to life in the small green room, forcing him to notice things he'd missed while daydreaming about how incredible his life had become. The trail of goosebumps decorating the slope of Autumn's neck, she'd become restless on the couch, her hips rocking in a slow tempo, the notebook forgotten on her lap. Her skirt had ridden up enough to make Blake's cock grow thick with lust. Was that a garter belt holding her stockings to her thighs?

"Autumn..."

Still she didn't turn, but her breathing picked up, shoulders lifting and falling.

Her nerves were getting the better of her. Blake's intuition where Autumn's sexual needs were concerned had been honed as sharp as a goddamn axe. If she didn't want to turn around and talk through her fears with him, she wanted him to obliterate them. Make them cease to exist. And so he would.

Quietly, Blake closed and locked the door behind him, the energy of the crowd fading into nothing. Her set wasn't due to begin for ten minutes, he could work with that. Even if the room had to wait, so be it.

His footsteps creaked as he approached Autumn, his gaze trained on the pulse at the base of her neck. She gasped when he stepped into her periphery, attempting to stand. But he caught a fist full of her hair, instead, half-dragging, half-guiding her across the room.

Autumn's palms flattened on the wall, head turning to the side so Blake could see the outline of her chewed lips. Seeing the proof of her nerves, his heart squeezed. Slowly, though, a certain power began pumping in his veins. A power she'd granted only him. "You think you can just make everyone wait, Blondie?" He caught her earlobe with his teeth and lowered his zipper, the sound extra punctuated in the tiny room. "All men wait for you, don't they? Girls who look like you show up when they please and we just accept it. We need to look at you, we need to pretend we've got a shot at *fucking* you. Too bad I'm tired of waiting and thinking. I'm taking this pussy however I can get it." Using his upper body to keep her pressed to the wall, Blake hiked Autumn's skirt up around her hips and jerked her thong to one side. *Fuck.* Garter belts on both thighs. He didn't know whether to be thankful or put her over his knee, because surely a hint of these would be visible up on the stage.

"This is going to be fast, just like when I jerk off thinking about you. If you're not on stage soon, they'll come looking."

"No, please." She pushed off the wall and tried to twist away, but Blake surged forward to keep her pinned, then jerked her hips back and guided his cock between her thighs where he found her soft flesh soaking wet. "*Please.* I don't want this."

"Oh, you're *getting* it. Go on your toes and make it easier for me to hit that pussy. Unless you want this to take longer?"

"Maybe I do," she whimpered, molding her ass to Blake's lap under the guise of attempting to escape. "Maybe I don't want to go on stage," she finished, almost too quietly for Blake to hear. But he did, thank God. Instead of ramming home inside Autumn as he'd intended, Blake pulled back on the reins of his control at the last second and sunk in slowly into his tight girl, inch by inch. "Fuck," he breathed into her shoulder, the lines of their game blurring. Autumn's head fell back, their eyes met...and perfect, singular love connected them, communicating everything.

"I'm scared," she whispered. "Excited, but scared."

He pressed their mouths together, but didn't kiss her, badly as he wanted to. "Of course you are, but you're too brave to let it overwhelm you."

"How do you know?"

"Because you didn't give up on me. You made me want to

live better. You made the past seem like nothing, in comparison to spending one day without you." He gave in and kissed her temple, cheeks and nose. "You've tamed a beast, beauty. This is just another thing you'll conquer."

She sighed a laugh, her eyes rolling back in her head when he shifted inside her. "What if I don't? What if I bomb and everyone throws rotten produce at me?"

"Then we go home, I get in my best underwear and we regroup." A laugh shook her little body and Blake groaned, his cock wondering why there was a hold up. Looking into her eyes, he could see his words had found their mark.

"I love you, Blake."

"I love you too, Autumn." The stress lines around her mouth had faded. And when he angled her hips, bent his knees and pumped from beneath, her jaw dropped, erasing them even further. "Now who are these garter belts for?"

Autumn turned and pressed her forehead to the wall, releasing a harsh sob when Blake began fucking her in earnest, her ass slapping with rapid, obscene sounds off his stomach. "No one. I swear."

"Liar. You wore them to fuck with me." He snapped one against her thigh, before reaching around and delivering a rough slap to her pussy. "This is what happens now, when you tease. You give this up. You hand it over."

"Oh my *God*."

Jesus, they could keep this up for an hour. Blake filthy-talking her, bringing her to the brink and letting her suffer a come down before driving her toward orgasm again. It's how they spent their nights, weekends and occasional mornings when the cravings were too intense to deny. But now one of Autumn's dreams awaited her and Blake was determined to make sure she got the chance to see it through. She'd chosen the time, date and place. Now he supported her timing. Her decisions. A lesson he'd learned the hard way, but one he'd needed to learn, all the same.

Blake's fingers found Autumn's clit and went to town, rubbing fast without ceasing or changing directions. The climax built inside of her so fast she reared back against him, arching, twisting and whining, her thighs going wild beneath, feet connecting with the wall. His cock rifled in and out of her, his grunts cutting her cries of his name in half.

"Come on, little brat. You've never had it better, just let your pussy admit it."

"Oh God. *God.*" Her flesh seized around his cock, a long pause following her sucked in breath. That's when her shaking started, every inch of her spasming and shuddering. Blake bit down hard on his lower lip, liquid fire making a brutally fast ascent in his cock and filling Autumn. Claiming every inch. He gave a few final pumps, trying to rid them both of every detail of the ache, the pressure.

Moments later, they hung there against the wall, clothes in disarray, their breathing just beginning to return to normal.

Blake grazed her cheek with an open mouth. "How do you feel?"

She turned in his arms and gave him a dazed look. "Like I wouldn't hate making this a ritual."

"At your service, Fun-Size." He kissed her mouth, long and hard, while fixing her skirt and panties. "Now and always."

After a few more kisses and reassurances that she was going to do amazing, Blake gave Autumn a final look and left the green room, traveled down the hallway and re-entered the club. There was no end to the smirking when he took his seat beside Kevin and Elaine, but he could only flip them the bird. Because now he was nervous on Autumn's behalf, like the comedy version of sympathy pains.

"Did you tell her to break a leg, or just break her off?" Elaine asked, gouging him in the side with an elbow. "You dirty dog. I didn't think you had it in you. Public places and everything. Kevin, we need couple's therapy."

"Would you stop?" Kevin signaled the waitress for another round just as Autumn's name was announced on stage. "She's right, though, B-Money. I don't even recognize you, anymore."

Blake smiled. "Good."

When Autumn came out on stage, keyboard in her arms, Blake almost stopped breathing. God, she looked like a tiny angel up there. If anyone heckled her, he'd have to punch someone else in the face. It took Elaine tugging on Blake's sleeve to realize he'd been so knocked dead by the sight of her on stage, he'd forgotten to clap. Just as he started, everyone stopped. On stage, Autumn laughed watching it happen. She squared her shoulders and played her first few notes on the Casio…and a transformation came over her, one he'd watched play out for months, but it became solid in that moment. A thing visible to the naked eye.

Christ, he couldn't be more proud. Or grateful she'd chosen him.

"Good evening," she half-said, half-sang into the microphone. "I'm Autumn Reynolds and I'll be making you feel better about giving up on your dreams tonight."

There was a loud burst of laughter and Kevin muttered, "Here's hoping," and was promptly elbowed in the side by Elaine.

"So, you may have noticed I'm a woman, a female if you will," Autumn said with faux seductiveness. She pulled up one side of her skirt and exposed her stocking suspender. There was more laughter and some catcalling. It sounded good-natured and as though it was coming from Owen, so Blake let it slide. He was still nervous but he was also exhilarated, feeding off the pure pleasure emanating from his girl.

"And you know what females have…?" She beckoned the audience closer, one hand playing the Casio keyboard, producing the bright show-tune melody of her first song. "Periods."

The audience laughed and she gave them an arch smile. "I know, pretty crazy, hope I didn't trigger anyone's puberty with that sexy disclaimer, but I mention periods because I have a song about it. Want to hear?"

Blake's greatest fear had been that some wise-ass guy would shout 'no fuckin' way,' but the crowd cheered and clapped and if anyone heckled, you couldn't hear a thing.

"You got it," Autumn said with a wink and launched into 'Fucking on my Period (don't think about your dick bleeding to death).'

The crowd was soon in stitches and while Blake knew the alcohol and energy of the past performances had a hand in it, no one could deny the people in the theatre were enjoying themselves. He looked over at his friends. Elaine was watching Autumn, utterly transfixed and Kevin grinned at him. "She's good. Congratulations."

"Thanks," Blake said, almost overwhelmed with gratitude that his friends were here, that he hadn't been a pigheaded idiot all his life and let them both slip away. "I'm glad you're—"

"Oh my God, will you assholes shut up?" Elaine hissed. "I'm only trying to hear Autumn perform over here."

They shut up. Autumn's first song ended and his girlfriend took a short bow.

"Thanks guys, I really appreciate it," she said, taking a short sip from her water bottle. "So I have an ex-boyfriend. Who doesn't, right? I'm looking at you, the Pope. Anyway, the thing about my ex-boyfriend is he's a main character in a reality TV show called 'The UnReal World.' I am not making this up, he's an actor and he's *a main character on a reality TV show.* That should tell you everything you need to know about our former relationship."

Everyone laughed.

"We were together for quite a while and he cheated on me a bunch, because again, reality TV star. The way I found out about it was kind of funny in a terrifyingly bad way because…"

Blake zoned out a little during Autumn's Ian material and the subsequent song 'Delete Your Nudes (You Silly Cunt).' Not because it wasn't funny, but because if he thought about Ian for too long, it made his fists ball up. The guy was long gone, living on the west coast, 'acting' in that moronic TV show, but Blake was never going to buy him a beer after what he did to Autumn. The crowd loved the song, and when Autumn was done they clapped loud enough to bring the roof down, louder and longer than he'd heard in the venue before.

"Thanks," she said again and this time Blake was sure he could see the sheen of tears in her eyes. His chest contracted, bursting with pride.

"So my ex and I broke up," Autumn said, swiping a finger under her eyelids. "On the way out I told him that what he didn't know about vaginas could fill a million vaginas. That opened him up for some really great *'well it wasn't a million vaginas but it was quite a few'* gags. That's the problem when two people who think they're funny date, it's like this never-ending fight over who has the best lines."

She began playing a sombre tune, or as sombre as anything produced on a Casio keyboard could sound. "There is a real but misguided idea in bad relationships that if you could incinerate your partner with cutting logic, just give them a *really* sick burn, they'd see what a dick they are and accept you're right in all things. Sadly, this is not even remotely true. Here's a song about it."

As Autumn sang 'If You Loved Me You'd Admit What A Cock You Are,' Blake checked his watch. She'd been given twenty minutes but she was edging toward fifteen already. What if they didn't let her finish?

"Don't worry about it," Kevin whispered. "She's killing, they'd be insane to take her off."

"Shut. Up," Elaine hissed.

Autumn finished the song with two and a half minutes to spare. She seemed blissfully aware of her dwindling slot, smiling out at the audience like it was the happiest day of her life.

"So I have a new guy," she told the crowd.

There was a loud chorus of 'oooh's and 'ahh's'. Elaine nudged his side and Blake felt his face go hot. He'd known it was coming but it was still hard not to be self-conscious, especially with so many people he knew around him.

"He's not really what I had in mind for the big love of my life," Autumn said and began playing a light wandering melody Blake had never heard before. His brain froze. This wasn't the end of her act. He'd never heard this before.

"My new man is big and hairy and a little mean," Autumn said. "Not Zuckerberg mean, just kind of standoffish. He's the Beast from Beauty and the Beast. But he never turns into the guy from Downton Abby, he just kind of stays hairy and grumpy. I like it."

Elaine laughed loudly in his ear. "Glad someone does. This is quite a roast you're getting, Blake. We thought you weren't going to be mentioned."

"This isn't the end of her act," Blake said numbly. "I...I don't know what this is, she hasn't rehearsed this in front of me."

He stared up at her, wondering what the hell was going on.

"So some people think the beast Stockholmed Belle into loving him, I disagree and we can have a big fight about it after the show, but here's the takeaway; I don't think Belle fixes the beast. I think she brings out what was already inside him. I don't think you can change people. I couldn't change my ex-boyfriend into someone who is not an enormous dickheel, but when I met this guy, I understood that you don't want to change the right person, you just want to be where they are."

There was another loud 'awww' and Blake felt like his heart was moving out of his body, swelling too large to be contained by his chest.

"Autumn," he whispered. And then her gaze found his and she smiled. "I wrote this song for him, it's called 'Beast I Never Knew I Needed.' Would you like to hear it?"

"YES!" the crowd shouted as one.

"Yes," Blake said just to her.

She smiled, because she'd been looking right at him, and then she said, "Alright then. Here we go!"

As it turned out, Blake couldn't hear a lot of the lyrics. The sound wasn't great in the theatre, especially when everyone was clapping and cheering, but that didn't matter, he just watched Autumn's face and drank in that she was singing about loving him. He also caught something to do with his massive cock and Kevin and Elaine cackled like a couple of old hens. He didn't mind, though, he didn't think he'd mind anything ever again.

She played her final notes with a flourish and curtsied, her expression a mixture of hope and worry. They both gave way to relief as applause exploded in the room. Whistles, cheers, cell phone snaps. The tenants of his building hooted and cat called, because, again, they were his crazy ass tenants. Even audience members Blake didn't know leaned over toward one another and repeated one of Autumn's jokes, laughing at it a second time.

He could no more stop himself from getting up and marching toward the stage than he could rearrange the seasons. As soon as he got close enough, Autumn turned and fell backward into his hold, cradling her Casio to her chest and laughing. Blake carried Autumn out of the club to a sea of laughter and clapping, walking straight into forever.

The End

ACKNOWLEDGEMENTS

Tessa Bailey

More than anyone, I would love to thank Eve Dangerfield for making this process so fun. I've never laughed harder reading anyone else's books—and this time, I got to laugh at our very own slice of biblioheaven. I got to be a *part* of it and I'm so grateful. When I started authoring just over five years ago, I took risks in my writing without so much as a backward glance. And working with Eve put me back in that daring mindset, just like I knew it would. We wrote purely for our vaginas and hearts—and the vaginas and hearts of the readers. Fly peacock, fly!

Thank you to Eagle at Aquila Editing for reading the first version of Captivated and giving us your fabulous take. As always, your input was incredible.

Thank you to my Bailey's Babes, who've come on this Eve Dangerfield fangirl ride with me and are so damn excited for this book!

Thank you to author Skye Warren for pointing out Eve's shout-out to me in Open Hearts, which subsequently became one of my favorite books ever and inspired us to form our unholy union.

And as always, thank you to my family for being my biggest supporters and loves of my life.

Eve Dangerfield

Thanks have to go first and foremost to Tessa Bailey. When she said she wanted to write a book with me I almost chucked, I was so excited. Six-plus months and nine hundred zillion words later and we have a book! I still can't fucking believe it! Captivated will always be my proof that life, while often a bitch, can be truly wonderful too. Writing with Tessa was almost suspicious in its easiness and I rate it among the best writing experiences of my career (can I say career? Fuck it; *career*.) Seriously, I can't tell you how amazing it's been. I'm so glad we made it happen. Happy birthday to the ground, TB <3

Additional thanks go to Kole, who did an exceptional job of proofing, as always. Girl, your eagle eyes are so, so appreciated. Sorry about all the non-commas, but I stay being me

¯_(ツ)_/¯

Also, massive thanks to Letitia from RBA designs whose incredible design graces our fabulous cover. I fucking adore your work.

As always big love goes to my nearest and dearest who make me laugh and think and give me hugs and head-rubs and point out when I'm being an anus and wholeheartedly accept my apologies; all the essential human things. How lovely it is to be yours.

ABOUT TESSA BAILEY

Tessa Bailey is originally from Carlsbad, California. The day after high school graduation, she packed her yearbook, ripped jeans and laptop, driving cross-country to New York City in under four days. Her most valuable life experiences were learned thereafter while waitressing at K-Dees, a Manhattan pub owned by her uncle. Inside those four walls, she met her husband, best friend and discovered the magic of classic rock, managing to put herself through Kingsborough Community College and the English program at Pace University at the same time. Several stunted attempts to enter the work force as a journalist followed, but romance writing continued to demand her attention. She now lives in Long Island, New York with her husband of eleven years and six-year-old daughter. Although she is severely sleep-deprived, she is incredibly happy to be living her dream of writing about people falling in love.

Instagram: instagram.com/tessabaileyisanauthor
Facebook: facebook.com/TessaBaileyAuthor
Goodreads: goodreads.com/author/show/6953499.Tessa_Bailey
Amazon: amazon.com/Tessa-Bailey/e/B00BKMOZYO

Other Books by Tessa Bailey

Standalones
Getaway Girl
Follow
Baiting the Maid of Honor
Unfixable
Off Base

Line of Duty Series
Protecting What's His
Protecting What's Theirs
His Risk to Take
Officer Off Limits
Asking For Trouble
Staking His Claim
Riskier Business

Serve Series
Owned by Fate
Exposed by Fate
Driven by Fate

Broke & Beautiful Series
Chase Me
Need Me
Make Me

Crossing the Line Series
Risking It All
Up in Smoke
Boiling Point
Raw Redemption

Made in Jersey Series
Crashed Out
Rough Rhythm
Thrown Down
Worked Up
Wound Tight

Romancing the Clarksons Series
Too Hot to Handle
Too Wild to Tame
Too Hard to Forget
Too Close to Call
Too Beautiful to Break

Academy Series
Disorderly Conduct
Indecent Exposure
Disturbing His Peace

ABOUT EVE DANGERFIELD

Eve Dangerfield has loved romance novels since she first started swiping her grandmother's paperbacks. Now she writes her own tales about complex women and gorgeous-but-slightly-tortured men. Eve currently lives in Melbourne with the boy, a bunch of semi-dead plants and a rabbit named Billy. When she's not writing she can usually be found juggling a beer, her phone and a lipstick. Not literally, she's really bad at juggling. You can find details about this and more relevant things at www.evedangerfield.com.

She hath various social media accounts

Facebook: facebook.com/evedangerfield
Instagram: instagram.com/evedangerfield
Twitter: twitter.com/Eve_Dangerfield
Goodreads: goodreads.com/author/show/14427168.Eve_Dangerfield

She hath written other books

Something Borrowed

Something Else

Taunt

Open Hearts

Act Your Age

Locked Box

Degrees of Control